THE ART OF DECEPTION

PAM LECKY

Storm

This is a work of fiction. Names, characters, business, events and incidents are the products of the author's imagination. Any resemblance to actual persons, living or dead, or actual events is purely coincidental.

Copyright © Pam Lecky, 2021, 2024

The moral right of the author has been asserted.

Previously published in 2021 as *The Art of Deception* by Pam Lecky.

All rights reserved. No part of this book may be reproduced or used in any manner without the prior written permission of the copyright owner.

To request permissions, contact the publisher at rights@stormpublishing.co

Ebook ISBN: 978-1-80508-697-0
Paperback ISBN: 978-1-80508-698-7

Cover design: Ghost
Cover images: Adobe Stock, Shutterstock

Published by Storm Publishing.
For further information, visit:
www.stormpublishing.co

ALSO BY PAM LECKY

The Lucy Lawrence Mysteries
No Stone Unturned
Footprints in the Sand
A Pocketful of Diamonds

To Keith, with thanks
For a lifetime of friendship

PART 1

THE HANGMAN'S NOOSE

ONE

Phillimore Gardens, Kensington, London, Late April 1888

Lucy Lawrence was all aflutter. She hadn't been this nervous since... Had she ever been quite this anxious before? How would it feel to see him again? She twisted Phineas Stone's note through her fingers as she conjured up his image in her head. It was ten months since they'd met and much had happened in the intervening time. Her feelings towards him had not changed, but it was impossible to know his state of mind. She could only hope.

Since her return from Egypt almost six weeks before, Lucy's life had been a whirl, not only of emotions but of practicalities. To her immense disappointment, Phineas was out of the country. All she could glean from her friend Lady Sarah Strawbridge was that he was in Ireland on a case, and no one knew when he would be home again. Resigned to wait, Lucy had done her best to push all thought of him from her mind and concentrate on the more immediate need: that of finding a home.

As ever, her relationship with Lady Sarah was a godsend.

Her friend learned of a delightful house about to come on the market and had interceded on Lucy's behalf to persuade the seller to let Lucy see it first. Lucy made an offer on the spot. Since moving in the week before, Lucy's life had been dominated by furniture, wallpaper and hiring staff. Until this morning that was, when a beaming Mary, her maid, handed her Phineas's note.

He was back in town, wished to see her and would call this afternoon.

The doorbell chimed. He was here! His message floated to the floor, forgotten. She stood. Then quickly sat down again, her heart racing. *You are not sixteen*, she berated herself. *Calm down!* She heard the murmur of voices out in the hallway. The seconds ticked by far too slowly. Lucy sat on the edge of her chair, twisting her hands in her lap. Why was she so nervous? No member of the house of Somerville ever lacked courage, she chided herself: brains maybe, money often, but *never* courage.

The door opened and Mary appeared. 'Mr Stone to see you, ma'am.'

And then, there he was, striding across the room towards her.

Lucy stood up far too quickly, leaving herself light-headed. Phineas had stalled a few feet away from her. Was that doubt she read in his eyes?

But they couldn't stand in silence forever. Lucy held out her hand, determined to break the ice. 'Hello,' she said, unsure if she should be reserved or friendly. Where on earth did they stand?

Phineas exhaled deeply before stepping closer and taking her hand. He did not shake it, however, but clasped it between both of his as he gazed at her. A gaze that left her wondering if all the air had been sucked from the room. 'Are you well, Lucy?' he enquired at last.

'Why, yes. Never better. And you?' she managed to reply.

'I'm fine.' He dropped her hand as a frown settled between his brows. 'But also relieved.'

'Why so?' she asked, a little mystified.

'Because not that long ago, I half expected to be visiting your grave in Africa.' She detected a slight quiver in his voice. He swallowed hard, then turned away and walked over to the fireplace. She'd expected him to be angry with her, but with a start, she realised he was upset. He was trying to compose himself. That could only mean that he cared, surely? There *was* hope. She sat down and waited for him to continue, her hands clasped in her lap.

When he turned back to her, his expression was solemn. 'I was in India at the time of your exploits. I didn't even know you were in Egypt until I saw the reports in the newspapers on my return to England. From what I read, you were lucky to have survived. Robbery, murder, explosions, and then to cap it all, confronting a cold-blooded and insane murderer in a tomb.'

It sounded comical encapsulated like that. Lucy tried not to smile. 'You make it sound as if it was on purpose, but it just… happened to me.'

'But it could only just happen to you, Lucy. That is the point! I have been beside myself these last few months wondering if you were truly unharmed.'

'I'm fine. I assure you; never better.'

He ran his fingers through his hair. 'Yes, but when I made enquiries, no one could tell me where you were to be found, except to say you were still in Egypt and playing the tourist.'

'Well, that was true. After all that happened at Sakkâra, I needed to recuperate, so we travelled up the Nile to Abu Simbel. We took our time coming back, lingering in southern Italy for a while. But let me assure you, I'm fully recovered. Do please sit down, and I will ring for tea.'

Phineas nodded and sat down, while Lucy rose and rang the bell for Mary. She had no wish to argue with him, but she wanted him to understand. As she passed his chair, she laid a hand on his shoulder. It felt the most natural thing in the world to do. 'Don't you see? I had to try to solve M. Moreau's murder. He was both a friend and the leader of the dig I was funding. His death was vile.'

His features relaxed as he gazed up at her. 'I do understand. But it was alarming to learn of the danger you were in, particularly as I could do nothing about it.' His hand closed over hers, and he smiled. Lucy's heart skipped. 'But how did you end up in Egypt?' he asked. 'You told me you would be touring Europe.'

Lucy sat down on the sofa opposite him. 'That was indeed my plan, but a lucky meeting with M. Moreau in Nice resulted in my going to Egypt instead. He needed a patron and, well, I suppose I wanted an adventure. After all the trouble of the previous six months, I yearned for distraction. Between my husband and my brother, my world had turned upside down.'

'You appeared to cope admirably,' he said with a gentle smile. 'Though I could see you were restless.'

'Very much so. However, I'm sorry if my... venture alarmed you. Can we not just put this behind us?'

Phineas sighed, shook his head, and laughed. 'Absolutely. I have no wish to fight with you, Lucy. I trust you will settle back into London life and steer clear of any mischief.'

Lucy couldn't help but splutter. 'Based on the last year of my life, I very much doubt it. Mischief usually finds *me*.'

'That certainly appears to be the case,' he said, his voice almost strangled with emotion. Seconds later, he was beside her, taking her hands in his. 'Lucy, you little devil; I have missed you terribly, yet I fear you haven't missed me at all.'

'I have, Phin. Of course I have.'

His gaze deepened. Lucy held her breath. But just as he was about to lean in closer, the door opened and Mary entered the room bearing the tea tray. She stalled on the threshold. Phineas dropped Lucy's hands and moved further down the sofa. Mary flicked a glance between the two before breaking into a wide grin. She placed the tray on the table beside Lucy.

Lucy schooled her features and took up the teapot. 'Thank you, Mary; that will be all.' Once the door had closed after the maid, who practically bounced out of the door, they just stared at each other.

'Oh, dear,' Lucy said at last, but inside she was joyous.

Phineas was embarrassed, she could tell, but he recovered quickly. 'Two sugars, please,' he said, nodding towards the tray.

'I remember; you don't have to tell me,' she chided.

Their fingers brushed as she handed him the cup.

'My timing was off,' he said with a mischievous smile.

'Just a little.'

He put the teacup down and snatched her hand, bringing it to his lips. 'Did I tell you I missed you?'

'Ahem, yes.'

'Did I mention you are the most infuriating, headstrong and wonderful woman I have ever met?'

Lucy tilted her head and narrowed her eyes. 'Not to my knowledge; I would definitely remember that.'

'How remiss of me!'

'Indeed. However, I give you permission to rectify the situation, and the sooner the better.'

He gently squeezed her hand. 'Ah, Lucy, I don't know where to begin. Within five minutes of meeting you, I was intrigued. Not much longer after that, I realised I wanted to be a part of your life, but you were as elusive as a butterfly. When we last met, I had hoped we had reached an understanding.'

'I thought we had too. At least, that we could remain friends,' she replied.

He grimaced. 'That was never enough for me, and I have deeply regretted not declaring myself that day, but I could see that you needed a little time to get over all that had occurred. The months since have been torture. I worried you would meet someone on your travels and forget about me. And then Lady Sarah had to pass on that ridiculous story about Alice and my disappearance from London. Did you believe I had been enticed away by my ex-fiancée? Were you concerned about me?' he asked, his lip quirking ever so slightly.

Lucy could feel the colour rise in her cheeks, for she'd suspected exactly that, but to admit it wouldn't be wise in the interest of building bridges. 'Certainly not. You are well able to fend for yourself,' she countered.

His face lit up with a grin. 'I appreciate the compliment!'

'I'm being serious, Phin. I never doubted you were an honourable man, and whatever actions you decided to take were for a good reason.'

'Even if it was to abscond with another man's wife?' He sounded incredulous.

'I can't win this argument,' she admitted. 'Yes, I'm sorry. I did wonder. Alice is an incredibly beautiful woman; not to mention your prior history.'

'Thank you for being honest, Lucy. She's beautiful, certainly, but also one of the most deranged and manipulative women I have ever met. I thank God that she released me. Now it's best we draw a line under it. I'm sorry if the rumours gave you reason to doubt me.' Phineas sighed heavily. 'Can you forgive me?'

'Oh, I'm sure I will... eventually,' she said. The dismay in his gaze alarmed her. He was still unsure of her! She smiled and caressed his cheek. 'I'm teasing you, Phin—'

But he silenced her with a kiss. Followed by another one. And then several more.

It was at least ten minutes before either spoke. Phin planted a kiss on her fingertips before lacing his fingers through hers. 'Do you know where you stand now?'

'I believe so,' she said, resting her head against his shoulder with a sigh. 'Though, I'm terribly forgetful; I may need constant reminding.'

'Should I put something formal in my diary?' he asked.

'Absolutely, and for every day of the week!'

TWO

Three Weeks Later, Kent, England

Lucy's travelling companions, the Strawbridges, were perfectly at ease, but then they already knew the members of the Stone family and had visited Thorncroft on many occasions. Being dropped into the middle of a society house party wouldn't faze Lucy normally. But this was different. Her relationship with Phineas had blossomed into a fully-fledged romance. It was wonderful and much longed for. However, up to now, no one except Lady Sarah and Lucy's servants was aware of it. So, when Phineas asked her to come to his father's seventieth birthday celebration at the family home, she'd been surprised and delighted, if not a little terrified: a feeling which intensified as she and the Strawbridges journeyed into Kent.

The fact she'd been invited declared Phin's intentions clearly to all, and as a result, Lucy played out all the possible scenarios she might encounter at Thorncroft. Would she be treated like an exotic specimen in the zoological gardens? The thought made her shudder. The problem was she suspected most of the family wouldn't consider her *suitable*. The notoriety caused by her brother's conviction for fraud, her husband's unfortunate death, and her recent much-publicised activities in Egypt couldn't have escaped their notice. Although only a short while back in England, Lucy had received several snubs from what Lady Sarah termed the 'cats': those ladies of the first water who ruled Mayfair society. Lucy didn't care; it was nothing new. Her elopement at eighteen had already placed her on the outskirts of society for much of the previous decade. However, if it were to hinder the future with Phineas, it was regrettable and frustrating.

As the horse and carriage swept around a bend, a corridor of ancient fir trees drew the eye to a magnificent Queen Anne style house at the bottom of the hill. Lucy caught her breath. The Stone residence was red brick and glowed in the late afternoon sun. The dwelling was beautifully proportioned, as reflected on the mirror-like surface of a lake to the front of the property. Extensive parkland stretched out as far as one could see.

And in the distance was the sea. Lucy sighed with delight.

'It's superb, isn't it?' Lady Sarah Strawbridge remarked.

'Yes, it's a beautiful house,' Lucy replied, keeping her eyes fixed on the façade.

'Restoration, I believe,' Geoffrey Strawbridge said, peering out the window. 'Generations of Stones have lived here, including, if I'm not mistaken, Francis Stone, one of the Queen's most trusted advisers. I refer to Queen Anne, of course, not the present Queen.'

Lucy barely heard him as her thoughts returned to the only member of the Stone family who mattered. His childhood home was lovely, and in sharp contrast to where she'd grown up in Somerville Hall in Yorkshire: a mausoleum of a house, cold, dark and forbidding. In fact, the only similarity she could detect was the beauty of the grounds. However, Somerville was no longer in the family, having been sold to pay her brother's debts.

She'd been thinking of Yorkshire much of late due to some extraordinary news she'd received.

'Oh, I didn't tell you,' Lucy said to Sarah with a wry smile. 'My Uncle Giles is no longer at Blackheath with the Chancellors. He broke the news to me in his last letter. He's only left for Whitby with the old housekeeper from Somerville. The old rascal had not hinted about it in any of his previous correspondence. Giles is full of surprises,' Lucy said. 'I'm sure Mrs Hughes is at least ten years younger. I understand there will be nuptials shortly.'

'How extraordinary!' Geoffrey exclaimed.

Sarah laughed. 'Good for him!'

'Phin thought it was hilarious, too,' Lucy said. 'I wonder if anyone has told my mother. She would be horrified to learn her brother was marrying a Somerville servant. Overall, as a family, we're a huge disappointment to her.'

'But she was hardly a model mother, now, was she? Have you heard from her since your return?' Sarah asked.

'No, nor do I wish to have any communication with her. Phineas thinks I should try to mend our relationship, but I'm afraid I can't forgive her. I hate to admit it, but Phin is a far better person than me!'

The carriage pulled up. Instinctively, Lucy looked for Phin, but there was no sign of him, only a butler and several footmen hurrying down the steps.

Sarah reached across and patted her hand. 'You'll be *fine*.'

With a grateful smile at her friend, Lucy took a deep breath, suddenly finding her throat tight. Sometimes it was disconcerting how well Sarah understood her.

Facing down murderers is easier than this, she thought, as she contemplated the daunting prospect of meeting Phin's entire family in one afternoon. The steps were lowered, and before she knew it, Sarah and Geoffrey ushered her up the front steps and into the entrance hall, as if they feared she might flee.

Inside the grand hallway, their hosts stood together beside an imposing fireplace. The lady was pale and dressed in a startling shade of yellow. Sarah guessed that this was Gertie, Phin's sister-in-law. She must have been a great beauty in her day, Lucy thought, but a faded one now with her vacant expression. Even her blonde hair was dull and brittle, her eyes a watery blue. She looked tired, and Lucy felt a rush of sympathy for her. Beside her, a clean-shaven man in his early forties, with deep-set hazel eyes, gazed at Lucy stern-faced. This was the famous Andrew, Phin's eldest brother, and the man who would inherit the estate in due course. Lucy detected no resemblance to Phin.

Andrew took a step towards them. His wife appeared to hesitate, as if she were miles away. Lucy caught the fleeting dagger-look of annoyance Andrew bestowed on his wife before almost pulling her forward, his hand gripping her elbow.

Lady Sarah broke into the strained silence. 'Gertie! Andrew! How wonderful to see you both. You do look well,' she said, advancing towards the couple. Sarah threw an encouraging glance at Lucy. 'I don't believe you have met my friend.' With a raised brow, she said. 'Lucy, this is Mr Andrew Stone and his wife, Gertrude. Gertie, this is Mrs Lucy Lawrence, a *dear* friend of mine.'

'Oh!' exclaimed Gertie Stone, her eyebrows shooting upwards. Lucy found the lady's wide-eyed stare surprising and exchanged a questioning look with Sarah, who appeared to be struggling not to smile.

'Welcome to Thorncroft, Mrs Lawrence,' Andrew Stone said. His tone was cool and his bow perfunctory. 'I hope you enjoy your stay. Any friend of Sarah and Geoffrey is always welcome.'

Territory was being marked. With a sinking feeling, Lucy realised he refused to acknowledge her as a guest of his brother.

Lucy smiled at Gertie, then turned to Phin's brother. 'Thank you for the invitation, Mr Stone.'

Andrew nodded politely, but Lucy was keenly aware of his scrutiny. 'Our pleasure,' he said before quickly turning his gaze to Sarah. His face lit up. 'My dear Lady Sarah, it's always a delight to have you here,' he gushed.

Lucy felt the slight. Very well, he had known Sarah for years, but his greeting to her had verged on icy. It appeared her worst fears were confirmed. How she longed to see Phineas for reassurance.

'Geoffrey!' Andrew side-stepped the ladies and shook Sarah's husband warmly by the hand. 'It is good to see you again. If you have time, I'd like to discuss that Marsham Bill with you.'

'Of course, old fellow. Would be delighted,' Geoffrey replied.

'No better time than the present. Come into the library and we can have a chat,' Andrew said, and the two gentlemen disappeared. Gertie gazed after them, a frown appearing between her fine brows.

'I should have known they'd be off talking politics. Are we the first to arrive, Gertie?' Sarah asked their hostess, dragging the poor woman's attention back from wherever it had strayed.

Gertie gave her a puzzled look before saying, 'No, no. Andrew's aunt and uncle arrived this morning, and Lady Dot and the Vaughans arrived about an hour ago. They're resting after their journey. Our neighbours, the Hamiltons, will join us this evening.'

'Excellent. No doubt we shall meet them later,' Sarah replied.

'Yes.' Gertie Stone blinked at Sarah. 'Afternoon tea will be served shortly in the gallery, and we will have drinks in the drawing room at seven thirty before dinner.'

'How lovely.' Sarah tucked her arm through Lucy's. 'We'd like to freshen up. Perhaps we might go to our rooms too, Gertie?'

Gertie's brow cleared, and she beckoned to a maid who was standing by. 'Show Lady Sarah and Mrs Lawrence to their rooms, Jean.' The young maid bobbed and made for the stairs. Gertie waved vaguely towards the stairway before turning away and drifting into a nearby room.

Lucy was bursting to make a comment on their hostess's strange behaviour, but knew from Sarah's clenched jaw she would have to wait until they were in private. Luckily, their rooms were next to each other. Lucy left Mary to unpack her things and went next door. Sarah was sitting at the dressing table, while her lady's maid tidied her hair.

Lucy chit-chatted until the girl finished and left the room. 'Sarah, why didn't you warn me?' Lucy asked, sitting down on a chair beside the window. 'Mrs Stone is extremely odd!'

'Poor Gertie! She's a pet, really. Very... other worldly, I suppose. Probably for the best when your husband is Andrew Stone.'

'He does appear to be a very serious individual,' Lucy said. 'Phineas had hinted at it.'

Sarah snorted. 'Dullest man I've ever met and with no imagination. It's a mystery to me that he and Phineas are brothers. They do not get on, as I'm sure Phin has told you. I would imagine the last few months have been difficult with his brother Sebastian so ill and Phineas insisting on staying here to keep an eye on him. Harold, their father, is a dear man, but his health is failing. Andrew has been running the estate for him for the past few years. I understand he's very efficient.' Sarah rolled her eyes.

Lucy smiled back at her friend. 'Andrew has the look of a man who revels in efficiency.'

Sarah gave an exaggerated shiver. 'A cold fish. Try not to take offence. His welcome to you was less than gracious. In fact, it verged on...'

'Frosty!'

'Yes, well, I think he has always been jealous of Phin with his easy manners, and of course, his success.' Sarah put in an earring. 'Don't mind him. It is only Phineas that should concern you.' With a flourish, she twirled her fingers through the ringlets of hair on either side of her face and smiled at her reflection in the mirror. 'I'm glad you agreed to come, Lucy. Phin would have been devastated if you had backed out.'

'It was a daunting prospect, I will admit, but my curiosity, as ever, got the better of me.'

With a grin, Sarah turned around. 'You have nothing to worry about. It will be a lovely couple of days.' But then her expression clouded, and she sighed. 'We certainly needed the break. Geoffrey has been under a lot of stress lately.'

Lucy had wondered. Geoffrey had been uncharacteristically quiet on the journey down to Kent. 'Why is that? Nothing too serious, I hope.'

Sarah frowned. 'That's just it. I don't know. He won't discuss it with me, but I'm aware that there has been some difficulty regarding his late father's estate, coupled with raising funds for the next election campaign. Horrid death duties are crippling so many great houses. But any time I try to discuss it, he makes excuses or says he doesn't want to worry me.'

Lucy didn't know Geoffrey very well and had always found him to be a little reserved for her taste, but that he wouldn't talk about any problems with Sarah was unfortunate. It brought to mind her own relationship with her late husband, Charlie. The distance between them had grown to such a point that there were days she'd felt she no longer knew him. Hopefully, the Strawbridge marriage wasn't headed in a similar direction.

'Politics is a rich man's game, is it not? Does he not have friends who will back him? Forgive me, but I thought he was considered a rising star in the Tory party,' Lucy remarked.

'Yes, indeed he is. There may even be a seat at Cabinet at some point. He has been lucky so far in his career, attracting the attention of suitable backers. Worthy men, no doubt, but terribly stuffy for the most part. I often have to entertain them, both in town and at Sidley.' She waved a hand. 'I'm sure I'm worrying over nothing. If it were serious, I'm certain he would tell me. Anyway, I hope he finds the time to relax amongst the Stones' guests. One is always guaranteed splendid company here.'

Lucy pulled a face. 'Speaking of guests, I suppose it was inevitable they would include the Vaughans?'

'The families are awfully close. I've told you this before.'

'Have you seen Alice Vaughan lately? Has she been behaving in a rational fashion?'

'I have heard nothing to the contrary. The last time I met Lady Dot, she told me they were over in Ireland, visiting some relatives of Edward.' Sarah frowned. 'Cork, I believe.' She gave Lucy a knowing look. 'The fact you have been invited will have everyone's curiosity roused. Don't be too surprised if Alice reacts.' She reached across and squeezed Lucy's hand.

'I fear it's very possible. That's why I was hoping they wouldn't be here, particularly after all that fuss last summer and Alice's strange conduct. Phin was blasé about it but what if she makes a scene?'

'Typical man; but I don't doubt there is an element of face-saving going on, Lucy. With the families on such close terms, the Stones would feel an obligation to help Lady Dot. The poor woman has been worried about Alice's behaviour for some time. Alice hasn't taken to married life very well. In fact, I suspect that is why Lady Dot thought it best the couple live with her.'

'I see. Edward Vaughan can't be thrilled about that arrangement.'

Sarah shrugged. 'He appears happy enough. I'm sure he's glad he doesn't have to handle Alice on his own. From the rumours I've heard, Alice is a handful even still.'

'I can well believe it. It is such a pity she had to drag

Phineas into the quagmire of her marriage. What did she hope to achieve?'

'Lord knows, Lucy. I expect she can't help herself, and Phin is handsome, successful, and of course, they were engaged at one time.'

'Yes, but to flirt with Phineas at the Royal Academy in front of her husband and the public!'

'I know, and there was a deal of scandal as a result. But I'm trying to be kind, Lucy. I'm extremely fond of Lady Dot.'

'Then I look forward to meeting her, Sarah. Hopefully, Alice will not remember me. We met briefly at Verrey's restaurant, as you know, and she was hostile towards me whilst simpering at Phin. So much so he was embarrassed.'

Sarah laughed and shook her head. 'Of course she will remember you. I do recall the night in question.' Sarah cast her a mischievous look. 'That was the night you were so naughty as to dine with Phineas and your poor husband barely cold in his grave!'

'Don't! I still don't know what possessed me. I broke every rule that evening.'

'I understand completely. Curiosity, loneliness, a broken heart—' Sarah ticked off her fingers. 'Perhaps even a little rebellion?'

Lucy sighed. 'Perhaps.' She gazed out the window, down towards the lake. 'Is there anyone else I should be wary of?'

'No!' Sarah gave her a sympathetic look. 'Lucy, you knew full well how it would be here; but take heart. Phineas wouldn't have asked for you to be included unless he wanted his family to meet you. But don't despair. I understand his sister Clarissa is not here, which is a blessing, as she's a female version of Andrew. The other siblings, Sebastian and Elvira, are lovely and will put you at your ease. His father, Harold, too. I expect they will be terribly curious about you, but they will not embarrass you.' Sarah laughed. 'I can't believe how nervous you are.

After all you have been through, this should not daunt you at all.'

Suddenly restless, Lucy squared her shoulders and stood. 'You are right, of course. Ignore me; I'm only tired after the journey.'

Never mind that my future happiness may well depend on the next few days.

Lucy briefly touched Sarah's shoulder as she passed. 'Are you going down for tea?'

'No, my dear, I wish to rest for a little.'

'Are you unwell?' Lucy asked.

'No, not at all. I will see you in the drawing room before dinner.' Sarah smiled up at her. 'Make sure you dazzle, my dear. I'm depending on you to cause a stir.'

THREE

Lucy's book lay unread in her lap as she watched Mary potter about. There was something calming about watching Mary. Despite her youth, she was an extremely efficient lady's maid. Since Charlie's death, the poor girl had had to fulfil quite a few different roles due to Lucy's circumstances. But now things had changed for the better, and Lucy wished to hire additional servants for Phillimore Gardens.

'Mary, there is something I've been meaning to ask you.'

Mary closed the armoire and scooted across the room to where Lucy was sitting. 'And what would that be, ma'am?'

'Your Ned—'

'Oh, he ain't my Ned no more.'

Lucy's heart dropped. That would explain why Mary had been so subdued of late. 'I'm sorry to hear that.'

'Nothing to be sorry about, ma'am. The rascal found someone else while we were off in foreign parts.' Mary sniffed. 'Good riddance, I say. What was it you wanted to say about 'im?'

'Well, now that we're settled, I thought perhaps he might have joined us as coachman-cum-gardener.'

The colour rose in Mary's cheeks. 'That was a kind thought, ma'am, but...'

'Yes, he obviously doesn't deserve it. Don't worry, Lady Sarah has recommended an agency to me. When we get back to town, I will engage them to find the rest of the servants I require.'

Mary's face took on a dreamy quality. 'It'll be nice to have a bit of company of an evening, ma'am. 'Tis a big house for just us two.'

'Yes, I couldn't agree more, Mary, and I don't expect you to run it on your own, though I have no doubt you could handle it.'

Mary's chin went up. 'We have managed since the master died.'

'And I would have been lost without you, Mary,' Lucy replied with feeling. 'Now, I must get ready. I understand tea will be served shortly.'

On entering the long gallery for afternoon tea, Lucy was disappointed to see only Andrew Stone present. He put down his cup and approached her.

'Good afternoon, Mrs Lawrence,' he greeted her, unsmiling. 'I hope you have settled in.'

'Yes, thank you.'

'May I get you something?' Andrew Stone waved towards a table at the far end of the narrow room where a couple of servants stood over the tea and coffee pots.

'Tea would be lovely, thank you.'

Lucy walked over to where he had been sitting, resigned to being stuck making small talk with him. Hopefully, other guests would appear soon. As she waited, she looked about. The gallery was long and narrow, the walls covered in portraits: presumably the ancestral Stones. One wall was lined with windows looking down on the gardens.

All too soon, Andrew returned with her refreshment.

'This is a delightful room,' Lucy said.

'Yes, it is,' he said, settling back down in his seat. 'How long have you known Lady Sarah, Mrs Lawrence?' he asked.

'About four years. We met at the Royal Free Hospital whilst visiting patients. We have been firm friends since then.'

'Yes, Lady Sarah is renowned for her charity work,' he replied, his smile not quite meeting his eyes.

Lucy smarted. Was he insinuating that she too was a charity case for Lady Sarah? Gritting her teeth, she smiled back at him. 'She's an example to us all.' She took a sip of tea, willing herself to remain unruffled. 'The house and estate are very beautiful, Mr Stone, what little I have seen of it so far.'

'We're rather fond of it, certainly. If you like, I will ask my brother to show you around if the weather is clement tomorrow.'

'I'm sure Phineas would be a wonderful guide,' she said.

Andrew's face hardened. 'Phineas? Oh, no. My youngest brother Sebastian would be better suited to the job. Phineas will be busy with Lady Dorothy and the Vaughans. They're great friends, don't you know. *Old* family friends.'

Lucy's initial dislike of the man opposite was now ramping up. My God, if she didn't know where she stood with Phineas, this conversation would be enough for her to flee back to London at the earliest opportunity. What was prompting this nastiness? Was it jealousy of Phin or her perceived unsuitability?

The door opened, and to her great relief, in strode Phineas. As he approached, he beamed at her, and her heart lifted and her qualms dissolved. However, she gave him a warning look and greeted him formally. 'Mr Stone, how nice to see you,' she said as demurely as she could.

Phin's gaze flicked to his brother. 'And a pleasure to see you again, Mrs Lawrence.'

Andrew grunted.

'Was there something you wanted to say, Andrew?' Phin asked, an edge to his voice.

'No, no. I was just thinking what a small world it is! I'm sure you two have much to catch up on,' Andrew said as he rose. He looked down at her. 'I understand, Mrs Lawrence, that my brother managed to have your brother convicted for fraud.' With that, he walked away to the other end of the room.

Angry colour flooded Phin's cheeks. Lucy tugged his sleeve and whispered, 'Don't rise to it.'

Phineas hesitated for a moment before shaking his head. He sat down beside her. 'I can only apologise, Lucy. Was he beastly?'

'Just a tad, but you need not worry; I'm well able to deal with it. After all, you forewarned me.'

Phineas threw a dirty look at his brother's back. 'He's insufferable. We've been at each other's throats since I arrived, two days ago.' Then he turned back to her. 'My God, it is good to see you.' He reached for her hand. Lucy shook her head. Phineas quirked his mouth as he captured it anyway. 'No, Lucy. He must realise he holds no sway over me.' The defiant expression in his eyes gave her solace. She'd determined not to mention Andrew's nastiness to him to save his feelings, but as he had witnessed it himself, there was little she could do.

'I warned him to be on his best behaviour,' Phin said.

Lucy turned to him. 'Well, that wasn't very wise. You probably antagonised him.'

He sniffed. 'Andrew is a dullard. It's always best to speak plainly. Now, more importantly, how was your journey down?'

'It was very pleasant and all the more so for travelling with friends,' she replied.

'Excellent, I'm only sorry that I couldn't accompany you myself.'

Phineas had been summoned to Kent earlier in the week by

his father due to Sebastian taking a bad turn. 'Not at all, I fully understand.'

'And I should have been here to greet you, too, but I had to go into Hythe to send some urgent telegrams.'

'Ah, a case, no doubt. By the way, you never did tell me about your trip to Ireland. Was it to do with a case?' she asked.

'Yes, indeed. I have been investigating a series of art thefts over the last eighteen months, and a very frustrating case it is. The latest theft was from a house in Ireland.' He shook his head. 'All the hallmarks of the same thief. At first, I thought they were isolated incidents; now I'm convinced there is one person orchestrating it all.'

'That sounds fascinating. Tell me more,' she said.

'No, no. I will not talk about work while you are here,' he replied, much to her disappointment. 'I'd like to spend time with you. It feels like an age since I saw you last.'

'Phin, we had dinner on Wednesday!'

'Exactly, two days ago—an age!'

Lucy chuckled. 'You can be quite frivolous, sometimes.'

'That's your improving influence,' he replied, his eyes alight. He glanced around the room and frowned. 'I thought more guests would be here by now. I haven't even seen the Strawbridges yet.'

'Sarah will not be joining us until dinner. She found the journey very tiring and wants to rest. The last I saw of Geoffrey he was heading off with Andrew but I haven't seen him since. Do you know if he's in some kind of difficulty? Sarah is worried about him; says he is out of sorts. She hinted at some financial problems to do with his late father's estate.'

Phineas frowned. 'I hadn't heard anything of that nature, but then I haven't been in town much lately.'

'Well, she must be worried about it to mention it to me.'

'I would hope if Geoffrey was in trouble, he would come to

me. Though, he knows Andrew better. They were at Oxford together.'

'He may be too embarrassed to ask for help, Phin.'

Phineas nodded. 'I'll see if I can find out something, discreetly.' He treated her to a smile. 'Now, shall I fetch you more tea? That looks as though it has gone cold.'

'Yes, please.'

Just then Geoffrey and Edward Vaughan entered the gallery. Geoffrey nodded and smiled at Lucy and greeted Phineas warmly. Edward lingered in the background, barely acknowledging Phineas. He ignored Lucy.

'There you are, my dear,' Phineas said on his return. He stole a glance at the others. 'Hopefully, they will leave us in peace.'

'Thank you,' she replied, taking her tea. She too was relieved to see the men meander down the room to seats at the far end, where they joined Andrew. Now, she could relax a little. She knew the opportunities to be alone with Phineas wouldn't be many over the next few days.

'How does Sebastian fare?'

'Not well, Lucy. I was dismayed to see how much he has regressed since I was here last. The bouts of illness continue. I had hoped being at home would help him recover, but between a nurse he can't stand and my brother's fussing, he's a mere shadow of himself.' Phin's voice had a strained edge.

'Perhaps he would do better in London.'

'I'm considering that option, but Andrew thinks Seb's removal from the house would reflect badly on him. We have argued about it. Unfortunately, I do not believe Seb's welfare is foremost in Andrew's mind.'

'Saving face is not uncommon, Phin.'

He chuckled. 'And he has made an art of it! But wait until you meet the rest of my siblings. They're dying to meet you, and I hope you will like them. Sebastian is a lamb, and Elvira is very similar to Lady Sarah, always in good humour. Unfortunately, my other sister, Clarissa, has just presented her husband with another child and was unable to travel. As for my father, he will adore you. You will meet him before dinner—he has to rest up in the afternoons.'

Phin's words sent a thrill through her: he would follow his heart, no matter what. *I should not have doubted him,* Lucy thought.

'Sebastian will join us shortly; he's especially keen to meet you,' Phin said.

'And I him. Are you very attached?' she asked.

'Yes. We were close growing up and always in trouble, whereas Andrew has always behaved impeccably; from babyhood, if my father is to be believed. To add to *his* woes, Andrew finds my profession an embarrassment.'

'Despite your success?'

'Because of it,' he said with a smile. 'But you know all about family jealousies.'

'I do indeed, but thankfully, all of that seems a lifetime ago now, Phin,' she sighed.

'I'm glad you have put it behind you.'

'Yes, I have, and it was one of the reasons I wanted to get away from England last summer. There has been no word from my mother, as you know, but Richard has written to me a couple of times. Unfortunately, he is not coping well in prison.'

'I don't often feel sorry for fraudsters, but his sentence was excessive, in my opinion,' Phineas said.

'Everyone said it was harsh, and now his solicitor has advised it might be possible to have the sentence reduced, but Richard is reluctant to drag it all up again, for the sake of the family.'

'It's a pity he didn't consider his family in the first place,' Phineas said with a shake of his head. 'It's a bit late to grow a conscience.'

'Phineas, I know you have offered to speak on his behalf,' she said with a smile.

'Ah!'

'It is very generous of you.'

'Say no more about it,' he answered, clearing his throat.

At that moment, the door opened, and a slender young man entered. Although not as dark as his brother, Captain Sebastian Stone was equally handsome, Lucy thought, as she shook his hand on being introduced. He was painfully thin, though, with a slight yellow tinge to his complexion, but his brown eyes brimmed with good humour.

Sebastian slowly lowered himself down into a chair, clearly in discomfort. 'Delighted to meet you at last, Mrs Lawrence,' he said. 'Phin didn't do you justice in his letters, I have to say.'

Phineas rolled his eyes. 'Behave, Seb; you're not in the officers' mess now.'

Lucy smiled at the young man. 'I understand you have been ill. I hope you are feeling better?'

Sebastian looked at his brother before answering. 'Coming along, nicely, thank you. Mercifully, that dragon of a nurse has departed. Her services, or should I say methods of torture, are no longer required.'

Phineas straightened up, his expression stern. 'What? I knew nothing of this.'

'Don't worry, Phin. I'm much better now. Father sent her on her way this morning.'

'Ridiculous! We will discuss this later, Seb.'

Lucy thought it best to change the subject. 'I understand you were stationed in India. A fascinating country, I believe.'

'A wonderful place! Have you ever been there, Mrs Lawrence?'

Lucy shook her head. 'My only knowledge of the country is from books, I'm afraid.'

Sebastian leaned towards her, his face lit up. 'I enjoyed my time there very much. But I was unlucky enough to fall ill and require rescuing.' He smiled apologetically at Phin.

'And how was your voyage home, Captain?' Lucy asked.

'Verged on unpleasant a few times, Mrs Lawrence; but as you see, I survived, in no small part thanks to my brother and the redoubtable George. The food on the ship from India to Cairo was dire. Even my major would have turned his nose up, and he'd usually eat almost anything. Why, once when we were up country—'

'Seb, Mrs Lawrence does not want to hear about your gruesome exploits in India,' Phineas said with a warning glare.

'Another time, Captain,' Lucy said with a smile.

'You're a good sport, Mrs L, I can tell.'

'For the love of—' Phineas snapped. This caused the captain to roar with laughter, which ended in a fit of helpless coughing. Across the room, Andrew swung around and glared at his younger brother. Lucy exchanged a concerned look with Phineas as Sebastian bent over, desperately trying to catch his breath. As the bout eased, Sebastian straightened up, but his face was deadly pale, with a sheen of perspiration on his forehead. A footman appeared at his side with a glass of water, and Phineas stood over Seb as he drank it.

'So sorry… darned illness,' Sebastian wheezed.

Phin laid his hand on his shoulder and squeezed it. 'Nothing to apologise for, Seb.'

'As I was saying, Mrs Lawrence, anticipating the delights of home kept our spirits up. I say, I'm sorry about all that trouble you had in Egypt. Phineas filled me in. The man who was murdered, he was a friend of yours?'

'Yes, he was.'

'An Egyptologist, I understand. I always thought that must be a jolly interesting line of work,' Sebastian said, eyeing his brother.

'Yes, it is, and he will be a great loss to the profession. I was fortunate to have the opportunity to make his acquaintance, and to help fund his excavation. As it turned out, his greatest rival is now leading the dig.'

'Phin told me the murdered chap found a new tomb,' said Sebastian. 'I wouldn't mind seeing something like that myself. I may take a trip to Cairo when I'm feeling more the thing. You wouldn't put in a word with this fellow to let me have a look?'

'You are hardly well enough to be exploring tombs,' Phineas cut in, his brow creased and his voice rather firm.

'Oh, I don't know. A few more weeks of rest, and some edible rations, and I'll be ready for an adventure. You wouldn't believe the vile offerings that nurse produced on a daily basis. Why even Andrew's hounds are better fed. Anyway, my condolences on the death of your friend, Mrs Lawrence.'

'Thank you, Captain. I only wish I'd had the opportunity to work with him for longer,' she said, pleased to observe Phineas tense at her words.

'Well, at least all of that unpleasantness is over,' Phineas cut in. 'Now, of much more importance—are you feeling better, Seb? I can make your excuses for dinner tonight, if you wish.'

Sebastian grinned. 'Good Lord, I wouldn't miss this evening for anything. The old man would be so disappointed if I didn't take part. I have a few lively tales to tell if anyone will listen.'

Phineas turned to Lucy. 'Do you see what I have to put up with? And I hoped the army would be a civilising influence.'

Sebastian sucked in a breath, but his eyes belied the expression of offence on his thin features. 'My, but you have become crusty.' He glanced across the room and said in a low voice: 'And I considered old Andrew the staid one.'

'Be careful, or I will leave you in his loving care permanently,' Phineas retorted.

Sebastian's eyes popped. 'Ha! An empty threat—you wouldn't dare. You care too much to condemn me so. No, as soon as you plan on returning to London, I'll be jolly glad to join you. You're getting on a bit now; I reckon you could do with a younger man around to look after all the dangerous stuff. What do you think, Mrs Lawrence?'

Lucy spluttered with laughter as Phineas closed his eyes as if in pain. 'I think that is an admirable plan, Captain,' she said at last.

'Traitor!' Phineas ground out, but he was smiling at her.

'And you like a bit of an adventure too, Mrs L. I'd be more than happy to help you out if you needed rescuing from tricky situations.'

'*Mrs Lawrence* is quite capable of looking after herself—as she never tires of informing me,' Phineas rejoined. 'Now, cease your nonsense, Seb, please.'

'Very well, Phin, whatever you say.' Sebastian turned and winked at Lucy. 'Now, tell me all the gruesome details of your adventures, Mrs L.' He threw a glance at his brother. 'It seems I'm not to have any of my own.'

FOUR

Lucy laughed nervously. 'Will I do, Mary?' Disconcertingly, Mary didn't answer but continued to twitch at the back of Lucy's dress, tut-tutting under her breath. 'Mary?'

Mary straightened up and grinned at her in the mirror. 'Sure, you'll outshine them all, ma'am. You've nothing to worry about. Don't you always look well in green.'

Lucy sighed. 'Are my nerves so obvious?'

'Well, ma'am, it ain't my place to say, but since you returned from afternoon tea, you have been on tenterhooks—'

Lucy ran her hands down the front of her dress. 'This evening is important. I will meet the rest of Mr Stone's family.'

'Of course, ma'am. Sure, I know that well, but...' Mary was biting her lip.

'Mary, out with it!'

'Mr Stone wouldn't have invited you here if he weren't serious about you. He's no Ned!'

Lucy turned and clutched Mary's hand. 'Oh, Mary, don't think about that scoundrel. You will find someone more worthy; I have no doubt.' Lucy exhaled slowly and turned back to the mirror. 'The truth is, I'm terrified. What if they don't like me, Mary? My past is not ideal.'

'Does that matter if he doesn't care? Now, let's finish off with that nice pearl set you bought in Paris. It will set off your dress beautifully.'

Both Lucy and Mary turned on hearing the bedroom door open. An unfamiliar face popped around the door. 'Lucy?' the young lady asked. Two bright blue eyes twinkled at them.

'Yes.'

The vision in cream silk advanced into the room, holding out her hand. Her raven locks were piled high on her head, her willowy frame only adding to the picture of perfection. Lucy knew immediately she had to be Phin's sister. They had the same nose and mouth; the same mischievous expression.

'I'm Elvira. I'm sorry, but I was too curious to wait to meet you.' Lucy's hand was grasped tightly and her face scrutinised. Elvira beamed at her. 'My, I have always said Phin had excellent taste!' Unsure how to answer, Lucy spluttered her thanks. Elvira glanced at the clock on the mantle. 'We have time for a chat. Have you finished dressing?'

Mary stepped forward and placed the pearl necklace around Lucy's neck, then stood back. Elvira tilted her head and nodded her approval. 'Perfection!'

'Thank you, Mary,' said Lucy. The maid bobbed and scooted out the door.

Elvira sat down on the sofa and patted the seat. 'Lucy, I'm so glad you came. I don't get home often these days, and I have been longing to meet you. Italy is such a journey away.'

'Oh yes, Phin told me. How lucky you are to live there. It's a beautiful country,' Lucy said as she took the place beside her.

'Thank you. I was a little naughty, don't you know. I married an Italian count. But you will meet Luca later, and I'm sure you will agree he's the most delightful man. Quite swept me off my feet. The family have... well, truth be told, Andrew has only just come round to the idea. Father and the rest of my siblings were happy for me.'

'How did you meet him?'

'I was accompanying an elderly aunt on a holiday, you see, and I met Count Carmosino at a dinner party in Milan. Have you been there? Oh, you must visit me, I absolutely insist on it. We spend the summers up at Lake Como—it's a magical place.'

'I have never been to northern Italy. I had intended to visit last year, but my plans changed.'

'Ah, yes. Egypt! Phin told me all about it. How plucky you are! I can see why Phin likes you.'

Lucy blushed. 'Thank you,' she answered, very much warming to Elvira.

'Please be assured you are very welcome to Thorncroft.'

'Thank you, Elvira, it's so kind of you to go out of your way to welcome me,' Lucy replied.

Elvira wiggled her fine brows. 'I had to make sure someone did. I suspect Andrew treated you to a cool reception, and poor old Gertie barely knows what day of the week it is. Have you met Seb yet?'

'Yes, this afternoon.'

'A scamp, but harmless. Idolises Phin, of course. Has done since childhood.' Elvira frowned. 'That only leaves Papa. I have no doubt he will adore you. We all suspect Phin is his favourite, though he would never admit it.' Elvira paused for a moment as if trying to decide whether to say something or not. 'You do know the Vaughans are here?'

Lucy grinned. 'If you came to warn me about Alice—'

'Indeed, I have. It's always good to be forewarned!' Elvira pursed her lips. 'What a lucky escape Phin had from that little witch.'

'Phin told me all about their relationship,' Lucy replied.

'Good. I was concerned you might be ignorant of their past liaison. Alice is likely to misbehave, and the shame is neither that dolt of a husband of hers nor Lady Dot can control her.'

'I'm expecting some hostility,' Lucy admitted.

'And it's best ignored, my dear.'

'Don't worry. I do not intend to engage in a cat-fight in the drawing room.'

Elvira bit her lip. 'I have to admit it might be entertaining, for I suspect you would best her in any confrontation.' Lucy shook her head and laughed despite herself. Elvira stood up and offered her arm. 'Then let us go forth, Lucy Lawrence, and do battle!'

Despite being a large room, the drawing room at Thorncroft had a comfortable ambience, enhanced by the soft light emanating from the crystal chandeliers, and the deep burgundy of the walls. Scattered about were sofas and chairs in small groupings, and a grand piano stood proud in one window bay. The two bays with floor-length windows led out to a terrace, visible by the light spilling from the room. It was too dark to see the view beyond, but Lucy imagined it had to be of the sea, if her sense of direction were correct.

As she surveyed the room, she spotted Lady Sarah and Geoffrey in conversation with Andrew and Gertie and an older couple by one of the windows. At the other end of the room, Phineas and Sebastian were part of a large group. As ever, Phin was immaculately dressed. His glance warmed as their eyes met, and he acknowledged her with a subtle bow of his head. A corresponding warmth bubbled up inside her. Beside Phin, Lucy recognised Edward Vaughan's long face and surmised the lady in the wine-coloured dress facing Phin was Alice. Thankfully, Elvira steered her in the opposite direction towards an elderly couple sitting together to one side of the fireplace.

'Excuse me, Lady Dorothy, Papa; I'd like to introduce Lucy Lawrence to you,' Elvira said.

Lady Dorothy Muldoon bowed graciously to Lucy and held out her hand. Her handshake was firm. 'Mrs Lawrence, how pleasant to meet you.'

With a little difficulty, the grey-haired Harold Stone rose to his feet. Lucy turned to him with a smile and held out her hand, which was captured immediately. 'Ah, my dear Mrs Lawrence; it's a pleasure to meet you at last. May I call you Lucy? I feel as though I know you already. Phin has told us so much about you.' Lucy nodded as he continued: 'Forgive me for not welcoming you when you arrived. I'm under instruction from my physician to rest up in the afternoons.' Harold bent over her hand and kissed it. Such an old-fashioned gesture, but somehow all the more welcoming for that. Although his features reminded her of Andrew, he shared the same expressive dark eyes as Phineas.

'Not at all, sir. Your family has been extremely hospitable.'

'Do please join us, Lucy,' Harold said, indicating the chair beside his own. 'You must forgive us old folk. I haven't seen Lady Dot for some time. We were reminiscing; something we tend to do whenever we get together.'

'Less of the old, please, Harry,' said Lady Dot with a chuckle.

Elvira squeezed Lucy's arm. 'We will catch up later, Lucy. Now, I must find Luca.'

Phin's sister drifted off, and Lucy turned to her host as she sat down. 'May I congratulate you on your birthday, sir.'

'Thank you, my dear. I suppose seventy is a milestone, though I'd rather ignore it, but the family insisted we celebrate. Now, my dear lady, you must call me Harry,' he replied with a wink. 'No standing on ceremony in this house.'

'Thank you, Harry,' Lucy said.

'I hear you are fond of travel, Mrs Lawrence,' Lady Dot said.

'Yes, I spent last winter in Egypt. It was very pleasant. Cairo is a fascinating place.'

Lady Dot sighed. 'I do miss going abroad. Since my husband died, the only travelling I undertake is with my daughter, Alice, and her husband. However, it tends to be house parties here in England. Edward doesn't like the Continent. Too full of foreigners, he says. Such foolishness!'

'Dear Dot, you don't have to abide by his ideas on the matter. You could always entice one of your many relatives to travel with you as companion.' Harry wagged his finger at her.

'The truth is I'm too old to be gadding about, Harry,' Lady Dot replied with a frown.

'Nonsense. Young Lucy here has blazed a trail and put us to shame. Why she has experienced more in six months than either of us in a lifetime.'

'Oh dear, my secrets are out!' Lucy exclaimed, trying not to blush.

'I was enthralled by your adventures, Lucy,' Harry said with touching eagerness. 'Perhaps tomorrow you could tell me more about them. You remind me of Phin's dear mother; full of pluck!'

'Oh yes, Eleanor was always the bravest of us,' Lady Dot said. 'We miss her dreadfully.' She pointed up to a portrait hanging above the fire. 'Beautiful and brave.'

'That was painted for my wife's thirtieth birthday,' Harry told Lucy with a sad smile.

The picture must have been painted in this very room, Lucy thought, recognising the backdrop. A gentle smile tugged at the lady's lips, and her eyes sparkled with mischief. Lucy wished she could have met her.

'I see no reason why a woman can't travel to foreign parts,' Harry continued. 'Some frown on it, but there is nothing more beneficial to the mind than new experiences. I have always encouraged the children to explore the world. If my health were better, I'd whisk you off myself, Dot.'

Lady Dot leaned across and patted his hand. 'You are a dear, Harry.'

FIVE

The bell rang for dinner. 'At last,' Harry said, rising to his feet as Phineas appeared by Lucy's side. 'Just in time, Phin,' his father greeted him. 'I was torn as to which of these delightful ladies to escort into dinner.' He grinned at Phin. 'As it's my birthday, I could be naughty and take one on either arm!'

'But Lady Dorothy must take precedence,' Lucy said.

'I'll second that,' Phineas said, offering his arm to Lucy.

Harry laughed. 'I know when I'm defeated. Come along, Dot.'

Phin and Lucy followed his father and Lady Dot to the dining room.

'That colour suits you very well, Lucy. I don't think I've seen you wear green before,' Phin said, caressing her hand where it lay in the crook of his arm.

'That is because you have rarely seen me in anything but widow's weeds,' she replied.

'True, your mourning is over,' he said with a hint of a smile. 'I suppose there will be a stampede of gentlemen to your door now.'

Lucy sniffed as Phineas pulled out a chair for her at the

dining table. 'Only one gentleman is of interest. Mind you, there is always the danger that he will get lost or be side-tracked by an interesting case.'

Phineas took the seat beside her and said sotto voce, 'I must remember to invest in a map.'

'It might prove beneficial,' Lucy quipped.

'To my future happiness?'

Lucy threw him a sharp glance. Phin returned her gaze steadily. And there was something deeper in his eyes, making her catch her breath. But before she could reply, her attention was called away.

'Why, it is Mrs Lawrence, is it not?' Alice Vaughan called from the far side of the table. 'I'm so glad to see you survived your travels relatively unscathed. So courageous of you to travel unaccompanied; so unconventional too.' This was followed by a titter.

Lucy felt Phin tense up beside her. 'Thank you so much for your concern, Mrs Vaughan, but I can highly recommend foreign travel. It elevates the mind so.'

Alice pinched her lips. 'Indeed? Again, you amaze me with your liberal view on the matter. I'm afraid I'm not as... *brave*. Widowhood must be extremely liberating.' She turned to Andrew, who had taken the seat beside her. 'What do you think, Andrew?'

Andrew glanced at Phin; whatever he saw made him flinch. He cleared his throat. 'I haven't given the subject any thought.'

Clearly disappointed in Andrew's prevarication, Alice continued: 'Well, Edward and I are content to holiday here in England. There are so many respectable resorts to choose from. I'm particularly fond of the seaside.'

Lucy couldn't resist a little mischief. 'Yes, I understand Blackpool is a delightful spot, and one is sure to meet only the *best* of company there.'

Alice's cheek twitched and her colour rose. Lucy treated her to a benign smile and turned to her new neighbour, Geoffrey, as he sat down. He immediately engaged Lucy in conversation. Once Alice was distracted, Geoffrey grinned at Lucy, throwing a glance in Alice's direction. 'Did I miss all the fun?'

'It's hardly that. I can't imagine what is fuelling her animosity.'

'Ah, now, Lucy, of course you do. Alice can't bear to see Phineas happy with anyone else.'

'Phineas and I are friends, nothing more, Geoffrey, as well you know,' Lucy replied.

Geoffrey chuckled. 'And yet you are here and on such an occasion.' He winked. 'Only a matter of time, my dear. I have no doubt.'

After several increasingly heavy hints from Elvira, Gertie eventually rose from the dining table and led the ladies away to the drawing room. In a mellow mood, Lucy followed arm in arm with Lady Sarah. Despite Alice's sniping, she'd enjoyed the meal and the company. She did regret not being able to answer Phin's question about the future when he had posed it. It was the closest he had yet come to declaring his intentions. The moment had passed, and it was impossible to recapture it: at least, until they were alone again.

Alice made straight for the piano and made a show of settling down at the instrument. Lady Sarah quirked a brow at Lucy. 'All the better to be the centre of attention when the gentlemen join us, I do believe.'

'Silly girl; best ignored. Shall I fetch you your tea?' Lucy asked Sarah.

Sarah narrowed her eyes. 'That is very kind of you, Lucy, but why?'

Lucy dropped her gaze to Sarah's waistline. 'You barely

touched your wine at dinner, and you looked ill in the carriage earlier and you are never travel sick. What clinched it was you missing afternoon tea. You *never* miss afternoon tea. Perhaps there is to be an interesting event in the near future?'

Sarah grinned. 'How clever of you to guess. But you must not say anything.'

'Does Geoffrey know?'

'Yes, but it's early yet. I'm not due until October.'

'I can keep your secret,' Lucy said with a grin. 'Now, sit down, and I will be straight back.'

Gertie and a footman were dispensing tea. When Lucy approached the tea table, Gertie looked up at her with a puzzled expression. Lucy could have sworn the lady was struggling to recognise her.

'That was a very enjoyable dinner, Mrs Stone,' Lucy said. She turned to the footman. 'Two teas, please.'

'Ah, yes, Mrs Lawrence, isn't it? Sarah's friend,' Gertie replied at last. Her gaze drifted towards the piano. 'Perhaps you would be good enough to play for us after tea?'

'I play very poorly and would clear your drawing room with my singing. Best to leave it to others. I suspect Mrs Vaughan is very proficient and eager to entertain us?'

'Yes, a wonderful performer. When she was engaged to Phineas, she was here a great deal. I always looked forward to hearing her perform.'

'Gertie, do stop chattering and pour me some tea!' Elvira stepped up and exchanged an apologetic glance with Lucy. 'May I join you and Sarah?' she asked Lucy as Gertie handed over her tea.

'Of course.'

Once they were out of earshot, Elvira said: 'I'm sorry about that. Gertie isn't known for her tact. I doubt she realises you are here because Phin wished it. Andrew would have drawn up the guest list. She probably assumes you are just a close friend of Sarah whom she dragged along.'

'Don't worry; I know she didn't mean any harm.'

'Still, thank you for understanding.'

The ladies settled down with their backs to the piano. As Sarah sipped her drink, she shivered. 'Goodness, I was looking forward to this.'

'Are you cold? Shall I fetch your shawl?' Lucy asked. 'I was going to slip upstairs to get my own.'

'Would you? Yes, all of a sudden I felt a chill.'

As Lucy descended the stairs clutching Sarah's shawl, she could hear the voices and laughter of the men coming from the dining room. It sounded much more fun than the drawing room, she thought, with a smile. Just as she was about to go down the last flight of steps, the men's voices grew suddenly louder. The door must have opened. Someone was telling a ribald joke, which was followed by raucous laughter. Lucy hung back on the next landing. She heard a door close, and the sounds from the dining room were muted once more. Peering down from the darkness of the landing, she spotted Edward Vaughan and Geoffrey Strawbridge in the hall.

To her astonishment, Geoffrey grabbed Edward's arm. Edward tried to shake him off. A heated but whispered conversation ensued, but Lucy was too far away to make it out. After a couple of minutes, Geoffrey pointed down the hallway before letting go of Edward's arm. With an angry gesture, he strode off towards the dining room.

Then, as she watched, Edward took up a candle from a side table and stared off into space as if trying to get his bearings. Nothing strange in that, Lucy thought. Perhaps he wasn't familiar with the house? Except he was clearly uneasy and kept looking about before eventually taking off at speed down the corridor in the direction Geoffrey had indicated. Lucy stepped down into the hallway in time to see Edward slip through a door at the end of the passageway. As far as she knew, it led to another wing. What on earth was he up to?

With a shake of her head, she turned and made her way back to the drawing room.

SIX

It was two in the morning. Lucy tiptoed along the deserted hallway, a knot of anxiety in her stomach. When she reached Sebastian's suite, she tapped gently on the door. George answered and ushered her in.

'I got your message, George. How is the captain now?' Lucy asked him.

'Very poorly, ma'am. I'm sorry to summon you, but Mr Stone is beside himself with worry and with the nurse gone, I thought—'

'Absolutely. You were right to send the message. Lead on!'

A single lamp was lit in the far corner of the bedroom. As Lucy entered, Phineas, seated at the bedside of his brother in his shirt sleeves, started and rose. 'Lucy!'

'Hush!' she said, meeting him halfway. Phineas took her hands and squeezed them gently. Lucy looked down at Sebastian lying on the bed. 'How is he?'

'A little quieter now. The doctor has just left. What are you doing here?'

'George sent a message.'

'No! He should not have disturbed you.'

Lucy shook her head impatiently and went to the bed. Sebastian slept, but even in the faint light of the room the mark of fever was on his thin features. 'What did the doctor say?'

Phineas joined her and stared down at his brother. 'That it was to be expected; as if that is any help.'

'He seemed fine at dinner earlier, though a little quiet,' Lucy whispered.

Phineas shook his head. 'It was only when we were retiring that he admitted he was worse. A splitting headache, aching muscles and the shivers. With the nurse gone, I thought it best I leave him in George's care. George helped him to bed, but an hour later came to me. Seb was in the grip of a raging fever and was delirious.'

'And you summoned the doctor.'

'Yes, immediately. He administered quinine and gave him a sleeping draught. For the last hour, we have been doing our best to keep him cool.' Phineas pointed to a bowl of water and a cloth on the bedside table.

'The poor boy!' Lucy took the seat beside the bed. 'Why don't you take a break and I'll look after him for a while.' Phineas protested. 'Hush! You'll wake him.' Lucy gestured towards the door. 'Off with you—get some sleep. Let me help. Please. I'll call you if there is any change.'

Phineas mouthed *thank you*, and closed the door. Ten minutes later, George appeared, bearing a tray.

'I thought you might like some tea, ma'am,' he remarked, setting the tray down. ''Tis terrible to see the young man so ill. I'm sure a lady's touch will help soothe him.'

Lucy smiled up at him. 'I'll do my best, George. You just take care of Mr Stone.'

. . .

Two hours later, Sebastian's fever broke, and his discomfort eased. When George entered the room, Lucy smiled across at him with relief. 'I think the worst is over.'

George came across to the bed and felt Sebastian's forehead. 'Indeed, ma'am, I do believe you're right. The master will be relieved.' Sebastian muttered, turned over, and appeared to go into a deeper sleep.

'Do the rest of the family know?'

'The master didn't wish to worry them, particularly his father,' George explained.

'I understand. Is Mr Stone resting now?' Lucy whispered.

'Yes, ma'am, he's dozing—out in the sitting room. But he would want to know...'

Lucy stood and rolled her shoulders to ease the stiffness. 'I'll tell him the good news. Would you mind sitting with the captain for a few minutes?'

'Of course, ma'am!'

Out in the other room, Phineas was asleep, resting his head on the arm of the sofa. Lucy froze. She'd never seen him look so vulnerable... or so attractive. Stubble shadowed his cheeks, and his hair was dishevelled, standing up in little spikes. A wave of affection flowed over her. He must be exhausted, poor man. It seemed a pity to disturb him.

Taking a seat opposite, she studied his sleeping form for several minutes, trying to decide what to do. Why had she not realised the strain he was under? Lucy rested her head back and closed her eyes.

'Have you abandoned your post?' Phineas's voice brought her bolt upright a few minutes later. He was in the process of sitting up, running his hands through his hair.

'Sebastian is much better and I... it seemed cruel to disturb you. You looked so peaceful,' she replied.

Phineas gave her an odd smile. 'My sleep was *not* peaceful.

I dreamed of you!' He patted the space beside him and grinned. 'You are a goose, Lucy. Come over here.'

As soon as she sat down beside him, he scooped up her hand. 'Thank you for your help. The fever has passed?'

'Yes, he's sleeping now,' she said, trying to ignore the strange quiver in the pit of her stomach and the sudden dryness of her mouth.

'Thank you.' Phineas raised her hand and kissed her fingertips, undoing her momentary recovery.

'It was nothing I did. It must be the quinine.' Lucy was acutely aware that she was rambling. A mischievous glint crept into Phin's eyes, but he didn't reply. He just kept gazing at her. Lucy gulped. 'Is something the matter?' Phineas shook his head. Suddenly self-conscious, she realised that in her haste to answer George's summons, she'd grabbed a dressing gown to cover her night attire, not stopping to dress. The robe was a voluminous Paris creation of brocaded silk, but it was still a dressing gown.

'I've never seen your hair down,' he murmured, winding a finger through a tress which lay over her shoulder. Their eyes locked, and Lucy couldn't have moved, even if her life had depended on it. 'You have bewitched me, Lucy Lawrence,' he whispered.

'Even if I'm nothing but trouble,' she answered, half smiling.

'*Because* you're nothing but trouble!' His first kiss was a gentle brushing of lips, but it was enough to set Lucy on fire with longing. The second was more demanding. She cupped his face with her free hand and returned his kisses with equal passion. The answer she needed was in his eyes as he leant forward, gently pushing her back against the sofa.

The bedroom door opened. 'Sir, your brother is asking for you... Oh! I beg your pardon!' George withdrew with haste. But the spell was broken.

Phineas groaned in frustration as he drew back. His gaze was full of longing and regret. 'My sibling will be the death of me,' he said, his voice hoarse. 'I'm sorry, my dear. I'd better check on him.'

Lucy laughed up at him. 'Perhaps it's just as well.'

'Please remember this is unfinished business which will be completed at the first available opportunity.' He held out his hand. 'Come, let's see how the scamp does.'

George was lighting another lamp as they entered Sebastian's bedroom.

'Well, young man, what do you have to say for yourself?' Phineas said, approaching the bed.

Sebastian gave them a watery smile. 'Terribly sorry to be such a nuisance. I'd hoped not to go through anything like that again.' Lucy's heart nearly melted at his words and his expression. Malaria was a cruel disease.

'You don't need to apologise, but I think you must now agree sending the nurse away was a mistake.' Phineas squeezed his shoulder. 'Get some sleep, Seb.' Sebastian gave a weary nod and closed his eyes.

'Don't worry, sir, I'll stay with him for the rest of the night,' said George, not meeting Lucy's eye.

'That will not be necessary. I will escort Mrs Lawrence back to her room, and will return shortly to give you a break,' Phin said.

George cleared his throat. 'There is no rush, sir.'

'I... Oh, very well, George. But I won't be long,' Phin answered with a mischievous glance at Lucy.

Then he ushered her through the sitting room and back down the stairs to her room. They stopped outside her door. 'Thank you, Lucy.' Phineas pulled her into his arms and kissed the top of her head.

'You do realise, Phin, that George could just as easily have summoned Elvira or Gertie to help you?'

'That is a good point, Lucy. However, I suspect George saw

it as a perfect matchmaking opportunity,' Phin answered with a grin. 'He fears I shall die a bachelor.'

'And his master didn't suggest that to him as a plan?'

'Innocent as charged! Now, *Mrs L*, as my dear brother would say, do as you are told—go back inside while I still have some self-control. Get some sleep. We have a lot to discuss, but it can wait until the morning.'

SEVEN

Phineas's note, which was slipped under her door in the early hours, asked Lucy to meet him at nine o'clock down on the shore. Happy to oblige, Lucy trudged through the sand dunes, and for one brief moment, she was back in the desert in Egypt. Except, of course, it was definitely England, not Africa, and it was extremely chilly. Lucy smiled. Some of the guests would frown upon her indiscretion. Meeting a gentleman alone was not the done thing. Mary's expression of disbelief when Lucy had told her she longed for a walk by herself on the beach had almost undone her. Luckily, at so early an hour, after such a late night, most of the other guests were still in bed and not witnesses to her reckless behaviour. But after last night, Lucy was sure of Phin. That was all that mattered now.

As Lucy emerged from the dunes, a squall coming off the English Channel buffeted her, and she wished she'd used a few more hatpins, as the wind threatened to relieve her of her hat. Along the shoreline, the waves were crashing onto the pebbles with a thunder-like roar. There was no sign of Phin. Lucy glanced at her watch; she was ten minutes early. With a contented sigh, Lucy stood gazing at the scene in awe. Growing up in the country, the seaside had been a novelty and rarely visited. Was that why she loved the sea so much now? She always found it exhilarating.

However, the eddies of nerves in her stomach at this moment were disconcerting. The way she felt about Phin was such a surprise, and so different to how she'd felt about Charlie. With the wisdom of ten years of marriage and the unveiling of her late husband's true character, she now knew it had been infatuation and a strong desire to leave Yorkshire, not love, that had drawn her to Charlie Lawrence. Charlie had never understood her nature or given her the freedom to be herself. She'd conformed to his concept of an ideal wife, and in so doing, had smothered a part of her true nature. Phin, however, loved her as an equal. He would let her grow to be the woman she was destined to be. Phineas accepted her many faults with a generosity of spirit she found humbling, even though he frequently gave in to the temptation to point out those failings. Knowing she could do the same only cemented her conviction that they would deal very well together.

Light of heart, Lucy took off down the beach to the water's edge, her boots slipping on the pebbles as they shifted under her feet. With one hand shielding her eyes and the other gripping her hat, she scanned the horizon, but there were no ships or fishing boats in view. The perfect place for a rendezvous. Growing impatient, she turned and surveyed the beach, only to spot Phineas making his way down the dunes. A knot formed in her stomach.

'Good morning,' he said as he drew level. Seconds later, she was enveloped in a hug and being kissed soundly.

'Good morning,' she whispered back when released several minutes later.

Phineas laughed. 'I'm sorry. Did I startle you?'

Recovering her equilibrium, Lucy lifted her chin. 'Certainly not!'

'Fibber!'

'If you're going to be nasty, I'm going back to the house for my breakfast,' she replied tartly.

'No, you're not. This is the best opportunity I've had to be alone with you. Those blasted guests and my meddlesome family are everywhere!'

'And don't forget our servants popping up at inconvenient moments,' she said.

'Poor George,' Phin laughed.

'Yes, indeed. I hope you appreciate what a fine fellow he is and how lucky you are to have him.'

'I have thanked the Lord on more than one occasion, I can assure you,' he replied.

'And your family is lovely; I don't know what you are complaining about.'

'Even Andrew? Have you been at the sherry this morning?' Phin asked, frowning down at her but with a twinkle in his eye.

Lucy spluttered and shook her head before giving him a playful push. 'How is Seb? Is he any better this morning? You must be anxious about him.'

Phin caught her hand in his and they set off along the shore. 'Thankfully, he was sleeping when I looked in on him. Poor boy is exhausted.'

'Will they engage another nurse?' Lucy asked.

'I hope not, for it has been a disaster. Last night proves Seb responds better to George's care. As soon as he can travel, I will take him back to Westbourne Grove; I know Father will agree. Between us, we will overrule Andrew's attempts to save face. Geoffrey gave me the name of an excellent doctor in Harley Street. I intend to call him in.'

'That's a relief. It was awful to see Seb so ill last night.' They walked on in silence for several minutes. 'I don't want to sound selfish, but you will still call on me. Seb won't take up all of your time?'

'My dearest idiot! I love you to distraction. You will be sick of the sight of me, Lucy. That is a promise.'

'I don't think that is possible, Phin,' she replied. 'I like seeing you too much. I love you, too.'

He grinned down at her. 'Truly? I was afraid you might not wish to remarry after your experience with Charlie, and we didn't have the best of starts.'

'That is very true, but I have decided to forgive you.'

'That is generous of you, indeed.' But he said it with a grin. 'Let us be serious, though, for a moment. While we appear to be enjoying a period of understanding—long may it last—I think it's only fair to warn you that I intend to approach Richard for your hand. That is, if you are agreeable?' Phin pulled her into his arms and kissed her again. 'Will you do me that great honour?'

Lucy gazed up into his eyes, overwhelmed with happiness. 'Yes, Phin. I will.'

'Thank God! It's the only way I will ever know where you are or what you are up to at any given moment.'

An hour later, Lucy and Phin made their way back up through the woodland to the rear of the house, hand in hand. As they reached the edge of the trees, Lucy heard raised voices and exchanged a puzzled look with Phin.

'I believe it's coming from the summer house,' Phin said, pointing to the small garden building in the centre of the lawn. 'And it sounds like the Vaughans. Perhaps we should skirt around the woods to the other side of the house?' he said with a frown.

'Lord, yes,' Lucy replied, 'We don't want to get caught up in that.'

But before they could move, Alice Vaughan erupted

through the summer house door, Edward close behind. 'Alice, stop!' he bawled after her. 'We need to talk about this.'

Phin pulled Lucy back into the shadows under the trees.

Up ahead, Alice spun around and snarled at her husband: 'I don't wish to talk to you. You are always so beastly to me. I rue the day I agreed to marry you. All you think about is yourself and what *you* want.'

Edward shook his outstretched hands in a helpless gesture. 'What are you talking about? This is ridiculous!'

Alice took a step towards him, shaking with rage. 'Well, I'll tell you, then. I don't want to visit the horrid Hancocks next week. All you do is drag me around the country to visit your tiresome friends, and I'm sick of it. Not to mention that dreadful trip to Ireland. I'm not acquainted with those people, and what's more, I have no desire to know them. Pathetic women with no breeding and their bourgeois husbands ingratiating themselves. It's pathetic. I won't go to any more of those atrocious house parties. They are utterly dull. You may go on your own.'

'I can't. You know how odd that would look, and it would give offence. Do you not think we have given the gossips enough to talk about already?'

'You dare to throw that in my face?'

'Look, Alice. These people are vital to our interests. You need to grow up. And coming here of all places was foolish; I should have known it would unsettle you. You will never forget Phineas Stone, will you? He haunts our marriage.'

'Nonsense!'

'Nonsense, is it? I see the way you look at him. When will you realise the man does not have feelings for you any longer? He has moved on with his life. I'd put money on it he's pursuing the widow.'

Lucy huffed and folded her arms. Phineas grinned back at her, wiggling his brows.

The colour rose in Alice's face. 'That awful woman! No, I don't believe he would be so foolish. Besides, with her frightful past, the family would never allow it.' Alice shook her head. 'If I were free...'

'Well, you aren't!' Edward roared at her. 'You are married to me and will do as you're bid.'

'Oh, I wish you were dead!' Alice screamed back at him.

'Charming as ever, my dear,' Edward replied before sidestepping her and striding away towards the house, his shoulders hunched and stiff with rage.

Alice flounced back into the summer house. Lucy could hear her sobbing. 'Oh dear, Phin, you best go to her.'

'Me? Oh, no thank you!'

'Why, yes. She hates me. I'll only make things worse. We can't leave her alone in such a distressed state. I'll go around the other way. Lady Sarah will be wondering where I have disappeared to. We were supposed to meet for breakfast. Go on. I will see you later.'

Phineas held her at arm's length. 'Very well. I will tell my father what our plans are, but let us keep this to ourselves until I have Richard's permission.'

Lucy tilted her head towards the summer house. 'Agreed. Probably best not to announce anything with the Vaughans here.'

Phineas kissed her swiftly. 'Exactly! I've witnessed enough drama for one day!

EIGHT

A Week Later, Phillimore Gardens, Kensington

Lucy handed Sebastian his tea. 'I'm delighted to see you looking so much better, Sebastian. London must agree with you.'

Sebastian beamed back at her. 'It does indeed, Mrs L— Lawrence,' he corrected himself, flicking a glance at his brother. 'Kent was far too quiet. I need distraction and a bit of excitement, so London is just the ticket. George has been looking after me well, and since visiting Dr Shaw in Harley Street, I'm feeling more the thing. I only wish Phin led a more exciting life. He disappears out without a word or spends his time at home at his desk, mulling over a case. And there I was imagining we would be running criminals to ground and saving the day. And as for his social life, well...'

'I'm here in the room, Seb.' Phin eyed his brother with barely suppressed amusement before turning his attention to Lucy. 'My company is not, it would seem, sufficient to keep boredom at bay.'

'That's not fair, Phin. You are far too secretive about your work, so what other option do I have but to force you to be sociable? A fellow can't stay in London and not meet people. I'm fed up looking at the four walls. Westbourne Grove is rather small, you must admit that?'

'You can always return to Kent; I'm not holding you against your will,' Phin replied. Seb smarted.

Believing more bickering would ensue, Lucy jumped in: 'It's *exceedingly* good of you to call.' She'd waited in every morning, hoping Phin would visit. Another day, and she would have taken matters into her own hands.

'Did you not receive my note?' he asked with a look of surprise.

'Why, yes, I did, and I expected to see you two days ago. Luckily, I have been busy settling into the house and engaging more servants.'

'Forgive me; I did plan to visit, Lucy; however, I was called away to Wiltshire. Another painting has been stolen and the insurance company is exasperated. As am I.'

Lucy sat forward, her gripe forgotten and her curiosity to the fore. 'Whose painting was it this time?'

'Lord Halpenny,' Phin replied. 'A James Alexander landscape, and a rather fine example of his work. Left with an empty frame, just like the others.'

'How many paintings have been stolen?' Sebastian asked.

'Lord Halpenny's painting is the ninth.'

'But how do you know the thefts are connected?' Lucy asked.

'Normally, stolen paintings eventually turn up on the black market. These paintings have vanished into thin air. None of my usual sources have heard anything. As for the thefts themselves, there is no sign of forced entry into the houses, yet there is no evidence to suggest servants or family are to blame. In several instances, the paintings were in locked rooms, stolen and the room locked again.'

'You are dealing with an expert lock picker,' Seb said.

'Exactly,' Phin said with a sigh. 'But that knowledge does not help me in the slightest, for most lock pickers tend to be common burglars: men generally not recognised as art experts. Yet, the paintings stolen are always priceless. Each one is carefully removed from its frame—a skill in itself—and a visiting card left behind; that is what links them conclusively.'

'Does the card have a name on it?' Lucy asked, perplexed.

'If only life were that simple, my dear. No, only a moniker.' Phineas rooted in his jacket pocket and pulled out a card. 'Here is the latest one,' he said, handing it to Lucy. 'Identical to the others.'

It was blank on one side and on the other was the message: *With the compliments of Apollo*. 'The god of art and music,' Lucy said, running her finger along the edge of the card. 'How extraordinary!'

'Yes, our thief has an inflated ego. And, he's stealing to order. Other valuable paintings are left untouched. One of the stolen paintings was in a private collection over in Ireland.'

'The same card left?' Lucy asked.

'Yes. To taunt me, no doubt.' Phin's expression turned grim.

'Is it the same artist each time?' she asked.

'No. All different so far,' Phineas replied, taking the card back.

'A particular style or school?' Sebastian asked.

Phin shook his head. 'I have found no link between the paintings.'

'Other than they are in private collections and extremely valuable?' Lucy said.

'Exactly!'

'And how long has this thief been active?' she asked.

'About eighteen months now.'

Lucy narrowed her eyes. 'Why are you giving me all this information, Phin? You usually keep me very much in the dark about your cases.'

Phineas had the grace to look sheepish. 'I may need your help.' His words ignited a warm glow inside her. He trusted her... or was he just desperate? Lucy glanced over at Sebastian, who was staring at his brother, the glow of excitement in his eyes.

'I'd be only too delighted to assist,' Lucy answered quickly.

'As would I,' piped up Sebastian.

'I'm afraid this is a job for Lucy alone,' Phin said to Seb, whose mouth snapped shut.

Red-faced, Sebastian glared at Phin. 'I see. I would have thought a family member would be a better choice.'

Phineas laughed gently and reached across to take Lucy's hand. 'Lucy will be family soon enough.'

'Oh! I say!' Seb said, his expression clearing to a wide smile, his irritation forgotten. 'Congratulations, you two!'

'Thank you,' Lucy replied.

Phin pressed her hand. 'We have a lot to discuss, Lucy. I suggest we do so over dinner later.'

Lucy took her time with her preparations that evening. The fact that Phin had mentioned their engagement to Seb made her sure that he was going to formally propose. She sensed the ceremony of the occasion was important to him, even though she considered herself engaged already. In the intervening week, she'd worried that Phin wouldn't act without Richard's permission. Her only worry had been that Richard might refuse, and if he did, how would she overcome Phin's scruples?

At her suggestion, they were to dine alone at Phillimore Gardens. Mary, sensing something momentous on the horizon, was unusually silent as Lucy dressed that evening, and for once, Lucy wished she could pour her heart out to her. But it wasn't something one did with one's maid, no matter what adventures and near-death experiences they'd survived together. With no sister and Lady Sarah visiting family in the country, Lucy had no one to confide in.

Bubbling with nervous energy and a great deal of happiness, Lucy supervised the laying of the table by the new maid, Janet, and had to restrain herself from interfering with the chef, only newly appointed. On her appearance in the kitchen doorway, Pierre Lacroix made it quite clear that the kitchen was his domain. Having enjoyed his culinary skills for several days and being relieved not to have to endure Mary's cooking any longer, she retreated, muttering under her breath, to the safety of the drawing room to await her guest. She couldn't afford to antagonise Lacroix. She'd poached him from a household in Mayfair and was determined to keep him under her roof.

Phineas arrived promptly, his demeanour calm, in sharp contrast to her own thumping heart. An affectionate greeting left her in no doubt as to his continued admiration, and it was with great reluctance that the couple disentangled themselves when dinner was announced. However, several glasses of wine and a splendid meal helped Lucy relax. As they sat over coffee chatting, Phineas produced a letter.

'I received this from Richard this morning,' he said.

Taking a deep breath, Lucy scanned it quickly. She looked up from her brother's letter, her eyes brimming. Across the dining table, Phin returned her gaze with a sympathetic expression.

'It's rather sweet of him,' she said, swallowing the lump in her throat.

'And thankfully in the affirmative,' Phineas replied.

'Did you doubt he would give his permission?'

'I will admit to a few anxious moments. If his response had been negative, it would have been extremely awkward for us.'

Lucy handed him back the letter. 'Perhaps, but I would marry you, anyway.'

Phin chuckled and shook his head. 'I suppose you would drag me to Scotland to be married over the anvil?'

'Something along those lines,' she replied. 'But seriously, Phin, society might not agree with me, but I believe Richard forfeited any right to have a say in my future. He was happy to throw me in jail to cover his fraudulent activities.' Lucy inhaled deeply. 'He may be head of the family, but he's wallowing in prison.'

Phineas rose and came around to her side of the table. 'Happily, his refusal is not an issue.' He drew a small velvet-covered box from his pocket, placed it on the table in front of her, and pulled out the chair beside her. His gaze intensified as he sat down and reached for her hand. 'Dear Lucy, I know we didn't have the best of starts that afternoon in the mortuary.'

'Don't remind me! You were so arrogant and not a little scary,' she replied.

'Was I? It was only because I suspected you were heavily involved in Charlie's shenanigans.' Phin held up his hand as she began to protest. 'Of course, I know differently now, and despite my suspicions, I knew that day you were someone out of the ordinary. You have never been far from my thoughts ever since, you know.'

'If only you had trusted me more,' Lucy whispered, breaking into a grin.

'And you me, my dear. I must admit no woman has ever driven me to despair as often as you have, and my grey hairs are testament to our turbulent past. However, that aside... Please stop smiling at me like that, it's putting me off... *That aside*, you can be in no doubt as to my feelings. I love you and can't picture a future without you by my side.'

To her surprise, his hands shook slightly as he picked up the box and opened it. She'd not expected him to be nervous. The ring lay nestled in white satin: a sapphire and diamond engagement ring, twinkling up at her in the candlelight.

She gasped as Phin slipped it onto her finger. 'That's not one of the maharajah's sapphires, is it?'

Phineas's shoulders shook with laughter. 'No, *they* are safely back in Kashmir. But I felt one was appropriate: to remind you of our first case.'

Lucy found there was a lump in her throat yet again. 'It's beautiful. Thank you. And of course, my answer is yes.' It was several minutes before she was free to speak again. 'I do have one proviso.'

Phin froze, and his eyes widened. 'Which is?'

'That we are equal partners, Phin. I want to be part of your life *and* your work.'

His shoulders relaxed, and he began to laugh. 'You *are* my life, and I doubt I could keep you away from my work, even if I wanted to.' He cleared his throat. 'I'm only too aware of your tenacity. However, I also have a stipulation.'

'Oh, you do?'

'Yes. When it comes to my professional life, if I feel you are in danger, I will insist that you heed my advice. That may constitute not being involved at all on some occasions, Lucy.'

Lucy nodded slowly. 'Very well, that sounds reasonable.'

He eyed her with suspicion. 'I have your word?'

She held out her hand. 'Let us shake hands on it.'

'Oh, no! I have a much better way of sealing a bargain!'

An hour later, a proud Lucy finished showing Phineas around her new home. Although only resident there a few weeks, she'd become very fond of it and hoped Phin would be equally enamoured. It was much larger than her old home in Abbey Gardens, and she particularly liked the rear garden which backed onto the Holland Park estate.

'I fell in love with the house on sight, but I don't mind if you'd rather we bought something together. Would you be happy to live here?' she asked, as they headed back to the drawing room.

'Yes, you chose well,' he replied. 'It's a fine house.'

'And you won't miss those bachelor rooms of yours too much?'

'Well, I could always keep them on as an office,' he said with a challenging gaze.

'Oh, so you can keep me at arm's length from your work. I don't think so!'

With a grin, he said, 'It was worth a try.'

The drawing room fire had almost died in their absence. Phineas grabbed the poker and did his best to revive it. Lucy watched him from the sofa with contentment, thinking how domestic a scene it was.

'I may have to hire more staff,' she said as he sat down beside her. 'I can't expect Mary and Janet to cope with such a large house.'

'I'll leave that business in your capable hands,' Phin remarked with a shudder. 'Once I have my George, I'm happy.'

'We will need a butler, and I thought perhaps George could fulfil that role as well. He's more than capable.'

'As you wish. I shall put it to him in the morning. Shall I put a notice of our engagement in *The Times*? Richard is not in a position to do it,' Phin asked.

'Certainly. I see no reason to delay any longer.'

'Do I detect eagerness, my dear?' She kissed his cheek in answer. 'And the wedding?' he asked.

'The autumn might be best. Charlie will have been dead for two years and fewer eyebrows will be raised.'

Phin grunted. 'That's five months away; could we not do it sooner?'

How eager he was, she thought, delighted. 'Ha! Scotland might not be such a bad idea, after all,' she teased in response.

Phin's expression turned forlorn. 'I suppose you are right.

Very well, the autumn it is. That just leaves the matter of where. Yorkshire is out of the question with Somerville sold. How would you feel about us getting married in Kent?' he asked. 'We could have the wedding breakfast at Thorncroft.'

'That's a wonderful idea, Phin. But would your brother be agreeable? I had the distinct impression he disapproved of me. He barely spoke to me all weekend at Thorncroft.'

'It's not his house, yet. He may disapprove all he likes,' Phineas replied with a frown. 'My father liked you, and that is all that matters to me.'

For several minutes, they sat, hand in hand, in companionable silence. 'When you were here earlier with Sebastian, you mentioned you might need my help with your case,' Lucy prompted.

'Hmm,' he replied, but his tone didn't hold much enthusiasm. 'As I told you this afternoon, I haven't been able to find any connection between the nine thefts, and none of my sources have heard even a whisper of what is going on. However, yesterday George was approached in the street by an urchin and handed this note.'

Phin handed over a crumpled piece of paper. Lucy flattened it out. *Wite Gallerie*, misspelt, was scrawled across the paper in pencil. Lucy glanced at Phin. 'Does the name mean anything to you?'

'I know of it. In fact, it was one of the many small galleries I visited, trying to track down the paintings. I spoke to the owner about six months ago.'

'And you are taking this information seriously?' Lucy asked.

Phin shrugged. 'I have no leads, Lucy.' He sat forward, lacing his fingers. 'I suspect someone is organising the thefts for a private collector, a man who must have extremely deep pockets. Who better to orchestrate such business than a gallery owner or art dealer, knowledgeable in his field and possibly aware of the contents of private collections throughout the country?'

'But you say this is a small gallery.'

'Yes, but it's exclusive. St John White, the owner, is well connected. Rent in the Royal Arcade isn't cheap.'

'Perhaps it's merely a case of his being successful and selling a lot of art.'

'Absolutely, that is entirely possible,' Phin replied, looking at the piece of paper, 'But why would someone try to point me in his direction.'

'Mischief?'

'That is certainly a possibility, but it can't do any harm to check.'

Lucy smiled. 'Have you no idea who sent you this?'

'I do, but I'd rather not say for now.'

'Very well, you had best tell me what it is you wish me to do,' Lucy said.

Phin made a show of looking about the room. 'Your walls are extremely bare. Such a shame!'

'Yes... I see. You want me to go shopping at Mr White's gallery?'

'I'd really appreciate it, Lucy. You would be welcomed with open arms. A rich widow wishing to adorn her new home with some very special artwork—how could he resist?'

'As you so helpfully point out, I do need to purchase a few paintings. But to flush this man out, would I not need to ask for something we know is in a private collection?'

'It would be best to buy a painting from the gallery first, so he believes you are a genuine customer. Then at the close, make the special request.' Phin rubbed his chin. 'Though it might be wise to wait for a second visit to introduce the subject.'

'Phin, I know so little about art. Surely he would see through me?'

'Not at all. Your request would not surprise him. Most of his clients buy what is popular to show off to their friends. Art is a symbol of wealth to these people, not knowledge of the finer things.'

'Very well. If you have a painting in mind, you better tell me all about it.'

'I do, as it happens. There is a rumour that Montgomery Stewart recently bought a highly sought-after Tissot painting called *Goodbye, on the Mersey*. Do you know anything about James Tissot?'

'Yes, I do. He lived in St John's Wood. Caused quite a stir with his live-in mistress. It was said he never recovered from her death and subsequently moved back to Paris a few years ago.'

'That's the chap. Have you seen any of his work?'

'Yes, quite exquisite.'

'Would you recognise his style?'

Lucy frowned. 'I'm not sure.'

'Don't worry. I have catalogues I can show you to help refresh your memory. There is a risk White might test you by showing you prints.'

'And who is this Mr Stewart? I've never heard of him.'

'You wouldn't have. He's a rich industrialist from the north with a fondness for art. Stewart owns a large estate outside Liverpool.'

'Hence his interest in that painting,' Lucy mused. 'He'd hardly want to part with it.'

'Exactly. Hopefully, our art thief, Apollo, will savour the challenge once White gives him the commission.'

'And you would be lying in wait, I suppose,' Lucy said.

'That's the idea, if I can persuade Stewart to help me. We have some mutual acquaintances, so I'm optimistic. My plan is to let Apollo take the painting in the hope he will lead me to the others. I want to find out who this unscrupulous collector is and retrieve those stolen paintings.'

'But you can't be sure White will take the bait, Phin.'

'No. But I have every faith in you, my dear,' Phin answered, kissing her fingertips, a gesture that sent a thrill through her.

NINE

A Few Days Later, Old Bond Street, London

Dressed in the most fetching of her Parisian visiting outfits, Lucy stood across from the entrance archway of the Royal Arcade, doing her best to ignore the butterflies in her stomach. That very morning, Phineas had called to tell her that Mr Stewart had agreed to be part of the plan. Although nervous, Lucy was delighted Phin trusted her with this mission. Their future together looked very promising indeed.

The entrance to the arcade had a charming façade, with the dear Queen's image adorning the top of the arch and beautiful reliefs in a Greek style positioned below. As soon as there was a lull in the traffic, Lucy made her way across the street and passed under the archway. White's Gallery was almost halfway down. A quick glance through the window told her the gallery was empty of customers. Perfect. A bell tinkled as Lucy entered. She glanced around the room. The white walls were adorned with paintings in a huge range of styles and sizes, an Aladdin's cave of art. In the far corner, an elderly and rather corpulent man sat at a desk. He regarded her unsmilingly for several moments before easing out of his chair.

'Good afternoon, madam,' he said with a bob of his head. His voice held the lilt of the Highlands. 'St John White, at your service. I don't believe I have had the pleasure of meeting you before. May I be of assistance?'

'Good afternoon,' Lucy replied, holding out her hand, his sickly-sweet tone turning her stomach ever so slightly. And whatever lotion he used smelled strongly of lemons. 'I'm Mrs Lawrence, and I do hope so. You have come highly recommended, you see. I have recently returned from abroad, and my new home is sadly wanting in decoration. Someone suggested you might have something to my taste in the line of paintings.'

'I'm gratified that you would consider my gallery, madam. I pride myself on always having the finest art in stock for my clients. Might I ask who recommended me?'

Lucy had to think quickly as she hadn't expected such a question. 'Now, let me see... Do you know, her name escapes me? It was at a soirée at Lady Muldoon's a few weeks ago.'

This appeared to satisfy him, and Lucy breathed a sigh of relief. 'Is there a particular style you like, Mrs Lawrence,' he asked, sweeping his arm in a grand gesture which encompassed most of the wall space.

'Well, sir, I must admit to not knowing a great deal about art; however, I do know what I like.'

'Of course. Please take your time and have a good look around. If you have any questions, do not hesitate to ask.' He bowed and returned to his desk.

Aware of his gaze following her, Lucy slowly surveyed the paintings. No prices were on display, and for a moment, she cursed Phineas. She had no idea about the value of the work before her, but hopefully admitting to her ignorance wouldn't make White suspicious of her choices. Would it be crass to ask?

Luckily, she came across a seascape which she would be happy to have on her drawing room wall.

'Madam is fond of maritime scenes?' White asked from right behind her.

Lucy jumped. How on earth had he crept up so quickly and quietly? 'Why, yes. Very fond indeed. I'd like to take this one, please. Do you have anything else by the same artist?'

White pointed to another landscape. 'An earlier work of Miller's, Mrs Lawrence.'

The man's closeness was making her uneasy. Lucy moved away on the pretext of examining the other painting. 'Yes, this is also to my taste. Perhaps you could arrange to have these two delivered to my home?'

White's smile was perfunctory. 'Certainly, Mrs Lawrence, my pleasure. If you could just furnish me with your address? Do take a seat.' He waddled back to his desk and opened a ledger, pen poised.

Lucy gave him the address and watched him scratch it down in his order book. She managed not to baulk when White looked up and told her the total price. As she retrieved her cheque book from her bag, Lucy heard the shop bell chime, but she didn't turn around. She wrote the cheque and handed it to White.

'Most satisfactory, madam,' he said, her cheque disappearing into the desk drawer with lightning speed. 'The paintings will be delivered in the morning.'

'Thank you, Mr White,' Lucy said. Her heart was thumping. Would now be a good time to bring up the Tissot?

'Good gracious! As I live and breathe, it's Lucy Somerville!'

Lucy turned around with a start. It was at least a decade since she'd seen him last, but she instantly recognised Thomas Hardwicke. His hair was now greying at the temples, his face florid, and he was chubbier around the middle than she remembered. What bad luck that an old beau should turn up here of all days!

'Thomas, how lovely to see you.' Lucy rose and stepped forward to greet him, hoping to make a quick escape. With an effort, she subdued her disappointment. The Tissot plan would have to wait for another day.

Hardwicke bowed over her hand. 'Ah, but if I recall, you deserted me for that scamp, Charlie Lawrence.' Thomas's breath reeked of whisky, and his words were ever so slightly slurred. Surely it was too early in the day to be imbibing?

'Yes, indeed, your memory is excellent.'

Hardwicke frowned. 'But I say, aren't you a widow now? Dashed sorry to hear about his demise. Tragic accident, wasn't it?'

'Yes, on Regent Street. Almost two years ago.' Keenly aware that White was listening, Lucy tried to change the subject. 'And you, Thomas, did you ever trip down the aisle?'

'Deary me, no. Confirmed bachelor, Lucy dear.' He looked around the room and said sotto voce, 'My first love was art, and it's still my passion. My brother has, I hate to admit, a finer collection, but he was good enough to point me in the direction of Mr White.' Thomas glanced across at the gallery owner. 'This is one of my regular haunts, is it not, White?'

'Yes, indeed, sir. Always delighted to see you,' White replied smoothly.

'I still recall that day you were so kind to escort my mother and me to the National Gallery,' Lucy said. 'It's always a pleasure to have an expert's view.'

Hardwicke beamed back at her. 'Well, my dear, it's very kind of you to say so.' Then he frowned. 'By Jove, I have just remembered. I saw your name in *The Times* the other day. I believe congratulations are in order.'

Lucy's heart sank. *Please don't let him say Phineas's name or the game will be up.* 'Thank you. How observant of you.' Lucy glanced at her watch. 'Good Lord, is that the time? I really must go. It was lovely to meet you again, Thomas.'

'I can't believe how unlucky I am. You have managed to slip through my fingers once more,' Thomas said, her hand held firmly in his grasp. 'I don't suppose I could tempt you to meet me for afternoon tea some day this week. Would love to chat over old times.'

Surely he must know such a meeting would be frowned upon, even though she was a widow? However, she was desperate to escape before he ruined it all and answered, 'I'd love to, Thomas. Shall we say tomorrow at four, at Brown's Hotel?' She could always send him a note to cancel.

'Splendid, splendid. Well, farewell, my dear Lucy. I hope that chap Stone realises how lucky he is.'

Phineas's Rooms, Westbourne Grove

'Phineas, I'm so sorry; there was nothing I could do. The game was up.' Lucy thumped the cushion as she plonked down on the sofa, still raging that their plan had failed so miserably.

'It's certainly unfortunate,' Phin replied with a grunt. His gaze was sympathetic, which just made it worse.

'Hardwicke didn't mention your first name, but the way White's head snapped up when he heard your surname, I knew he had made a connection.'

'And it will be easy for him to verify it. Not to worry, my dear. I will have to think of something else,' Phin said, sitting down beside her and taking her hand in his. 'At least you hadn't shown your hand regarding the Tissot.'

'There is that, I suppose. It's so annoying; it was such a good idea. Perhaps someone else could approach him looking for that painting?'

'Yes, it would be a shame to miss this opportunity, particularly as Stewart is willing to be bait.'

'Exactly! How about Lady Sarah? I'm sure she would be game,' Lucy said.

'And Geoffrey would kill me for putting her in danger. I don't think so, Lucy.'

She huffed. 'You were happy enough to use me.'

'That's different,' he replied with a smile. 'I know you can think on your feet in a tricky situation.'

Slightly mollified, Lucy smiled back at him. 'Charmer!'

Phin's gaze deepened as he leaned over and kissed her cheek. 'Siren!'

Several minutes later, Lucy pulled away. 'I do not come to you entirely empty-handed,' she said, reaching across to pick up a parcel from the table. 'I saw this in one of the shops in the Royal Arcade and thought it would be the perfect engagement present for you.' She handed it to him and watched as he unwrapped the cane. 'A less utilitarian one than your swordstick, but I'm always a little uneasy when you have that one with you.'

Phin quirked a brow. 'Does my swordstick inhibit your argumentative side?'

Lucy sniffed. 'Hardly!'

Phineas shook his head and beamed. 'That's a shame. However, this is perfect, thank you.'

'It was the Egyptian design that caught my eye. The shopkeeper assured me it's a unique piece made from the finest ebony. The inlay is malachite and mother-of-pearl.'

'I say, Phin, did you see my book? I know I put it down somewhere. Oh! Pardon me, Mrs L, I didn't know you were here,' Sebastian said, bounding into the room. The colour rose in his face as he exchanged a glance with Phineas. 'Perhaps you wish to be alone?'

'Not at all, Sebastian. You are just in time. You can help me persuade Phin that an intimate dinner for close friends and family is the best way to celebrate our engagement. Lady Sarah wishes to host a grand party at her home. I know full well she'll invite half of London,' Lucy said. 'What do you think?'

'Ah, Mrs L! No party? No, no. I can't condone that sort of timid stuff. The family were almost in despair that he'd ever get married. I say the bigger the party, the better,' said Sebastian, grinning across at his brother.

Phineas sighed. 'For once, I have to agree with you, Seb.'

TEN

The Strawbridge Residence, Mayfair, 8th June 1888

Lucy was almost light-headed with happiness as she glanced down at the ring glittering on her finger. Tonight was their engagement party, their wedding only a few months away. Despite her reservations—Lucy's appeal for a quiet dinner with friends had failed—she had to admit Lady Sarah had outdone herself. It bothered her greatly, though. Lucy hadn't forgotten Sarah's previous comments about possible financial difficulty. When she'd delicately put it to her friend that perhaps it wasn't a great idea, Sarah had pooh-poohed her concerns, telling her all was well. Certainly, no expense had been spared this evening. Sarah was always the consummate hostess, and this evening's party was a triumph. Even now, well past midnight, the champagne was still flowing, the party spilling over into several of Lady Sarah's reception rooms.

Phineas had been particularly keen that the evening went ahead. Lucy was unsure if Phin's enthusiasm stemmed from a desire to establish her with the upper echelons due to her less than perfect past, or because of his disastrous entanglement with Alice Vaughan. Unfortunately, for the sake of appearances, it had been necessary to include Lady Dot and the Vaughans on the invitation list. It was best not to give the society columns any more ammunition. But Andrew's and Gertie's absence, citing a prior engagement, was more damaging. Phineas had been furious, but Lucy had been relieved, even though she knew tongues would wag. Lucy didn't care for her own sake, but she could tell how hurt Phineas was by their neglect.

And now, although she'd avoided Lady Muldoon's group all evening, Lucy could do so no longer. With some reluctance, for she enjoyed his company very much, Lucy turned to Harry Stone. 'Please excuse me, sir, I must circulate again.'

Harry patted her arm. 'Of course. Don't worry about me.' He raised his glass of whisky with a grin. 'I have everything I need, and two fine sons to look after me when this runs out.' He glanced over at Phineas and Sebastian, now deep in conversation on the sofa opposite. Harry leaned in closer to her. 'Do you think Seb looks better? I'm ever hopeful he will make a full recovery. I suspect Phineas keeps the truth from me, as he does not want me to worry. But I can't help it.'

'As far as I know, there have been no other relapses since he came back to London with Phin. The new doctor he's seeing is pleased with his progress.'

'Excellent! That eases my mind. Now, off you go and enjoy the rest of your evening,' Harry said with a smile.

Phineas touched her hand as she passed and smiled up at her. 'Where are you off to?'

'Lady Dot.'

'Ah!'

'Don't worry, I'll be on my best behaviour,' she replied.

'I don't doubt it,' he replied with a knowing look.

Lucy soon spotted the Muldoon party and headed towards the French doors and the startling plumes of Lady Dot's head-dress. The doors opened onto the terrace, allowing a delicious, cool breeze to enter the crowded room. If only she and Phin could slip out and disappear into the darkness. Lucy sneaked a look at her watch. Twenty past twelve. Surely they could make an escape soon?

Lady Dot greeted her kindly, Alice with an icy stare. At least the vacuous Edward was missing. After a few minutes of stifling chit-chat, Alice piped up: 'I understand you have moved into your new home, Mrs Lawrence.' Her smile didn't quite reach her eyes. 'And not far from here. It must make a pleasant change from living out of a suitcase.'

The lady's words dripped venom-like from thin lips. Digging her nails into her palms, Lucy smiled back. 'Yes, indeed it does. It was Lady Sarah who heard the owner was thinking of selling and introduced us. It's a wonderful house, and Phillimore Gardens is delightful.'

'But, forgive me, that was before your engagement to Phin. Will you stay there when you are married?' Lady Dot asked.

'Yes. Phineas likes the house very much.'

'What a shame!' cried Alice. 'I'm sure he will miss those divine rooms of his in Westbourne Grove.'

'But my dear, those are only suitable for a single gentleman,' her mother said, frowning at her in a meaningful way.

Alice scowled. 'That may be the case, but I will always have happy memories—'

Suddenly, a series of screams rent the air, sending a shiver down Lucy's spine. It sounded like a woman in terrible distress. Alice gasped and her crystal flute hit the floor with a thud, its contents quickly becoming a dark stain on Lady Sarah's prized Persian rug. Lucy stepped back hoping to avoid damage to her dress. Silence descended on those near enough to the doors to hear the cries and puzzled glances were exchanged. Lady Dot stood blinking at Lucy, whose heart was now pounding. Something was wrong. No one in the Strawbridge house would scream like that without good reason. Could little James have taken ill?

Lucy scanned the room. Neither Lady Sarah nor Geoffrey was present. She really ought to find them and let them know something was amiss. Of course, she was rather interested to know what was going on, too. Around her, the gentle murmur of conversation started up again. Lucy made her excuses and moved towards the door. Just as she got to it, the butler entered. Lucy noticed his cheeks were ashen as he beckoned over one of the footmen.

'Where is the master?' he asked.

'I think he may be in the library,' the footman replied.

The butler's concern was obvious as he muttered under his breath and exited the room. Lucy's curiosity was now alight. Something *was* wrong. She had no choice but to follow.

The entrance hall was busy with guests as she made her way towards the library. She greeted those she knew but kept moving. Turning a corner, she caught sight of Geoffrey and the butler ascending the staircase, two steps at a time. Heart thumping, she hitched up her skirts and followed. To Lucy's surprise, they didn't stop on the second floor where she knew the family bedrooms were but continued up another flight, which was accessed through a door at the end of the landing. They were heading up the back stairs to the servants' quarters.

Lucy stalled at the bottom of the steps. She shouldn't follow: it must be a domestic situation with a servant. Relieved it wasn't anything to do with little James, whose health was a constant concern to his parents, she turned away. But she was reluctant to leave just yet. Leaning on the banister, Lucy breathed deeply and relaxed. It was lovely and cool up here. The voices from the party below were muted, and she felt a pang of guilt. As a guest of honour, she should really go back down. It was her engagement party, after all. But would it be so selfish to enjoy a few moments of quiet?

Lucy's reverie was suddenly shattered as the door at the end of the landing burst open and Geoffrey almost fell out.

'Oh my God, Lucy!' he exclaimed, his eyes bulging. His hand shook as it flew up to his mouth.

'What is it? What has happened, Geoffrey?' Her host stumbled towards her. In all the years she'd known the Strawbridges, she had never seen Geoffrey lose his composure. 'Tell me!'

'It's too ghastly,' he spluttered. Then he gripped her upper arm. 'Get Phin, quickly now!'

'But—'

'Just do as I ask, Lucy, please,' he replied, his voice shaking. 'He'll know what to do.' Geoffrey pulled a handkerchief out of his pocket and mopped his brow.

Lucy didn't hesitate. She flew down the flight of stairs. As she reached the next landing, Geoffrey leaned over the banister and called out: 'Don't say anything to Sarah.'

Lucy frowned up at him. 'But she'll know something is wrong if she heard those screams.' Geoffrey waved her on and turned to talk to his butler, who had now rejoined him.

Pausing outside the salon, Lucy calmed her breathing. She must present herself as unruffled so as not to startle the other guests. On entering, she spotted Phineas straightaway on the far side of the room, standing, chatting to Seb. When she reached him, she slid her hand through his arm while smiling at Seb. 'I wonder if I could entice you away for a few moments, Phin?'

Phin's glance was sharp, and as she surreptitiously squeezed his arm, his brow shot up. Thankfully, he read the signal correctly. 'Certainly.' He turned to Seb. 'Excuse us. We will return shortly.'

'Of course.' Sebastian grinned at them both before waving them off. 'You too lovebirds! Can't keep away from each other.'

Phineas threw him a warning look before turning to Lucy. 'Lead on.' Once they were outside the salon door, however, he tugged her to a stop. 'What's the matter, Lucy? Your cheeks are flaming. Are you unwell?'

She answered, suddenly flustered: 'No, no! We must hurry. Geoffrey needs your assistance.'

'With?' he asked.

'Phin, he wouldn't tell me, but he's terribly upset. It must be something ghastly. Please hurry. He's waiting for you upstairs.'

The second-floor landing was empty. Lucy gestured towards the door standing open. 'They must have gone back up to the servants' quarters.'

Phin nodded and hurried towards the door. At the bottom of the steps, he turned. 'Go back downstairs, my dear. There is no need for you to wait. I won't be long.' With that, he disappeared up into the darkness.

Lucy stood smouldering. He might be her fiancé, but he was ordering her about. *And we aren't married yet*! Sarah was stuck somewhere below with the guests whereas she was on hand. If there was a crisis with one of the servants, and that cry had been from a female, a woman's help would be vital, she reasoned. Decision made, she followed Phin.

The stairwell was dark and smelled of carbolic soap. As Lucy drew near the top of the stairs, she could hear the men's voices coming from one of the rooms. A footman stood about halfway down the narrow corridor. As she approached, he glanced nervously at her.

'Best not, ma'am,' he choked out as she tried to pass him. His hand shook as he tried to bar the way.

Undeterred, Lucy pushed past him and into the small bed chamber. Huddled in the corner on a chair was one of the maids, sobbing hysterically, her head in her hands. Geoffrey and Phin were staring down at the bed.

'You must call the police, Geoffrey,' Phineas said.

Lucy side-stepped around them, then wished she had not, as the scene came into full view. She gasped in horror.

Phin swung round and cursed before grabbing her around the waist and pushing her back outside the door. But it was too late: Lucy had seen it all in vivid detail. A man was sprawled face down across the bed. A gentleman, she discerned from his evening attire. A guest. The deceased's hand was clutching the bedspread. The bedclothes and the wall were splattered with blood, and the side of his skull was bashed inwards. But she could see enough of his face to recognise him. It was Edward Vaughan.

And if she wasn't mistaken, the cane resting on the counterpane next to the body—covered in something... vile—was a distinctive ebony walking stick inlaid with malachite and mother-of-pearl.

It was her engagement present to Phin.

ELEVEN

Phillimore Gardens, 9th June 1888

Shocking and Brutal Murder of Edward Vaughan at the Residence of the Eminent MP, Geoffrey Strawbridge was the headline in *The Times* that morning. Lucy lowered the newspaper with a sigh. How had the papers picked up the story so quickly? Someone must have gone straight to them. It was disgusting how people tried to make money out of tragedy. Lucy rubbed her eyes, which were dry and gritty. Her head was splitting too: a consequence of too much champagne the night before, and, oh yes, a vile murder. She pushed aside her uneaten breakfast as the scene in the maid's room flashed yet again before her eyes.

Now she was worried about Phin. Morose and distracted, he had accompanied her home, and they'd parted in silence, a peck on the cheek the only sign that he was aware of her company. With a mind full of disturbing thoughts, sleep had been fitful at best, even though she'd been exhausted when her head hit the pillow. When Mary had entered her room to start the day, all cheerful chatter, Lucy had lain despondent, with a heavy heart and some troublesome questions playing havoc with her composure. Who had murdered Edward Vaughan, probably the dullest and most insignificant man of her acquaintance, and worst of all, could Phineas really be implicated?

Lucy couldn't help but relive the scenes from the night before. When she closed her eyes, she could still see Edward sprawled on that bed with half his skull smashed and Phin's cane beside the body. She recalled Phin's anguished face as he had pulled her out of the room to the sound of the maid's sobs. Geoffrey had stumbled out of the servants' room after them and promptly cast up his accounts. Geoffrey's butler ran to his side, patting his back in an awkward way, his eyes straying to the room where Edward lay. Dead.

Phin regarded Geoffrey with an unsympathetic look and shook his head. 'This isn't helpful,' he had muttered under his breath, rubbing his hands. 'We must act quickly.'

'Oh, but Phin, this is dreadful!' Lucy cried, clutching his arm. 'And that poor girl.' Phineas gave her a puzzled look. 'The maid, Phin. We can't leave her in there with the body.' Lucy pushed past and went back into the room, deliberately avoiding looking at the bed. Lucy pulled the servant to her feet. 'Come now, you must calm down, my dear. You'd best accompany me.'

As they passed Phin out in the passageway, he stalled her. 'Thank you,' he said, caressing her cheek. But she could tell his mind was already occupied, running through the implications of the murder. He turned away and strode down the corridor to the footman guarding the room. The poor fellow wore a bewildered look. Phin told him to send a message to Chief Inspector McQuillan at Vine Street Station and the footman shot off, clearly relieved to get away. When Phin turned back to Lucy, his expression was bleak. 'We must inform the family. When you have found someone to look after the maid, go to Lady

Sarah and explain what has happened. Tell her to persuade Alice and her mother to join us in the morning room on some pretext. Let us break the news there, away from prying eyes and ears.' With that, Phineas turned away and began to instruct the butler to seal off the servants' quarters and to ensure no guests left the house before the police arrived.

Twenty minutes later, they gathered in Sarah's morning room to await Alice and her mother.

'What is going on?' Alice asked on entering the room, all smiles. 'This is all very cloak and dagger.'

Lucy squirmed at Alice's unfortunate remark and threw a bleak glance at Phin. However, he was staring off into the distance, his mouth a grim line.

'Alice, my dear, and Lady Dot, please sit down,' Geoffrey said. 'I'm afraid I have some dreadful news.'

'Should we not wait for Edward to join us?' Alice asked, her fine brows arching, giving her pretty face a haughty aspect. Lucy pushed down her dislike. After all, the woman was about to learn her husband was dead.

Meanwhile, Alice's words caught Geoffrey off guard, and his expression crumbled. 'My dear young lady, my news concerns your husband.'

'What has happened?' Lady Dot asked, grabbing her daughter's hand. 'Tell us, at once, Geoffrey.'

'Edward is dead. He was found a short time ago. I'm so dreadfully sorry.'

Lady Dot gasped and Alice went rigid. 'Was he murdered?' she asked at last.

'Yes, it would appear so.' Geoffrey shifted on his feet. 'The police are on their way.'

Lucy and Phin exchanged glances. Why had Alice assumed it was murder? Lucy's mind began to whirl. Geoffrey had said he was dead: he had not mentioned the possibility of foul play.

Then to everyone's astonishment Alice brushed off her mother's hand and dashed over to Phineas who was standing by the fireplace next to Geoffrey. She flung her arms around his neck and cried out, 'Oh no, Phin, why did you do it! Was it for me? For us?' Geoffrey's eyes popped and his mouth dropped open. Phineas's face, above Alice's head, drained of colour. He stood awkwardly, his arms encircling but not touching Alice. *As if she were a stick of dynamite*, Lucy thought.

On the sofa beside Lucy, Lady Dot gasped, her hands flying up to her face. Lady Sarah swiftly crossed the room and put her arm around the trembling woman's shoulders. A tiny part of Lucy's brain went numb, and for a moment, she couldn't think or move. When she did look up again and met Phineas's gaze, she smiled tentatively, as if to say *this is nonsense, I don't believe it*. The answering look of disappointment he gave almost undid her. Phin had sensed her split-second of doubt.

'Ma'am?' Mary's voice interrupted Lucy's less than sanguine thoughts. 'The chief inspector is here, ma'am. Will you see him now?'

'Yes, of course, Mary. Show him in, there's a good girl,' Lucy replied, composing herself as best she could.

'Chief Inspector,' she said as a weary-looking McQuillan approached. With dismay, she noticed he had aged: the grey hairs now outnumbered the red curls, and the lines around his eyes had deepened. The previous evening, she'd been too tired and distraught to observe the changes a year had wrought on her favourite policeman. 'Please do sit down. You look exhausted. Have some breakfast, or at the very least, some coffee.'

'I have eaten, thank you, but coffee would be most welcome,' he replied. McQuillan sat down with a sigh.

'Mary, fetch some fresh coffee, please, then see we're not disturbed.'

'Yes, ma'am,' Mary replied, her eyes flicking towards the policeman before she bobbed and quit the room. Mary had an in-built distrust of officers of the law, as Lucy had learned over the years. However, Lucy had a great fondness for the chief inspector, for he had helped her out of a very tricky situation the year before. 'Did you get any sleep last night?' Lucy asked him.

With a dismissive wave of his hand, he replied, 'I doubt I'll see much of my bed for some time. The powers that be are... well, you can probably guess.'

'Yes, of course. A murder in an MP's home is not an everyday occurrence. The government must fear a scandal,' she said. Lucy nodded towards her discarded newspaper. 'The headlines are ghastly already.'

'That's it, in a nutshell, Mrs Lawrence.'

Mary entered with the coffee. 'Thank you, Mary. I'll look after it.' Lucy poured McQuillan a cup and returned to her seat.

'Thank you,' he replied with a weary smile.

'I feel dreadful, as does Phin. The Strawbridges were so kind to host our engagement party, only for this to happen. Poor Lady Sarah was particularly upset, and in her present condition, we're all concerned for her welfare.'

'Ah, yes, I see.' McQuillan cleared his throat. 'I was there earlier and gave my consent for Lady Sarah to go into the country, if she so wishes.'

Lucy gave a sigh of relief. 'Thank you.'

'By the way, my congratulations to you and Phineas. It was not appropriate for me to say so last night.'

'I understand. Thank you, Chief Inspector,' she replied with a smile. 'Now, hadn't you best ask me those burning questions?'

'If only everyone were as generous with their time,'

McQuillan said with a shake of his head. 'Several difficult interviews already this morning, and it's only eleven thirty.'

'I will help you in any way I can; however, there is something that has been bothering me. What on earth was Edward doing up in the servants' quarters? I can't see a reason for it unless he was lured there. Of course, it's the quietest part of the house if one were inclined to murder someone and didn't wish to be heard.'

The chief inspector pulled out a notebook and pen and gave her a wan smile. 'Indeed. We have so far ascertained that Edward Vaughan was in the general company up to about eleven, at which point he received a message, delivered by a footman, and left the main salon.'

'Aha!'

The chief inspector raised a brow. 'Yes, quite. My problem is that the witnesses are unreliable, giving different times for this occurrence.' He treated her to a knowing look. 'Everyone appears to have had a lot to drink at that stage of the evening. Did you, by any chance, see Vaughan depart the room?'

'I'm afraid not. After dinner, I was circulating in both the salon and the drawing room.' Lucy frowned. 'I don't recall seeing Edward at all after dinner. If I'm honest, he was someone I would generally avoid.' Lucy leaned forward. 'I gather you have some idea of a time of death, then?'

McQuillan quirked a brow. 'Yes, though it helps us little as it could have been any time between eleven when he was last seen and twelve twenty when the maid discovered the body in her room.'

'What about the footman who delivered the message? Surely he could give you the information you require?'

'That is also a problem. He appears to have vanished.'

'And the note that lured Edward upstairs?'

'There is no trace of it. I assume the killer took it with him and disposed of it. The Strawbridges are of the belief that the murderer was one of the hired servants. Once the dinner was over, many of the hired staff left. I have an officer following up with the agency this morning.'

'Good.' A horrible thought struck her. 'Could Edward have known one of the maids? I hate to speculate, but if he had a dalliance with a maid or worse still had forced himself…?'

'You think he was murdered by a maid or other servant in self-defence? I suppose it's a possibility, but so far, we can find no connection between either of the two maids who share that room and Mr Vaughan.' McQuillan cleared his throat and glared at her momentarily. 'You have given the situation some thought. At this juncture, I suppose I need to remind you not to meddle.'

Lucy sat back with a sigh. 'I'm sorry. But I can think of little else.'

McQuillan gave a humourless laugh. 'I know only too well I will have the same problem with Phineas. It's the type of messy case I would gladly have his input on; however, for his own sake, it's best he keeps well out of it. I would appreciate if you would emphasise that to him when you speak to him.'

'You don't seriously think Phin—'

'The weapon was his.'

'Circumstantial. The murderer could just as easily have picked another. The cloakroom is at the back of the entrance hall and easily accessed.'

McQuillan licked his lips. 'Phineas was absent for at least fifteen minutes during the evening.'

Lucy's heart dropped. 'I was not aware of that. Are you sure?'

'His own brother confirmed it. But, as you said yourself, you were circulating. How could you know who was moving in and out of the rooms all night?'

Lucy closed her eyes for a second as anger bubbled up inside. 'Yes. It would be impossible for me to say with any certainty who was where at any time. Also, I will concede I wasn't keeping account of Phineas. But, Chief Inspector, you are acquainted with him far longer than I. Do you seriously consider him a suspect?'

'I can't treat him differently to anyone else, nor would he wish me to do so. I must concentrate on the evidence. Who had a motive and an opportunity?'

'As for opportunity, most of the guests probably left the rooms at some stage over the evening for various reasons. I visited the room set aside for the ladies to freshen up after dinner, as did many of the other ladies. I'm sure I was absent for about ten to fifteen minutes. Why not suspect me?'

The chief inspector harrumphed. 'What motive would you have? Besides, would you have had the strength?'

'I don't see why not. If I caught him unawares from behind. A good swing of the cane and—'

'But motive, Mrs Lawrence?' Oliver McQuillan shook his head. 'No. This is not helpful; a flight of fancy. Now, if it had been Mrs Vaughan found murdered...'

With a smart, Lucy sat up straight. 'I won't deny she's an annoying creature with her hysterics and constant dramas, but I don't wish her dead.' She clasped her hands in her lap. 'But I cannot and will not believe Phineas guilty. What would he have to gain by murdering Edward?' To her dismay, her voice shook.

The chief inspector sucked in a breath. 'I had an enlightening conversation with the widow's mother, earlier.'

'Chief Inspector, Lady Dot would most likely try to save face; I doubt she would tell you everything that would be pertinent. And as for her daughter, Alice, she is deranged. You know the history between her and Phineas. She broke off their engagement, then discovered she was still in love with him, though I believe *obsessed* describes her state of mind more accurately. Despite that, she went on to marry Vaughan. Foolishly, she has made a spectacle of herself on several occasions and in public, too. You must have heard about what happened at the Royal Academy last summer?'

'I'm aware of it, but I can't ignore Mrs Vaughan's claims, Mrs Lawrence. Even her mother believes them to some extent. Mrs Vaughan is convinced Phineas wanted to help her gain her freedom. That he still... loves her. I have the impression Edward Vaughan was not a kind or generous husband.'

'That is pure poppycock. I didn't like Edward, but the man was to be pitied. Alice's behaviour has been tiresome. As far as I know, Alice spent some time last year *resting her nerves*, as the family put it about. Probably in an asylum somewhere. She's infatuated with Phineas, don't you see, and convinced herself that he's her knight in shining armour.'

'Perhaps he returns those feelings?' the chief inspector asked, ever so softly.

'Phineas is engaged to me,' Lucy ground out. 'And a more honourable and honest man it would be hard to find.'

'I must look into it, all the same,' McQuillan said, not meeting her eye. 'Now, shall we continue?' Lucy answered with a stiff nod. 'Did you notice anything strange when you went into the maid's room?'

'Other than the dead man?'

'Mrs Lawrence!' The policeman's eyes glinted dangerously.

Lucy smarted, but he was right: now was not the time for levity. 'No, Chief Inspector. The maid was distraught and sitting on a chair in the corner, head in hands. Geoffrey and Phineas were looking down at Edward. As I entered the room, Phineas was urging Geoffrey to call the police. Of course, I spotted Phineas's cane on the bed. I gifted it to him only a few weeks ago. It was obvious... from the blood on it... that it had been used to kill Edward. Immediately after that, Phineas ordered the servants' quarters be blocked off and that no one should leave the house until the police came. I escorted the maid back downstairs and took her to the housekeeper; then I found Lady Sarah and broke the news to her. Phin and I had a brief conversation with Geoffrey and Lady Sarah, and it was decided that Alice and her mother should be taken aside and informed of what had occurred.'

'Was there anyone loitering, someone who looked out of place? Either on the upper landings or in the hallway when you followed Mr Strawbridge and his butler.'

'Not upstairs, no. There were servants and guests down in the hallway as I passed through. When I followed Phineas to the servants' quarters, there was only a footman doing his best to guard the room. He's known to me, for I visit the house quite often. I doubt he was involved: he was shaking like a leaf and barely able to function.'

Oliver McQuillan grunted. 'Anything unusual happen over dinner earlier in the evening? Did Vaughan appear to be his normal self?'

'I wasn't paying him much attention. He never says—said—much, in any case. A taciturn man at the best of times.'

'I'm sorry, I must ask this. Up in the servants' room, how did Phineas appear to you? How did he react?'

'Shocked, as was I. It was a nauseating sight. But you know him well. Phin is a man of logic, and I think he was struggling to be objective and do the right thing. When I entered the room, he was urging Geoffrey to call you and trying to preserve the scene as best he could.'

'Yes, it was quite a vicious slaying, one of the worst I have seen in recent times. But Phin appears to have held his nerve,' he said, his gaze boring into her.

'How can that be a negative?' Lucy asked, outraged. 'Someone had to take charge. Geoffrey was temporarily indisposed and his servants no better. Phin is no more used to seeing dead bodies than I, Chief Inspector. He investigates fraud and theft in his line of work, not murders. He did his best in very difficult circumstances.'

'And how did he react when Mrs Vaughan accused him?'

'Alice's accusation upset him greatly, as is only natural. The Muldoon and the Stone families are long-standing friends. I imagine he was hurt that Alice could believe such a thing about him. On the way here last night, he barely spoke a word. I could tell he was troubled, and I have no doubt it was genuine.'

McQuillan took a deep breath. 'I apologise, but I do need to ask this. Do you think there is any significance in the murder being perpetrated at your engagement party?'

Lucy blinked at him. 'I don't see how there could be. Well... other than it being a perfect situation.'

'What do you mean?'

'There were lots of people around, some strangers in the house, and as you said yourself, most present being a little inebriated. That makes it more difficult to investigate, does it not?'

McQuillan grunted and wrote something in his notebook.

'Chief Inspector, Edward's murder is a heinous crime, and would be no matter where it had taken place. We deeply regret the inconvenience and upset this has caused the Strawbridges. As a Member of Parliament, Geoffrey can't wish for scandal or gossip. It could jeopardise his career.'

The chief inspector looked up at her with a surprised look. 'No one suspects the Right Honourable Mr Strawbridge, Mrs Lawrence. What motive could there be? No. Someone with a strong motive carried out this murder. It was premeditated, too.'

Not entirely happy with where this was leading, Lucy piped up: 'Well, then I suggest you take a very good look at Alice Vaughan. I'm convinced she holds the key to this.' Lucy quickly told him about the argument she and Phineas had overheard between the couple at Thorncroft.

McQuillan wrote it down and in conclusion said, 'Obviously, I will challenge Mrs Vaughan about this when she's in a fit state for more questioning. However, as Phin's fiancée, I can't discount the possibility that you may be trying to protect him.'

Shaking with rage, Lucy stood and McQuillan had to follow suit. 'I *never* lie. I think we're done, Chief Inspector,' she snapped.

'For now.' With a sad smile, Oliver McQuillan turned on his heel and left.

TWELVE

Westbourne Grove, Kensington

Phin's valet helped her slip out of her coat. 'Good afternoon, George,' Lucy said. 'How are you, today?'

'Very well, madam, thank you,' he answered, folding the coat over his arm. 'The master left about an hour ago to escort Mr Stone senior to the station. I expect he will return shortly. However, Mr Sebastian is here if you care to join him.' His gaze shifted towards the drawing room.

'Yes, thank you, George.' Lucy was disappointed not to get a chance to say goodbye to Harry. But she delighted in Seb's company. Over the past few weeks, she'd grown extremely fond of Phin's brother.

'Would madam care for tea?'

Lucy beamed back. 'That would be excellent, George; you read my mind.'

George hesitated. 'Madam, I just wished to say thank you. The master informed me that you wish to include me in your new household as both valet and butler.'

'It would mean the world to us both, George.'

George gave a little bow. 'It would be my pleasure, madam.' He turned away on a smile.

'Hello, Seb,' Lucy called out as she entered the drawing room. She found him with his nose in a book.

With a cry of delight, he jumped up to greet her. 'Good afternoon, Lucy.' He kissed her cheek. 'I suppose George told you Phin and Father have left for the station?'

'Yes. Such a pity; I would have liked to wish him a good journey.'

'Father was anxious to say goodbye to you too, but Phineas felt it was best he went back to Kent as soon as possible.'

'Because of Edward's murder?'

'Well, yes. Father found it very upsetting. Lady Dot is a close friend, as you know. It took some time to persuade him not to dash over to her this morning. Well, with Alice's accusation hanging in the air, it would have been terrifically awkward.'

'Indeed!' Lucy replied, entertaining some far from pleasant thoughts about the awful Alice.

'Shall I call for tea?' Seb asked.

'Not necessary; the inimitable George has already suggested it.' Lucy said with a smile as she sat down. 'I must admit I think my household will run much more efficiently when he's part of it.'

'Butlers! Very dull stuff, Lucy, today of all days,' Sebastian said, sitting down. 'Of much more importance: what do you make of last night's events?' There was a decided sparkle in Seb's eyes.

'Tragic, my dear Seb. All the more so because of where it happened and who will be dragged into it,' she answered with an impatient sigh. 'None of it makes sense to me and why would Alice implicate Phin?'

Seb scoffed. 'To cover her own guilt. I wouldn't be surprised if she did it. She was always a rum 'un. Even when we were children, she behaved badly. The number of times the little witch pinched me till I cried or told lies to get me into trouble. She tended to pick on me because I was the youngest. I used to dread their visits to Thorncroft.'

Lucy chuckled softly. 'Are you trying to convince me you were a saint growing up?'

'Of course not, but you don't expect girls to be so mean.'

Lucy couldn't have disagreed more but moved the conversation on. 'Notwithstanding her strange behaviour, I don't think she could have done it.'

'Why?'

'I saw the body. There would have been a lot of blood. The murderer couldn't have prevented getting blood splatters on their clothes; I don't see how they could have avoided it. Her dress was spotless.'

'You checked?' Seb asked with raised brows.

'Oh, yes! And not just Alice.'

'You're amazing!'

'No, just observant, Seb. I also pointed it out to McQuillan last night, though more for Phin's benefit than Mrs Vaughan's. His clothes were without blemish too.'

'There is the possibility that the murderer was able to change their clothes, I suppose.'

Lucy nodded. 'If it were premeditated, they may well have brought a spare change of clothes, assuming it was a man. A change of dress would be rather a different matter, if it were a woman. Where would you hide a bulky dress in a house you might not know very well? Or have two identical dresses, come to that.' With a sigh, Lucy dismissed the idea.

'Well, Alice is still on top of my list. Couldn't she have covered her dress with something to keep it clean?' Seb asked. 'Even an apron. She could have taken one from her maid, done the deed, then hid it somewhere in the house or taken it home with her and destroyed it.'

'Perhaps.' Lucy gazed at him and smiled sadly. 'You've given this some thought.'

'Of course. I know Phin is innocent,' Seb replied with a fierce look.

'As do I, Seb. No need to glare at me.'

'Sorry. Very well, I can see you are sceptical about Alice, but I believe she's deranged enough to do anything. Phineas would never hurt anyone, and let's face it, no one could take her claim seriously. Rescuing that little minx from a disastrous marriage, when he has you?' Seb snorted. 'He would have nothing to gain and would run the risk of losing you and his life. Just daft! 'Tis all in her mind.'

'Thank you, Seb. However, I believe the chief inspector *is* taking it seriously, and therefore we should be concerned.'

'But we're agreed it wasn't Phin, so the only other logical conclusion is that Alice did manage to do it.'

'Unfortunately, I can't see how. However, there is another possibility. It may not have been Alice who swung that cane into her husband's head, but she may have encouraged someone else to do it for her.'

'I hadn't thought of that. Gosh! I wonder who.'

'It's only a possibility. I mean, she's the one with the most to gain from Edward's death. From what I witnessed at Thorncroft, their marriage wasn't exactly happy. She may have wanted her freedom, and I can't imagine the Muldoon family would countenance divorce. However, she's a rich woman in her own right and may have found another solution.'

Seb's eyes popped. 'Do you think she might have paid someone to do it? What an awful thought!'

'Stranger things have happened. Accusing Phin is an effort to shift attention away from herself. We both know Phineas has no motive. I did try to persuade McQuillan that was the case when he came to see me this morning.'

'You're a good egg, Lucy. I've no doubt you defended Phin to the hilt.'

'Of course, but I'd rather not be in this position. The sooner this is cleared up the better.'

'McQuillan paid us a call too and took our statements. Not a man I would wish to cross.'

'Perhaps not, but he's one of the best detectives in London. I've heard Phin say it many a time. I, too, hold him in high esteem; however, I'm afraid we didn't part on the best of terms this morning,' Lucy said with a sad smile. 'It's all so terribly unsatisfactory.'

Seb straightened up. 'You're never considering investigating?'

'No, absolutely not. I must place my trust in McQuillan. He's very experienced. Besides, I have had my fill of murders and murderers I can tell you.'

'Your adventures in Egypt?' he asked, and she nodded. 'Oh, I see. Very well... but you know if you should change your mind...'

'You are a dear. Let us hope it doesn't come to that.'

'Come to what?' Phineas asked, entering the room and eyeing both with suspicion.

Sebastian blushed and exchanged a startled look with Lucy. 'Oh! I was just telling Lucy I might consider going back to India, unless something more interesting happens here in London.'

Phineas didn't look convinced as he stooped to kiss Lucy's cheek. 'You are hardly well enough to consider returning yet,' he replied as he straightened up.

'We shall see.' Sebastian harrumphed. 'Did Father make the train?' he asked, suspiciously breezy.

Phineas accepted the change of topic without comment. 'Yes, and luckily Major Williams was taking the same train. They're travelling together, which is a relief. I sent a telegram to ensure Andrew has the coach to meet him at the station.' Phineas looked across the room towards the door. 'Thank you, George, you may leave the tray. We will help ourselves.' George nodded to Phin and floated back out the door. Phineas remained by the fender, staring down into the empty grate.

'Don't brood, Phin. It puts me off my rations,' Seb quipped, sharing an arched-brow glance with Lucy. 'Shall I do the honours?' he asked Lucy, nodding towards the teapot.

'Certainly,' she said. But her stomach plummeted as she regarded Phin. He had the look of a man too familiar with lack of sleep or unhappy thoughts.

With a grunt, Phineas eventually sat down beside her and accepted his tea from Seb.

'Are you well, Phin?' she asked.

'I've had better days, my dear. Oliver was here first thing. We may have some unpleasant days ahead.'

'He called on me, too. I put him right on certain matters,' Lucy said fiercely.

Phin picked up her hand and kissed the back of it. 'I don't doubt it.'

They chatted over their tea, but Lucy couldn't help but feel despondent. It was almost a relief when their conversation was interrupted by the entrance of George again. They all looked up as he coughed discreetly before handing Phineas a telegram.

Phin read it quickly and sighed. 'I'm to present myself to Chief Inspector McQuillan at Vine Street, first thing Monday morning,' he said, before scrunching up the telegram and flinging it into the grate.

THIRTEEN

Two Days Later, Vine Street Police Station

Chief Inspector Oliver McQuillan groaned as Lucy entered his office; this was quickly followed by a smile of embarrassment as he rose to greet her.

Lucy glared back at him, standing before his desk. She was not in the mood to be patronised or cajoled. Matters had taken a dramatic turn for the worse. 'I demand an explanation, Chief Inspector. This is outrageous! Why are you holding Phineas here?'

McQuillan held up his hands as she drew breath. 'He's helping us with our enquiries, Mrs Lawrence.' The chief inspector's expression turned sheepish. 'There is enough evidence—'

Lucy clenched her fists by her sides. 'Nonsense! Phin is no more guilty than you or my maid!'

'Please sit down and let us discuss this calmly.' Oliver waved towards a seat, his expression pleading.

Lucy threw him another scolding glance. 'I'm not feeling

particularly calm.' With a harrumph, she sat down. 'I want to know what is going on.'

McQuillan laced his fingers and stared down at them. 'A credible accusation has been made by Mrs Vaughan.'

'Good gracious! She is not well!'

'Their relationship history gives her claim some credence, you must admit,' he said.

'Nonsense. Phin had a lucky escape from her clutches. And I might remind you, he is now engaged to me.'

'That's as maybe, but—'

'If you are going to accuse me of being biased, then yes, I am. But you of all people know Phin is an honourable man.'

'Perhaps it was that very honour that prompted him to help her,' Oliver said, his voice low.

'That is an appalling notion, Chief Inspector, and unworthy of a friend.'

'Is it? After all, did he not help you when you were in distress?'

'The circumstances were entirely different.' Lucy clasped her hands in her lap. She needed to keep calm and convince McQuillan to let Phin go. 'I can't imagine that Mrs Vaughan's... accusation is sufficient grounds for an arrest.'

'True, but when you add in the other evidence, such as Phin's absence from the party and his cane being the murder weapon—'

'There must have been over sixty people at the Strawbridge House on Friday night, between guests and servants. Any of them could have taken that cane. It may have been the first to hand in the cloakroom and be no more sinister than that. And as for him following Edward Vaughan, that is ridiculous. Phineas insists he was freshening up. I'm sure someone could confirm that. One of Lady Sarah's footmen would have been in attendance.'

The Chief Inspector sat back. 'I'm afraid not. The man in

question does not recall seeing Phineas. I'm afraid, at the moment, every clue we have points to Phineas. We have no other suspects at this time.' McQuillan paused and cleared his throat. 'My superiors have insisted that Phin be questioned at the very least.'

'The evidence is entirely circumstantial. You have been too hasty,' she replied.

The chief inspector sighed. 'You must understand a murder in an MP's house attracts a lot of attention. Particularly a rising star in the ranks such as Geoffrey Strawbridge.'

'Ah!' Lucy straightened up. 'We get to the nub of it. Are you suggesting that Geoffrey Strawbridge has demanded Phin's arrest to avoid a scandal? Poppycock! I don't believe that for a second. The Strawbridges are close friends of ours. So, it must be someone else: someone in the Cabinet. Is the Home Office putting pressure on you to close this as quickly as possible?' The colour rose in McQuillan's face: the only answer she needed. 'Phineas is your friend,' she ground out in disgust.

'Indeed, he is, and I can assure you we will investigate this thoroughly. I will leave no stone unturned.'

Overcome with rage, Lucy had to take a few deep breaths before she could speak. 'I wish to see him, please. Immediately!'

'I don't think that is a good idea,' McQuillan replied.

'On the contrary, I think it's an excellent idea... and, furthermore, I *insist*.' Lucy stood, forcing McQuillan to do the same. Chin up, Lucy stared at him, determined to have her way. 'We need to discuss suitable legal representation and to expedite his release.'

'Very well. You can have ten minutes with him. That is the best I can offer.'

The interview room was familiar. Almost exactly a year before, it had been the setting for that awful row with Phin when she'd returned to London with the stolen sapphires. *Not auspicious,* Lucy thought as she sat and waited for Phineas to be brought to her from the cells. She drummed her fingers on the pitted and scratched tabletop in an effort to control the anger which was stampeding through her veins like a wild beast. But she wasn't sure who she was angriest with: Alice, McQuillan or the mysterious powers that be? Lucy clenched her fist so hard her fingernails bit into her palm. But anger was such a useless emotion in the circumstances. They would all have to keep cool heads if this mess was to be sorted out quickly. Lucy sucked in a breath as the dismal thought she'd kept at bay all day broke into her consciousness. Now, sitting in Vine Street, it was impossible to ignore what a conviction for murder meant: if they couldn't prove his innocence, Phin would face the noose. A tremor of panic almost undid her. She could not... would not lose him now.

As the door opened, Lucy straightened up, doing her best to project a serenity she did not feel. McQuillan entered first, followed by Phin.

'Well, here he is,' Oliver said with an attempt at a smile. He turned to Phin. 'I'm sorry. I can only give you ten minutes.'

'Thank you, Oliver,' Phin replied.

Lucy kept her gaze locked on Phin.

As soon as they were alone, Phin sat down opposite her with a sigh. He looked composed, but he was pale. 'At least I was spared the indignity of handcuffs,' he said with a quirked brow. 'I'm glad to see you, Lucy.'

'And I you. I came as soon as I could. Sebastian sent me a telegram to say you had been detained.'

'Were you really that surprised? The summons could only have meant one thing.'

'I suppose so, but I was still shocked. No one could seriously believe you had anything to do with Edward's murder,' she said.

'And yet, we find ourselves in this tricky situation. We need to discuss what is best in the circumstances.'

'I couldn't agree more. What do you want me to do?' she asked, leaning forward with eagerness.

Phineas let out a slow breath and a look of pain momentarily flickered in his eyes. 'I have given the situation some thought, Lucy. It might be best if we broke off our engagement.'

Stunned, Lucy could only stare back at him. 'You can't mean that,' she whispered at last, shaking her head. 'I will not abandon you.'

Phin stretched across and grabbed her hand. 'Don't be foolish. People would understand. If the worse should happen... I don't want you dragged into this debacle.'

Lucy scoffed. 'My reputation is already well and truly tarnished, Phin, thanks to Charlie. Besides, I'm already *dragged* into this. Did you not see this morning's papers?' He shook his head and suddenly his shoulders sagged. Alarmed by the look of defeat, she clasped his hand in both of hers. 'Phineas, look at me. We will get through this together. Whatever it takes to prove your innocence I will do and do willingly.'

Phin pulled his hand away and clenched his fist, his knuckles white. 'It's a shame we're not already married, for at least then I could forbid you to do anything as foolish.'

A surge of pure anger almost choked her. 'Oh, really? And what about *for better, for worse*? As far as I'm concerned, the wedding is merely a formality. We have made a solemn promise to one another.' Lucy waved her hand. 'None of this changes that—for me.' Breathing heavily, Lucy had to pause to compose herself. 'Phineas, you can't work on this case from a cell, but I can, under your guidance. Don't you see? And I know Sebastian will help.'

Phin closed his eyes as if in pain. 'No, Lucy! Do not involve Seb in this. He's not well enough. Nor yourself. Please, Lucy, listen to me. Meddling will only make it worse.'

'Meddling! I'm trying to help.'

'I know, Lucy, I know you are. But we must be patient. We're dealing with extremely dangerous people. If you— I couldn't bear to see you hurt.'

Lucy frowned. 'Why would anyone wish to harm me? I don't understand.'

'You must listen to me, Lucy. I can't explain it any further.' With a heavy sigh, he continued: 'The danger is real.'

'Why can't you tell me?' Phineas looked away. 'I promise I will be careful,' she said in dismay. 'But I would risk the danger for you, as you would for me!' Phineas looked horrified at her words. She carried on. 'Time is of the essence. If they hold you for much longer, they will have to charge you. Phin, you know vital evidence may have disappeared already. How do we know Oliver is following all the leads? What about the agency servants who conveniently melted away or the fact that anyone at the party could have taken your cane and used it?'

'And Alice's accusations,' he said with a grim look.

'Exactly! Someone needs to confront her.' Lucy sniffed. 'I'm more than willing to do that.'

'I was afraid of that.' He held up his hand. 'Lucy, I don't want you involved in the scandal.'

'The scandal, Phin, is the way this whole affair is being handled!'

'No doubt you have left Oliver in no doubt as to that,' he said, trying to smile.

'Of course.' Lucy leaned towards him. 'But I'm concerned, Phin. He appears to be under pressure to solve this quickly. He could crumble and charge you even though the evidence is so tenuous.'

'Please don't take it out on Oliver. He's in an impossible position. However, I have every faith in him to clear me in due course.'

Lucy was taken aback. 'I'm not sure I share your optimism. This is far too serious to leave to chance.'

The colour suddenly rose in Phin's cheeks. 'Lucy, I beseech you. Do not even contemplate investigating.'

'But—'

'Give Oliver some credit. I hold him in high esteem. He's one of the most experienced detectives I have ever known.'

'But what if he's impeded in his investigation? What then? Will you just accept your fate?' Lucy exhaled slowly, searching his face for a clue to his thoughts.

'He's perfectly capable of juggling whatever pressure is brought to bear while doing his best to get to the truth. This is not the first investigation he will have undertaken with Whitehall snapping at his heels.'

Lucy wasn't entirely convinced, but decided on another tack. 'What harm could it do if I were to help him?' she asked. 'After all, I know almost everyone who was at the party. People might be more willing to talk to me than to a policeman.'

'I'm certain he would refuse the offer, my dear. He barely tolerates my help as it is on cases where our interests cross.'

'Then I shall not tell him what I'm doing until I find the evidence to clear your name.' Phin groaned and Lucy smarted; his lack of trust in her abilities was disappointing. 'If our roles were reversed, you would already be out there, trying to find out the truth,' she said, with an angry movement of her hand. 'Admit it!' Phin winced, then gave her a disconcerted look but didn't respond. Lucy was mystified. Why was he behaving like this? What was he keeping from her and why? But she knew she wouldn't get answers from him today. 'Now, of more immediate importance is your legal representation. Who is the best?' she asked.

'That is taken care of. Andrew has already made arrangements. My dear, it would be best if you were to leave London for now. Why not go to Judith up in Yorkshire? Only a few days ago, you spoke of it as a possibility.'

'But I can't leave while this hangs over you,' she said, all too aware of the pleading tone she had used. Phin's expression was, to her surprise, blank. He swallowed hard, not meeting her eye. He drew breath as if he were about to say something when Oliver appeared in the doorway. The moment had passed. Phin stood, sharing a strange glance with McQuillan, who raised a brow.

Phineas turned back to her. 'Think on what I said earlier, Lucy,' he said, his voice full of pleading. 'It isn't too late to extract yourself from this situation. The law must take its course.'

Without further ado, Phineas followed Oliver out of the room.

FOURTEEN

Bow Street, the Following Day

Lucy made her way to Bow Street Magistrates' Court in a state of shock. Early that morning she'd received a telegram to inform her that Phineas was to be charged with murder and was to appear before the magistrate that very afternoon. She'd promptly burst into tears. The nightmare clearly wasn't over. How was she to help him? She hated to feel powerless and was consumed with anger that McQuillan had succumbed to the political pressure to charge Phin when the evidence was so weak.

On arrival at the courthouse, Lucy wasn't too surprised to see the crowds. Public interest in the case was intense. As she made her way inside, she was jostled in the packed corridor leading to the courtroom. Lucy suspected it was a mix of the public and the press but hoped she'd come early enough to secure a seat in the public gallery.

The newspapers that morning had been full of the sensational news that the famous Phineas Stone was to be charged with murder. Although still upset and not a little frightened for

Phin, Lucy was determined to show the world, and her fiancé, that she had every faith in him and his innocence. However, the first person she encountered amongst the throng of press and voyeurs was Andrew Stone, standing granite-like outside the courtroom. He seemed surprised she'd come and questioned the wisdom of it. Too preoccupied with the unfolding horror of the day, Lucy barely replied to his sharp comment. He must have travelled up from Kent on an early train. Then, with relief, she spotted a friendly face as Sebastian pushed his way through the throng to her side. George was right behind him.

Andrew treated Seb to an angry glare. 'Why are you late?' he demanded.

'Traffic,' snapped Seb before turning to her. 'Are you all right, Lucy? Come with me.' He tucked her arm through his before bestowing a nasty look on his brother.

What a comfort he is, Lucy thought. *And such a contrast to Andrew.*

'Father was too distraught to come up from Kent,' Seb whispered to her as they sat down. He glanced at Andrew who took the seat on Lucy's other side. Andrew remained bolt upright and unspeaking. Lucy almost felt sorry for him for he was clearly mortified to be present.

Sebastian snarled: 'I'm surprised *he* came. When he arrived this morning at Westbourne Grove, he ranted and raved all through my breakfast. Dashed bad form. My God! We nearly came to blows. I told him he had to come today to support Phineas, no matter what.' He gave her a sweet smile and squeezed her arm. 'I knew *you'd* come.'

'I had to, for Phin's sake. Besides, we need to know what we're up against,' Lucy whispered back.

Seb's eyes lit up. 'Are we going to—?'

Seconds later, Sebastian stiffened beside her as a hush fell over the courtroom. She gripped his arm as her heart began to gallop. Phineas had appeared from the depths of the court up into the dock. Two policemen accompanied him. Lucy had to bite her lip as her eyes welled up. She still couldn't believe it had come to this. This was all Alice's fault! In that moment, Lucy truly hated her.

Phineas appeared to be composed, but he was deadly pale. His eyes roamed the court, seeking her out. She caught her breath as he cast her one sad smile before his gaze shifted and his expression became fixed. Perhaps it was the only way he could cope. Was he terrified? she wondered. She certainly was!

Sebastian leaned in. 'You have to admire his stoicism, Lucy.' She nodded. 'That's our counsel, Mr Finlay, down there, and we have managed to retain Sir Wilfred Clark, QC. If it goes to trial, Phin will have only the best of representation.'

'Let us hope it doesn't go that far, Seb.'

'All rise!' rang out, and the magistrate entered the courtroom.

Soon, the proceedings were underway with the chief inspector being called to the stand. Lucy sat rigid with anger as McQuillan outlined the evidence on which the charge was based.

But there was worse to come.

Alice Vaughan was called next. The public gallery watched as one as the widow floated across the courtroom, swamped in black. Lucy clenched her teeth. What a pathetic figure Alice was as she slowly walked towards the witness box. But Lucy knew it was for effect. *Blast her! The grief-stricken widow just can't resist being in the limelight*, Lucy thought, biting down on her cheek. Did the woman genuinely believe Phin had acted in her interest or was this some kind of revenge? Whatever it was, Lucy determined she would get to the bottom of it.

Alice gave her evidence amidst many pauses to sob her heart out. 'Poor, poor Edward. He didn't deserve to die in such a brutal and cruel way!' she exclaimed.

Sebastian rolled his eyes, his face flushed with anger as the widow's words dropped like nails into Phin's coffin.

'Phineas was desperate to help me. He knew how cruel a husband Edward was.' There was a dramatic pause while she sobbed once more into her lace handkerchief. 'I pleaded with him not to do anything... rash.' She turned ashen-faced towards Phin in the dock, the handkerchief grasped tightly at her bosom. 'I still can't believe he did it. He just loves me too much, I suppose.'

The courtroom erupted, Seb cursed under his breath, and Lucy struggled not to cry. Phin's glance in her direction almost broke her heart. But then the whole procedure had been utterly grim so far.

Whilst the magistrate called for order, Lucy spotted a constable entering the court. His face was flushed, and he was breathing hard as though he had run a great distance. He went straight up to McQuillan and handed him a note. An intense conversation ensued for several minutes. As Lucy watched, McQuillan grabbed Phin's counsel by the arm and another heated interlude took place. Then the prosecution lawyer joined them.

Lucy drew Seb's attention to what was going on.

'Golly! I wonder what that's all about,' he whispered.

Just then the magistrate also appeared to become aware of the activity around Phin's counsel. 'Mr Finlay, would you care to explain what is going on or may I proceed?'

'I apologise, Your Worship, but may we approach the bench?' Mr Finlay said. 'There has been a significant development in the case.'

Lucy gasped and gripped Seb's arm, her heart racing. Dare she hope?

The magistrate didn't look pleased but beckoned Finlay and the prosecution lawyer forward. Eventually, after a brief debate, the magistrate nodded, scowled at the chief inspector who was still standing near the dock and was heard to mutter, 'Very well.' The men returned to their seats.

Sebastian turned to Lucy, his eyes full of apology. 'I don't suppose you could let go of my arm, Lucy. That is quite a grip you have.'

'Sorry,' she murmured, not daring to take her eyes off Mr Finlay, who looked as though he was about to speak.

'I wish to call Chief Inspector McQuillan to the stand again, Your Worship,' Mr Finlay said.

Holding her breath, Lucy watched as Oliver McQuillan made his way across the courtroom.

'I understand, Chief Inspector, that further evidence has come to hand?' the magistrate asked, his tone terse. 'Would you care to inform the court?'

'Yes, Your Worship, thank you. The blood-stained clothes of a waiter were found in the dustbin of a house close to the Strawbridge residence by a housemaid this morning. The owner of the property, guessing the significance of the find, sent a message to Vine Street. A servant of the house has confirmed that he saw a fair-haired man of short stature lurking in the grounds close to the bins on the night in question. He and the butler ran the man off, thinking him a burglar.' McQuillan glanced at the note in his hand. 'They both confirm the incident took place just before midnight.' Lucy could have sworn McQuillan's colour rose. 'We have various witnesses who can confirm that Phineas Stone was in the Strawbridge residence at that time. Based on this new evidence, Your Worship, the police case against Phineas Stone no longer—'

Whatever McQuillan said was drowned out by the eruption of the court once more. Several of the press men ran from the courtroom. Lucy stared at Phineas. Slowly, he turned towards her. Shock and relief crossed his features in quick succession. Then he smiled.

'Good Lord!' exclaimed Andrew.

Seb kissed Lucy's cheek. 'He's in the clear! The magistrate will have to throw the case out now.'

Lucy beamed back at him as relief flooded through her, but then she noticed Alice Vaughan staring across at her from the far side of the court, and a shiver ran down her spine.

Alice's glare was laced with hatred.

FIFTEEN

Lucy and Seb waited outside a side entrance of the courthouse for Phineas to be released. Unfortunately, so did most of the London journalists, anxious to get a scoop. Andrew Stone took one look at them, shuddered and disappeared without a word. Lucy was disgusted but not surprised at his behaviour. She hoped Phineas wouldn't be too upset that he hadn't bothered to wait. The newspaper men crept closer again, trying to catch their eye.

Lucy turned her back on them. 'What a nuisance they are,' she muttered to Seb.

'George, can you do anything about those fellows?' Seb asked in exasperation. 'Mr Stone won't want to speak to them.'

'Very good, sir,' George replied.

The valet drew the men aside and spoke to them in urgent tones. Whatever George said had the members of the press scurrying away down the street.

'Well done, George!' Seb exclaimed. 'How did you manage that?'

'I told them, sir, that I understood Mrs Vaughan was to be found talking to a *Times* reporter over on Russell Street.'

'How clever of you, George. Thank you,' Lucy said. 'And is she?'

George smiled. 'I very much doubt it, madam.'

However, it was almost twenty minutes later before Phineas finally appeared. 'I say, old man, that was a close-run thing! I don't think I'll be the better of that for a week,' Sebastian exclaimed, slapping Phineas on the back. 'Thank goodness that new evidence turned up.'

'Fortuitous, indeed, brother,' Phin replied, but he was smiling broadly at Lucy. 'Thank you for coming, my dear. The sight of you kept me from despair.' He flicked a glance at Sebastian. 'You too.'

Sebastian, looking a tad uncomfortable, averted his gaze. 'Not at all. We're family.'

Phin looked around. 'Where is Andrew?'

'Oh, he wanted to catch a train back to Kent. To, eh, tell Father the good news in person,' Seb lied, with a surreptitious glance at Lucy. Luckily, Phin appeared to accept this at face value.

Lucy slipped her arm through Phin's as they walked towards the waiting carriages George had procured. 'You must be exhausted, Phin. Did you get any sleep last night?'

'A few hours. My only hope was that the evidence the police had was too circumstantial for the magistrate, and he would throw the case out.'

Lucy paused. 'And so he might have, if Alice hadn't taken the stand!'

Phineas wrinkled his nose and sighed. 'I have to admit I'm mystified by her behaviour.'

'Well, I for one, am not!' Seb piped up. 'She's a witch and always was. I've a good mind to confront her about it.'

Phin shook his head. 'No, no, Seb. It would achieve nothing. Don't forget she's grieving. The funeral is only a matter of days away. And all was well in the end. I told you to trust Oliver.'

'I agree with Sebastian. You are far too forgiving, Phin. She was determined to see you charged for Edward's murder,' Lucy said, shaking her head. Then immediately regretted her words as Phin sucked in a breath, clearly distressed. 'Now, off home with you and get a good night's sleep. We can discuss things in the morning.'

'Yes, my dear. I'll call on you early,' Phin replied with a weary smile as he climbed into the carriage.

Seb squeezed her hand before jumping up into the vehicle after Phineas.

'Ma'am?' It was George, waiting to hand her up into the second vehicle that would take her home.

'Thank you, George. The best outcome, thank goodness,' she said.

'Very much so, madam. Let us hope that is the end of the matter,' he replied as he closed the carriage door and rapped on the side.

Lucy was still puzzling over his comment as they pulled out into the late afternoon traffic.

Lucy sat over her solitary dinner, exhausted. She pushed her plate aside, her food barely touched. Lacroix wouldn't be pleased, but it might as well have been dust and straw on the plate. Even now, hours afterwards, Lucy couldn't shake off her anxiety. The nightmarish quality of the afternoon had taken its toll on her state of mind. Perhaps an early night would help. They would all be in a better frame of mind in the morning to tackle the mystery of Edward's murder and Alice's false claims against Phin.

Halfway up the stairs, Lucy heard the doorbell chime, followed by knocking. Mary appeared from the nether regions to answer the door, her grumblings floating upwards. 'Now, who on earth is a-calling, this time of night? Inconsiderate is what I call it!'

Curious, Lucy stayed where she was, peering over the banisters down into the hall.

More banging on the door followed, sounding more urgent this time. 'I'm comin',' Mary said, raising her voice to be heard above the noise.

Lucy grew anxious and called out to her to be careful just as Mary opened the front door. A dishevelled Sebastian fell into the hallway. 'Where is your mistress?' he cried to Mary. 'Quickly now!'

Mary stood, hands on hips. 'Why she has retired for the night, young sir. Exhausted she is, and no time for *your* pranks.'

Sebastian looked at her as if she were mad. 'You must fetch her directly!'

'What is it, Seb?' Lucy asked, rushing down the stairs towards him. 'What has happened?'

'You must come at once. Phin has been shot!'

St Thomas' Hospital, Lambeth

Lucy sat in the dimly lit room watching Sebastian pace up and down. It was almost midnight, and the hospital was eerily quiet. On arrival they'd been told very little other than Phineas needed urgent surgery to remove a bullet from his shoulder; however, they feared there were other injuries as Phineas had arrived at the hospital unconscious. For the last hour, they had waited. He was still on the operating table.

'Do you know anything about what happened, Seb?' she asked.

Seb sat down heavily. 'Very little. He was going into his club on Pall Mall when some scoundrel ran up and shot him.'

'But why was Phineas out? I thought he'd have a quiet night at home.'

'So did I, but it was a long-standing commitment, he claimed. I think it was something to do with a case.'

'But why would someone try to kill him?'

He shook his head. 'I wish I knew. Luckily, the porter heard the shot and ran out. He scared the attacker off. Seemingly, he was aiming to shoot Phin again as he lay on the ground.'

Lucy swallowed hard, her stomach twisting at his words. 'Oh, my God!'

'First I knew, there was a constable at the door.' Seb dragged his hands down his pale face. 'Someone wants Phin dead.'

Lucy frowned at him. 'Yes, but who? Could it have anything to do with him being cleared earlier today?'

'Lord knows, Lucy.' He thought about it for several minutes. 'I don't know how there could be a connection.'

'I don't like coincidences, Seb. I'm sure Phin has made enemies over the years by exposing fraudsters and thieves but for anyone to want him dead... well, it doesn't seem likely.'

'And yet the attempt has been made.'

They both looked up as the door opened. It was Chief Inspector McQuillan, his face creased with concern. 'I came as soon as I could. Is there any news?' he asked.

Lucy shook her head. 'Not yet. He was extremely lucky, Chief Inspector. But I'm concerned. Do you think whoever it was will try again?' A horrible idea popped into her head. 'Maybe even here?' she asked.

Oliver McQuillan took the seat beside her. 'My dear Mrs Lawrence, I'm concerned too, I must admit. But do not worry. I have arranged protection for him here. There will be a constable guarding his room until he's discharged. No one will get near him again.'

Lucy gave him a tremulous smile. 'Thank you. And well done today. I didn't get a chance to thank you earlier. That evidence couldn't have shown up at a more serendipitous moment.'

The chief inspector gave her a wry smile. 'I couldn't agree more. If only we had discovered it a day sooner, we wouldn't have had to put Phineas through a court appearance.'

'Well, at least it went no further. Phineas has enough to worry about if his life is under threat,' Seb said.

'Agreed, Captain. If he had ended up in Holloway, an assassination would have been even easier.'

Lucy turned to him, horrified by his words. 'Chief Inspector, do you believe this has something to do with Edward Vaughan's murder?'

He quirked his mouth. 'I can't rule it out. I have my best officers on it, Mrs Lawrence. We have already interviewed all the witnesses outside the club.'

'Did anyone get a description of the assassin?'

'The porter caught a glimpse. Fair-haired and stocky and, it would appear, fast on his feet.'

'But that sounds like the man in Lady Sarah's neighbour's garden,' breathed Lucy. 'Edward Vaughan's murderer.'

A nurse appeared in the doorway and Seb leapt to his feet. 'Well? How is he, nurse?'

To Lucy's relief, the nurse smiled. 'If you follow me, sir, the surgeon will speak to you now.'

SIXTEEN

The surgeon's prognosis was hopeful. Phin had been lucky; the bullet had been safely removed from his shoulder. However, it was suspected that Phin had hit his head when he fell, for he had not regained consciousness. They thanked the surgeon and Lucy begged to see Phineas. One brief glimpse of him was all they were allowed. Lucy was overcome when she saw Phineas lying so still in the bed. She touched his hand but there was no response.

Seb moved up beside her and put his arm around her shoulder. 'Poor old Phin!' he said. 'Don't you worry, he will be fine. You heard what the surgeon said. He'll be fighting fit in no time. Come now, let me see you home.'

Lucy sighed and squeezed Phin's fingers once more before letting Seb lead her away. Only for the presence of a constable at the door of his room, Lucy would have refused to leave.

The journey home in the hansom through the almost deserted streets reminded Lucy of a similar journey with Phineas on the night he had brought her back from Yorkshire, a recently freed woman. The night she suspected she fell in love with him.

'Lucy?' Seb asked, cutting into her thoughts. 'You are miles away, but you must not worry so. Phineas is strong. He will pull through.'

'Sorry, of course, you are right,' she replied. 'But I can't help worrying about him.'

'That's only natural. But look, I was thinking. With Phineas indisposed for the moment, we should try to get to the bottom of things. I can't sit easy knowing that little witch, Alice, tried to set him up.'

Lucy blew out her cheeks. 'But why did she do it, Seb? That is the real question.' She sighed. 'All right. She hates me and obviously is upset that Phin and I are to marry. I just don't understand her. If she was still truly infatuated with Phin, why send him to the gallows? Surely she would save him instead?' Lucy threw Seb an anguished look. 'Could she be behind this attempt on his life as well?'

Seb whistled. 'Blimey! That's a shocking idea.'

'But why not?'

'Well... I don't rightly know,' he replied with a frown.

'If she's capable of having her husband killed, it isn't such a leap, now is it?' Seb shook his head. 'Perhaps this is about me.'

'What do you mean?' he asked.

'If she can't have Phin, she wants to ensure I can't have him either.'

'That would make her insane, Lucy.'

'I don't think there is any doubt about the state of her mental health. She believes what she said in court today. She's totally deluded, of course.'

'Deluded? Tosh! She's an evil little... madam, and no mistake! She's made it all up.'

'If you are right and we challenge her, she could spew out

more of her lies and stir up more trouble for Phin. I just wish I knew what was motivating her.'

Seb shrugged, casting her a woe-filled glance. 'I can't answer your questions, Lucy. I can't see the logic at all. What do you suggest we do?' he asked.

'I will try to see her, get her to explain,' Lucy replied.

'But the Muldoon house is in mourning. You won't be admitted.'

'Ah, that is where Lady Sarah may come in useful. There are few doors that remain shut to her.'

Mayfair, the Next Day

The sudden June heatwave was testing everyone's patience, but was particularly tiresome for Lady Sarah in her present condition. Lucy discovered her friend was not her usual sprightly self on arrival at the Strawbridge house. Wilting in her drawing room, Sarah had perked up at the idea of getting out in the fresh air, but once outside, Sarah quickly apologised. Although the Muldoon and Strawbridge residences were only streets apart, she was incapable of walking the distance required in the heat. But now, sitting opposite her friend, Lucy realised the carriage was probably worse, for Lady Sarah's face had a greenish tinge as the equipage trundled along over the cobbled streets. She regretted dragging Sarah along but knew the only way she could gain access to Lady Muldoon and Alice before the funeral was through her friend. Lucy's only thought was Phin's predicament.

'You do look unwell. Do we need to stop?' Lucy asked Sarah as they lurched over yet another dip in the cobbles.

After a pause in which Sarah swallowed several times, she replied, 'No, my dear. We're nearly there. I will be better presently.'

'Why didn't you say you felt so wretched travelling this way?'

'It's not usually so bad, Lucy. Besides, you need my assistance. Poor Phin. I do hope he recovers quickly. I was never so shocked when I saw the report of it in the newspapers.'

'He's a fighter, and I'm sure he will be fine,' Lucy answered with a sigh. 'I'm sorry to ask this of you, but I fear Alice is out to destroy Phineas with her vile lies. I want her to tell the truth. And until he regains consciousness, someone must do something.'

'I understand, Lucy, and I'm happy to help. However, I wonder... have you thought this through? It's unlikely she will want to help. She will be fuming after the result yesterday. All she did was make herself look foolish,' Sarah said.

'But that's just it. Some of the papers believed her and are daring to say that the new evidence was planted: that it's too convenient. And Phineas is in no position to defend himself, poor lamb.'

Sarah reached across and patted her hand. 'I'm sure he will be fine, my dear.'

Lucy took a calming breath. 'I think she had something to do with the attempt on his life.'

'Lucy! That is outrageous! You're not going to accuse her, are you? I will not be a party to that.'

'No, of course I won't, but you have to admit, it's all very odd.'

'Phineas wouldn't want you to get involved,' Sarah said with a knowing look.

'I know.'

'You have no faith in the police?' Sarah asked.

'McQuillan, and indeed Phin, seem very reluctant to admit that Alice may not be as innocent a party as she portrays. Besides, the police are unable to find this mysterious assassin.

How many more murders must he carry out before they catch him?'

'Do you think he may be hiding in the basement of Muldoon House?' Lady Sarah shook her finger at her.

'Nooo,' Lucy drawled, but she couldn't help wondering if it was a possibility.

'Lucy, Lucy. This is madness. You should heed Phin's request not to investigate. He must have a good reason to ask it of you. He's concerned for your safety. You can't just go around chasing down murderers.'

'And why not?'

Sarah shook her head. 'Lucy!'

'Oh, if he had his way, I'd be on my way to Yorkshire to stay with Judith. As if I would leave at such a moment with his life in danger.'

'It's a dreadful situation,' Lady Sarah said. She wiped her brow with a delicate sweep of her handkerchief. Then she frowned across at Lucy. 'I think you underestimate Phin. You need to trust his judgement more. As I said, he must have a good reason to want you to leave London. Perhaps it's as he says, he doesn't want the gossip to touch you. Or maybe he has another reason. But one thing I'm certain of, it is because he cares for you so much.' Sarah paused and raised a fine brow. 'Phin also knows what you are capable of if left to your own devices. Indeed, we all do.'

Lucy smarted but laughed despite herself. 'Yes, he's terrified I will go *a-meddling*. As for gossip and scandal, I'm immune to it. Though I deeply regret the scandal this has caused for you and Geoffrey when you have shown us nothing but kindness.'

'It isn't your fault Edward Vaughan was murdered in my servants' bedroom. Blast him!'

'Yes, it was rather inconsiderate of him!'

Sarah scowled. 'Lucy, don't! And as for scandal, yes, the newspapers have been quick to condemn us all with their nasty insinuations and speculation. Geoffrey is finding the sudden attention bewildering, and now the irony is that having been ignored by Lord Salisbury for the last two years, Geoffrey was summoned to Downing Street yesterday afternoon.'

'Good gracious. The Prime Minister!' Lucy exclaimed. 'And?'

'And, he came home and locked himself into the study for an hour. He refused to discuss it afterwards other than to say the PM was not pleased. Hopes of a Cabinet seat are now dashed. Well, for the lifetime of this government at least.'

Lucy's heart sank. She hated to see her friends affected.

Sarah looked out the window and said a little too brightly: 'Thank goodness, we're here at last.'

Lucy followed her gaze. There was no mistaking it; the Muldoon residence was a house of mourning. The hall door ornaments were draped in black crepe and the shutters closed over in all the windows. A flashback of Abbey Gardens after Charlie's death blurred her vision for one moment. For all her worry about Phin, she was about to enter a grieving household. There could be no barging in and making demands. Alice's behaviour may be strange, but she'd lost her husband, and Lady Muldoon her son-in-law, through violence. Lucy would have to balance respect for their mourning and her need to glean the truth from Edward's wife. The desire to pin Alice to the wall and demand she retract her accusation would have to remain the stuff of daydreams. *Am I really that wicked?* Lucy thought as the carriage came to a stop.

Sarah nodded to her footman who climbed the steps to the front door, Sarah and Lucy's visiting cards clasped in his gloved hand. He tapped on the door. As they waited, Sarah turned her gaze back to Lucy. 'We may not be admitted by the butler, Lucy. We really should not be here. You know it is frowned upon to visit the bereaved so soon.'

Lucy leaned over and squeezed her arm in gratitude. 'I

wouldn't ask unless it was so important. Alice must withdraw her accusation, Sarah.'

'I know, my dear, but we must tread carefully.' Sarah followed this with a stern look. 'Don't let fly, no matter how tempting it may be.'

Lucy pulled a face. 'I promise I will be on my best behaviour.'

'Hmm.'

The footman reappeared at the carriage door. 'Lady Muldoon will see you, ma'am.'

Once on the pavement, Lady Sarah took a few deep breaths, and a healthier colour flooded her cheeks. With one more plea to Lucy for restraint, Sarah climbed the steps towards the waiting butler. Lucy followed close behind.

The drawing room they entered was far too warm. In the dimness of the room, Lucy could make out Lady Muldoon sitting over the coals. Lucy's heart dropped; poor Sarah would die in this heat. Worse, there was no sign of Alice. Lady Dot looked up as they were announced. A smile hovered momentarily on her lips before fading, and her chin wobbled as Lady Sarah approached.

Swamped in bombazine, Lady Dot had aged since Lucy had seen her last. The fire of avenging anger in Lucy's heart spluttered and died to be replaced by an overwhelming urge to hug the poor woman. Not being as well acquainted with her as Sarah, however, she hung back. The situation required delicacy.

'Dearest Sarah!' Lady Dot exclaimed, holding out her hands. 'How good of you to come. And Lucy, too. You are both very welcome. Come and sit with me.' Sarah hugged her, then sat down opposite. Lucy shook her hand, then took the seat beside Lady Dot. 'I have never understood the custom that dictates no one should call on the bereaved. It is the very time you need your friends around you,' Lady Dot sniffed and settled back in her seat with a sigh. Then she shivered and began to rub her hands together. 'I can't seem to get warm. It is very odd.' Lucy exchanged a look with Sarah: the room was stifling.

Lady Dot continued: 'Alice has taken to her bed, of course. Giving evidence yesterday was too much for her. I pleaded with her not to go, but she wouldn't listen to me.' Lady Dot sighed. 'I suppose she felt she owed it to Edward.'

Lucy squirmed at her words as Lady Sarah leaned forward after giving Lucy a warning glance. 'How is she now?'

'The doctor has given her a sleeping draught. She's inconsolable and making very little sense. I do hope we don't have to send her *away* again.'

Lucy raised her brows at Sarah. Did the asylum beckon for the widow? It would be inconvenient in that Lucy wouldn't be able to question her, but perhaps it would be a blessing as she wouldn't be able to spread any more lies about Phineas.

'I'm so sorry to hear Alice is so taken down by it all. It's a terrible tragedy, Lady Dot,' Sarah replied. 'Geoffrey and I are so sorry for your loss. Edward was far too young...' She trailed off. There was little in the way of good things to say about Edward. Quiet and sullen-faced, he had always disappeared into the background. It made his murder all the more inexplicable. *Except, of course, if one were married to him*, Lucy thought, *and desperate for your freedom*.

'My deepest sympathies also, Lady Muldoon,' Lucy said, catching Lady Sarah's meaningful glance.

'Thank you both. It is indeed terrible. Poor Edward. To die in such a way.' Lady Dot fell silent, and Lucy and Sarah exchanged glances over her head.

'Lady Dot, I hate to be the bearer of more unfortunate news, but I'm afraid there was an attempt on Phineas Stone's life last night,' Lady Sarah said.

Lady Muldoon straightened up, her face ashen. 'Phin? Is he...?'

'No, no, he will be fine but must remain in hospital for the present.'

'I'm sorry to hear of this, truly.' She glanced at Lucy. 'My dear, this is shocking. I don't understand any of this. Two fine young men...' After a deep sigh, she continued: 'Edward wasn't the ideal husband for Alice, of course. I tried to talk Alice out of it, but well, she is and always has been, headstrong. Edward was far too easy-going. Alice needs a firm hand.' Lady Dot shook her head. 'I was so disappointed it didn't work out between Alice and Phineas. He would have known how to curb... Oh my dear, I'm sorry,' she said, turning to Lucy and taking her hand. 'I'm just a foolish old woman; please ignore my ramblings.' With that, she burst into tears.

Fighting the lump in her own throat, Lucy consoled her as best she could, but it was several minutes before Lady Dot gained her self-control. Lucy kept hold of her hand and looked about the room, trying to avoid looking at Sarah, who was dabbing her own tears. The mirrors were covered, the clock stopped, and all the pictures were face down on the sideboard. No wonder the poor woman was distraught, left all alone in such a room of misery. Guilt crept over Lucy. She should not have come, not yet at least, and it was clear there would be no opportunity to confront Alice.

'Lady Muldoon, I'm sure you would like a few minutes with Lady Sarah,' Lucy said, rising. Casting a meaningful glance at Sarah, she said goodbye. 'I just wanted to convey my condolences. I'll wait out in the carriage, Sarah.'

Her friend nodded her approval and took Lucy's vacated seat beside the grieving old lady.

. . .

Twenty minutes later, Lady Sarah joined Lucy in the carriage. Lucy was alarmed to see her pasty complexion and the sheen of perspiration on her brow.

'My dear, are you well?' Lucy asked, as the door closed.

Sarah sank into the squabs with a deep sigh. 'Too warm,' was all she could say.

Lucy tapped the roof with her parasol, and the carriage swept out into the morning traffic. After several minutes, Sarah opened her eyes. Her expression was grim.

'It's not good news, Lucy; it's not good news at all.'

SEVENTEEN

Lucy watched as Sarah's footman obeyed his mistress's plea that he let some cooling air into the house. Sarah sat down by the open window, fanning herself, gazing down into the street below. Lucy realised she was avoiding eye contact with her, and her anxiety grew even more. Whatever Lady Dot had said had upset Sarah, but what on earth could it have been that was so bad?

'Is Mr Strawbridge still at home?' Sarah asked the servant as he handed her a glass of water.

'Yes, ma'am. I believe he's in his study with Mr Cartwright.'

She frowned up at him. 'Please ask him to join us when he has concluded his business.' Lady Sarah dropped the fan on the windowsill; she appeared distracted.

'Is anything the matter, Sarah?'

'It's Mr Cartwright, our steward. I can't imagine why he's here.' Then her brow cleared. 'It must be something to do with Sidley. Odd, though. He rarely visits us here in town. Geoffrey must have summoned him.'

Lucy made a sympathetic remark, but Sarah's dire comment in the carriage was foremost in her mind. Her heart pounded as she said, 'You had better tell me the worst, Sarah. What did you hear at Lady Dot's?'

'It is best Geoffrey is here too,' was all her friend would say, her gaze fixed once more on the streetscape below.

They sat in silence for several minutes, Lucy's stomach in knots.

At last Geoffrey hurried into the room, going straight up to Sarah. 'My love, are you well? You are terribly pale. You should not have exerted yourself so,' he said, casting Lucy an irritated look. Lucy shifted in her seat, knowing full well his rebuke was deserved.

'It is merely the heat, Geoffrey. I will be fine. No need to fuss. Please take a seat, my dear, this is important. You need to hear this too.'

Geoffrey sat down close to his wife, his brow creased with concern. 'How did you fare with Lady Dot?'

Sarah glanced at Lucy—it was almost a look tinged with apology—then she turned to her husband. 'She's distraught, as is Alice. The shock and the manner of Edward's death were devastating.'

'That is understandable,' Geoffrey said with a nod, his face grim. 'Murder is a nasty business. I still can't believe it happened.'

'Well, it did!' Sarah snapped, the colour rushing into her cheeks. 'And in our home, and now we're left to deal with the consequences of it all. I only thank God that little James is too young to know what is going on. If travel didn't affect me so badly at the moment, I would take him back to the country and away from this.'

Geoffrey made comforting noises and hugged her. 'Now, my dear, you must not get upset,' he said. 'And travel is out of the question for you right now.'

'And what about Phin? He's the one lying unconscious in hospital with all these question marks hanging over him?' Lucy piped up, her own temper beginning to fray. What on earth had Sarah learned for her to react like this?

'Indeed.' Sarah straightened up and took a deep breath. 'Something worrying came to light during my conversation with Lady Dot.' Her gaze landed on Lucy. 'Something which casts a very different light on Alice's accusation concerning Phineas.'

Geoffrey's brows shot up. 'Good Lord!'

Lucy froze. 'What exactly did Lady Dot say?'

'Two days before your engagement party, Phin visited Lady Muldoon with his father.'

'What of it? Harry and Dot are old friends,' Lucy said.

'Yes, they are. However, Phineas and Alice spent quite some time together, alone, out in the garden. When the Stones left, Alice was positively gushing about Phin and what a wonderful man he was… and that he was going to help her with a delicate problem she had with Edward.'

Geoffrey stiffened and flicked a glance at Lucy. 'Gosh! That's sounds rather ominous in the circumstances. What was the issue?'

'Alice refused to tell Lady Dot,' Sarah answered. 'Though Lady Dot admitted to me that she knew their marriage was in trouble. Well, after that fiasco last summer…'

'But she could have meant something innocuous,' Lucy said. 'She could have been seeking his advice on any number of topics.'

Sarah gave her a pitying glance. 'Oh, Lucy, don't be so naïve. You know well how manipulative Alice can be. Unfortunately, I must tell you I witnessed something disturbing at Thorncroft. I didn't want to say anything about it, but in light of what Lady Dot told me today, it is best you should know.'

'Go on.' Lucy clenched her hands in her lap.

Sarah sighed and glanced at Geoffrey. He nodded encouragement. 'I think there may be some basis for Alice's claim because I believe there is something going on between Phin and Alice.'

Lucy laughed. 'That's ridiculous!'

'Please hear me out. One of the mornings at Thorncroft, I happened to be in the drawing room with Gertie waiting for you. No one pays the poor woman the slightest bit of attention, particularly Andrew. Anyway, that is beside the point. As I sat there making small talk, I saw Alice and Edward come out of the summer house. I couldn't hear what was being said, but it was obvious they were engaged in a spectacular row. There was lots of dramatic hand waving, and then Edward stormed off. As he approached the house, I could see his face. Edward was livid. Alice, deeply distressed, dashed back inside the summer house. I assume to lick her wounds. All highly dramatic stuff, and I could hardly take in what Gertie was saying to me. Then, what should I see but Phineas going into the summer house. What I witnessed next was quite shocking.'

'Oh, let me guess. She flung herself into his arms, weeping and wailing, and he consoled her,' Lucy ground out.

'Why, yes. How did you know?'

Lucy rose. 'Because we too witnessed that row, and I was the one who urged Phin to comfort her. We were afraid she would do herself some harm. I didn't go with him for, as you know, Alice dislikes me intensely. Instead, I made my way back into the house to give them some privacy.' Lucy took a deep breath, her rage spilling over. 'I would have to ask why, if you consider yourself my friend, you kept this so-called questionable behaviour of my fiancé from me?'

'Lucy!' Sarah got to her feet, the colour draining from her face. 'I... I didn't want you to get hurt. I'm sorry. Of course I should have said something at the time, but you were so blissfully happy that day telling me about Phin. I didn't want to ruin it, and frankly, since then I have been too ill to even remember it.'

'How can we be friends, Sarah, if you are prepared to believe the worst of the man I intend to marry? Even you, Geoffrey. I can see it in your eyes, you think he did have something to do with Edward's murder, don't you?' Geoffrey clamped his mouth shut and glared at her.

Holding back tears of rage and sadness, Lucy dashed for the door.

Westbourne Grove

'Here, you need this, by the look of you,' Sebastian said, handing Lucy a glass of brandy. 'I can't believe the Strawbridges consider Phin guilty. Dashed bad form.' Miserable, Lucy could only sip her drink and nod as he continued: 'It goes to show you never really know people. I've a good mind to go over there and put them straight.'

'It would be a waste of time and effort.' Lucy attempted to smile back at him, but suspected it looked more like a grimace. 'What on earth are we going to do, Seb? We can't let Alice get away with these lies.'

Sebastian's eyes lit up, and he leaned forward. 'Are you suggesting we do a spot of digging? In fact, in court the other day, I thought that was what you were suggesting.'

Lucy swallowed another mouthful, savouring the warmth of the alcohol. At last, she'd stopped shaking. 'Most definitely.'

'Well, I'm game. Can't let Phineas down,' he said, sitting back. 'But, eh, where do we start?'

'I'm not sure. If only we knew what Phin and Alice discussed that day at Lady Muldoon's. I wouldn't be surprised if Alice were making that conversation out to be more than it was.'

'Well, yes, that would be true to form for her, the little madam,' he said. 'She'd say anything to be the centre of attention. Cares only for herself.'

'Unfortunately, Alice or her mother will have mentioned that incriminating nugget of information to the chief inspector.'

'Gosh! Yes, Lucy, of course, but McQuillan knows he's innocent now,' Seb said, chewing his lip.

'Yes, but if it became common knowledge—say the newspapers got hold of it—he would have to look into it. For now, we're in the dark,' she said, feeling rather glum. 'I'll have to ask Phin about it when he regains consciousness. Has there been any further news since early this morning?'

Seb shook his head. 'No, there's been no change.'

For several minutes, Lucy gave in to gloomy thoughts, but catching Sebastian's anxious gaze, she pulled herself together. 'Sorry, we must not give in to despair. There is always something that can be done.'

'Any ideas?'

'A few. We will have to be careful, though. If we go snooping, it might get back to McQuillan. The chief inspector has already warned me off, and I know Phineas would be mad at me for even thinking of getting involved.'

Sebastian grinned back at her. 'You're not tied to him yet, Lucy. Phin can't order you about. And at the moment he can't stop you from doing anything.'

'True, but we have an agreement of sorts. However'—she smiled sadly—'that was before he was shot.'

'Phin won't want me involved, either. He still thinks of me as his little brother,' Seb mumbled. 'He seems to forget I'm ex-army. I could tell you about some of my adventures in India. Blood-curdling stuff, I can assure you! My commanding officer complimented me on my bravery, I'll have you know.'

'I don't doubt it. You have nothing to prove to me.' Lucy attempted to smile. Seb's distress was almost undoing her. 'What a pair we are!' Lucy finished off her drink. 'However, we need to use logic, Seb, if we're to clear his name.'

Sebastian stared into the empty grate. 'It seems to me that

we have to prove Alice guilty to prove Phin completely innocent.'

Lucy quirked her lips and leaned her head back against the sofa. 'My dear Seb, that's it in a nutshell.'

'What could her involvement be?' he asked.

'Well, if she was behind Edward's murder, she had someone do the dirty deed for her.'

'Our blond-haired assassin?'

'Yes, whoever he is. With her resources, she could afford to pay someone a great deal of money to get rid of her problem husband and old suitors.'

'I have no idea how one goes about hiring an assassin,' Sebastian replied after a few moments.

'But I know a man who probably does,' Lucy said, perking up. 'I think we need to take a little trip this evening to the East End.'

Sebastian's face began to glow. 'Jolly good.' Then he frowned. 'After dinner, though? I do my best sleuthing on a full stomach.'

EIGHTEEN

Lucy stood staring at her reflection in the mirror. *Have I gone completely mad?* she asked herself, sweeping her hands down the dull skirts of her old mourning attire. To venture into the unknown in search of a man she barely knew, and with Phin's brother in tow, must be the craziest thing she'd ever attempted. Lucy suspected, for all his bravery, Sebastian was about as clueless as she was. The only problem was it was the only plan that came to mind. Consulting Phin as to a course of action was impossible until he recovered, and besides her pride, she was not prepared to sit and wallow at home while his reputation lay in McQuillan's hands.

Lucy heard the door knocker. That would be Seb.

Minutes later, Mary burst into the bedroom. 'Captain Stone is here, ma'am. I've shown him into the drawing room. What should I tell him? Should I not send him home?'

Lucy swung around. Mary's tone left her in no doubt as to her maid's opinion of the proposed outing. When Lucy had informed her of her plan to venture into the Nichol that night, Mary had been aghast. 'Certainly not, Mary, thank you. I'm ready. Just hand me that hat with the veil.'

Mary sniffed as she handed it over. 'I never thought that would see the light of day again or the rest of that tatty outfit.'

Lucy bit her cheek to stop herself from smiling. Mary had taken on some snobbish notions lately; the outfit Lucy was wearing had been her 'best' mourning attire barely a year before. 'It is serviceable. It is unlikely I will be recognised, but I don't want to take the chance of word getting back to the gossips or the press.' She pulled the veil down over her face. 'See?'

Mary cleared her throat. 'Ma'am, I don't think you should go. Even the polis don't go in there at night. Gawd almighty, it's the most dangerous part of the city. They say it's even worse than the Monto back in Dublin, and that's saying somethin'.'

'You could always come along to protect me, Mary.' Lucy thought that would put a stop to her gallop.

The maid's chin went up. 'Well, I will so! I don't want to have to be explaining your lynchin' to poor Mr Stone. Better I die with you.'

Lucy burst out laughing. 'Oh, Mary! You are a tonic!'

But Mary frowned back at her. She was serious. 'You are my responsibility, ma'am. What with Mr Stone inconvenienced, at present.'

'That's one way of putting it, Mary. Very well, you can come along. Go put on your dullest garb. We don't want to stand out.'

'I will so,' Mary answered, and sped out the door.

Seb greeted Lucy as she entered the drawing room. Lucy was relieved to see he had taken her advice and dressed in a subdued fashion. 'Evening, Lucy. Are you all set? I have to say I haven't been this het up since my first foray out of base camp when I was stationed in India.'

'Let us hope it's a tamer environment, Seb.'

Seb chuckled. 'I don't expect to see any tigers, that's for sure.'

With a sniff, Lucy gave him an amused look. 'Not tigers, but I believe there is wildlife of a particular kind.'

'I say! Ladies shouldn't mention such things.'

'I expect not, but I'm nothing if not a realist. Now, are you sure you are prepared?' she asked, trying to keep a straight face.

Seb brandished Phin's swordstick. 'I thought this might come in handy. By Jove, George made quite a fuss about me taking it. I had to make all kinds of promises.'

'You didn't tell him what we're up to, I hope.'

Seb reddened. 'That's jolly unfair, Lucy. Of course I didn't. George thinks I've gone to my club.'

'Dressed like that? George would never fall for such flimflam.'

'No. I waited until he was busy in the kitchen, and I ran out the door. Our secret is safe for now. Shall we go?'

'Shortly. I've asked my maid to come along. She's getting changed,' Lucy said.

'Any particular reason you asked her? I will look after you, you need not worry.' Sebastian sounded hurt.

'Mary would only be mithered stuck here at home, and if she became worried, I wouldn't put it past her to telegram McQuillan.'

'Ah! I see. Good decision,' he said with a harrumph.

Lucy tilted her head at the sound of footsteps out in the hall. 'That's her now. If you are ready, we should set off. It's almost ten o'clock. We don't want to get there and find the place closed.'

'Gosh, no, that would be a disaster.' Seb paused. 'Though I suspect hostelries in that part of the city never close.'

'And you were able to hire a suitable carriage? We don't want to stand out,' Lucy asked.

Sebastian flashed her an irritated glance. 'I found the oldest one at the stand. I don't know which is more pitiful a sight: the horse or the cabbie.'

'Very good, Sebastian, thank you,' she replied.

With a nod, he strode towards the door.

Lucy ran her hand over her handbag as she followed him out. It was a comfort to feel the outline of her pistol beneath the cloth. She only hoped she wouldn't have to use it.

Bethnal Green Road

The hackney coach pulled into the kerb. Mary, sitting opposite Lucy, rolled her shoulders, her lips tightly clenched. Tellingly, over the forty-five-minute journey, Seb's flow of conversation had gradually ceased. And, if she were honest, Lucy's nerves were jangling too. Was this wise? It wasn't too late to tell the cabbie to turn around and go home. Lucy glanced out the window. Leading away into the darkness was an alleyway, three posts cutting across the entrance. Beyond was a dark tunnel, formed by looming buildings on either side. Whatever lurked within the rookery and its vicinity was well hidden.

Seb cleared his throat. 'Best get on with it. Are you ready, Mary?'

'Aye. You wait here, ma'am. We'll bring this fellow to you,' Mary said to Lucy.

'If you can find him,' Lucy replied. 'You do remember what he looks like?'

Mary's laugh was without humour. 'I should think so!'

'And you are sure this public house... the Unicorn, is where he will be?' Seb asked.

'Phin happened to mention last year when we had all that trouble with Marsh, that the headquarters of the gang was at the Unicorn in the Nichol. The incongruity of the name stuck in my mind. It's a funny name for a hostelry in such a notoriously dangerous area.' Seb gave her an uneasy look, and she regretted her words. 'If you tell him you are Phin's brother, there won't be a problem.' Seb's cheek twitched, but he made no comment.

Mary nodded. 'The locals will know him and where he's to be found, don't you fret, ma'am.' Then she treated Lucy to another one of her stern looks. 'But best you stay 'ere, as agreed. You'd stick out like a sore thumb, you would, even in those old weeds. I'm used to these kinds of places. Sure, my sister lives just yonder in Spitalfields.' Mary jerked her head towards the other side of the street.

Not sure whether to laugh or scold, Lucy waved them on. 'Very well. Off you go. And, I promise to be good.' Lucy watched as her two companions were swallowed up by the darkness of the lane. Suddenly, the enormity of the risk they were all taking almost had her jumping out and calling them back. But how would that help Phin? No, they had to do this. The carriage moved forward slightly, and she heard the cabbie calming the horse down. A shiver of apprehension danced down her spine.

Half an hour later, a figure with a swaggering gait materialised from the shadows and approached the carriage. He opened the door, hopped in, and closed the door behind him. From the corner of her eye, Lucy saw Seb and Mary hanging back at the edge of the lane. Seb nodded to her, but his expression was wary.

Lucy directed her gaze at Coffin Mike. A year at the helm of the most notorious gang in the East End had wrought some change. Gone were the patched clothes and greasy hair. The man sitting opposite was almost dapper—except, of course, the scar still stood out livid on his cheek.

'I'm sorry to drag you away from your evening's...' Lucy trailed off. 'Thank you for coming.'

Mike sat back against the squabs and crossed his legs. 'Your friends'—he nodded out the window to where Seb and Mary were standing—'were persuasive. Particularly, the female.'

'Yes, she can be on occasion. I'm sure you are a busy man, so I will be brief. I need your help. Well, it's Phineas Stone who needs it, really.'

'Aye, I heard he's been in a spot of bother lately with the polis and now he's in the 'ospital.'

'Yes, he was attacked, and an attempt made to kill him. I believe it is the same person who murdered a friend of ours.'

'Not sure what I can do for you.' Mike's eyes narrowed.

'Don't worry. I'm not here to suggest anything untoward. I'm looking for information.'

Mike quirked a brow at her. 'I see.'

'I don't think the police are doing a good enough job. I want to—'

'Investigate?' Mike's brow creased. 'I thought the Paddy was doing that.'

'Who?' Lucy stared at him, confused. 'Paddy who?'

Mike rubbed his chin, his eyes suddenly hooded. 'My mistake. What do you want?'

'It is my belief that the man's wife was behind his murder and that she hired someone to do it for her.'

'And you're hoping I can supply the name of this man? I'm no nark, Mrs Lawrence.'

Fighting her disappointment, Lucy frantically tried to think of anything which might persuade him to help. Did he have a conscience?

'Mike, Phineas helped you when you wished to overthrow Marsh. You wouldn't be where you are now without that assistance. He negotiated a deal with the police, and you benefitted from that.'

Coffin Mike sniffed. 'That's as maybe, but I don't grass up no one.'

'If that assistance were to become common knowledge...?'

Mike's head snapped up, and he gave her a look which curdled her insides. 'I don't take kindly to threats, no matter who you are.' The words dropped like ice in the confines of the carriage, and for a moment, Lucy feared she'd gone too far.

But she held her nerve and stared right back at him.

'Who is the lady?' he asked, at last. 'I'll see what I can find out.'

So relieved she could barely answer, Lucy nodded, swallowing hard. 'The lady's name is Alice Vaughan. Her husband was Edward, a man about town, but we're not aware of him having any enemies. His murder makes little sense except—'

'It's handy for his missus.' Mike pursed his lips and chuckled. 'I'm thinking Mr Stone has met his match in you. You're a wily one, but of course, I knew that when you escaped from me on Regent Street that day.'

Lucy smiled at the memory and held out her hand. 'No hard feelings?'

Mike returned the handshake. 'None. You'll hear from me soon.'

And with that, he disappeared back out into the night.

Vine Street Police Station

On her way to the hospital the next morning, Lucy stopped off in Vine Street. Just as she reached the station entrance, McQuillan emerged in the company of another man, and they were in deep conversation. The man was tall and fair and extremely well-dressed. As Lucy paused at the bottom of the steps, the stranger's gaze swept over her as if he were taking in every little detail. When the chief inspector noticed her, he raised his hat in greeting and gave her a cheery smile.

'Good morning, Chief Inspector,' she said, keeping her tone cool as she approached.

'Good day to you, Mrs Lawrence,' he replied. The chief

inspector glanced at his companion, who nodded to Lucy and continued down the steps. 'How is Phineas?'

'No change as far as I'm aware, Chief Inspector; I'm afraid he is still unconscious.' Aware that the stranger was now observing her from the pavement, Lucy turned back to Oliver McQuillan and asked in a low voice: 'How fares your investigation?'

McQuillan's brows shot up and his gaze darted about before coming to rest on her. 'Fine, fine.' He leaned down towards her. 'Best not discussed in public, eh?'

'Well, I have some ideas I'd like to discuss,' she replied.

'I'm afraid that is out of the question, Mrs Lawrence, but suffice to say our enquiries are ongoing.'

Then McQuillan straightened up and strode back into the station.

Lucy stood, consumed with anger and not a little shocked at his abruptness. 'Well!'

NINETEEN

St Mark's Church, North Audley Street, Mayfair

Two days later, the funeral service for Edward Vaughan was punctuated by Alice Vaughan's muffled sobs. Lucy glanced across the aisle to where the Muldoon family was seated. Alice's head was bent, and her mother was trying to comfort her. It was almost as if the widow were truly grieving. With a flash of guilt, Lucy had to swallow her prejudice. Perhaps, just perhaps, Alice was genuine. Lucy had to look away and concentrate on the trio of stained-glass windows above the altar. As the vicar's voice droned on, she thought about Coffin Mike's reply, which she'd received that very morning. He claimed his enquiries had come to nothing. But was he to be trusted?

Lucy felt Mary shift in her seat in the pew next to her. Being a Catholic, Mary had objected strongly to entering the church, but Lucy had insisted she needed her help. They had to observe the mourners carefully, and one of Mary's many talents was a keen eye. Maybe she was clutching at straws, but Lucy hoped someone would give something away. Unfortunately, many of those present were unknown to her. How would she know what was significant? A shifty glance, a recoil, anything which might suggest... With a sigh, Lucy realised she was letting her desperation cloud her judgement.

A few rows ahead, she saw Lady Sarah and Geoffrey. It grieved Lucy to have fallen out with them, but her loyalty was to Phineas. Their doubt in him had hurt her deeply, and it would take time for her to forgive—if she ever could. They, like everyone else, would have to apologise by the time she was finished and Phin's name was cleared. Just how she was to achieve this happy outcome, she wasn't a hundred per cent sure...

A few minutes later, she heard Mary's sharply indrawn breath. Her maid was frowning, staring at someone on the far side of the church. Mary's lips were tightly clamped. Intrigued, Lucy followed her gaze and pulled up short. The familiar face of McQuillan was no surprise, but half hidden in the shadows under the marble columns supporting the upper balconies, was the stranger she'd seen with the chief inspector on the steps of Vine Street station. Although in profile, Lucy was sure it was the man who had sized her up so carefully. Why was he provoking such a reaction in Mary? And what on earth was he doing at this funeral? Confound it! It was not the time or place to ask Mary. Pulse racing, Lucy had to be content to wait until the service was over.

Half an hour later, Lucy still didn't know what had disturbed Mary, although she was certain it was McQuillan's companion. Much to Lucy's frustration, the mourners filed out of the church with painstaking slowness. Once outside, Lucy scanned them from the top of the steps. Further down the pavement, she spied the stranger, standing back a little from the crowd. If she didn't know better, she would believe he too was studying the funeral congregation.

Lucy quickly pulled Mary aside and whispered, 'What did you see in the church? Who was that man you were staring at?'

Before Mary could answer, Sebastian had joined them. 'Hello,' he said. 'I thought I spied you in the church.'

'It's good to see you, Sebastian,' Lucy replied, shaking his proffered hand. 'But before you say another word, Mary spotted something in the church. She was just about to tell me.'

'Oh, I say, what is it, Mary?' Seb asked, leaning forward.

Mary puffed up. 'Well now,' she declared, 'it was a sight I thought I'd never see this side of the Irish Sea.'

Lucy and Sebastian exchanged a puzzled glance. 'Go on, Mary,' Lucy said with an encouraging smile.

With a sniff, Mary looked about before continuing. 'It was Jabber Kincaid; the very man himself. I'd swear to it on me father's grave, so I would.'

'But who *is* he?' Lucy ground out.

'Why only the meanest, shiftiest sleeveen of them all!'

'*Mary*,' Lucy warned.

'Do tell, Mary,' Sebastian said with a coaxing smile. 'We're not acquainted with the gentleman.'

'Huh! He's no gentleman.' Her nose in the air, Mary pointed him out to Sebastian, then paused—no doubt for effect. Lucy struggled to hold on to her temper, the temptation to give Mary a dig almost impossible to ignore. 'A 'G' man,' Mary announced at last. 'A Dublin Metropolitan Police inspector, loathed from one end of Dublin to the other.'

'What would a Dublin policeman be doing here?' Lucy asked.

'Kincaid was kicked out of the DMP a few years back, ma'am, for God knows what awful shenanigans,' Mary said. 'The rumours were something shocking. No one cried in Dublin when he left, I can tell you. It was good riddance!' Mary's expression turned even more sour. 'A dark devil, he is. Don't be fooled by those schoolboy looks.'

'By Jove, Lucy, I've seen him before,' Sebastian said.

'Do you know him?' Lucy asked, grabbing his arm.

'No, no, but he called to Westbourne Grove a few evenings ago. I came in from my club just as he was leaving.'

'Did you ask George who he was?'

'Yes, of course. Said he was a friend of his... This is odd, is it not?'

Lucy smarted as possibilities began to form in her head. 'Very, and I suspect I might know what is going on.'

Sebastian shrugged. 'I'm glad someone does. I'm totally confused.'

With a sigh, she turned to Mary. 'Can you wait in the carriage, please, Mary?'

'Yes, ma'am. Are we going to Kensal Green?'

'No. I'm sure only close family and friends would be welcome at the burial.' Lucy watched Mary slip away through the mourners before turning back to Seb. 'I assume you are here with Andrew?'

Sebastian nodded towards the carriages below. 'Yes, we're going to the cemetery. You could always come with us, if you wish.'

'Best not, Seb. I don't think your brother would appreciate my presence.'

'Pooh! What makes you say that?'

'Sebastian, we're talking about *Andrew*.'

'Yes, I suppose you're right. But he will come round to your engagement, eventually. I mean, it's dashed silly of him to object. There was the most frightful row at Thorncroft after you left. I don't suppose Phin would have told you about it. Thought they would come to blows, but Father intervened. It was almost funny to see Andrew eating humble pie. Father actually told him not to be an oaf; that he thought you were smashing, and if he were young enough, he'd pursue you himself!' Sebastian laughed, but then his face fell. 'You wouldn't abandon Phin because of old Andrew, would you?'

'Certainly not! If anything, it makes me more determined to be your sister-in-law.'

'Good for you! You've a lot of gumption, Lucy Lawrence. No wonder Phin is dotty about you.'

'Is he?' she asked, trying not to smile.

'Gosh, yes. Absolutely smitten.'

'I'm glad to hear it because I'm absolutely smitten too. Now, if you will forgive me, I need to interrogate Mary as to this fellow Jabber Kincaid's history. What an extraordinary name.'

Sebastian tilted his head and grinned. 'Suggests he is handy with his fists.'

'Oh, I see. An interesting moniker. I wonder what he could be up to here in London.' Down below, through a gap in the mourners, Lucy could see Andrew speaking to Lady Dot. 'What did you think of the service?' she asked Seb, as she turned back to him.

'Extremely sad, wasn't it? Alice is very taken down. Lady Dot was telling us she didn't think Alice would be able to come at all. The doctor had to give her something this morning so she could get through the service.'

Acting lessons, perhaps? Lucy had to shake off the treacherous thought.

Sebastian touched her arm. 'It was good of you to come... in the circumstances.'

'No more than your family.'

'Aye, it's all very awkward. Still, Lady Dot is delighted we came.' Seb glanced about then lowered his voice: 'You know, Lucy, I think... Well, the thing is... I really don't think Alice could have been responsible.'

'I'm slowly coming around to that opinion too, albeit reluctantly,' Lucy said with a self-effacing smile. 'I suppose it was too easy a solution. Best you see this.' She rooted in her bag and handed Sebastian Coffin Mike's note.

Sebastian grimaced as he read it and passed it back to her. 'I guess that confirms it. It's unlikely she had anything to do with Edward's demise. If Coffin Mike doesn't know about that hired assassin, that leaves us with no leads.' He looked at her closely. 'Am I right, Lucy?'

A plan of campaign was forming in Lucy's head. 'Perhaps not. Come to dinner tomorrow evening—alone. We can thrash out a strategy between us.'

Sebastian frowned down at her. 'Yes, of course. As it happens, Andrew returns to Kent in the morning. He hates it here in town, and with no change in Phin's condition, he doesn't see any reason to stay. Council of war, what?' He rubbed his hands together and grinned. 'Just the ticket.'

TWENTY

Lucy looked up from her desk as Mary appeared in the doorway. Lucy had been trawling through her backlog of correspondence before her planned trip to the hospital.

'Ma'am. Lady Sarah Strawbridge is here. Are you receiving visitors?'

Lucy sprang up. 'Of course, Mary. Please show her in.'

Her split-second internal argument about whether or not to be standoffish vanished as soon as Lucy saw Sarah's pale face. Lucy rushed up to her and hugged her. 'Oh, my dear, Sarah, you should not have come if travelling does this to you.'

'Don't fuss so, Lucy. I'm fine, but I had to come. I couldn't bear for us to be at odds for even one more day,' Sarah answered, her eyes suspiciously bright. 'What news of Phineas? Is there any improvement?'

'I don't believe so, but I'm due to visit the hospital later this morning.'

'I deeply regret if I gave the impression... that I accused Phineas of anything. I was ill and upset. It has been nothing but a nightmare, Lucy. Geoffrey pretends nothing is wrong, but I can see how much stress he's under, and it is getting worse since the murder. He barely eats, and when I retire at night, I can hear him pacing the floor. Oh, Lucy, the press will not leave us alone. If only we could retreat to Sidley, but I'm sure they would follow us even there.'

Lucy's heart ached for her friend. She gently nudged her into a chair before ringing the bell.

Mary appeared within minutes. 'Yes, ma'am?'

'Tea, Mary, please and ask M. Lacroix to provide us with something delicious. We're in great need of a treat.'

Mary glanced over at Lady Sarah and grinned. 'Certainly, ma'am. Won't be a tick.'

'She's a treasure,' Lady Sarah said, as she delicately wiped her brow. 'Oh, will this heat never end?'

'Yes, I know. It must be very trying in your condition.'

'It is, but I didn't come to discuss that, my dear Lucy. No, no, let me continue.' Sarah held up her hand as Lucy protested. 'Geoffrey and I wish to apologise.'

'Sarah, please don't. I'm just as much to blame for our falling out. I'm stubborn and stupid, and let's say no more about it.' Lucy gave her a self-effacing smile before continuing: 'I would have called on you in a day or two, I promise, but I have been trying to do what is best for Phineas. My investigations have continued into the possibility that Edward's death was orchestrated by Alice.'

Sarah's mouth dropped. 'Lucy, you can't be serious! No woman could perform such a vile act. Did you not see the state she was in at the funeral yesterday?'

'Yes, I did, but I think you underestimate our own sex, Sarah. Women are just as capable of violence when pushed beyond their limits. However, I must admit, I no longer believe she did it... Though there is still the chance she may have engaged someone else to do it for her.' Lucy drummed her fingers on the arm of her chair. 'Unfortunately, the trail has gone cold.'

Sarah sat forward. 'You can't believe that of Alice. That is a dreadful notion, and I can't give it credence. I've known the family all my life, Lucy. You must be mistaken.'

'At the very least, the possibility had to be ruled out,' Lucy answered. 'There is no room for emotion in these matters, only logic.'

'That, my dear Lucy, sounds like something a man would say.'

With a chuckle, Lucy nodded. 'And I think you can guess which man in particular.'

Sarah was pensive for a moment, then slowly nodded. 'Yes, of course, Phineas is correct. Logic must always be used to solve the crime even though passion may have initiated the foul act of violence.' She smiled. 'But these days I'm all emotion. Can't think clearly at all. I would make a terrible policeman.'

'Oh, so would I!' Lucy exclaimed. 'I couldn't bear the discipline and would always be in trouble with my superior officer.' This, to her relief, coaxed a smile from Sarah.

Mary came in with the tea tray and set it down on the table in front of Lucy. She bobbed and left the room.

'Lacroix has done me proud. These biscuits look delicious.' Lucy offered the plate to Sarah as she inhaled the aroma of cinnamon.

'I must admit, I agree. I have such a desire for sweet things lately, which is so unlike me. Geoffrey teases that I will grow fat.' As Lucy poured the tea, Sarah munched on the biscuit. 'Good Lord,' she said, staring at the biscuit in awe. 'This is divine; it just melts in your mouth. Where did you say you found him again?'

Lucy tut-tutted. 'My lips are sealed and don't you dare try to poach him.'

'Don't worry, I don't have the energy for such a campaign at the moment,' Sarah replied with a wan smile. 'But be warned, once baby arrives, I shall rally.' Sarah drank her tea and looked at Lucy above the rim of the cup. 'Tell me, what do you plan to do next if your trail has run cold?'

'I'm not quite sure at the moment. I hope that when Phin wakes up, he will direct us. By the way, is Brown's still good for afternoon tea?'

'Why, yes. Why do you ask?'

'I bumped into an old beau a few weeks ago, and we arranged to meet there for afternoon tea. As it happened, he had to cancel at the last minute as his brother was ill and he had to travel to Edinburgh.' Lucy glanced towards her desk. 'I received a note from him this morning. Thomas is back from his trip and wishes to renew the engagement. At the time, I suggested Brown's on the spur of the moment—it was a tricky situation, and I needed to get away quickly—and it was the first place that popped into my head. Anyway, I just wondered if it was still as good.'

'Very much so. An old beau? Would you care to tell me who the gentleman is?'

'Thomas Hardwicke. Do you know him?'

'Hardwicke. The name *is* familiar, but I don't think it was a Thomas I met. It was some time ago, down at Sidley Manor. One of Geoffrey's supporters, if I remember rightly. An odd man, as I recall; not particularly talkative, but Geoffrey insisted on inviting him to stay for the weekend. Luckily, we had a full house, so he was lost in the crowd, if you know what I mean. I remember I remarked on it at the time to Geoffrey, which didn't please him one bit. The man contributed funds to Geoffrey's election campaign, so Geoffrey would hear no ill of him. Now, what was his first name? I'm sorry, it escapes me at present.'

'Don't worry; I'm sure Thomas will acquaint me with his family history. He's probably the most loquacious man I ever had the misfortune to meet.'

'That does sound fun, my dear,' Sarah said with a flash of her old mischief. 'Won't Phineas be jealous when he finds out?'

Lucy stared at her friend. 'He already knows all about him. Though, I have to admit to feeling guilty. Why should I have all the pleasure of meeting Thomas? It would be perfectly acceptable if you were to accompany me.'

Sarah looked as though she was about to object when the door opened and Mary bounded into the room. 'This just arrived for you, ma'am. Shall I take the tea things away now?'

'Yes, please, Mary.'

The maid handed Lucy a telegram.

'Oh, it's from Seb,' Lucy said, gazing with relief at his message. Then she read it out to Sarah: *'Phin awake and asking for you.'*

TWENTY-ONE

St Thomas' Hospital

On the journey to the hospital, Lucy collected her thoughts. There was no point in avoiding it. As much as she hated having to do it, she had to challenge Phin about Alice and their time spent alone at Lady Muldoon's home. Could it be significant? Why had he not mentioned the encounter to her? Her heart sank. How prepared was she for disquieting answers? No, she had to trust him. If he hadn't told her about it, it was because it was unconnected with the murder or so insignificant that it didn't matter. Such a shame that they'd not been able to find evidence relating to Alice, though. It would have strengthened her argument to let her help him in his investigation. Despite the lack of evidence, however, Lucy still questioned Alice's motivation in implicating Phineas. It had to be deliberate. After all, Alice had the most to gain from Edward's death and had wished the poor man dead in their hearing.

Lucy was determined to show Phineas she was calm and capable. It was imperative he agreed to let her help. From their previous brief exchange in Vine Street, she knew Phin wanted her out of London, away from the scandal and possible danger, so how could she persuade him otherwise? With no obvious progress by McQuillan to find the assassin, she would have to argue that it was going to fall to her and Seb to speed things up. Particularly as Phin could do nothing from his hospital bed. Surely that would be reason enough to accept her assistance? She was confident he would have plenty of ideas as to how to proceed.

Lucy shifted uneasily on the hard seat of the hansom. What if news of her sojourn to the Nichol had reached Phin's ears. He would be furious. She'd put herself, Seb and Mary in danger. But how else was she to track down the killer? As she'd lain awake in the early hours, she'd realised how fruitless a quest it had been because she couldn't quite shake off the notion that Mike knew more than he was letting on, despite his communication claiming he couldn't find any so-called assassin hired by Alice. Was Coffin Mike's loyalty to Phineas, or as Phineas had previously claimed, would Coffin Mike always sell his soul to the highest bidder? Not that she regretted asking him. If anything, McQuillan's lack of progress vindicated her actions.

Perhaps she might have to consider hiring a private detective just in case Coffin Mike wasn't to be trusted. Did they advertise in *The Times?* She would discuss it with Seb.

The constable nodded to Lucy and opened the door to Phin's room. 'Oh, you poor thing!' she exclaimed on seeing his woebegone expression. A large purple bruise on the side of Phin's face contrasted sharply with his pale cheeks. A bulky bandage peeped out from the collar of his pyjamas. But he managed to smile at her as she rushed to his bedside.

'How do you feel?' she asked, caressing his cheek.

'A thumping head and a painful shoulder, but otherwise I'm fine. It is good to see you, Lucy,' Phineas said, taking her hand and raising it to his lips.

She frowned at him. 'Phin, this is all so dreadful. What if

that awful man had succeeded? At least, McQuillan has left some protection for you,' she said in a rush.

'You must not worry about me,' he said. 'It is unlikely another attempt would be made here.'

'But what about when you are discharged? Will you still have protection? I should talk to McQuillan about it.'

'As you wish,' he replied with a smile.

'Is there anything you need?' she asked as she settled into the chair beside his bed.

'No, no. George brought everything I require.'

'When can you leave?' she asked. 'We can always arrange a nurse for you in your rooms. I'm sure you would be far more comfortable at home.'

Phin laughed. 'I'd be an even worse patient than Sebastian. I will discuss it with the doctor later, but I imagine I will be here for a few days at least. In the meantime, I plan to use the time productively, you will be delighted to hear. I intend to catch up on my reading. Not the most ideal circumstances,' he said with a smile. 'But needs must. There is no point in wallowing in self-pity.'

'Phin, how can you be so calm? Someone tried to kill you. We need to investigate.'

'We?' There was an edge to his voice.

Lucy gave him an impatient look. 'Don't trot out those old arguments, Phin. You're in no fit state to do it. Seb and I, however, are more than willing.'

'It's far too dangerous, Lucy. Promise me you will resist the temptation. McQuillan will deal with this.'

'Is that so? Tell me, what exactly *has* McQuillan done?'

'Oliver does not discuss it with me; it wouldn't be appropriate.'

Lucy was instantly suspicious. She didn't believe him. The men were firm friends and had worked together for years. 'Then I shall tackle him, myself,' she replied.

'Please don't. I know this is difficult for you. You will have to trust me.'

So, he was determined to keep her in the dark. Unlucky for him that she had a fair idea of what was going on. 'I suppose you leave me little choice.'

Straightening up, Phin smiled at her again. 'You are a welcome sight. How are you? You know I don't expect you to visit every day. In fact, I had hoped you would—'

'Remove myself from London and the temptation to investigate?'

'Lucy!' He sighed. 'It would be best.'

'I'm not leaving London, not even to visit your sister Elvira.' His reaction, a jolt of his head, screamed guilt. Lucy continued: 'I received a suspiciously timely invitation from her in the post yesterday. However, as much as I would love to stay with her in Italy, I have no intention of leaving London for now.'

Phin didn't exactly meet her eye. 'She isn't known for her subtlety, but she's well intentioned.'

'Phin, really!'

'I had to try,' he said quietly.

'I know well you want me out of the way.'

Phineas pursed his lips. 'I do, my dear. I have only your welfare at heart.' His tone was flat.

Lucy raised her eyes to the ceiling and let out a slow breath. She would have to choose her words wisely or he would thwart her endeavours entirely; not that she was about to admit she was doing anything he wouldn't approve of—such as trips to the Nichol late at night.

When she glanced back at him, she thought she detected a trace of humour in his dark eyes. *Damn him, he reads me like a book.* 'Phineas, you must not worry about me.'

'I can't help it, my dear, I know you only too well,' he replied, his gaze suddenly intense, causing her stomach to flip.

How unfortunate she would have to destroy the intimacy of

the moment, but she couldn't help but wonder if Phin was deliberately trying to steer her away from unpleasant topics. Very well, she would press on. 'By the way, Lady Sarah and I called on Lady Muldoon. We felt it would be a kindness to offer our condolences in person.'

'That was good of you, Lucy. I'm sure the family is devastated,' he replied, his expression guarded again.

'Why, yes; however, we only saw Lady Muldoon. Alice was indisposed. The family physician had been in attendance.'

'That does not surprise me. Alice is an emotional creature and feels things deeply. The poor girl must be overwhelmed.'

'But Phin, we witnessed a relationship in trouble, surely? Can her grief be genuine?'

'You refer to that argument at Thorncroft? I would imagine most couples have flare-ups like that. I wouldn't read too much into it.'

'We have never fought like that,' she replied, wondering why he was playing the incident down.

A smile tugged on his lips. 'But we might in the future.'

Lucy sniffed. 'Only if you were unbearable! However, I'm sure I would never behave in such a manner or say such things. Seriously, Phin. She wished him dead. That is difficult to ignore.'

'Just words, Lucy, in the heat of the moment.'

'And yet McQuillan took her words—her accusation against you—seriously. Have you told him about that incident? I still think she merits investigation.'

'Of course I told him, and if we had ended up in court, my defence would have used it to discredit her.' Phin sighed. 'I'm only glad Alice was indisposed, or you would have interrogated her, I suppose—grieving widow or no.'

'I wouldn't do anything so crass,' she snapped. 'I'm sure Oliver will question her when she's in a better state of mind.'

'He will. Do not doubt it. After her display at Bow Street,

his antennae are twitching. Oliver is treating her statements with due scepticism.'

'This is no petty crime she accused you of, Phin.'

'I'm aware of that, my dear. Again, I stress you must be patient.'

'I'm doing my best.'

'Really?' That damned eyebrow of his rose.

Well, now was as good a time as any. She had to know. 'Phineas... I must be honest with you. I'm deeply concerned. It has come to my attention that you and your father called on Lady Muldoon last week. I was surprised you had not mentioned the visit to me, and the fact that you and Alice spent a considerable part of the visit alone, according to Lady Dot.'

'Ah! And you have put two and two together—' He threw her a doleful glance. 'You do not trust *me*?'

'I do, of course, but must admit at this moment, I'm struggling to understand why you didn't mention it.'

'I'm sorry. Yes, perhaps I should have; however, I would point out that you do not inform me of every social call you make. You are reading far too much into what was a routine morning call.'

Lucy kept her gaze fixed on his face. He looked away first, and her heart sank. 'What did you talk about?' she managed to get out.

Phineas sat back against the pillows which made him wince. 'I honestly can't remember. General chit-chat, most probably. I wanted to give Father time to talk in private with Lady Dot. They seldom meet these days, and Alice tends to dominate any conversation. Meeting old friends is one of the few pleasures left to Father now he can no longer hunt or fish.'

'I see. By the way, I attended Edward's funeral service, and it was ghastly. Alice was distraught in the church,' she said. 'I believe she collapsed at the graveside.'

'Yes, Seb told me. My dear Lucy, I know you doubt it, but

I believe she truly loved Edward. Her greatest fault is a love of the dramatic, which comes from being an only child and being pampered for most of her life. Entirely Lady Dot's fault.'

Lucy shook her head. 'I don't doubt there is an element of that, but her behaviour since her marriage to Edward has bordered on irrational and scandalous. Might I remind you it was a scandal you were drawn into only last year.'

'Those were the actions of a spoilt child.'

'You can dismiss it so easily? I can't believe you are prepared to excuse her behaviour,' Lucy said, miffed.

'I have moved on, Lucy. In fact, the day I met you was the exact moment she ceased to mean anything to me.'

Lucy tilted her head, her curiosity piqued. 'You did care for her, then? You did regret she broke off your engagement?'

'Of course, I did—at the time. I loved her and assumed we would spend the rest of our lives together. I wouldn't have proposed to her if I hadn't had strong feelings for her.'

'Oh!' Lucy struggled momentarily with a little green-eyed monster.

'Or, at least, I *thought* I loved her. However, the ease with which you captured my heart makes me question what the nature of my feelings for her were in reality.'

Lucy spluttered. 'There you go, trying to charm me again.'

'I'm only being honest,' he said. Lucy was amazed to see the colour rise in his cheeks. Phin cleared his throat. 'Anyway, what were we talking about? Ah yes, the funeral. I knew you wouldn't be able to resist going. But far more pertinent is what other mischief have you been up to?'

Lucy schooled her features. 'Why, nothing at all. Just sitting at home, worrying about you.'

Phin's eyes flew wide. 'Touché!' But then his eyes crinkled, and his mouth twitched. 'You will be the death of me,' he said.

But she was not to be swayed. Lucy couldn't help herself.

'No, my dear. I think you have me confused with Alice Vaughan.'

A flash of dismay crossed his face.

'Phin? What is really going on? I know you are hiding something from me, no doubt in the erroneous belief that it is for my own good.'

'No, no.'

'Then who is Jabber Kincaid?'

'Who?' he asked, not meeting her gaze.

'Malcolm "Jabber" Kincaid.' She enunciated his name slowly. 'The private detective you have working for you. Don't deny it. I'm happy to produce all my evidence.' Phin licked his lips but said nothing, his gaze steady. 'Very well. I have seen the man twice. Once at Vine Street with the chief inspector. And he was at St Mark's at the funeral, skulking about in the shadows, doing his best to look inconspicuous. However, Mary happened to spot him and became extremely agitated. It would appear he was instrumental in having her cousin incarcerated on a trumped-up charge back in Dublin.'

'Merely coincidence,' Phin said, somewhat weakly.

'Indeed? Mary pointed him out to Sebastian only for him to exclaim he had seen him in Westbourne Grove with George. That was the most telling occurrence of all. What could the man want with George other than to question or liaise with him?' Phin gave a half-hearted shrug. 'Mary has kindly given me something of the man's history from when she knew of him in Dublin. Based on that, I asked Mary to find out what he's doing in London through her contacts in the Irish community in Spitalfields, where her sister and family live.'

'Do enlighten me,' Phin replied.

'Certainly. It would appear he was expelled from the DMP under a cloud and has been living here in London for the last few years. He set up a private investigation bureau, situated in Battersea of all places, and has established himself with quite a reputation. Ruthless, efficient and discreet. Need I say any more? Or perhaps I should visit the gentleman and ask him myself?'

'Very well, Lucy. You have found me out.'

'Is he investigating Alice?'

'No. Alice is, as you witnessed at the funeral, a grieving widow,' Phineas replied. 'Kincaid has taken over the Apollo case for me, for now.'

Lucy let out a slow, steady breath. 'I don't understand, Phin. What has that case got to do with any of this?'

'Everything, my dear, absolutely everything.'

TWENTY-TWO

Lucy stared at Phineas, her thoughts tripping over each other as she tried to fathom it all out. How did Edward's death relate to the theft of all those paintings? And why did Phin need the likes of a seedy private investigator to pursue the case?

'Phin, you had better explain it to me,' she said with some reluctance. 'I must be missing something, for this isn't making sense.'

'What do you want to know?'

'Everything!'

Phin settled back against the pillows with a sigh. 'Initially, the murder of Edward Vaughan, looked at in isolation, made no sense to me. McQuillan's enquiries indicated Edward had no enemies, no outstanding debts and no connections to criminals. Who could have a motive? At first, it appeared the only motive might well be my desire to rid the world of Mr Vaughan and to help a lady in distress: a theory offered so helpfully by Alice that night.'

'Yes. I still say she has questions to answer.' Phin raised a brow. 'Well, she does, Phin. If you were being set up, the use of your cane was not by chance either.'

'Yes, indeed, that was rather clever of them. So, all the circumstantial evidence pointed to me. But even McQuillan thought it was all a bit *too* convenient. As you surmise, the only logical conclusion was that the murder had been carefully planned to ensure the police *would* suspect me. However, what the murderer or murderers didn't count on was that McQuillan and I are old friends. We quickly realised that Edward's murder was a red herring. The true intention behind the murder was far more sinister.'

Lucy mulled this over for a few moments, then gasped. 'I see... to frame you... because you were getting close to discovering the Apollo syndicate. But then Alice is *not* involved.'

'You sound disappointed, my dear.'

'Hmm.'

Phin cast her a knowing look. 'You must abandon that theory.'

'But what changed? Why did McQuillan decide to charge you?'

'With no evidence to clear me, the chief inspector's hand was forced by his superior, and he had no choice but to let things take their course. I must admit, I was worried for a while. McQuillan cut it fine producing that evidence.'

Lucy sat back, flabbergasted. 'It was an extremely clever plan. But it went awry when you were cleared. Is that why you were shot?'

'I would think so, yes.'

'Do you or McQuillan have any idea who the real murderer might be?' she asked.

'McQuillan's enquiries are ongoing. Trust me, he's working night and day on it. We can be certain now that our assassin was one of the hired servants, placed in the house that night by whoever is behind those art thefts. However, although the agency Lady Sarah used provided names and addresses of the hired staff that night, half of them have proved to be false.

Seemingly a common enough occurrence. Whoever the perpetrator was, he has slipped back into the gutter without a trace. For all we know, he may have left the country.'

Lucy straightened up as fear began to bubble up. 'But unless we find him, how can we fully clear your name? I hate to tell you this, but the papers are saying that last-minute evidence may not be legitimate.'

'Let them speculate away. The charge has been dropped. We have some time, Lucy. Kincaid is helping too. He owes me a favour. I helped him with a case in Dublin some years ago.'

'Can he be trusted?' Lucy asked.

'Needs must, Lucy,' he replied with a sigh.

This didn't give Lucy much comfort, so she turned her attention back to the night of the murder. 'If what you say is true, your cane was used as the murder weapon deliberately.' She shook her head. 'You see, I was sure it was random, that the murderer just happened to grab it from the cloakroom.' An awful realisation hit her. 'I didn't help matters by giving you such a distinctive gift.' Lucy sucked in a breath. 'The cane shop was directly opposite White's Gallery. The shop fronts in the arcade are all glass. White may have seen me make the purchase.'

'Or checked with the proprietor to see what you had bought when you had left the arcade,' Phin said. 'Though I suspect they were following me, anyway. I used that cane every day before the engagement party.'

'Either way, it played right into their hands. How nasty!' Lucy exclaimed.

'We're not dealing with honourable individuals, that is certain,' Phin said.

'And you did have a feasible motive—freeing Alice from her supposedly horrible husband,' Lucy added.

Phin grimaced. 'Most likely they thought they'd hit on the perfect plan.'

'So, they chose Edward to murder as it was public knowledge that you and Alice had been engaged and that the lady appeared to still have feelings for you. Whoever planned the murder is privy to London gossip, Phin. They knew about Alice's breakdown last year, and they also must have known of our engagement party at the Strawbridge residence.'

'Yes, whoever is behind this is well informed.'

'Our engagement wasn't taken very seriously, it would appear, if it were felt it was plausible you would put Alice's interests above mine.'

Phin quirked his brow. 'We played down our engagement, my dear, and perhaps it was assumed it was not a love match by some.'

Lucy smarted. 'By the gossips? Yes, I would believe that. The syndicate's plan was neat and ingenious. One would almost admire its audacity.'

'I'm not sure I'd go that far,' Phin said. 'It was my neck on the line.'

Lucy patted his hand. 'But... forgive me, Phin, but does it not seem to be unnecessarily complicated? Why didn't they have you assassinated in the first place? Why go to all the trouble of killing Edward?'

Phineas rubbed his chin. 'My assassination in the beginning, as you suggest, would have been easier, but would have merited an investigation: something which would have run a greater risk to Apollo's network. The engagement party in a house full of people was the perfect location for the murder. It was easy for the real murderer to mingle and slip in and out without being noticed. Edward and I were guaranteed to be in attendance. The beauty of it was that by framing me for murder, the Crown would do the job of killing me for them. No doubt revenge added a certain piquancy. There is a very twisted mind behind this. Unfortunately, my dear, your visit to Mr White's gallery was the trigger. They realised I had uncovered

White's involvement in the gang. Once White made the connection between us, he must have panicked... or his paymaster did. Edward was just unfortunate enough to be Alice's husband and a useful tool in our friends' plans for me to stand on the gallows.'

His words made her shiver. 'And then Alice was so helpful with her hysterical allegations,' Lucy said. 'Stupid woman!'

Phineas cast her a pained glance. '*Whoever* is behind this wants the trail to go cold on the painting thefts, and that will only happen if I'm out of the way,' he said. 'My only consolation is their desperation indicates my hard work was beginning to pay dividends. However, my reputation for tenacity may well be my undoing. The attempt on my life was inevitable.'

'Just like poor Charlie! Don't joke about it, Phin,' Lucy said with a shiver. 'If you are correct, then White had something to do with this. Why has he not been questioned?'

'There is no evidence to link him, and besides, he's only the middleman,' Phin replied. 'The collector is the brain and the money behind this enterprise, and McQuillan and I agreed he's the one we must concentrate on finding. We have no idea who he is or where he is. If McQuillan takes White in for questioning, the collector will disappear, along with all those paintings. All my work will have been for naught. We know he's extremely powerful and with useful connections. Our best chance of catching the members of the gang is if another theft occurs. They're doing their best, Lucy; both McQuillan and Kincaid. White is under surveillance,' Phineas said. 'If he tries to abscond, he will be arrested. McQuillan doesn't have the manpower, so I called in a few favours with our friends in the East End.'

'Coffin Mike's network?' Lucy asked.

'Why, yes, as it happens. Fancy you remembering him,' Phin said, his gaze laced with suspicion.

Lucy felt the colour rise in her cheeks. 'How could I forget the man who chased me across half of London?' Lucy paused and threw Phineas a dirty look. 'At your behest, as I recall.'

Phin grinned. 'But you bested him.'

'Yes, I did, and that is why you must let me help. I'm no helpless female,' Lucy said.

Phineas stared at her for several seconds. 'Very well, there may be something you can do.'

PART 2

UNTANGLING THE KNOTS

TWENTY-THREE

The Tea Rooms, Brown's Hotel, Albemarle Street,
Wednesday, 20th June

Although Phin had made steady progress over the last few days, Lucy didn't doubt that Phin's life was in danger. However, while he was still in St Thomas' he was safe at least. With great eagerness, she agreed to help in whatever way she could. Phineas wanted her to liaise with Kincaid, and that very morning, Lucy had sent the private detective an invitation to come to Phillimore Gardens. Sebastian would also attend. Lucy had persuaded Phineas that it was foolish to leave Seb out when he was so keen to help. For now, however, she had to put the forthcoming council of war aside as she entered Brown's Hotel. When she'd mentioned her intention of cancelling the appointment with Thomas Hardwicke, Phineas had urged her to reconsider. Thomas Hardwicke was a regular customer of White and might have information that would be useful. Surely she could glean something from Thomas? He was such a prattler.

Lucy glanced around the wood-panelled room, seeking her host. The aroma of tea and cakes reminded her she'd not eaten since breakfast, and her stomach gave a gurgle of reproach. At least the din of lady chatter drowned it out. Lucy patted it surreptitiously and looked around again. There was no sign of Thomas. Most of the tables were occupied by society women, and she recognised some familiar faces. None, however, looked friendly as their glances slid away. Lucy smothered a sigh. Being engaged to a man recently accused of murder had its advantages, she thought, as she progressed through the room and through the archway to the rear salon: she no longer had to pretend to like these women. Perhaps Thomas would also feel the need to curtail their meeting. Now, that really would be a joyous thing.

However, in the next room, she spotted her old beau. To Lucy's surprise, Thomas was not alone. As he stood to greet her, another gentleman, seated opposite, rose to his feet.

'My dear Lucy, I'm so glad to see you,' Thomas said, rushing forward to shake her hand. 'Let me introduce my brother, Menzies.'

Lucy could detect a slight resemblance as she shook hands with the elder Mr Hardwicke. Taller than Thomas and with a slighter build, he was a handsome man, though a trifle pale. Piercing blue eyes in a sombre face sized her up. Whereas Thomas was clean-shaven, Menzies had a full beard, flecked with grey. Lucy reckoned he must be at least sixty.

'It's pleasure to meet you, Mrs Lawrence,' he said, releasing her hand, his smile cool. 'Thomas has spoken of you often.'

'Oh, I say, Menzies, don't give away all my secrets, old chap,' Thomas said with a nervous titter, blinking rapidly. 'Please, Lucy, do sit down. Shall I order tea?'

'Yes, please,' Lucy said. Thomas waved to the hovering waiter as she continued: 'I do hope I haven't kept you waiting. The traffic was heavy along Hyde Park. The hansom crawled along.'

'Did you have far to come, Mrs Lawrence?' Menzies asked.

'Phillimore Gardens; it's about twenty minutes away.'

'I'm afraid I do not know London well, Mrs Lawrence. I have lived in Scotland my entire life.'

Lucy realised he must be the brother who had been ill. It would account for his pasty complexion and the touch of gauntness in his cheeks. 'It's a beautiful part of the world, sir. My late husband hailed from Edinburgh, and I always enjoyed visiting the city.'

'Is that so? I live outside the city now but know most of the Edinburgh families. What was his name?'

'Charles, Charles Lawrence. His parents reside in the New Town, but they live a retired life and venture out little. I doubt you would know of them. And you, Mr Hardwicke? Where do you live?'

'You will not have heard of it, Lucy. Menzies lives on a small island off the coast, north of Edinburgh,' Thomas pitched in.

Lucy turned a questioning gaze upon Mr Hardwicke, catching the flash of irritation he directed at Thomas. Lucy thought he was not a particularly patient man, but then Thomas was a bit of an oaf. Menzies took out a handkerchief and coughed. Lucy wondered just how ill he was as she noticed the faint sheen of perspiration on his forehead.

'It's a remote old manor house on the water's edge,' Menzies said, putting away the handkerchief. 'I bought Kinnock Island about ten years ago. When my wife passed away, I couldn't bear to live in the city any longer. The peace and quiet suits me perfectly.'

'I'm sorry to hear about your wife,' Lucy said.

'Well, I don't know how you stick the place. Particularly in the winter,' Thomas said. 'When it's stormy, you are cut off for weeks at a time. I couldn't bear it.'

'It suits me perfectly, Thomas. I have no need for gallivanting at my age,' Menzies replied, his eyes hardening as he glared at his brother.

To Lucy's relief, the tension was interrupted by the arrival of the waiter with the tea tray. Lucy picked up the tea pot. 'Shall I pour, gentlemen?'

The conversation centred on safe topics for a few minutes before Thomas turned to Lucy, frowning. 'Lucy, I was sorry to read of your... eh, trouble. It must be awful for you.'

'I'm fine, Thomas, thank you. Of course, I knew all along Phineas was innocent. The whole thing was preposterous.'

'But why was your fiancé shot?' Thomas asked.

'It is under investigation.' Lucy smarted at the implication in his question as Thomas and his brother shared a glance. Irritated, she sipped her tea. They obviously believed the stories in the newspapers. But she could hardly explain the real circumstances to near strangers.

To give him his due, Thomas blushed and turned to his brother. 'You will never guess where we bumped into each other, Menzies, after all these years. Only at White's Gallery. I couldn't believe it when I spotted Lucy.' Thomas turned to her. 'I do hope White provided what you required. You know I would be happy to advise... any time you wish. Though,' he laughed, 'Menzies here knows far more about art than I do. In fact, he was the one who told me to go to White when I was looking for a set of Richardson sketches for my collection. Very rare, you know, but White came up trumps.'

I bet he did! Lucy thought. 'Mr White appears to be very knowledgeable and successful. Has he been in business for some time?'

'I've no idea, Lucy. I don't know his history,' Thomas answered. 'Why do you ask?'

'Oh, just idle curiosity. I wondered if he had any famous clients.'

'Would you know anything about him, Menzies?'

'I'm afraid not,' his brother replied. 'I only met him once.'

'But he must be very successful, to have such a well-known gallery in this part of town?' she asked.

Thomas shrugged. Menzies studied his fingernails before looking up at her. 'There are many such galleries in London, I would imagine, Mrs Lawrence. Mr White was recommended to me by a gallery owner in Edinburgh, but as I said, I only had dealings with him once.'

'Oh, yes, I remember now,' Thomas said. 'That Hicks painting that hangs over your fireplace. That must be ten years ago now.'

'I see.' Lucy was disappointed. It didn't look like she would get much information from Thomas or his brother.

'What did you purchase from him, Mrs Lawrence?' Mr Hardwicke asked, clearly being polite and judging by his tone, not interested at all.

'Two seascapes,' Lucy answered. 'Unfortunately, the artist's name escapes me at the moment.'

'Gosh, it was you!' Thomas exclaimed. 'I've had my eye on those for some time.' He looked across at his brother. 'Those Miller paintings I told you about. I was hoping White would drop the price. How funny that you should whip them out from under my very nose, Lucy. I don't suppose you would consider parting with them?'

'No one in their right senses would part with them, and Thomas, I don't think that is an appropriate request to make of Mrs Lawrence,' his brother snapped. Thomas's face went livid, but he didn't respond. Menzies turned to Lucy. 'You have a good eye, Mrs Lawrence.'

'Pure luck, I assure you, sir. I know little about art. I have always loved the sea, and those paintings caught my eye for that reason alone. I have recently returned from abroad and purchased a new home, you see, and wanted something to brighten the place up. There is nothing worse than bare walls, isn't that so?'

'I couldn't agree more, and you must allow me to advise you in future,' Thomas piped up.

With a sinking feeling, Lucy smiled and nodded.

'I told you about Lucy's trip to Egypt, Menzies.' Thomas smiled across at her, adoration plain to see. Lucy's heart sank, and she did her best to smother her irritation. Did he think she would drop Phineas in his favour? Furthermore, she was sure his brother had no wish to learn about her exploits. The man couldn't have looked more indifferent.

'An intrepid explorer as well as a connoisseur of the finer things. I congratulate you, Mrs Lawrence. Your fiancé is a lucky fellow.' Menzies finished his tea and silence fell.

Growing uncomfortable in the continuing silence, Lucy asked: 'I believe you are acquainted with some friends of mine, Mr Hardwicke?'

Hardwicke's brow rose. 'Indeed?'

'Yes. The Strawbridges?'

Thomas's brother frowned and Lucy noticed the perspiration on his forehead had increased. 'I'm afraid the name is unfamiliar.' Menzies cleared his throat. 'My apologies. Will you excuse me? I'm afraid I'm feeling a trifle unwell,' he said, rising stiffly.

'Do you need help?' Thomas asked his brother.

'Certainly not, Thomas. You must entertain your guest.' Menzies bowed over her hand. 'Good day, Mrs Lawrence.'

Thomas's gaze followed his brother out of the room. 'You must excuse him, Lucy. He has been poorly. I suspect Menzies is in considerable pain, though he would never admit it to me.'

'I'm sorry to hear it,' Lucy replied. But something was niggling at the back of her mind. She was sure Menzies had lied about knowing Sarah and Geoffrey. No one who had met Sarah would forget her, even if it had been years before. Neither would a man forget a political protégé whose campaign he had funded. Thomas only had one brother; of that she was certain. Menzies must be the gentleman Sarah told her about. It didn't make sense, unless his illness had affected his memory. What an odd pair the Hardwicke brothers were. With a little guilt, she wondered how soon she could escape. Kincaid's visit this evening was of far more importance.

Catching Thomas's expectant glance, Lucy pulled herself back to the moment and asked, 'That was the reason you went to Scotland, was it not?'

'Indeed. I was shocked when I saw the state he was in, and I insisted he accompany me back down to London to see a specialist. It took some convincing, but in the end, he gave in. He saw a fellow in Harley Street this morning. I don't think the news was good, but he won't discuss it with me. I'm concerned he intends to return to that awful mausoleum of a place. I've been in cheerier funeral vaults, Lucy.' He gave an exaggerated shudder. 'Kinnock House is far too big for just one man and a handful of servants, and it is incredibly isolated. However, my invitation to stay in London for a few weeks only made him cross.' Thomas gnawed at his lip. 'Menzies was always a difficult fellow. Why, he even took a room here in the hotel when I have plenty of space at my home. We're opposites, but I reckon you have worked that out for yourself, eh, Lucy?' Thomas's smile died. 'I wish he would reconsider, though, and come to live in London. There's only the two of us, and Scotland is such a journey away.'

'Will he stay for a few days at least?'

Thomas's mouth turned down. 'He plans to return tomorrow, as far as I know.'

'Perhaps you could tempt him to linger by offering to show him around the galleries and current exhibitions. Edinburgh can hardly compete when it comes to art.'

'I agree with you there, but to be honest, he would probably say he has seen it all before rather than admit he doesn't have the stamina for it. Besides, he's a dreadful snob about art.' Thomas patted her arm. 'Though it might be worth a try. Thank you.' His eyes fell on the plate of cakes. 'These are quite delicious, are they not? Hard to resist!'

While Thomas munched away, Lucy's gaze strayed to the clock above the fireplace. Politeness dictated she stay at least another fifteen minutes. With a barely suppressed sigh, she turned the conversation to Miller and his seascapes. She might as well learn something about her expensive wall hangings.

TWENTY-FOUR

Some hours later, Lucy sat at her dressing table. Standing behind her, Mary was in a foul mood. Her tirade on hearing that Kincaid was coming to dinner had taken Lucy aback. Now tight-lipped, Mary pulled the comb through Lucy's hair without mercy.

'I'd like to have some hair left for the wedding, Mary,' Lucy muttered.

'Wedding, is it? Sure, the way things are going, there'll be no nuptials for you. You let that gombeen under this roof, and you kiss goodbye to your future.'

Lucy swivelled around. 'Now, Mary, you must stop this nonsense.'

Mary drew in a deep breath. 'Have I not said it often enough? Kincaid is the very devil himself.'

'I think you are a tiny bit biased, Mary, because of your cousin,' Lucy replied, now growing tired of Mary's attitude.

This was answered with a snort. 'Tommy did naught! Was it his fault he was in the wrong place at the wrong time? But Kincaid needed the arrests, see. Had a reputation to maintain.

You mark my words. That man uses people for his own ends. He'll not care about you or Mr Stone. Haven't I told you before? His shenanigans back in Dublin caught up with him in the end, and they kicked him out. And let me tell ye, it takes a lot for a 'G' man to get fired.'

'Mr Stone trusts him, and that is good enough for me. Now, if you are quite finished venting, ask Lacroix to bring the menu for this evening to me in the morning room. And Mary?'

'Yes, ma'am,' Mary said, with a wary look in her eyes.

'I want this evening to go smoothly. Mr Stone is depending on us. Is that clear?'

Mary's nose twitched. 'Very. But don't come cryin' to me when Jabber does his worst!'

Exasperated, Lucy watched her maid flounce out of the room. Picking up the comb, Lucy completed the process of twisting her hair up, pinning and tucking, knowing full well it would soon be in disarray without Mary's expert touch.

Both gentlemen agreed to dispense with brandy and cigars in the dining room and followed Lucy to the drawing room. When Mary entered with the coffee tray, Lucy held her gaze to ensure she behaved. Kincaid, to his credit, had sensed the maid's icy tone on arrival and had gone out of his way to be pleasant to her whenever she appeared. Lucy had been vastly amused to see Mary trying to suppress her natural instincts.

Over dinner, talk had been sensible and surprisingly comfortable. Lucy liked Kincaid. A little devil inside asked was it because he was a handsome fellow. Like the Metropolitan Police, the DMP recruited their men tall and well built. Blessed with cherub-like features, the fair-haired Kincaid also knew how to dress. He was well spoken with a subtle, soft lilt to his voice which Lucy assumed was a more well-to-do Dublin accent compared to Mary's often harsh tone. Even Sebastian appeared to be impressed by the private detective. Kincaid was a natural storyteller and regaled them with some of his more interesting tales of villains, rogues and charlatans. By the third course, the trio were laughing and joking as if they'd known each other for years.

Now, however, the conversation had to take a more serious turn.

Kincaid accepted his coffee from Lucy. 'Thank you, Mrs Lawrence.' He flashed a glance at Sebastian. 'I assume you are up to date on the situation regarding the Apollo case?'

'Yes, Lucy explained it all to me when I arrived. It would appear we were on the wrong track, chasing shadows,' Sebastian replied. 'But to be fair to us, it was logical to assume Mrs Vaughan had been up to mischief, based on our knowledge of her and what she will gain by her husband's death.'

'And the fact that she was so quick to blame Phin,' Lucy cut in.

Kincaid nodded. 'I understand completely. Particularly as Mr Stone had not enlightened you with the facts; or perhaps, I should say his *theory*.'

'Phin thought it best we didn't know the connection between the murder and the Apollo case, Kincaid,' Lucy said. 'Not wishing to put us in danger.' Kincaid nodded, but she could tell he had doubts. 'Do you think it possible Phineas has misinterpreted the situation?' she asked.

Kincaid took a moment to answer. 'It's always best to examine every possible explanation, I have found. I do not doubt his analysis makes sense. From the little involvement I have had in the Apollo case, it is clear the syndicate is well connected, well informed and highly dangerous. They will not take kindly to anyone attempting to curb their activities. Perhaps, Mr Stone *was* getting too close. However, when it comes to murder, those who have most to gain must always be investigated thoroughly.'

Sebastian threw a satisfied smile at Lucy. 'Alice!'

'Yes, Captain Stone,' Kincaid replied. 'Mrs Vaughan will benefit; however, both your investigations and mine can find no evidence to link her to the crime either directly or indirectly. My latest intelligence is that she has taken ill.'

'Oh!' Lucy exclaimed. With a pang of guilt, she realised she'd not even attempted to keep in touch with poor Lady Dot. She would have to remedy that first thing in the morning and send her a note.

Kincaid was still speaking, and she had to focus on him. 'We must therefore give Mr Stone's theory sufficient weight and assume Edward Vaughan was collateral damage.' Kincaid set down his cup. 'I'm curious, Mrs Lawrence. What changed Mr Stone's mind? Why has he involved you both at this stage?'

'I left him with little choice. I suspected he was keeping me in the dark about something. Your presence at Vine Street and then at the funeral set me thinking. My maid Mary recognised you and knew a little of your history.'

'Ah!' Kincaid smiled.

'Tell me, how long have you been working on the case for Phin?'

'Mr Stone first approached me before he left for India last year. Asked me to keep an eye out for any further thefts which appeared to have the same modus operandi.'

'And were there?' she asked.

'Yes, as it happens. But, as in the other cases, no clues were left other than the calling card. Apollo simply vanished back into the shadows along with the paintings. And, of course, at that time we were unaware that White was involved. The irony is, *that* was only confirmed by Vaughan's murder. If they'd held firm and not acted, we might have dismissed White from our enquiries.'

'A mistake at last, eh?' Sebastian said. 'What do you suggest we do now? Neither Lucy nor I are good at kicking our heels, don't you know?'

'My latest report from Coffin Mike is that there has been a lot of activity at the Royal Arcade at night, these last few weeks.' Kincaid looked at Lucy. 'I understand you had to abort your attempt to entrap White?'

'Yes, pure bad luck,' Lucy admitted.

'Indeed, as it most likely triggered Vaughan's murder. However, I think we could still give it another try. White is our only lead.'

'White would recognise me; I couldn't do it,' Lucy said, putting down her cup.

'We shall have to find someone willing to help,' he replied. 'Do you happen to know anyone who might be willing?'

'There is someone, actually,' Seb said. 'Me.'

'Are you sure? It could be dangerous, and you would have to use an alias.' Kincaid exchanged a glance with Lucy before turning back to Seb. 'We will only have one more chance for this to work.'

'I understand completely. I'd be only too glad to help.' Sebastian smiled and wiggled his brows at Lucy.

'Won't someone need to notify Phin's contact with the Tissot?' Lucy asked.

'Montgomery Steward is the man, I understand,' Kincaid said. Lucy nodded, and he continued: 'I shall telegram him to expect me as soon as we know White has taken the bait. We will need someone at the house in Liverpool if Apollo turns up to steal the painting.'

Sebastian's eyes lit up. 'Gosh, absolutely. We must catch the fellow.'

'But we don't want to catch him, Captain Stone, that's the point. We want him to lead us to White and from there to the Collector. Once the painting is stolen, I shall telegram you immediately. You will need to watch White's gallery, just in case I don't make it back on time.'

'Yes, of course.'

'Discreetly!'

'Oh yes, indeed,' Sebastian replied, his colour rising. 'You can rely on me.'

'Perhaps I could help with that? What else can I do?' Lucy asked, determined not to be left out.

'You might relay our plans to Mr Stone and the chief inspector. Vine Street may be under surveillance, so it is best I do not go near it again. Your visits, however, would be expected. Apollo's network could include police officers, which is why telegrams or letters would be risky.'

'Do you believe they're so devious that they have policemen working for them?' Lucy asked.

'Of course. They need to know what the police thinking might be to enable them to stay a step ahead. Police pay is poor and the temptation all too great. It was a problem in Dublin, I can tell you.' Lucy briefly wondered if *he* had ever taken a bribe. She'd have to ask Mary if that was the reason he was fired. Was the charm a little too practised? However, more importantly, the concept of an insider working at Vine Street made her uneasy.

Kincaid cast her a sympathetic glance. 'Don't be concerned, Mrs Lawrence. I'm sure the chief inspector is being careful.' Kincaid accepted the offer of another cup of coffee. As he stirred in some sugar, he said: 'There is a possibility that we must be prepared for, and that is that the Collector may not even be in this country.'

'How can we find out? Is there any way we can check if White is exporting paintings?' Lucy asked.

Kincaid grinned. 'Not without checking his order books. We may have to consider a spot of spying if it comes to it.'

Lucy swallowed hard. Was he suggesting breaking into White's office? Still, if it were to help Phin, she would have to go along with it. 'It *would* be interesting to know who his clients are.' Another idea popped into her head. 'What if there is more than one collector involved in the network? They could be located anywhere,' Lucy said.

Kincaid took a moment before answering. 'That is quite possible. It could even be an international network. From a financial point of view that would make sense, particularly if you had foreign individuals with their beady eyes on paintings located here in this country.' He gave a soft chuckle. 'That will make it even more difficult to trace the stolen paintings. I hope Mr Stone likes to travel.'

'It would not deter him,' Lucy said, a trifle peeved at the jibe on Phin's behalf.

'I'd say! He often goes abroad on cases,' Sebastian said, giving Kincaid a hard look.

Kincaid smiled but didn't respond, and Lucy grew wary. Sebastian, however, was rattling away, seemingly oblivious.

'Can we be sure that White would even contemplate sourcing something for a stranger like me? Do we not run the risk of tipping him off?' Sebastian asked.

'An excellent point. But we have little choice but to try. Without knowing Apollo's identity, we can never close down the network.' Kincaid sat forward, looking directly at Lucy. 'We must trust your fiancé has good instincts. He believes this is the best way to find those paintings. At the moment, I can see no other option.'

'Agreed. But do we not have an obligation to try to solve the murder as well?' Lucy asked, as an unbidden image of Alice in distress popped into her mind. They should not lose sight of the fact that an innocent man had died.

'That would be an added bonus, of course,' Kincaid replied. 'But the chief inspector may not take kindly to any intervention in that matter.'

Was he sincere, Lucy wondered? She knew he would only

be paid to solve the thefts as a sub-agent of Phin. With a mental shake, she realised she was letting Mary's mistrust seep into her mind. However, it would be no harm to keep an eye on the man, just in case.

TWENTY-FIVE

Two Days Later, Royal Academy of Arts, Piccadilly

Everything had fallen into place. Phineas's contact, Mr Steward, agreed to revive their original plan to be bait for Apollo, and Lucy secured McQuillan's agreement to their proposal. Lucy hoped Sebastian would succeed where she'd failed. Her frustration at their lack of progress was growing.

Lucy and Kincaid had spent the previous evening rehearsing with Sebastian. Seb would use an alias, and he had been rather proud to announce he had surreptitiously pocketed several visiting cards from the hallway of his club the night before. He would assume the identity of one of the younger gentlemen as they would be unlikely to be clients of White already. If challenged in any way, he would flash the card at White, if necessary. The only stumbling block had been which address to give White if the man agreed to secure the painting. Again, Seb came to the rescue, suggesting the painting be sent to the alias at his club. If everything went to plan, they could always let the real cardholder know what they were doing to retrieve Steward's painting. Now, a tiny part of Lucy was jealous of Sebastian. She hated being a spectator.

By agreement, Lucy and Kincaid were waiting for Sebastian at the Royal Academy, not far from the Royal Arcade. For the past twenty minutes, they'd strolled through the Summer Exhibition, passing time. To any observer, they hoped to give the impression of a couple out for the afternoon, enjoying the display of new artworks. Now, however, both stood gazing up at one particular painting entitled *The Lady of Shalott*. Kincaid's overnight bag lay at his feet in preparation for a speedy departure to Liverpool if Sebastian was successful.

After a few moments, Lucy realised she'd been holding her breath. 'It's magnificent,' she said, turning to Kincaid.

His eyes were roaming over the painting. Suddenly, he leaned closer to it and read out the name on the label at the base: 'J. W. Waterhouse; do you know of him?'

'No, to my shame. I really do wish I knew more about art, Kincaid. This painting is wonderful,' she breathed.

'You are not alone, Mrs Lawrence, but it's a rich man's interest. I couldn't afford such a work.'

Recalling how much she'd paid White for her two seascapes, Lucy nodded out of sympathy. Only two years before, she couldn't have afforded it either. 'But it isn't difficult to see how someone with the resources could become obsessed with these paintings. I would love to have this hanging in my home. I would stare at this for hours. Tennyson's poem is one of my favourites,' she said.

'It's fine poem and a magnificent painting,' he agreed.

'Look at her expression, Kincaid. She accepts her curse so stoically. I cried the first time I read the poem. My governess was bewildered, for I usually escaped the schoolroom at the merest hint of poetry. But those verses were different. They touched something in me. Even now, those lines make me shiver.' An image flashed into her mind: of a day she'd stared out the window in Abbey Gardens, waiting for Charlie to come home and knowing it was unlikely. Years of loneliness encapsulated in one fleeting memory. Thank God Phineas had rescued her from *her* fate.

'Tragedy and romance intertwined; it's a very powerful thing,' Kincaid said, still staring up at the lady's face.

Was he mocking her? Lucy couldn't tell by his expression. 'You think I'm foolish to be affected by such things?' she asked.

Kincaid glanced up at the picture again and shook his head. 'Not at all.'

Finding a lump in her throat, Lucy had to blink several times. 'I suspect you are a romantic, Kincaid, beneath that professional demeanour.'

'You have found me out, Mrs Lawrence,' he replied with that charming grin of his. 'But you see, we Irish love a good story and one with a tragic ending even more.' There was an unmistakable glint in Kincaid's eye.

They were straying into uncomfortable territory. 'Let us hope there are no tragedies today. Shall we continue?' Lucy asked, stepping away.

Kincaid offered his arm, and they moved forward through the crowd. 'You are worried about young Captain Stone?'

'I fear his enthusiasm may override the necessary caution for such an undertaking,' she said.

'He's certainly eager.'

'But White is wily and may guess what Sebastian is about.' Lucy gnawed her lip. 'If anything should go wrong, Phineas will never forgive me.'

'Don't worry. The worst that can happen is that White runs him out of the gallery.'

'Surely you underestimate White? You said yourself these men are dangerous,' she replied.

'In broad daylight with the public close by, White will not do anything to harm the captain.'

'He might follow Sebastian here,' she said in a low voice. 'White would recognise me, and the game would be up.'

Kincaid gave her an amused look. 'White does not strike me as the type for that kind of legwork. Could you see him keeping up with the nimble Captain Stone? Yes, if his suspicions are aroused, he may have Sebastian followed, but it will be some young fellow, not the portly Mr White. Besides, I warned Sebastian to ensure he wasn't tracked when he leaves the gallery. He will take a circuitous route here.'

Only slightly mollified, Lucy checked her watch. 'Thank you. Seb should be here soon.'

'And if our luck is in, I can head for Euston straightaway. There should be a Liverpool train on the hour. We were lucky Mr Steward was happy to assist us.'

'Yes, indeed; we would be lost without him. Wouldn't it be something if our plan works?'

Kincaid chuckled. 'And to succeed where Phineas Stone has failed would be quite a coup.' Lucy threw him a sharp glance. 'Oh come, Mrs Lawrence, you must see that.'

'We're not engaging in this to boost your career, Mr Kincaid. We must focus on retrieving those stolen paintings and revealing Edward Vaughan's murderer, if at all possible.'

'Of course,' Kincaid said at last. He looked contrite, but that charming smile soon twitched on his lips.

Mary was right: the man *was* a rogue, Lucy thought, but at least she was wise to him. 'I have to admit I'm dying to know Apollo's identity,' she said, turning the conversation.

Kincaid laughed. 'As are half the police forces and insurance companies in the country. The scoundrel has given everyone the slip for far too long.'

Lucy stopped dead. 'You are not he, by any chance?'

Kincaid's eyes flew wide. Then he burst out laughing. 'I'm deeply flattered, Mrs Lawrence, but no, I'm not Apollo.'

'I'm sorry. That was unforgivably rude of me,' Lucy said, feeling the heat rise in her face.

'Oh, no, you have nothing to apologise for. You are more than quick-witted, Mrs Lawrence. That mind of yours is always trying to work out the possibilities. I admire you for it. I do hope your fiancé appreciates how lucky he is. I must admit to being surprised that he decided to keep you in the dark about my involvement, initially.'

As this touched a nerve, Lucy had difficulty quelling a sharp response, but she was determined not to rise to his bait. Was Kincaid trying to drive a wedge between her and Phineas? And if so, to what end? Did he hope she would reveal something Phin was keeping from him?

'Phin's reasoning was sound, Kincaid. If the Apollo gang thought they'd neutralised him, they might make a mistake, perhaps steal another painting and leave a clue. Obviously, the fewer people who knew, the better. And now, his safety is my *only* concern.'

'Of course,' Kincaid replied, patting her arm where it lay on his.

Lucy bristled in silence.

TWENTY-SIX

The Royal Academy, Piccadilly

Lucy knew as soon as she set eyes on Sebastian that their plan lay in ruins. With drooping shoulders and avoiding eye contact, he approached them slowly through the throng of people. At her side, Kincaid sighed and muttered something under his breath. She was disappointed too, but she wasn't sure which was worse: their failure—condemning Phin to continued speculation—or the fact that all their hopes had hinged on White leading them to Apollo and his syndicate.

'Hello,' Sebastian said, his glance shifting between them. 'I'm sorry. White feigned total ignorance. I had to abandon the whole thing.' Lucy glanced at the small rectangular parcel under Seb's arm. 'Oh yes, I had to buy this so he would think I was a legitimate customer. Couldn't leave empty-handed, now, could I?' Seb asked, his misery all too evident. 'Damage limitation.'

'That was good thinking, Captain Stone. Let's hope he wasn't alarmed by your request regarding the Tissot. The last thing we need is for the operation to close down when we're getting close.' Kincaid looked about. 'Best we discuss this somewhere more private, I suggest.' Looking none too pleased, Kincaid headed for the exit.

Lucy hung back, her eyes on Kincaid's retreating back. She wondered if his displeasure related to his own hopes of besting Phineas rather than a failure to help Phin clear his name. And what of Edward's murder? Kincaid appeared to have no interest in investigating that. That niggled. Surely it was another way to track down members of the gang? If indeed Phin's theory was correct, and Edward had been murdered to set him up.

With a sympathetic smile, Lucy tucked her arm through Sebastian's. 'Don't worry, Seb. You tried. We will just have to come up with another plan. Let us adjourn to Phillimore Gardens,' she said softly. 'All is not lost.'

They made a glum party in Lucy's drawing room. Sebastian sat, staring out into the garden. Kincaid sat opposite, his expression somewhere between grim and annoyed. Lucy was equally disappointed but determined not to dwell on it.

'Seb, take this. You look like you need it,' Lucy said, handing him a goblet of brandy.

'Thank you, Lucy,' the young man said, trying to smile up at her and failing.

Lucy put a hand on his shoulder. 'Don't worry, Seb. We will find another way to help Phin,' she said.

'You kept to the script we agreed?' Kincaid asked, taking a glass from Lucy, and ignoring her scolding glance.

'Yes, the fellow just looked askance at me, as if I'd asked for the crown jewels. I felt six inches tall, I can tell you.'

'White's caution is telling, though, isn't it, Kincaid?' Lucy asked, sitting down. She hoped Kincaid would stop making poor Seb feel worse. 'White must be worried for him to pass up on an opportunity to make more money. Perhaps he will do something rash.'

Kincaid blew out a slow breath. 'That is my hope, certainly. They're being cautious; there have been no further thefts. I only hope Apollo will not be able to resist the temptation to get back to work soon.'

'But we have no notion where he might strike if we do not orchestrate it,' Lucy said. 'We must find out who he is.'

'But how? We must give up on that idea and take a different tack,' Kincaid said, swirling the brandy in his glass.

'Do you have a plan?' Seb asked, sitting forward, all eagerness.

'There was a strong possibility White wouldn't fall for our ruse. I believe there is only one option left to us, but you may not like it.'

'What?' Lucy and Seb asked in unison.

'We must break into White's premises and do a search.'

'Blimey!' Seb exclaimed, wide-eyed. 'Oh, sorry, Lucy. Excuse my language.'

Lucy dismissed this with a wave of her hand and turned to Kincaid. 'Of course, yes,' Lucy said. 'You are right. There may be a clue to the other members of the network in his records.'

'Even the faintest trace could be all we need,' Kincaid said with satisfaction. 'There is one difficulty, however.'

'McQuillan! He will never agree to it,' Lucy said.

'Correct, Mrs Lawrence. We can't tell him of our intent.' Kincaid gave her a steady look. 'Are you prepared to break the law?'

'I'm prepared to do anything to help my fiancé,' she replied, returning his stare.

Kincaid smirked. 'Such loyalty is commendable, but you must be sure. This is no light undertaking.'

Lucy's chin went up. 'I say we do it, and the sooner the better; however, I'm due to visit Vine Street in the morning. I'll have to tell the chief inspector today's mission failed. Naturally, he will want to know what we plan next.'

'Then best we strike this evening. Ignorance is bliss, is it not? Hopefully, you will have something useful to impart to McQuillan in the morning.' Kincaid set down his empty glass.

Sebastian leaned forward. 'I say, are you sure, Kincaid? I'm not sure we should involve Lucy in something so dangerous.'

Lucy glared at Sebastian. 'Just try to stop me!'

The Royal Arcade, Saturday, 23rd June, 1.15 a.m.

After a quick reconnaissance, it was obvious that the only way they could access White's office or basement was through the main gallery. Lucy watched closely as Kincaid picked the lock. *Oh! If my mother could see me now,* she thought, *she would have a fit!* Still, anything was better than sitting at home worrying. The risk of being spotted by a member of the public or a diligent policeman was high, even at this hour of the morning. Though the entrance was stepped back slightly, framed by the curving front windows of the gallery, they couldn't risk being caught. Luckily, they'd taken the precaution of wearing dark clothing.

With a click, the door swung open, and Kincaid ushered them inside. Lucy pointed to the nearby desk, but Kincaid shook his head and mouthed: *too dangerous, too visible.* Seb shrugged at Lucy. Kincaid tried the door at the centre of the back wall. It was locked, but it only took him a few seconds to open. *He's rather good at that*, Lucy thought—a practised lock-breaker. *Something I should probably mention to Phin.* Lucy and Seb followed him through. The door closed noiselessly behind them. Seconds later, the gas light popped into life, casting a dim glow. They were in a narrow corridor. It was bare except for a slender stairway which led both upwards and down.

'Should we split up?' Lucy whispered to Kincaid. She

watched as he lit his lantern. He slid a shutter across the bulb to mask the beam.

'No. I only have one lantern. We can't risk showing a light. Let's check the basement first.'

With the limited glow from the lantern, Lucy could see the basement ran the full length of the gallery above. Stacks of paintings leaned against the walls. Some were wrapped, ready for despatch; others must be stock to replace sold items. It was unpleasantly stuffy. Kincaid looked up. A small grille in the ceiling let in faint light from the arcade walkway above. He turned to Lucy. 'I'm going to risk opening up the lantern. It will be too dim for us to work otherwise.'

The additional light illuminated a quantity of cobwebs, but more disconcerting was the scuttle of tiny feet. Mice. Lucy shuddered. There would have to be mice.

'What are we looking for, Kincaid?' Seb asked, standing in the centre of the basement.

'Check any of the paintings ready to be delivered. Take a note of the names of the purchasers on the labels.'

'Do you hope the Collector might be among them?' Lucy asked Kincaid, who was sorting through a stack of large canvasses. 'But how will we know?'

Kincaid straightened up. 'The clue will be the number of paintings, I would imagine. A large consignment to one person should be a red flag. Yes, I know, it is clutching at straws. The order books might be a better source of information, if White is foolish enough to record everything that comes through the gallery. But we have time and I like to be thorough. We might as well check.'

'Kincaid! There is a large box here. Should I open it?' Seb called from the other side of the room.

'What about the label?' Kincaid asked, hurrying across to join him.

Seb shook his head. 'There isn't one, I'm afraid, but there must be at least four frames inside judging by the size of it.'

Kincaid sighed. 'Without a label, it is useless to us. Very well, keep looking,' Kincaid replied, his tone flat.

Ten minutes later, they'd checked the entire stock in the cellar.

'Let's hope the office bears better fruit,' Kincaid said with a heavy sigh, leading the way back up the steps. He stalled at the top of the stairs and tilted his head. Lucy waited patiently behind him. The silence was broken by distant voices and laughter. Late-night revellers on Albemarle Street, Lucy supposed.

'All right, let's continue,' Kincaid whispered once silence had descended once more. 'I will have to extinguish the lantern; we can't risk showing a light in the office window.'

They emerged onto a small landing with a skylight in the roof. Straight ahead was a solitary door upon which a sign proclaiming 'White's Gallery' was discernible. Kincaid left the lamp down on the ground and tried the door handle. It gave a faint creak as he pressed downwards. Kincaid froze and grimaced at Lucy before gently nudging the door open. The first thing that hit Lucy was the smell. It was White's distinctive citrus lotion, which she'd found deeply unpleasant the day she'd met him. But there was another odour underlying it. A metallic one.

Lucy squeezed up beside Kincaid in the doorway and peered into the office. It took a few seconds for her eyes to adjust to the gloom as the curtains were half pulled across the window. But there was enough light from the street and arcade to make out the outline of the room's furniture. Near the window, there was a large cabinet. The sight of it cheered her up. Hopefully, it would contain some proof or clue to the Apollo gang's activities.

Kincaid took a step forward, then froze, Lucy running into

his back. He held out his hand as he leaned into the darkness towards the back of the room. He was sniffing the air; she was sure of it. Did he detect that same sickly-sweet odour?

'What do you see?' Sebastian whispered from behind Lucy.

'Shh!' Kincaid answered. 'Grab that lantern and light it, Captain. Something's not right.'

Lucy heard the match being struck and stood back to let Sebastian move up beside Kincaid. Sebastian held up the light. The now-illuminated office held an unpleasant surprise.

'Oh, bloody hell!' Sebastian cried.

Lucy stood stock-still, her body suddenly as cold as a Yorkshire winter. Head down on the desk, with a pool of blood staining the papers scattered across it, was White.

His throat had been cut.

TWENTY-SEVEN

The Royal Arcade

Lucy knew they were in deep trouble. Once her heart had stopped pounding, she'd felt an overwhelming urge to cry. Suddenly exhausted, she suspected the next few hours would be extremely unpleasant. Kincaid sucked in a breath before shooing Lucy out of the office. Then he took the key from the inside of the lock, closed the door rather firmly, and locked it.

'Damn and blast it!' he growled, slamming his hand against the wall.

'I know,' Lucy said. 'It is dreadful, but what are we going to do? We can't just leave.'

'Agreed. We must fetch the police,' Kincaid answered. 'We have no choice.'

Lucy glanced at Sebastian who was standing ashen-faced across the landing. The young man's grip on the top post of the stairs showed white knuckles.

Whatever Kincaid was going to say to Sebastian died on his lips. 'If you are all right, Mrs Lawrence, I'll track down a constable. You two best wait down in the gallery.'

Ten minutes later, Kincaid returned. 'I've sent a constable scurrying to Vine Street. Best McQuillan deals with this. If you want to leave, Mrs Lawrence, they need never know you were here.'

'No. I will stay. We're in this together.'

'You have guts, Lucy Lawrence, I'll say that for ye,' Kincaid replied with a grin.

Sebastian smiled across at her. 'I'll second that.' After a moment, he continued: 'Do you think we will get the blame, Kincaid?'

'No, of course not. What reason would we have for killing White?'

Lucy hoped his reasoning was sound.

They waited in near silence for the nightmare to descend. Sure enough, half an hour later, Chief Inspector McQuillan arrived. He walked past them without a word and headed up the stairs, two policemen on his heels. Another constable took up position at the front door, two more at either end of the arcade. Lucy thought longingly of her bed and wondered if there was any chance she might see it tonight. She needed to concentrate on mundane things. The alternative was re-living the scene in the room above. No more than Edward's murder, it had been a vicious assault. She was unlikely to forget the sight of so much blood any time soon.

All three of them looked up as they heard footsteps out in the hallway. Lucy took a shuddering breath as McQuillan entered the gallery.

The chief inspector stared at each of them in turn before concentrating his gaze on Kincaid. Lucy gulped, thankful the glare Kincaid was being subjected to was not focused on her. But to his credit, Kincaid crossed his arms and stared right back at the policeman.

'Chief Inspector,' Kincaid said, as if he were greeting him casually on the street.

McQuillan raised his eyes to the ceiling. 'Would you care to explain, Kincaid?'

'Certainly, Chief Inspector, but perhaps Mrs Lawrence might be allowed to go home? It has been a trying evening for her.'

Lucy threw Kincaid a dirty look. She didn't take kindly to being dismissed as if inconsequential. 'I'm fine,' she said. 'And happy to answer any questions the chief inspector may have.'

McQuillan turned his focus back to her. 'Nonetheless, Mrs Lawrence, your statement can wait until tomorrow. One of my constables will see you to a carriage.'

Sebastian looked up from the floor. 'No, please, Chief Inspector, I should do it. After all, Mrs Lawrence is almost family.'

'I'm afraid that is out of the question, Captain Stone. You will be helping me with my investigation.'

Sebastian frowned at him, but then his shoulders sank. 'I suppose you have some questions for me?'

'I certainly do,' replied McQuillan. He called to the constable on the door. 'Please escort Mrs Lawrence outside.'

'Sir!' The constable gestured for Lucy to go ahead of him, out the door.

Miffed, Lucy stood her ground. 'Chief Inspector, I'm more than happy to stay. We're equally responsible for tonight's... adventure.'

'Please do not try my patience, Mrs Lawrence. I have just about enough fortitude to deal with these two. You may report to the station in the morning. *Goodnight*,' McQuillan said, his eyes boring into her.

Lucy smiled apologetically at her co-conspirators before following the constable out into the arcade to the Old Bond Street end. At least she'd tried.

. . .

Several police carriages were waiting at the entrance and a small group of men stood a little further down the pavement, deep in conversation. It was too dark to see their faces, but Lucy assumed they were more of McQuillan's men. When the constable opened the door of the nearest carriage, inviting her to enter with a wave of his hand, she stepped up with relief and sank onto the seat.

'Someone will escort you home, ma'am,' the constable said before closing the door of the carriage. Then he disappeared from view. It was a bit much insisting she was escorted home. Did McQuillan not trust her to go straight there? Where would she go at two in the morning?

Lucy was vaguely aware of voices outside the carriage. But she was so tired. Leaning back against the squabs, she closed her eyes. Still feeling guilty to leave the others behind, she hoped McQuillan wouldn't be too hard on Seb and Kincaid. Surely McQuillan would realise they were not to blame? It was bad luck stumbling on yet another murder, of course, but after all, they were only doing what he should have been doing: investigating White. Really, she'd have to give the chief inspector a piece of her mind when she saw him in the morning. Of course, she'd also have to face Phineas at the hospital. She almost groaned as she thought about Phin's reaction when he'd hear of her latest catastrophe. He'd probably recommend McQuillan lock her up for all their sakes. There might even be talk of breaking off the engagement again...

She was aware of the carriage door opening and her eyes flew open.

'Lucy?'

To her astonishment, it was Phin. 'What on earth—?' Lucy exclaimed.

'Sorry, my dear. I didn't mean to alarm—'

Lucy interrupted him by flinging herself into his arms as he sat down opposite her.

'Ouch! Watch the shoulder,' he cried, half laughing.

It was several minutes before either of them could speak.

'What I was going to say—' Phin cleared his throat '—was that McQuillan thought it best I come along when he heard you were involved in Kincaid's escapade.' He rapped on the roof, and the carriage moved away from the kerb and out into the street.

Lucy was confused. 'This is madness! What are you doing here? Are you well enough to be out of hospital?'

'I'm fine, Lucy. A little sore.' He hunched his shoulder. 'But I can heal just as quickly at home under George's care.'

Lucy treated him to a sharp glance. 'Then that is where you should be, not here! You just want to be able to investigate, admit it.'

His mouth twitched. 'Perhaps. I managed to persuade the doctor I would be better off at home when he arrived on his round this evening. I went straight to Phillimore Gardens, but you were not home. All Mary could tell me was that you had gone out with Kincaid and Seb. Then I went to Vine Street to see if McQuillan knew what was going on.'

'Oh!'

'Lucy, I can understand why the three of you thought this was a good idea, but you must see now how dangerous this gang is.'

'I do, of course. But we had to try something. Our attempt to entrap White this afternoon failed. Poor Seb was so disappointed. He really wanted to help you.'

Phin grunted. 'He's the best of brothers. I could never see Andrew breaking and entering for my sake!'

Lucy managed a smile. 'Gosh, no! If he ever hears of this, Phin, I will be persona non grata, for sure.'

'Andrew's opinion on any subject means nothing to me,' he said fiercely. 'Don't take any notice of him.'

'It's all right, Phin, I understand how you feel. We just need to give Andrew time.' She sighed. 'I wish the outcome had been different tonight. You see, we hoped to find some clue to either Apollo or the Collector's identity to present to you.'

'I don't doubt your motivation, Lucy,' Phin said. 'Well, it was lucky I was still with McQuillan at Vine Street when he was summoned to White's Gallery.' He smiled. 'It was like old times, sitting up half the night discussing a case. Only, this one is so much more personal. Naturally, when I heard Kincaid's name mentioned, and I knew you were with him, I insisted on coming along.'

'I'm glad you did. But, Phin, if news of your discharge comes out, as surely it must, your life will be at risk. You must leave London,' she urged. 'Go home to Kent.'

Phin shook his head. 'That is out of the question. I will not hide, Lucy. I'm more determined than ever to solve both the art thefts and Edward's murder.'

'Then you must promise me to be careful,' she said.

'I will do my best.'

'But how are we to progress? With White now dead, there is no one who can lead us to the Collector. It was awful tonight, finding White like that. The man was disreputable, certainly, but he didn't deserve to die in such a ghastly way.'

'I hope you do not have nightmares as a result. I will have words with Kincaid, for he should not have involved you in such a dangerous operation.'

'I insisted.'

'Hmm, I don't doubt it. However, I must admit I would probably have done the same as Kincaid tonight. Searching the gallery for a lead, however faint, was the only possible next step.'

'Yes, it was.'

'But White was obviously on his guard when Seb made his play and thought it too risky to agree to source a painting for someone he didn't know. You can be sure the Collector would have told him to be extra careful.'

Lucy grimaced into the darkness of the carriage. 'And then ordered his murder!'

'Yes. The man is ruthless, whoever he is.'

'We must find him, Phin, whatever it takes. I will help in any way I can.'

'I know,' he replied with a sigh as he scooped up her hand. 'And I will involve you as much as I can and only if it does not pose *any* risk to your life.'

'Really? You promise?'

Phineas grinned in response. 'If at all possible.' Then he swooped in for a kiss.

Eventually, Lucy pulled back. No matter how glad she was to see Phin, what she'd witnessed at White's Gallery was still far too fresh in her mind. 'Why do you think White was murdered?' she asked.

'It has to be connected to the syndicate. The real question is why *now*?'

'Is the Collector trying to get rid of anyone who might lead you or the police to him?'

Phin blew out his cheeks. 'Probably.'

'Did the Collector panic? Could your discharge earlier have triggered this?'

Phineas shook his head. 'I don't see how it could have. Only a handful of people know of it. Unless, of course, he had someone at the hospital keeping an eye on me.'

'Don't! Kincaid even suggested that there might be a spy at Vine Street.'

'It's possible.'

'Are you serious? I hope you are wrong. The very thought of it will give me nightmares.' Lucy nibbled on her bottom lip.

'Phin, I know you will think me silly, but I cannot but conclude that my original visit to the gallery may have been the catalyst for both murders.'

Phin put his arm around her shoulder and drew her close. 'You must not blame yourself. Anyone who becomes entangled in such schemes must know the risks.'

'Well, we found nothing to prove White's involvement, even though we searched through the stock in the basement quite thoroughly.'

'Yes, but his murder rather proves it.'

'True, and there may still be evidence. We didn't get to search the office at all.'

'Yes, dead bodies are a bit off-putting,' Phin remarked with a grim expression.

'I'd do it if I had to! And let me tell you, there were mice down in that basement, but they didn't put me off.'

'How brave you are!'

'Now, you're just teasing me,' she answered with a frown. 'We were only doing what we hoped would help your case.'

'I don't doubt it, my dear, and I'm grateful. Mice or no, tomorrow I intend to do a thorough search of the premises. Hopefully, the killer didn't remove anything of interest that might help us.'

'And I will assist,' she said, clutching his hand. To her surprise, he nodded. 'In fact,' she continued, 'I wish to stay near to you at all times.'

Phin's brow shot up. 'That might give rise to talk!'

Lucy threw him a dirty look. 'You know very well what I mean.' He just grinned in response. 'You should know, I still have the pistol you gave me.'

'Good,' he replied. 'However, I should warn you that you may have to fight Sebastian for the role of bodyguard.'

Lucy tried not to laugh as the carriage came to a stop. 'Well,

I'm warning *you*, if you go and get yourself murdered, I'll be extremely cross.'

That produced a smile from Phin. 'I will bear that in mind. Now, my dear assistant, get some sleep. I will call for you in the early afternoon, for we have paintings and a murderer to track down.' Phineas handed her down to the pavement, kissed her cheek and stood by the carriage door as she made her way up the path to her door.

Lucy was still grinning as she put her key in the latch. He wasn't, as she'd feared, leaving her out of the investigation.

TWENTY-EIGHT

The Next Afternoon

Phineas handed Lucy up into the hansom cab. 'We need to make a slight detour, my dear,' he said. 'Lady Dot sent a message to Seb at Westbourne Grove first thing this morning, requesting to see him. For her to do so, suggests it is rather urgent and important. George sent a telegram to inform her I would call at her home instead.'

'Do you know what she wishes to discuss?'

Phin shook his head and tapped the roof with his cane, and the hansom swept forward. Lucy noticed he was using his old swordstick again and was somewhat relieved. She was concerned about his safety but knew he would be irritated if she were to bring up the topic again. Safer ground was needed. 'And how is Sebastian? Did McQuillan keep them long at the Royal Arcade?'

'Seb arrived home just as I did. A little shaken, I believe, but it may, hopefully, discourage him from such wild pranks in the future.'

'Oh, come now, he has been a great support to me and

desperate to help you. I hope you weren't too hard on him, or that he suffers because of our late-night escapade. He's still not entirely better, is he?' Phin pursed his lips but didn't reply. She continued: 'And Kincaid was very... persuasive, you know. I fully agreed that it was necessary when Sebastian's attempt to lure White to procure the Tissot failed. You have already admitted you would have done the same.'

'Yes,' he answered, not quite meeting her eye. 'He's quite the charmer, Kincaid.'

Lucy quirked her lip. 'He certainly believes himself so.'

Phin's brows snapped together. 'Do I detect dislike?' he asked with a smile.

'More distrust than dislike, if I'm honest.'

'Did he at least behave as he ought?'

Was Phineas jealous? she wondered in astonishment. 'Absolutely, and I might add, I was never alone with him. Mary put me on my guard, you'll be glad to know. Her opinion of him is rather low. Something about a cousin of hers back in Dublin who had less than pleasant dealings with him.'

Phineas relaxed back into the squabs. 'Mary has good instincts; do not dismiss them. However, I hired him for his mind. Some would say he engages in methods most would not condone. That probably indicates how desperate I am to solve this case. The sniff of a reward from the insurance companies involved, once highlighted, had him eager to help.'

'Kincaid sees this as a challenge, then. He wishes to beat you to the reward.'

'Probably,' he replied with a smile tugging at his lips. 'I can't condemn him for that, Lucy. It is how I make the bulk of my living, too.'

'I suppose so, but you do not come across as mercenary, whereas he does. Is that why Kincaid was discharged from the DMP? Could he have been receiving bribes?' she asked. 'Mary hinted at trouble.'

'I don't know the details, my dear, but I imagine the fact he left Ireland for London speaks volumes.'

'Then I suggest you keep a close eye on him,' Lucy said.

'I intend to.'

'Good. Has McQuillan made contact since last night? Has he made any progress with White's murder?' she asked.

'I've heard nothing as yet. I will call on him later if he isn't at the Royal Arcade when we get there.' The hansom pulled into the kerb. 'Ah, we are here at Lady Dot's,' Phin said, pushing open the flap and climbing down.

Lucy hesitated. 'Shall I wait for you here?' she asked.

'No, no, come with me,' he replied to her relief, handing her down. 'Lady Dot may feel more comfortable with you present.'

The prevailing atmosphere of gloom Lucy had experienced on her last visit to Lady Muldoon's house had not diminished. As she and Phin followed the butler across the marble entrance hall, Lucy's mellow mood was sucked away. On entering the drawing room, the sight of Lady Dot's drawn and pale features touched Lucy's heart, and she rushed forward to greet her, Phineas close behind.

'Dear Lucy and Phin, it is so good to see you both,' Lady Dot said; then she gasped, staring in dismay at Phin's sling. 'It is such a relief to see you up and about, Phin. I thought you were still in the hospital. That is why I asked Seb to visit me. I couldn't believe my eyes when I read about the shooting. Who would do such a terrible thing?' She grabbed Phin's good hand and glanced at Lucy. 'And all of this coming so soon after your court appearance. My dear boy, it's all so awkward. Alice's accusations against you... I don't know what to say. Please believe me when I say I never believed them, not for a second.'

Phineas smiled kindly, taking a place beside her on the sofa and patting her hand. 'A misunderstanding as you say, and now it's all cleared up with the police. Let us not speak of it again.'

Lucy was tempted to rebuke their hostess; after all, it was partly her testimony that had led to Phin's arrest. But it was best to be circumspect, and it was Phin who had been wronged, not her.

'I hope you do not mind my asking for help, Phineas, but I'm in a quandary and don't know who else to turn to,' the elderly lady said.

'Lady Dot, you know well I'm always happy to be of service to you,' Phin replied.

Lady Dot shook her head and gazed at Lucy with a sad expression. 'Still, I would hate to impinge on you after what Alice has done. Please don't hate her. She's bewildered and so unwell. Edward's death has... unsettled her.'

'Where is she, Dot?' Phin asked gently.

'Alice left for Broadmeadows directly after the funeral. It was all too much for her.' Lady Dot looked across at Lucy. 'It's a private establishment near St Ives. Complete rest is what she requires.' Then she turned to Phin. 'But I miss her company so much, Phin. The house is empty now. Worst of all, it is left to me to deal with Edward's affairs.'

'Can his solicitor not handle these things?' he asked.

'Well, yes, the financial and legal matters. But his personal effects... That is why I have called on you, for I'm puzzled.'

Phineas's brows snapped together. 'There is something in particular that concerns you?'

Lady Dot's gaze dropped to her lap. 'Yes, Phineas, but it is probably best I show you.'

They followed Lady Dot up to the second floor and into a large bedroom. The windows were shuttered, and the air in the room was stuffy. Their hostess tut-tutted and pulled back the shutters, then remained at the window. Lucy sensed she was struggling. The elderly lady's hands were clasped tightly together, and she looked on the verge of tears.

'This is Alice and Edward's room,' she explained. 'I asked my housekeeper, Mrs Pugh, to remove Edward's things so that when Alice returns there won't be anything to distress her or remind her of Edward's murder.'

'An excellent idea,' Phin said. But Lucy could sense the tension in him as he stood beside her. He was scanning the room, his nose almost twitching.

'In the circumstances, I told Mrs Pugh to give his clothes to charity, as opposed to offering them to the male servants. Again, I do not want Alice to be confronted...' Lady Dot's shoulders sagged a little. 'Oh dear, it's all rather ghastly.'

Lucy's patience was beginning to wane, and she could imagine Phin felt the same. However, it would be too rude to ask the woman to get to the crux of the matter.

'Did the servant find something unusual?' Phin prompted.

Lady Dot nodded, then slowly crossed over to the large armoire and pulled open the doors. 'This is what she found.'

They moved to stand on either side of Lady Dot. At first, Lucy was puzzled. The wardrobe was empty except for one item, leaning against the back. It looked to Lucy like a roll of heavy cloth. It was tied with a ribbon.

Lucy heard Phin gasp. He leaned in and pulled it out. 'Untie it, Lucy,' he demanded, struggling to hold it with one hand.

Lucy did as she was bid. The material unravelled with a whoosh. Phin held it at arm's length.

'Good grief! A canvas!' Lucy exclaimed.

'And not just any painting,' exclaimed Phineas. This was significant, if the sparkle in his eyes was anything to go by.

But Lady Dot groaned and staggered over to the bed. 'What

possible reason could there be for its presence in my house; hidden in a wardrobe?'

Lucy rushed to her side and took her hand. 'Are you unwell? Shall I call for your maid?'

Dot shook her head, impatiently shaking her off, her eyes fixed on Phineas. 'No, indeed, Lucy, I am well.' Her voice changed, firmer now. 'Phineas, I had such a bad feeling when my housekeeper showed it to me. Why would Edward have put that there? Even I can see it's an expensive piece of art.'

'Yes, extremely expensive,' Phin said. Lady Dot groaned once more. 'I'm sorry, but there is no good explanation for its presence,' he said gently. 'This is Lord Halpenny's stolen painting. A James Alexander landscape. It was removed from his library in the middle of the night, several weeks ago.'

'Oh, dear Lord, no!' exclaimed Lady Dot.

'This is a most unfortunate discovery,' Phin said as he sat down beside Lady Dot. 'You knew there could be no good reason for this being in your house. You have called me here because you fear that Edward was involved in something nefarious.'

Lady Dot's shoulders sagged, and she nodded slowly. 'What other conclusion could there be?'

Lucy's mind was a whirl. Edward a thief? Was it possible? 'Phin, you don't think Edward was Apollo?'

Phin flashed her a smile above Lady Dot's head. 'If he wasn't, then he's a close associate.'

Lucy's heart began to race as the implications of the find took shape in her mind. At last, some progress and a possible alternative explanation for Edward's murder. This was the first positive lead they had.

Half an hour later, they were sitting back downstairs in Lady Dot's morning room. A restorative glass of brandy had done the trick, and Lady Dot's colour had returned to normal. However, it was clear the news had shaken her.

'Had you any idea he was up to mischief?' Phineas asked her.

'No... well, I suppose there were times when I wondered about him. I did my best to discourage Alice from marrying him, as I'm sure you know. His connections and his financial position were not what I would have hoped.'

'Did you fear he was after her fortune?' Lucy asked.

'Yes, indeed. Alice is a very wealthy young woman. But she was determined, and as she was of age, I could do nothing to prevent their union. I was only thankful her funds are tied up for another two years. They remained living with me at my request. Edward didn't object. In fact, I think he was relieved, for he soon realised that Alice could be difficult to manage. It seemed the sensible solution, and I could keep an eye on them. Alice's behaviour was giving me cause for alarm, and I wanted to be sure that Edward was doing right by her.' Clearing her throat, she threw an impassioned glance at Phin. 'It was such a shame she broke off her engagement to you, for I know you would have been perfect for her. Alice needs a firm hand. She's far too prone to flights of fancy.'

'It was not to be, Lady Dot,' Phin muttered, looking uncomfortable.

What else could he say? Lucy thought as she murmured her agreement and hoped it would encourage Lady Dot to divulge more.

Once composed again, Lady Dot continued: 'Then about a year ago, the arguments began. I suppose they'd probably bickered on and off, as most couples do, but this was different.'

'How so?' Lucy asked.

'They argued in front of me and with increasingly regularity.'

'And what were these arguments about?' Phin asked.

'The constant travelling. I'm a sociable creature myself and often accompanied them, but it was peculiar. When they first married, they didn't travel at all. Suddenly, Edward was receiving invitations to house parties all over the country. I believe, at first, Alice enjoyed them. She's always admired for her great beauty, you know, Lucy.'

'Of course,' Lucy murmured.

'But it was becoming tiresome. Alice no longer wanted to accompany him, but Edward would insist. You must understand that Alice has a low threshold for boredom. Unfortunately, it led to a lot of unpleasantness.' Lady Dot paused, her gaze fixed. 'Then I noticed other changes. Suddenly, Edward appeared to have money. He began to wear more expensive clothes and some of the gifts Alice received from him were extravagant. Alice, of course, didn't question it, but it made me uneasy. To the point that I tackled him about it.'

'How did he react?' Phineas asked.

'Edward told me he had been lucky with the horses, which I knew to be a lie. He had no interest in such things. I never heard him speak of attending a meet in all the months he had lived in this house. When I questioned Alice about it, she was delightfully vague.' Dot looked up, her face tense. 'Phineas, you must be honest with me. What do you think he was involved in?'

Phineas shared a glance with Lucy before he spoke. He tapped the rolled-up canvas on the table beside him. 'I suspect, based on the presence of this painting, that Edward was working for a group of people who are involved in the theft of priceless art throughout the country, and indeed, even over in Ireland. Edward used his position in society, helped in no small part by being married to Alice, to gain access to houses where the gang knew or suspected particular paintings were housed. In other words, Edward found the paintings they wanted and either informed the gang, or in fact, came back at a later date, and stole them.'

'And that was the source of his income,' Lady Dot said with a sigh. 'Dear Lord, the scandal this will cause.'

'Please don't be concerned. The police may wish to speak to you and to Alice, but I will do my best to keep his involvement from the press. As he's deceased, that may be possible. I must, however, take the painting. It must be returned to Lord Halpenny immediately.'

Lady Dot teared up. 'Thank you, Phin. I knew I could rely on you.'

Phineas frowned at her. 'I must admit, I'm puzzled, for I wouldn't have thought Edward particularly knowledgeable about the art world. Can you shed any light on that?'

'Oh, but Phineas; didn't you know?' Lady Dot cried. 'His grandfather was the famous Irish artist, Tandy Robinson. Edward grew up in his house after his parents died in a boating accident when he was just a child.'

TWENTY-NINE

The Royal Arcade

A small crowd had gathered outside White's Gallery. The presence of the police was causing quite a stir, Lucy thought, as they approached the entrance. Some curious glances were directed at them as Phineas politely made his way through. The constable standing guard at the front door of the gallery stood aside and nodded to Phineas as he passed inside. The gallery, however, was empty.

'Is the chief inspector, here?' Phineas turned and asked the policeman.

'Yes, sir. He's up in the office on the first floor.'

McQuillan sprang up from behind White's desk as soon as he saw them come through the door. 'Mrs Lawrence,' he greeted her, unsmiling. 'Phineas.'

'Chief Inspector,' Lucy replied, doing her best to assume a meek countenance. She had no doubt she was due a tongue-lashing for her part in the fiasco of the early morning. A quick scan of the desk revealed that all signs of White's murder had been removed. However, it still made her shiver to remember the sight and smell of the room from earlier.

'I hope you have suffered no ill effects from this morning?' the chief inspector asked, an edge to his voice.

'None, thank you, Chief Inspector. I have recovered,' she replied. McQuillan nodded. Then his gaze moved to Phineas who was now standing at the window, looking down into the arcade below.

'You have drawn quite a crowd,' Phineas remarked. 'The news of his demise spread quickly.'

'White was well known around here—and popular it would appear,' McQuillan said. 'The first we knew of him was your assertion that he was implicated in Edward Vaughan's murder.'

Phineas grunted. 'I still believe that to be the case. He had to have been the middleman. Once he tipped off the Collector that I was getting close, it set the wheels in motion. Unfortunately, now White is dead, it will make it harder to link him to whoever is controlling the syndicate.'

'Someone is eager to obliterate any trail that might lead to his door,' McQuillan remarked with a sigh. 'I should have brought White in for questioning when I had the chance.'

'But you had no evidence, Oliver. His solicitor would have whipped him out of Vine Street with lightning speed, and all trace of a connection to the Collector would have been obliterated. You can be sure of that.'

McQuillan shrugged. 'It won't stop the chief from jumping up and down on my head when I meet him later.'

Phineas gave him a sympathetic look. 'Have you made any progress since I saw you last?'

McQuillan leaned against the desk with a weary sigh. Lucy felt sorry for him: he must have been here since the early hours. 'Not much. The owner of the cane shop across the arcade said he saw White in the gallery at about half past six yesterday evening when he was closing his own shop. He appears to have been the last person to see White alive.'

'Did White have other staff on the premises?'

'Yes, a young lad who handles deliveries and such. He works down in the basement and clocks off at half past five.'

'And what did the police surgeon estimate for time of death?' Phineas asked.

'He reckons between nine last night and midnight.'

'And what time did you and Kincaid arrive?' Phineas asked Lucy.

'It must have been one o'clock and there was no one else around, at least not in the arcade,' she answered.

'And nothing suspicious about the place?' the chief inspector asked.

'No, and there was no sign of a forced entry.' Both men swung round to stare at her. Colour flooding her face, Lucy continued: 'Kincaid had to pick the lock for us to... enter.'

McQuillan frowned at her. Phineas's chin twitched in amusement.

'That's important, is it not?' she continued in a rush. 'It means whoever killed White was known to him. Someone he let into the gallery himself. Oh! Unless someone hid in the basement earlier in the evening before the gallery closed.'

'I'm afraid that is entirely possible, too, Lucy,' Phineas said. 'Or the murderer is an expert lock picker.'

'Agreed. But it doesn't really help us figure out who did it,' McQuillan said in a gloomy tone.

'My sources are few in this case; however, as I told you, Oliver, someone had pointed me in White's direction already in connection with the art thefts. The fact White was so brutally murdered suggests that information is correct. Innocent gallery owners aren't butchered as a rule. White must have been involved in shady dealings of some sort. My guess is our friendly neighbourhood assassin has been at work again. Perhaps he's a member of the syndicate? As you have speculated, Lucy, it is likely White knew his killer and let him in, never suspecting that person's intent. What better place to meet your cohorts than here in the arcade in the evening when it is quiet? It may even have been a pre-arranged meeting.'

'This case will be the death of me!' McQuillan grimaced. 'I can't afford to make any assumptions. Theories are all well and good, but I need concrete evidence.' With that, he threw a fierce glance at Phineas. 'It would help if I knew what I was looking for. I have an increasing body count, an irate superior, and very few clues.'

Phin flashed him a sympathetic look. 'We need to unravel the chain of command, linking all the people we know are involved, right up to the Collector, whoever he is.'

Oliver snorted. 'You make it sound so easy, Stone. I suppose you'll be after my job next.'

'Far from it, my friend.' Phin smiled at him, but the chief inspector only grunted in reply. Phineas frowned at him. 'It is not like you to give in to despair. Together we can solve this. What we need is some luck.' Phineas crossed his arms, staring at the desk. 'No more than Edward Vaughan, White must have made a mistake or threatened to expose the syndicate.'

'What has Vaughan to do with this?' McQuillan thundered, straightening up.

'Ah, sorry, Oliver. We have just come from Lady Muldoon's house. Her housekeeper made quite a discovery,' Phin replied. 'I should have mentioned it straight away.'

'And what might that discovery be?' Oliver ground out, his eyes flashing with impatience.

'Edward Vaughan was in possession of Lord Halpenny's stolen painting,' Phin said. 'I would hazard a guess that *he* was Apollo.'

'Oh, was he now!' exclaimed the chief inspector, folding his arms. 'Good of you to share that, Phin!'

'But of course!' Phineas flicked an amused glance at Lucy. 'I will need to find more evidence, however. But it makes sense that he was the thief, with his access to the quality of house that often has priceless art adorning the walls. We also learned from Lady Dorothy that he was very au fait with the art world. He must have been reporting back to White or directly to the Collector, informing them of what painting was where.'

'Oh, good Lord!' Lucy exclaimed. Both men stared at her. 'Edward! When I was at Thorncroft, I saw him wander off that evening on his own. Perhaps he was scouting for art?'

'And you didn't think to mention that to me?' Phin asked.

'Well, I had entirely forgotten about it. Sorry,' she replied. She could have kicked herself. *Too wrapped up in your happiness that night, my girl.* 'How can you prove he was Apollo?' Lucy asked.

'It may not be that difficult. I will need to link the Vaughans' visits to the houses in question to the timing of the thefts. I will ask Lady Dot to give me Edward's diaries. In fact, this would be an excellent job for Sebastian to undertake.' Phineas broke into a smile. 'It will also keep him out of mischief.'

'Uncovering Apollo's identity is certainly an interesting development.' McQuillan frowned across at them. 'Could his murder have been connected to that fact, and not, as we first believed, purely to incriminate you?'

'Indeed. What is that awful expression?' Phineas asked as he sat down on the chair recently vacated by the chief inspector.

'Killing two birds with the one stone?' Lucy offered.

Phineas quirked his mouth as he pulled open a drawer. 'Yes, exactly, my dear. Vile, but I suspect accurate in this case. It is certainly something we must consider, as it suggests Edward was no longer of use to the Collector or—' Phineas broke off as he rummaged through the drawer.

'Or?' Lucy prompted, stepping closer.

Phineas pulled out a large leather-bound book and placed it on the desk. He looked up at her. '—had threatened to pull out of the arrangement. If Alice was protesting about visiting all those houses, he may have wanted a quieter life. You saw for yourself how volatile Alice can be. And Lady Dot did tell us that they were quarrelling about it. The other possibility is that he asked for more money, and the Collector was not pleased by his greed. Whatever the reason, it can be no coincidence that since Edward's death, there have been no more art robberies of the same character. No more Apollo calling cards.'

'Do you really believe he would have been motivated by money, Phin? I suppose he could have grown rather fond of a luxurious lifestyle,' she surmised. 'But having married Alice, surely he didn't want for funds?'

'I'm not sure. Lady Dot is nothing if not astute. I suspect the couple were kept on a tight rein. Alice doesn't come into her full fortune for at least another two years, as Lady Dot informed us. Why do you think they agreed to live with Lady Dot?'

'Ah!' Lucy exclaimed. 'There's his motivation, then, without doubt.'

'That or boredom,' he answered without looking up. 'Ah, nothing in the diary for yesterday evening. How disappointing!'

'I had already checked,' growled McQuillan.

'As I knew you would have, Oliver.'

The strain was plain to see in the chief inspector's face, and Phineas wasn't helping matters. 'It seems to me, Phin, that I would be better employed checking White's diary,' Lucy said. 'Just tell me what to look for. Why don't you search through the paintings down in the basement? You are familiar with the stolen canvasses. We rummaged through White's stock last night but found nothing untoward.'

'Illegally, I might point out,' the chief inspector interjected. Lucy squirmed and cast him a self-effacing smile.

'*But*, I would point out, Oliver, for a good cause: namely, proving my innocence,' Phineas said. 'Very well, Lucy. Take a note of any regular appointments or frequent names that pop up. That sort of thing,' he said, standing up and ushering her into the chair. 'You might look for an address book for his clients as well. That should make for interesting reading. The Collector must be amongst that group.'

'There is a client register in that cupboard on the far wall, Mrs Lawrence,' Oliver McQuillan said.

'Thank you, Chief Inspector,' Lucy replied meekly.

'Now, if you are amenable, perhaps I could take a look around?' Phineas asked McQuillan.

'Be my guest! We're finished here for now. I need to talk to White's widow next.'

'I don't suppose...'

'No, Phineas, you may not come along.'

'But you will tell me if she relates anything of interest?'

McQuillan grunted an affirmation before pulling on his overcoat. 'Well, it would appear I'm surplus to requirements.'

'On the contrary, my friend,' Phin replied.

'Are you coming back to Vine Street?' the policeman asked.

'No. I can't hide forever, Oliver. Kincaid has proved inadequate. I must take this investigation on once more; if for no other reason than to stop my fiancée from falling over any more dead bodies.'

'You're too kind!' Lucy muttered under her breath.

McQuillan guffawed. 'You're a brave man, Phineas Stone!'

Phin smarted. 'Be off with you, McQuillan. I'm certain you have much more important work to do. Let us help you here. If we find anything of interest, I'll send you a message. And Oliver...'

'Yes?'

'I suggest you try to get some sleep.'

'Noted. Phineas, I must warn you that I do not have the men available to provide you with protection outside the hospital. For God's sake, man, be careful. You can be confident word is out already that you are no longer there. Nothing I can do about that. For now, all I *can* do is leave the constable on the door here to keep out the gawkers and the press.'

'Thank you, Oliver,' Phineas answered as they shook hands.

McQuillan coughed and Lucy looked up. 'I will need a statement from you, Mrs Lawrence, regarding your activities here last night. Perhaps you could call by the station later today?'

'Yes, of course, Chief Inspector,' she replied. 'I shall do so as soon as we're finished here.'

With a grunt and a nod, the chief inspector left.

Half an hour later, Phineas reappeared from the basement. He sat on the edge of the desk before reaching out and caressing Lucy's cheek.

'I have missed you,' he said softly.

'And I you,' she replied before sitting back. 'These last few weeks have been dreadful. And now I'm worried about you. When the Collector finds out that you have been discharged, what is to stop him trying to have you killed?'

'Nothing, I suppose. But at least I am forewarned. Please don't worry about me,' he said.

'That's easy for you to say. How can I make plans for our wedding with this hanging over us?' she asked.

'I'm as anxious to clear up this mess as you are, my dear.' Phin glanced down at the open diary. 'Now, have you found anything of interest?'

Lucy sighed. 'It reads like a *Who's Who* of London society. White was very well connected. A few names pop up more than others. I've made a list,' she said, handing Phin a sheet of paper with names and addresses.

Phineas scanned the page. 'No sign of Edward, though.'

'No, but wait until you see what I found in one of the drawers, half wedged down the back.' Lucy handed him a visiting card which was all too familiar. 'I don't know how McQuillan missed it.'

'Exhaustion, my dear; the poor man didn't get any sleep last night.' Phin's face lit up. 'At last, we can link Edward and White!'

'Yes. It looks old.'

Phin twisted the card through his fingers. 'Yes, it is yellowed with age but still, this Apollo card links them.'

'But not the Collector and White which is the connection we really need to find.'

'True. Still, it is progress. I may go back to Lady Dot's and do a thorough search, if she will let me. I may find something to link Edward to a possible art connoisseur or collector.'

'And did you discover anything in the basement?' she asked.

'No. I had hoped to find a canvas reframed and ready for despatch, but no luck.' Phineas stood up. 'Very well, my dear sleuth, let us leave here. I can drop you off at Vine Street, and I will go back to Lady Dot.'

'How kind you are!' she said, dreading the interview to come.

'Anything for you, my pet,' he replied with a grin as he held the door open for her. 'But it isn't as if you haven't helped the police with their investigations before!'

THIRTY

Westbourne Grove, Later that Evening

Although not quite as good a chef as M. Lacroix, Lucy had enjoyed the meal George had provided. She was just happy to be in Phin's company once more. Sitting opposite, Sebastian's face was grey with dark circles under his eyes. Despite this, he too appeared to have benefitted from Phin's return and had regaled them with some slightly risqué stories from his time in India. It was a relaxing evening, which they all needed badly.

'Will that be all, sir?' George asked as he cleared away the rest of the dishes.

'Thank you, George. We can help ourselves to coffee,' Phineas said.

George coughed delicately. 'May I say, sir, that it's a pleasure to have you back in residence.' He threw a glance at Sebastian. 'You were missed.'

Phineas schooled his features. 'Thank you, George. I hope my absence didn't... inconvenience you?'

'Indeed not, sir.'

As soon as George quit the room, Sebastian grumbled. 'I suppose he was getting a dig in at me. Well, I'm no schoolboy to be bossed about.'

'No indeed, Seb. However, I would point out that I treasure George highly and would be very put out if he were to leave my service. Now, let us leave it at that.'

'Lucy will tell you—anything I did was to try and save you from the noose,' Seb replied, shoulders hunched.

'It's true, Phin. Seb has been a great support,' Lucy said. This earned her a grateful smile from Seb.

'Hmm,' was Phin's reply.

'And what does that mean, pray?' she asked.

'Between you, you have upset Coffin Mike and Oliver McQuillan, given rise to gossip that Alice Vaughan had despatched her husband, and been caught breaking and entering a business premises which contained a dead gallery owner. None of which has reaped any rewards.'

'That's jolly ungrateful, Phin, I must say!' exclaimed Seb. 'I've a good mind to go back to Kent, if that's the way you're thinking.'

'I wouldn't blame you, Seb,' Lucy said with a dangerous edge to her voice, 'We have been trying our best, Phin, following what leads we had.'

'But you can't seriously have thought Alice murdered Edward?' Phin said.

'Well, I still think she warrants further investigation. Until such time as Edward's murderer is caught, Alice must remain a suspect.' Lucy sat back with her chin in the air.

'Hear, hear,' Seb joined in. 'All that strange behaviour she indulges in could be play-acting.'

'Whether it is or not, there is no proof that she either killed Edward or paid someone to do it,' Phin said with a meaningful look at Lucy.

She smarted. Her East End friend had betrayed her, but she wasn't surprised. 'Did Coffin Mike inform you I paid a call?'

'Of course. That was an extremely dangerous thing to do.'

'Mary and I were with her, and I can tell you, I know how to protect my future sister,' Seb piped up, highly indignant.

'Thank you, Seb,' Phin said with a sigh. Lucy suspected he was too tired to argue and wanted to placate Seb whose high colour was alarming her a little also.

'Now, as it happens, I have a very important job for you to do,' Phineas told Seb.

'Am I to be your bodyguard?' Sebastian sat up, eyes sparkling.

'Eh, no. I don't need one. This task is far more important. In fact, it could crack the case.'

'Tell me!'

'I need you to go through my case notes on all the art thefts and cross-reference the dates to any visits by the Vaughans to those houses. Lady Dot kindly gave me Edward's diaries for the last two years. You see, it looks as though Edward was our thief. Lady Dot found one of the stolen paintings amongst his effects.'

'No!' Seb exclaimed. 'Well, that's jolly unexpected, I must say. Edward a common burglar! How ghastly for Lady Dot.'

'Yes, it's a surprise, but you do see how important it is to connect these events, Seb?' Lucy asked.

Seb beamed back at them. 'I can start right now.'

'No, no, Seb, that isn't necessary,' Phineas said with a smile. 'The morning will be fine. You've had a long day; we all have. Best to get some sleep and start afresh, first thing.'

'Yes, I must admit to being tired,' Seb said, giving Lucy a sheepish look. 'Between Kincaid's little outing and my visit to Vine Street, it's been an eventful day.'

'I couldn't agree more. Though all they did at Vine Street was take a statement. I didn't have to stay long,' Lucy said. 'The chief inspector was more than magnanimous about the whole affair, which I have to admit, surprised me. I fully expected to be charged with something.'

'I told you not to worry as I dropped you off,' Phin said, annoyingly.

'Still, by rights, he probably should have charged us with breaking and entering. I wonder how he treated Kincaid?'

'The same, Lucy. I received a message from him earlier. We are to meet tomorrow,' Phin said.

'You see, it pays to have Phineas on your side,' said Seb with a grin. 'Now, don't you worry; I'll do what is required with those diaries. You'll have your proof.' Then his face dropped, and he looked suspiciously at his brother. 'Though I honestly think you stand more in need of a bodyguard. They have already tried to kill you once. With Edward, and now White, dead, someone, somewhere, isn't happy.'

Lucy jumped on this. 'He's right, Phineas. The Collector is doing his best to obliterate all links to himself.'

Phineas nodded. 'Unfortunately, I do believe you are correct, Lucy.'

'Then you need to take care,' she replied. His response was a bland smile. How could he be so blasé about his safety? But she knew by his expression that he did not wish to discuss it, possibly because Sebastian was present.

'How was Lady Dot? She was so miserable when we visited this afternoon. I really pitied her,' Lucy said to change the subject.

'In much better spirits. Alice had arrived home shortly before I called,' he replied.

'You're not serious! So soon? Why did she come back?'

'She said she was bored,' he replied. 'It wasn't an asylum, Lucy. She was free to leave at any time.'

Lucy was flabbergasted. In her opinion, the woman should be locked up permanently. 'How was she? Did she act oddly?'

Phineas answered with a shrug. 'Not at all. She was quiet

and appeared to be perfectly rational. As you can imagine, it was all very awkward.'

'Did you tell her about Edward? What he had been doing?' Lucy asked. 'How did she react?'

'There was no need to tell her; Lady Dot had done so already.'

Lucy leaned forward. 'Did you question her about Edward?'

'No, Lucy,' he said with a look of surprise. 'It didn't feel appropriate. In fact, she appeared highly embarrassed. My name being cleared made her accusations incredibly foolish, of course. Though she didn't exactly apologise, even when Lady Dot asked it of her.'

Lucy sat back with a frown. 'I hope she will formally retract them.'

'Is it not enough that I am a free man? Let it lie, Lucy. Once I had the diaries, I made my escape.'

'And Alice was agreeable to you taking them?' Lucy asked, surprised. 'She'd hardly want you to prove her husband was a common thief.'

'Lady Dot had already given them to me before Alice joined us. She had little choice but to acquiesce. And perhaps that was her way of saying sorry.'

'Huh!' Lucy exclaimed. 'You are far too forgiving!'

'We can call in a day or two... and you can be my bodyguard, as well as judge and jury.'

Lucy glared back at him. 'It is not a matter for joking.'

Sebastian spluttered. 'If you two have finished sniping, tell me this. How does the case stand, Phin? Besides getting proof of Edward's involvement, what can we do?'

Phineas rubbed his temples. 'Honestly, Seb, I don't know. This case is exasperating.'

Lucy was surprised to hear him so defeated. 'No one would blame you if you walked away,' she said. 'Least of all me. I'd rather have you alive. But I know it would drive you mad not to solve this.' Phineas shrugged. She reached out and touched his hand. 'At least we know who Apollo was. It is some progress. Now, gentlemen, if you don't mind, I'm in great need of sleep, and I suspect the same can be said of you. Shall we reconvene in the morning?'

THIRTY-ONE

Phillimore Gardens, Sunday Morning

Lucy awoke to shrieks of distress. Heart pounding, she scrambled out of bed, dragged on her wrap and flew down the stairs. Down in the hallway she found her chef and kitchen maid staring at Mary, who was crying uncontrollably.

'Whatever is the matter, Mary?' Lucy called out in an effort to be heard above the wailing.

The chef turned to her and threw his hands in the air. 'She's not sensible, madam,' Lacroix said. 'All this crying and wailing, it upsets me. How am I to create wonderful dishes in such an atmosphere? I'm an artist. *C'est impossible!*'

'I will look after her, M. Lacroix. Please go back to your duties,' Lucy announced from the bottom step of the stairs.

Lacroix threw her a pained look before heading back down to the kitchen, nose in the air. Janet followed him down the hallway with a bemused expression on her face.

'Now, Mary, please stop crying and tell me what is wrong,' Lucy said, putting an arm around Mary's shaking shoulders.

Mary continued to twist her apron in her hands. 'Oh, ma'am. It's all my fault!'

Lucy guided her gently to a nearby chair and coaxed her to sit. 'Best tell me, Mary. I'm sure you have blown whatever it is out of proportion.'

'Ah, God, ma'am, I haven't. 'Tis terrible!' She began to cry again.

'Mary! Please pull yourself together and explain.'

'You know it was my evening off yesterday?' Mary managed between sniffles.

'Yes?'

'Well, I must have left the kitchen door unlocked when I came in last night. It's the only explanation I can think of.'

'Mary, I have no idea what you are talking about!' Lucy exclaimed, slowly losing patience.

The maid's chin wobbled as she nodded towards the drawing room door. 'I went in there first thing, like. To check if everything was as it should be. That's when I discovered—' With a gulp, she continued: 'In there, ma'am. Oh, my!' With that, she buried her face in her apron and howled.

Totally baffled, Lucy patted her shoulder before stepping inside the room alone. She looked around in puzzlement. Nothing appeared out of place. The curtains had been opened; the grate had been cleaned and polished; the cushions had been plumped on the sofas; and there was no sign of dust or clutter. What could have caused Mary's distress?

Bewildered, she turned to leave the room and stopped dead. On the far wall, where her two Miller seascapes had pride of place, only two empty frames were to be seen. Stunned, Lucy could only stare for several minutes as she processed the theft and its implications.

Her mesmerized state was broken when Mary crept into the room. 'You see, ma'am, it's my fault some rascal got in and took your lovely paintings.'

. . .

An hour later, Phineas sat down as if in a daze, his eyes fixed on the empty frames. Lucy watched him closely, trying to figure out what might be going through his head. Eventually, his gaze shifted back to her. He blinked, then burst out laughing.

'I don't see what's so funny,' Lucy snapped.

'Oh, my dearest Lucy. This case becomes more and more bizarre.'

'But what about my paintings? They were expensive, I'll have you know.' Lucy sat down with a huff. 'Now, all I have left are two beautiful but empty frames.'

'Did you not insure them?' he asked.

'No, I forgot with everything else that has been going on.'

Phin shook his head and gave a weary sigh. 'That is unfortunate. Did you find a card?'

'Yes,' she replied, and jumped up to retrieve it. 'I found it here, leaning against the clock on the mantle.'

Phineas glanced at it and handed it back. 'The same Apollo card as the others. Damnation! I had hoped it might just be someone copying what the syndicate was doing. The ins and outs of it are common knowledge in the criminal community at this stage.'

'But how can this be? Edward is dead.'

'Either there is more than one Apollo or Edward performed a different role. Perhaps all he did was find the paintings and someone else did the actual robberies.'

'Yet he had that painting in his possession,' she replied. 'Surely only the thief would have a canvas? It wouldn't have been at Lady Dot's if Edward was merely a finder of art.'

'I agree,' Phin said with a groan.

'I'm baffled,' Lucy said.

'As am I!'

'Tea or something stronger?' she asked as she rang the bell.

'Much as I'm tempted, it is still only morning. Tea would be best,' he said, grinning back at her in a way that made her stomach somersault.

'You rang, ma'am?' Mary asked from the doorway a few minutes later. Her face still showed signs of her earlier distress, her eyes red-rimmed.

'Tea, please, Mary,' Lucy replied.

Mary gave Phineas a self-effacing smile and left.

'Poor girl blames herself,' Lucy explained. 'I don't suppose you could reassure her. I've tried several times, but it just ends in more tears.'

'Could she have left the door unlocked?' he asked.

'It is possible, but she's usually very security conscious. Especially after our encounters with Marsh and Coffin Mike. Remember that nasty incident with my cat?' Lucy shuddered.

'I do,' he said. 'What about your other servants?'

'Again, feel free to question them, but my conversations with them yielded nothing. Both went to bed early and heard naught.'

'It was the same in the other cases. No sign of a broken lock or window and all carried out in absolute silence. Indeed, it has crossed my mind that I may be dealing with a thieving ghost!'

'Nonsense!' Lucy said with a reproving look. 'Why would a ghost be interested in art?'

Phin burst out laughing and wagged his finger at her. 'Let's try to stick to logic for now. We can explore the fantastical only when all other possibilities have been exhausted.'

'Agreed.' Lucy gave Mary an encouraging smile as she entered with the tea tray. 'Thank you, Mary. That will be all for now.'

Mary bobbed and departed. Lucy could have sworn she heard a sniffle. 'Very well. How do we go about solving this new puzzle?' She poured his tea and handed it to him.

'Was anything else taken?'

'No, only the Miller canvasses.'

Phin grunted. 'And the modus operandi is exactly the same as the others,' he muttered. 'However, you only acquired them recently. Who could have seen them? Who knew you had purchased them?'

'White and his employee, I suppose. And the only visitors to the house since I bought them have been you and Sebastian,' she replied. 'Oh! And Kincaid and Lady Sarah.'

'It is highly unlikely to have been either of them.' He put down his cup a little carelessly, splashing tea into the saucer. 'Hold on, they were purchased from White's gallery. If the Collector had wanted them, all he had to do was ask White, so he can't have ordered this.'

'Unless White refused. Perhaps that's why he was killed?'

'I doubt anyone refuses that man what he wants. Those paintings were valuable, Lucy, but nothing on the scale of the other paintings. I don't believe the Collector would have wanted them for himself.'

'Are you questioning my taste?' she asked with a sniff.

'Not at all. Art is a very subjective thing.'

'Then you believe someone else wanted those paintings? When they discovered they were sold, they asked White to organise their retrieval?'

Phineas nodded slowly. 'Yes, that is also possible, but that doesn't help us. It could have been any of White's clients. This suggests that my theory that the syndicate was organising these thefts for a number of clients could be correct. The Collector most likely gets a cut on the thefts for other people.'

'So, in effect, there could be several collectors involved?'

'Yes, I'm afraid so—no more than quite a few thieves and several art fences like White. It may even be international,' he said with a grimace.

Lucy was disheartened. 'Dear Lord! It's hopeless, then.' Phin nodded and sat back, his expression one of gloom. Lucy sipped her tea, her mind churning. 'My goodness!' she cried, hastily putting down her cup. 'There is one person who knew I bought those paintings. He commented on how he had been interested in them himself and complimented me on my good taste.'

Phineas sat forward, his eyes glowing. 'Who?'

'Thomas Hardwicke!'

'Was this in the gallery? You met him there that day, if I recall,' Phineas said.

'No, it wasn't in the gallery. He didn't know what I purchased that day. It was at Brown's Hotel. Don't you remember? You encouraged me to meet him to see if he knew anything about White's clandestine activities. When I arrived, his brother was there too, so I couldn't question Thomas about White too much. But we did discuss my paintings, and he said how he had wanted them too.'

'Remind me of your history again,' Phin said.

'My mother viewed him as an eligible match for me during that rather disastrous season of mine. In fact, it was on an outing with Thomas and my mother to the National Gallery that I met Charlie. He rescued me from a very dull afternoon. Thomas's knowledge is extensive, but he has the unhappy knack of making your ears hurt the way he drones on.' Lucy paused again as an idea formed in her head. 'You don't think *he* could be the Collector? I mean, he's a ridiculous man, but there can be no doubt he's obsessed with art. The day I met him at White's he indicated he was a regular visitor, and White certainly fawned over him. It's difficult to see him as a ruthless individual, ordering murders and thefts on a whim, though. I've always considered him a buffoon.'

'Well, Lucy, something I have learned over the years is never to trust outward appearances,' Phin said. 'He warrants further investigation.'

'Should we pay him a call?' Lucy asked.

Phineas's brows shot up. '*We* will do nothing of the kind. Haven't you been listening to me? The Collector is a dangerous man. We must be careful. A visit to Thomas, if he's involved, could trigger even more mischief.' Phin waved towards the empty frames. 'I think the Collector knows I'm out of hospital. Perhaps this was a further warning to me to drop the case?'

'Dear Lord! A threat? All the more reason to follow through on this. We can't ignore that Thomas could be involved, Phin. I will go mad if I can't do something. I know Thomas socially—you do not. If you were to call on him, and Thomas was involved in the thefts, Thomas would be on his guard straightaway. Whereas, if I were to make a casual morning call, he's unlikely to question my motives.'

With a sigh, Phineas said, 'I suppose so. What pretext could you use?'

Lucy mulled this over. 'I could tell him my paintings had been stolen and seek his help. But, no. That's too weak, and mentioning it might silence him. Perhaps I could pretend I still had them. I could tell him how wonderful the paintings are and ask him to help me source more of them. He did offer to help me if I was ever looking for more art. That might just work. Based on his reaction, I would know if he had a guilty conscience. Someone as dim as Thomas would be bound to give himself away.'

'Or I could just make discreet enquiries?'

'Phin, I can do this. Though obviously not today, being the Sabbath.'

'Indeed not. It would be highly irregular and would ignite suspicion.'

'As it happens, I plan to call on Lady Sarah tomorrow morning anyway,' Lucy replied. 'Thomas's house is not far from there.'

'All right, my dear. But please take Mary with you, and for goodness's sake, be careful.'

Lucy beamed up at him. 'I promise.'

As he passed her chair, he swooped down and planted a kiss on her cheek. 'You do still have that pistol?'

'Why, yes! I told you the other night.'

'Take it with you whenever you leave the house.'

As the door closed behind him, those parting words gave her pause.

THIRTY-TWO

The next morning, Lucy entered Lady Sarah's boudoir and was dismayed to find her hostess lying down in a dressing gown on a chaise longue close to an open window. Sarah's skin glowed with a faint sheen of perspiration. Her arm lay outstretched and limp beside an ivory fan on a small table by her side.

Lucy rushed over to her. 'My dear Sarah, are you still suffering from the heat?' Sarah struggled to sit up. Lucy forestalled her. 'Please don't disturb yourself on my account if lying down helps.'

'I don't think it makes much difference. I'm sorry, Lucy. I'm afraid I'm not finding things any easier. I'm utterly exhausted. It is good of you to call.'

Lucy sat down close to her friend. 'Tell me, what does the doctor say?'

Sarah discreetly mopped her brow. 'That I must stay in town and rest. The man repeats it as if it were a mantra. Huh! A doctor he may be, but he has no idea what it is like to be in this condition. It is so frustrating, for I'm convinced if I could just manage the journey to Sidley, I'd be much more comfortable there in the country with lots of fresh air. But he disagrees. He believes travel in a carriage could be dangerous, and Geoffrey holds him in such high esteem that he will not entertain the idea of disobeying him.'

'Oh, dear,' Lucy said. 'I'm sorry to hear that. Perhaps in a week or so you will feel up to the journey. This impossible weather can't last forever.'

Sarah twisted the handkerchief in her hands. 'I do hope so. The thing is, there is something else that prevents me from going.'

'Oh?'

'It is Geoffrey. I told you before about all the fuss over... Edward's death... and the newspapers. I've never seen him so anxious. He's acting quite out of the ordinary. Why only yesterday he berated me for buying new clothes for James. The child desperately needed summer clothes. I couldn't just ignore that. But you would swear we were facing imminent dunning the way Geoffrey reacted.'

'Most uncharacteristic, I would have thought,' Lucy replied. 'But he hardly acted that way because of Edward's murder?'

'Lucy, I don't know. I can think of little else but that awful occurrence. However, I believe the real reason Geoffrey doesn't want to leave town is that he's under considerable pressure from within the party. Things are delicate, politically, for him just now. Geoffrey dares not leave. He won't even contemplate accompanying me down to Sidley and returning immediately. When I suggested it, he was apoplectic.'

'Surely the press has ceased to pursue him? He had nothing to do with the murder; merely unfortunate enough for it to occur in his house. Best to ignore the newspapers. Since Charlie's death, I certainly do. I would have thought the Prime Minister is well used to this kind of situation. MPs are often hounded in the newspapers; I believe it's a type of sport.'

'I know, but the slightest hint of scandal and people become nervous, especially down in the constituency, and just when things were looking favourable for him. It was a tight run thing in the last election, but he had managed to turn things around.'

'I'm sure he can do so again, Sarah. Everyone knows how hard he works.'

'And that is why I must be a good wife and stay in town, for there are rumours of a reshuffle coming in the autumn.'

'Ah! Is there any hope for him?' Lucy asked.

A pained expression crossed Sarah's delicate features. 'I don't believe so, but Geoffrey refuses to give up hope.'

'Well, good for him,' Lucy replied. 'He has done nothing wrong. Before Edward's demise, he was being hailed as a rising star, was he not?'

'Yes, he was.' Lady Sarah smiled and pulled herself upright. 'Now, tell me all your news. I must say we were so relieved to hear Phineas was cleared of Edward's murder, but why on earth did someone shoot him?'

Lucy shrugged. 'We now think it is connected to a case he's working on. Phineas has made some discoveries regarding Edward, but I'm afraid I can say no more than that at present. But you need not fear; he will solve this. I have every faith in him, and once he has, the press interest should die down. For all of us.'

'It all sounds terribly dangerous. Do be careful, Lucy.'

'Don't worry; I'm taking precautions,' she replied.

Lady Sarah gave her a wan smile. 'If I'm honest, I just want to forget about the whole ghastly business. I still can't bear to go up to the servants' quarters.'

A maid entered the room, carrying a jug of lemonade and glasses on a tray. 'Perfect, Ellen, thank you. You can leave the tray with me,' Sarah said. 'Can I tempt you? I find it wonderfully refreshing.'

'Yes, please.' Lucy took the glass from her friend and cocked a brow. 'You know, you could just disobey all these men and go to Sidley if you believe it will help your condition.'

Sarah chuckled. 'I'm not as brave as you, Lucy. And, if I am to be completely honest, I'm not sure I'd have the energy for a full-scale rebellion.'

Lucy was torn. She wanted to help Sarah and offer to accompany her out of London. Didn't Phin want her out of harm's way? He would think it very convenient. However, she couldn't bear the thought of missing out. She was determined to do her bit in solving the case. But then she looked across at her friend and realised how miserable she was.

'But what if you had a partner in crime? Sarah, if you wish, I will travel down to Sidley with you and little James.'

Her friend perked up. 'Oh, would you, Lucy? Geoffrey might agree to that. I didn't want to ask it of you, for I know what a busy few months you have ahead, preparing for your wedding.'

'Nonsense! The wedding will be a quiet affair with only close family and friends. Phineas has suggested the wedding takes place in Kent, so most of the work will fall to Gertie.'

Sarah burst out laughing. 'You can't be serious, Lucy. She's incapable of organising even the simplest of events.'

Lucy shrugged. 'The church is the most important part of the day, and Phineas will see to that. Anything else will be a bonus. I only hope you will be well enough to be my matron of honour.'

'I'd love to be, but I'm likely to be the size of a small building by then.' Sarah blinked at her. 'My goodness, you really do love him, don't you? To leave all the arrangements to chance and Gertie Stone.'

'You know me. I like to live dangerously!'

Sarah chuckled. 'I don't suppose Phineas knows what he's really taking on. I almost feel sorry for the man.'

'Oh, thank you very much! Ah, Sarah, I do love him so. Don't worry. I know how lucky I am to get a second chance with someone so wonderful. After the devastation Charlie left, I thought I would never trust a man again.'

'All your friends are happy for you: for both of you.'

'Thank you. You and Geoffrey have been wonderful. Now, you must tell me—when would you like to travel? Would Friday suit? I have a few errands to run today, and I shall have to clear my diary.' Lucy reached across and squeezed Sarah's hand. 'Are you game?'

The answer was a beaming smile from her friend.

THIRTY-THREE

Mayfair

Fifteen minutes later, Lucy consulted Thomas's visiting card before glancing up at the imposing façade of his townhouse. To live on this particular street, Thomas had to be far wealthier than she'd realised. She smiled. Her mother had obviously known his worth all those years ago.

Lucy turned to Mary. 'Now, remember what I said. And Mary...'

'Yes, ma'am?'

'Be subtle. We need to be careful, for I don't know what manner of man I'm dealing with.'

'Don't you worry, ma'am. I'll wheedle what I can out of them, and they won't even realise they're giving up their secrets,' Mary replied with a wink before heading down the area steps to the basement servants' entrance.

Steeling herself, Lucy trotted up the steps and rang the bell. A minute later, an elderly butler appeared in the doorway. 'Mrs Lawrence to see Mr Hardwicke,' she said with far more confidence than she felt. Was she entering the lion's den?

'Certainly, madam. Do come in, and I will see if the master is at home.'

Lucy stepped across the threshold into a beautifully appointed hallway. White marble floors and panelled walls gave it a bright and cheerful aspect. But she spotted two enormous trunks near the front door. Thomas must be about to depart on a trip. Now, that was very interesting! Lucy watched as the butler disappeared down a long corridor towards the rear of the house. As soon as he was out of sight, she scurried over and examined the label on one of the trunks. Waverley Station. That was the main station in Edinburgh. So, he was running off to Scotland?

Hearing the murmur of approaching voices, she moved back across the hall, stepping closer to a large painting which dominated one wall. She made a show of examining it. The gilding on the frame had dulled with age, but the painting itself looked almost newly painted. Lucy guessed Thomas had had it cleaned and restored. It was an impressive piece of art. Something an aficionado would display to show the world how knowledgeable he was; what distinguished taste he had. With a disgruntled quirk of her mouth, she reflected that her dear fiancé would probably recognise the work before her immediately. Was it acquired legally, she wondered, and could the rest of the house contain even more precious art, including her lovely seascapes?

'My dear Mrs Lawrence! Lucy! To what do I owe this pleasure?' Thomas asked, rushing towards her. As ever, his colour was high and there were dark circles under his eyes. Had he been up to mischief?

'I do apologise for arriving unannounced, but I was visiting a dear friend close by...'

'Not at all, my dear Lucy. Do come in. You must forgive me, however, for I'm due to depart shortly. My brother has taken a turn for the worse, and I must return to Edinburgh.' Thomas tucked her arm through his and walked her into a sitting room. She caught the faint whiff of whisky from him.

'I have no wish to delay you, Thomas,' she replied, taking a seat. Other than a grim-faced elderly lady staring down from a large painting above the fireplace, the room was bright and beautifully proportioned. If her mother had succeeded, she would have been mistress here. The thought almost made her laugh: Thomas would have been an even worse husband than Charlie.

Thomas glanced at the mantle clock. 'I'm not due to leave for an hour. I missed the express at ten o'clock, don't you know? Rather a late night, last night and the night before. Well... you know how it is when you are with friends. Went to see that new show at the Adelphi after dinner at the club on Saturday. I can highly recommend it.'

Why was he telling her this? Was he trying to establish an alibi?

'Now, do join me for some refreshment.' Thomas glanced across at the butler, who was hovering in the doorway. 'Tea, please, Groves.' Thomas raised a brow at her. 'Unless you'd like something stronger?'

Lucy smiled. 'Tea would be perfect, thank you.'

Hardwicke waved his hand at the butler. 'Of course, sir,' Groves replied, closing the door.

Thomas remained standing by the fireplace, rubbing his hands together as if he were cold, yet the room was overwhelmingly stuffy. *Guilty conscience?* Lucy wondered. *I think I have rattled him by showing up.*

'I'm sorry to hear your brother is unwell again. You had such hopes that a London physician might improve his condition.'

'Indeed, I did.' At last, Thomas sat down: he was making her nervous, hovering like that. 'The man came highly recommended by an acquaintance of mine. However, the trip down to London appears to have exacerbated Menzies' condition.'

Thomas's mouth turned down. 'I think he holds me accountable.'

'Oh, surely not, Thomas? That is hardly reasonable on his part.'

'Menzies does not have the easiest of dispositions at the best of times. Since his wife died, he has become more... aloof. Forbidding, even. You know, he sold a very beautiful home in the New Town for that mausoleum of an old manor house on Kinnock Island. Never could understand it,' Thomas said with a shake of his head. 'Well, I have been summoned to Scotland, for he wishes to settle his affairs.' He cast her a grim look. 'I'm dreading the visit, if I'm honest. I do not know how he will receive me, but it may be my last chance to see him.'

'You are right to go, if it's as bad as you have been led to believe.'

A sullen-faced maid entered with the tea tray and set it down on a table beside Lucy. As she departed, she threw a curious glance at Lucy, then averted her eyes just as quickly.

Lucy poured two cups, and Thomas came across the room to receive his tea. 'Not to worry. Your visit has cheered me up. You are a ray of sunshine, Lucy, I have to say. I have often thought back on our time together. If only that rascal Charlie Lawrence hadn't spotted you first, I might have had a chance.'

Notwithstanding the fact that Thomas was much older than her, she'd never felt drawn to him, even though her mother had touted him as London's most eligible man during Lucy's spectacular failure of a London season. Once Charlie appeared in her orbit, Lucy had eyes for no other, despite her mother's increasingly frantic attempts at matchmaking. Now Lucy was amazed. Thomas was recalling their scant acquaintance in a false light, but there was little to be gained by correcting him. 'We were all young and foolish, then, Thomas.'

He guffawed so loudly that Lucy nearly spilt her tea. 'Perhaps,' he said at last with a drawn-out sigh. 'However, I remember those days fondly.'

If Lucy didn't know better, she would think there was something forced about his behaviour this morning. Thomas was on edge. Now that was intriguing. Dare she bring up the Miller paintings or was that playing with fire? Yet, there was little point in her coming if she did not.

'As do I,' she murmured. 'Especially that lovely afternoon we spent at the National Gallery. Do you recall? I was so impressed by your knowledge of art. Actually, that is one of the reasons I wished to call on you this morning: to seek your advice.'

Thomas perked up. 'Oh, yes?'

'As you know, I'm due to be married in the autumn, and I have had the most marvellous idea. My fiancé, Phineas, has greatly admired those two lovely seascapes I bought that day in Whites. Do you recall?'

Did he just lose all colour in his face?

'Oh, yes, my dear girl, of course I remember. Two Millers—exceptional pieces.'

'Yes, that is correct. I'd love to find another one and present it to him as a wedding gift. Would you happen to know where I might find one?'

Thomas's mouth worked silently for a moment. 'Well, now, my dear, I don't recall seeing any of late. But, if you wish, I could put the word out.'

'Could you?' she said, giving him her most winning smile. 'I would be so grateful. I would have asked Mr White, but of course...'

'Yes, his murder! What a dreadful business!' This time the colour flooded into Hardwicke's cheeks. His gaze rested on the clock. 'Dear me, but the time has flown! I'm afraid I really must get ready to depart for King's Cross.'

'Of course. I have no wish to detain you,' Lucy said, placing her half-drunk cup of tea down and rising. She held out her hand.

Thomas kissed it.

'Always the gallant, Thomas,' Lucy said. 'I wish you a pleasant journey, despite the sad circumstances.'

'You are very good, Lucy, indeed... and I will of course... I will do my best to source that painting for you.'

Lucy had barely pulled back the half door of the hansom when Mary burst out: 'Ma'am, that is the strangest house and the oddest bunch of people I have ever come across.'

The cab pulled out into the traffic. 'Do tell, Mary,' Lucy said with delight.

'That butler, for starters; such a gloomy man, and the maid, Sally, is terrified of him. I think they all are. Him and the master are like that,' Mary said, holding up two fingers side by side. 'He's the only one allowed in the master's office, which is kept locked at all times. Sally was given a warning one day just cos she lingered outside, and Groves caught her.'

'Why is it kept locked?' Lucy asked.

Mary made a face. 'Sally didn't know. But she's likely to leave soon. Says she's a good Christian girl and doesn't like the carry-on. Strangers calling at all hours, and his nibs is rather fond of his drink.'

'That's interesting. And do these nocturnal visitors go into the office?'

'Yes. But she's too cowardly to try to find out what they're up to. Now, if that were me...' Mary blushed. 'Not that I'd listen at *your* door, ma'am.'

Lucy grinned. 'Of course not. Anything else?'

'Not really. Oh, she did mention the brother. She didn't like 'im either.'

'Nor did I, Mary, the one time I met him. A rather cold man. Although, he is very ill, which may account for it.'

'And then there was the incident,' Mary declared darkly. Lucy glanced at her maid. Mary loved a bit of drama: she'd been saving this juicy piece of gossip for effect. Amused, Lucy schooled her features. 'Well?'

'Early hours of Sunday morning, it was.'

'Was it now? Go on!'

'Sally woke up in the middle of the night to find the butler knocking on her door and urging her to get up!'

'Oh! Not Mr Hardwicke? It was definitely the butler?' Lucy asked.

'Yes, he wanted her to make tea and something to eat for the master and a guest. Mr Hardwicke had just come in and was the worse for wear. Drunk as a lord, she said he was. It was the only time in her entire time in the house that she has been let into the office.'

'I don't suppose she happened to see a couple of paintings in there... my paintings?'

'Well, I could hardly ask that directly. But the stupid girl was half asleep,' Mary said in disgust. 'She could barely describe the room to me. However, Hardwicke's guest was a woman.'

'Oh, my goodness! I wonder who she was.'

'Sally didn't get a good look at her: the woman was veiled; but I got the impression she thought she was as good as she ought to be!'

'A lady of the night?' Mary nodded and pursed her lips. Lucy smiled in satisfaction. She'd been right to call on him. 'How intriguing. This gets better and better.'

'Glad to be of service, ma'am,' Mary replied with a satisfied smile.

'I knew I could rely on you. A very satisfactory visit, I think, Mary.'

'Yes, ma'am, but does it tell us who broke into your house and stole your paintings?'

'No, but if nothing else, we know Hardwicke was out and about in the early hours. Could he have had the maid woken up to provide him with an alibi?'

'I didn't think of that, ma'am. That's fierce clever of 'im.'

'I'm more inclined to think it is foolish. I do wonder if it's an act he's putting on so we will discount him, for whoever is head of the syndicate is extremely clever.'

'The scoundrel is trying to mislead you?'

Lucy gave a little shrug. 'Something isn't right, of that I'm certain, Mary. For some reason he was keen to tell me about his late-night antics. A gentleman wouldn't normally do so. It shouldn't be too difficult to find out if he was at his club or at that show. I'll get Mr Stone to make discreet enquiries to see if anyone saw him there. Did you ask which club he frequents?'

'The Imperial, ma'am.'

'Good work, Mary. We have learned more than I had hoped, but I wish we knew the identity of that woman.'

THIRTY-FOUR

Phillimore Gardens, that Evening

Lacroix had outdone himself. Lucy guessed she would have to increase his wages if she were to hang on to him for much longer. The first dinner party she would hold, the Mayfair cats would be on the prowl, throwing out lures. Phineas was in a mellow mood over dinner, so it was with some reluctance that Lucy brought up the investigation. It could be ignored no longer. As she described her visit to Thomas's house, Phin's expression grew more troubled.

'And it is just as well I acted this morning, Phin, as he has left for Scotland, and in a bit of a rush too,' she said. 'If I had not called, we wouldn't know where he was going.'

'Do you believe he has left because of your call?' Phineas asked with a raised brow.

'No, of course not. His trunks were already in the hall and labelled for the north. He was definitely shaken by my visit, though. And why was he so keen to give himself an alibi?' She gave him a half-conciliatory smile. 'It would be easy enough to check it, would it not?'

Phineas sighed. 'Yes, I will ask George to make enquiries at his club and in general. We do know he was a regular client of White's Gallery.'

'Yes, very much so. He appears regularly in White's order books. But if he were the Collector, surely he wouldn't be buying paintings at all?'

'A good point, but...' Phineas trailed off and thumped the arm of his chair. 'I keep going round in circles. Misdirection, red herrings and bluffs. What is the truth, and who is telling the truth?'

Lucy gave him a sympathetic smile. 'It is quite a web of deceit.'

'Still, he knew about your paintings, so he could be involved.'

'Hardwicke's behaviour does raise some questions, and I would dearly love to know the identity of the woman he was entertaining,' Lucy said.

'I wouldn't set too much store by it. He may have a mistress; it is not uncommon,' Phineas said.

'I suppose not,' she answered, thinking how unpleasant a role that would be for the woman involved. 'But you must admit, Thomas Hardwicke could be our man. I wonder if my lovely paintings were in those trunks.' Lucy frowned. 'The only problem is I can't see him as a house burglar. He's rather tubby to be squeezing through windows and the like.'

Phineas grinned. 'Isn't that a little unkind? Besides, he may well be an expert lock picker. It would explain the lack of evidence of break-ins in all the cases, including yours. In several instances, the paintings were held in locked rooms. Apollo locked those doors behind him.'

'But what was Edward's role in all of this if Hardwicke is the thief? And if Hardwicke *is* the thief, who is the Collector?'

'They're not mutually exclusive, but I admit, it puzzles me. There must be more people involved.'

'Did Sebastian have any success with his task?'

'Yes. Bar one of the thefts, the Vaughans had stayed at the properties in question in the months before the paintings were taken. In the other case, the Collector himself may have visited the property or knew about it from another source.'

'From White, perhaps, or a friend of his could have mentioned it? These art fanatics probably talk of little else.'

Phineas gave a tiny shrug. 'It's too much of a coincidence. Edward must have been Apollo. However, that leaves us with the question of who stole your paintings?'

'Perhaps he had an apprentice?'

'Anything is possible,' he replied.

'I hate this case,' Lucy said. 'All we do is go round in circles, as you said.'

'I won't be sorry when it's over. But we desperately need some luck to solve it.'

'It's a pity Kincaid didn't work a little bit harder.'

'Yes, it has been a disappointing experience. Kincaid is ambitious and is angling to take over some of my work; however, I wouldn't consider him a threat. Goodness knows, there is enough fraud to keep us both busy,' Phin replied. 'I called on him this morning to discharge him.'

Lucy drained her wine glass. 'Shall we take coffee in the drawing room? You can tell me all about your meeting with him this morning.'

They linked arms as they strolled down the hallway towards the drawing room. 'There is little to tell, because he wasn't to be found,' Phin said. 'I shall try again tomorrow.'

'It wouldn't surprise me to learn that he's carrying out his own investigation, and he's unlikely to share any information with you. He wants to claim the rewards for recovering those paintings.'

'I can't blame him for that, Lucy. Of the eight paintings still missing, the rewards are substantial. Don't concern yourself; I will get to the bottom of it first thing tomorrow.' Phin came to a stop and sighed before planting a kiss on the top of her head. 'Now, it has been a long couple of days. Let us talk no more about business. I'd much rather discuss our nuptials. We must set a date.'

Before Lucy could respond, Mary came rushing up from the kitchen. 'Ma'am, sir, you must come at once to the kitchen. That maid has turned up, and she's in an awful state.'

'What maid, Mary?' Lucy asked, taking in the flush of excitement on Mary's face.

'The one from this morning who works in Mr Hardwicke's house. Sally Evans. I wouldn't bother you, only I think you will want to hear what she 'as to say.'

Lucy and Phin shared a surprised glance before following Mary back downstairs.

Thomas Hardwicke's parlourmaid was sitting at the kitchen table, a cup of tea clasped between her hands, a used handkerchief crumpled up in a ball beside her right hand. The girl's glance was fearful as she looked up.

'Now, Sally, the mistress here and Mr Stone need to hear what you just told me,' Mary said, sitting down beside the young girl. 'Go on, now!'

Lucy drew out a chair and sat down opposite; Phineas stood behind her. 'Please, Sally. You have nothing to fear from us. What has happened?' Lucy asked in a gentle tone.

Sally snuffled. 'When you and Mary left this morning, I got to thinking about it all, and I decided I'd had enough. I'm a good girl, I am. You ask anyone! The goings on in that 'ouse just ain't right.'

'Of course!' Lucy said, trying to contain her excitement. 'What happened to distress you so?'

'The master, he was to leave for up north. Old Groves had told us first thing this morning. In a fierce hurry he was and all. So, I went to him straight off and told him I was 'anding in my notice.' She took a gulp of tea. 'But he flew into one of his rages. I feared for my life, I did. He told me he was closing up the house anyway—just like that! Said I'd never get a reference from 'im neither. Well, says I, I know things about you, and wouldn't the newspapers love to know what kind of man you really are.'

'Oh dear. How did he react to that?' Lucy asked.

'Went and slapped me, he did.' Sally turned her head. There was a bruise on her cheek. 'In a proper temper, he was. Old Groves came in and shooed me out. I went straight up to my room and collected my things. When I came back down, the master and Groves were waiting for me in the servants' 'all. Groves 'anded me an envelope with a month's wages and told me to scarper, but I could only 'ave it as long as I told no one about the woman I'd seen with the master the other night.'

Lucy smiled at her. 'Did you agree?'

'Course I did! Ran out that door like the 'ounds of 'ell was after me.' Sally stared down into her tea for a moment. 'It was only when I was far away from the 'ouse that I remembered your Mary said that if I was ever in trouble to come and see her. And 'ere I am.' Sally gave Lucy a sly look. 'I reckoned what I had to say might be worth something.'

Lucy was disappointed. How could she be sure the girl was telling the truth if she was after money.

'You did right, Sally. Didn't she, ma'am?' Mary asked, her eyes wide with meaning.

'Absolutely. You may stay here tonight, Sally, and we can discuss recompense in the morning. Thank you for giving us this information. I don't suppose you can tell us anything about that woman who was with your master that night?'

Sally gave her a sad smile. 'Sorry, ma'am, but she was all in black and had a veil covering her face. She was young, though. Her gloves were off, and her skin was smooth and soft. I did hear her speak and her voice was a bit swanky-like. I reckon she was an opera singer or an actress,' Sally offered with a scowl of distaste. 'For no decent woman would be out with an old bachelor like 'ardwicke in the early hours of the morning, now would they?'

'No, indeed,' said Phineas, squeezing Lucy's shoulder. 'Can you recall what she said, by any chance?'

Sally frowned down at the table and gnawed at her lip. 'I was just coming in the door with the tray. It was something like: "I don't want to do this anymore." Didn't make much sense to me, sir. She said not a word more while I was in the room.'

Lucy was aware of Phineas's indrawn breath as he straightened up. 'Lucy, my dear, I think we had better discuss this further. Thank you, Sally. Mary will look after you.'

'I will, of course, sir.' Mary put a comforting arm around Sally's shoulders while beaming across at Lucy.

Lucy mouthed *thank you* to Mary before following Phineas back upstairs.

'I appear to have been blessed with the best of maids,' Lucy said on closing the drawing room door.

'It was lucky indeed that she befriended Sally this morning,' Phineas said, rocking back and forth on his heels before the fireplace, his eyes alight. Lucy could almost hear the cogs of his brain turning.

'And lucky indeed that I called on Hardwicke,' Lucy said with some satisfaction in driving her point home.

'Indeed.'

'Well, dearest fiancé, what do you make of it all?' she asked.

'Hardwicke is rattled. Closing up his London home and bolting to Edinburgh are not the actions of an innocent man. It's hardly a coincidence that all of this occurred in his house on the night your paintings were stolen when we know he's one of the few people who knew you had them.'

'The only other person in the syndicate with knowledge of my purchase was White, who has gone to meet his Maker. If you are right, then Hardwicke must be followed to Scotland,' Lucy said, settling down on the sofa.

'Yes, I shall follow first thing in the morning.'

'I think you meant *we*,' she said with a narrowed gaze.

'Did I? I hardly think so.'

'We had an agreement,' she said.

'Yes, and if you recall, I said if the danger were too great, I would exclude you. I'm certain you agreed to my terms.'

'You know I will follow you,' she said, almost in a whisper. 'Mary and I will be on that train too. I would remind you that we're not married yet. I'm a free agent.'

His features set, Phineas gave her a long, hard look. 'What if I were to beg you to stay in London?'

'It would be pointless,' Lucy replied, holding his gaze.

Phin looked away first and muttered, 'I thought as much!'

THIRTY-FIVE

To Lucy's surprise, for it was now well past ten o'clock, she heard the front doorbell chime. 'Who on earth is calling at this hour? It can't be a good thing. I think I have had enough drama for one day.' Phineas shrugged and remained standing by the fireplace, still looking very much put out. Lucy sighed. She hated arguing with him. 'Hopefully, Mary will do what she does best and turn them away.'

However, minutes later, Mary appeared in the doorway, a scowl marring her features. 'Mr Kincaid, ma'am,' she muttered with a roll of her eyes. 'Are you *at home*?'

Before Lucy could respond, Kincaid brushed past Mary and was boring down on her. Phineas cleared his throat, and Kincaid stalled, looking across at him. Kincaid actually blushed, but he recovered quickly. 'Ah, Stone, delighted you are here. Mrs Lawrence, how are you? No ill effects from our little adventure, I hope?'

From the corner of her eye, Lucy caught Mary rolling her eyes once more. 'That will be *all*, Mary, thank you,' Lucy said.

Kincaid took Lucy's hand and bowed over it, much to her disgust, before shaking Phineas by the hand. 'Well, this is indeed fortuitous and saves me having to visit you at your rooms tomorrow,' he said to Phin, taking up position beside him before the fireplace.

'You make a habit of visiting ladies at this hour?' Phineas asked, with an edge to his voice.

'Only when I have something of value to share... with you both, of course,' Kincaid replied, his eyes twinkling at Lucy. 'Some information has come to light that may help us solve these art thefts.'

Phineas raised a brow at Lucy before turning to Kincaid. 'You have my attention.'

'Before I say any more, I'd like your assurance that if this information leads to the resolution of your case, I get my fair share of the reward.'

Lucy huffed in anger, disgusted. How could the man be so mercenary? He had done so little to help Phineas. However, to her astonishment, Phineas nodded and said: 'Of course, we have an agreement; I do not see any reason to break it.' Why was Phin being so magnanimous? Earlier in the evening, he had spoken of dismissing Kincaid.

'Excellent! Well now, 'tis like this. I thought it prudent to keep an eye on White's clients. In particular, those who dealt with him on a frequent basis. I have a network of informers, you see. Very useful fellows, I find, on the whole. I'm surprised you don't employ the same tactic, Stone.'

Lucy knew well that Phin did, but to her chagrin, Phineas just shrugged. Was he holding fire until Kincaid gave them the information?

Lucy turned to Kincaid. 'And?' She dearly wished he would get to the point and leave them in peace.

'A fine gentleman by the name of Thomas Hardwicke has only closed up his house in Mayfair and left for Scotland under something of a cloud.'

Lucy glanced at Phineas, but he remained silent. 'And what is the significance of that, Kincaid?' Lucy asked.

A smug smile appeared on Kincaid's face. 'Ah, Mrs Lawrence, I believe the man is part of the syndicate your dear fiancé and I have been so keen to run to ground. Indeed, I have little doubt.'

'What evidence do you have to implicate him?' Lucy persisted.

'Shall we say he was a trifle indiscreet at his club last night? Hardwicke got into an argument with some other chap about art and was heard to boast that he could lay his hand on any painting he wanted, if the fancy took him. He went as far as to dare the other man to name a picture he wanted and swore he would get it for him. The other chap called him a fool and a rather heated argument erupted. Hardwicke was asked to leave and was, in fact, escorted off the premises.'

'Hardwicke's claim could just be talk, Kincaid,' Lucy said. 'He was probably inebriated.'

'And, as it happens, Kincaid,' Phineas revealed with some satisfaction, 'we had already reached the conclusion that he is in fact the Collector. You are not telling us anything new, I'm afraid.' Was that a hint of smugness Lucy detected in his tone? It wasn't like Phin, though she could hardly blame him: Kincaid was more than annoying.

But Kincaid ignored Phin. 'I would normally agree that it was just bluster, my dear Mrs Lawrence. However, when viewed in the light of other information I have in my possession, it is significant. I'm afraid your *guess* is incorrect, Stone. You see, Thomas Hardwicke is not the Collector. In fact, his brother is the head of the syndicate.'

'Menzies Hardwicke?' Phineas asked, frowning. 'Where is your proof?'

Kincaid gave him a self-satisfied look. 'The night your fiancée and I were at White's Gallery, I found a message to

Menzies Hardwicke attached to a consignment of paintings in the basement. It was a shipment addressed to Kinnock House which is Menzies Hardwicke's home. I would wager that was Thomas Hardwicke's destination earlier today.'

'What did the message say?' Lucy asked. 'Would you care to enlighten us?'

'Better than that; I can show you,' he replied. Kincaid slowly drew a card from his jacket pocket. Lucy gasped, for she recognised the front of the card. It was one of Apollo's.

'Well, it was more what the message was written on that caught my eye at first,' he replied with a grin, twirling the card between his fingers.

Lucy tried to recall their search that night. There hadn't been much light down in the basement. Kincaid could easily have found something and secreted it in a pocket. How sly he was!

Riled, Lucy jumped up, snatched the card from him, flipped it over and read it out. '*Menzies, I'm taking a sabbatical! A.*' The message was scrawled in black ink.

'Good Lord!' she said, handing the card to Phin. 'This is extraordinary. This links White and Menzies.' Kincaid's smile was smug. Lucy turned on him. 'Why didn't you share this with the rest of us the next day? The police would have been very interested in this.'

Kincaid guffawed. 'Dear Mrs Lawrence, this is business, pure and simple. Let us be realistic,' he said before turning to Phineas. 'No offence, Stone, but would you have shared this with me if you had found it? I think not!'

'You are only interested in the reward,' Lucy snapped.

Kincaid sniffed and turned to Lucy, his lips pursed. 'I'm sorry if an honest man making his way in the world offends your sensibilities, Mrs Lawrence, but a man has to make a living. I'd remind you, that is how your fiancé also survives in this harsh and cruel world we live in.'

Furious now, Lucy had to take a deep breath to calm down. 'What about the two murders? Whatever those men were involved in, they didn't deserve to die as they did.'

Phineas frowned at her. The smile died on Kincaid's lips, and Lucy almost groaned. What a slip up!

'Edward Vaughan was involved in the syndicate? You never told me this, Stone,' Kincaid ground out.

Phineas's gaze was steady. 'It only came to light very recently.'

'And what role did he play?' Kincaid snapped.

'As your involvement in this case has come to an end—at your request, I might add—your need to know that is now redundant.'

Lucy almost cheered as an angry glow crept into Kincaid's face. Mary was right: the man was obnoxious.

'Why are you coming to me with this now, Kincaid?' Phineas continued, his fingers drumming the mantle.

Kincaid took a moment to answer. 'I've no fancy for travelling up north, and it's your show after all. As I say, once I get my cut, I'm satisfied. Sure, I've plenty of other work to be getting on with.' With that, he held out his hand. 'It was a pleasure doing business with you, Stone. Don't hesitate to call on me again if you should get stuck on a case.'

After a flicker of hesitation, Phineas shook hands, but Lucy could sense he was only barely holding onto his temper.

'Mrs Lawrence!' Kincaid treated Lucy to a curt bow and left.

For several minutes, neither spoke.

'Do you think that is genuine?' Lucy asked at last, her gaze resting on the card in Phin's hand.

'Kincaid has no reason to fabricate this,' Phin said, waving it with a look of distaste. He glanced at the message on the back once more. 'I wonder if this demand for a break in their activities was the reason for Edward's murder.'

'Could the Collector—Menzies—be that cold-blooded?'

'Apollo was crucial to the entire operation. If he wanted to stop, it meant the whole thing would fall apart.'

'But Edward is dead, and my paintings were stolen just the same and in a similar manner. It doesn't make sense now, does it?'

'Little about this case does! Unless, of course, Edward wasn't Apollo.' Phineas sat down beside Lucy, his face drawn with tiredness. He ran his fingers through his hair and sighed. 'Tell me what you know of Menzies Hardwicke.' As Lucy described their meeting at Brown's Hotel, he listened intently.

Phineas smiled, much to her relief. 'I get the impression you didn't like him.'

'He came across as cold, reserved and a trifle taciturn—the exact opposite of Thomas, in fact.' She relived the discomfort she'd felt when Menzies had regarded her so sternly that afternoon. At the time, she'd put it down to a dislike of society women, when most likely it was her association with Phineas that was the issue. 'Thomas told me that he's a dying man. Do you think he's dismantling the syndicate because of that?'

'Not necessarily. He may wish to pass it on to his brother.'

Lucy shook her head. 'I don't see it. Thomas isn't capable of running something like that.'

'Have you ever considered that the persona he displays to the world may be false?' Phin asked.

'No, but I suppose we will find out soon enough what kind of man Thomas truly is. Had you never suspected his brother before this?'

'I'd never heard of him until you mentioned meeting him with Thomas, and I thought I knew who all the major collectors were,' he said. 'Thomas had come to my attention but not in a negative way: merely as a man with a great deal of interest in the art world and the possessor of some fine pieces.'

'I suppose Menzies living in so isolated a place and using

third parties to acquire the art he wanted, it was unlikely many knew of him. And now he has my paintings too, if Thomas has taken them with him to Scotland. I do hope we can get them back.'

'I will do my best,' he replied.

'And I will help you, of course,' she said, holding his gaze.

For a moment, Phineas looked as though he was going to argue and insist she stay in London. But then his expression cleared. 'Scotland it is, my dear.'

Lucy tried not to smile. It was a tiny victory, but a significant one. 'I hope Lady Sarah won't be too disappointed, for I shall have to defer our trip to Sidley.'

'You never mentioned it,' Phin said, his eyes alight.

Lucy could have kicked herself for now he would try to persuade her not to cancel. 'With everything else that has happened since I called on her, I had almost forgotten about it. The heat is unbearable for her, and she wishes to go to the country. Her doctor and Geoffrey have forbidden it.'

'Is that not odd? I would have thought the country is just the place for her,' he said with a frown.

'Well, he's adamant she's not to risk the journey, backed up by their physician.'

'And you are willing to incur Geoffrey's wrath?' he asked.

'Geoffrey can bluster all he wants. I care only for her welfare. Phin. If you saw how she's suffering you would have offered too.'

'Perhaps you are right. With luck, we should be back in a few days. You may not need to defer for too long.' Phineas planted a kiss on her cheek before rising to his feet. 'Don't be late in the morning. The express leaves at ten o'clock sharp.'

THIRTY-SIX

The Royal Hotel, Edinburgh, Scotland, Tuesday, 26th June

It was early evening. A weary Lucy wandered over to the window of her hotel bedroom whilst Mary bustled about, putting away her few belongings. She'd not brought much with her, for Phineas didn't think the investigation would take long to complete. Lucy, however, was unsettled, for she couldn't get the two murders out of her head. Surely the man who had orchestrated those would stop at nothing to protect himself? Hadn't he tried to eliminate Phineas already? Menzies Hardwicke was not shy about ordering a spot of murder when the fancy took him. Now his choice of living in an isolated manor house on an island made a lot of sense. The little she could find out about Kinnock Island didn't inspire hope of a quick resolution either. Would they be able to access it? The place was a few miles offshore, rugged, and even a colony of monks had abandoned it in despair in the past, the North Sea proving too much for even their hardy souls. When she'd voiced her concern to Phin, he had told her not to worry—which had the opposite effect.

Once they had been shown to their respective suites,

Phineas had popped his head around Lucy's door to inform her that he intended to make himself known to a local chief inspector who he hoped would provide some assistance. The man was an acquaintance of Oliver McQuillan. Without further ado, he had vanished, much to Lucy's vexation. There was little she could do except order dinner for them in her suite and await his return. That he was annoyed with her for insisting on accompanying him, she was well aware, but although she usually could charm him out of a mood, today she had been unsuccessful. Guilt crept in. Should she have stayed at home? She could tell he was anxious about the case, and now she'd added more worry by being stubborn.

Phineas had been consumed by this case for a year and a half. Perhaps he felt his reputation hinged on a successful outcome and her presence might jeopardise that? But no. She knew he was a proud man, but it was a burning desire to get to the truth that drove him, unlike Kincaid, who she was sure was mercenary to the core. But Lucy hated being at odds with Phin. Since becoming a widow, she'd tasted an independence few women were lucky enough to experience. And that was wonderful. But she would have to find a balance. Her life with Phin would be fraught if they were at cross purposes and constantly trying to outwit each other. She had learned that the hard way with Charlie: marriage had to be founded on honesty and mutual respect.

Lucy rolled her shoulders. She was still stiff from the eight-and-a-half-hour journey on the express. The only chance to stretch one's legs had been the thirty-minute stop for lunch at York. Overall, it had not been the happiest of journeys. Mary, whose detestation of travel anywhere outside London was well known to Lucy, made it abundantly clear at every opportunity that she considered Scotland a wild and dangerous place. Lucy tried to laugh it off, conscious of Phineas's growing irritation, culminating in his burying his head in a book. She realised it was a measure of the stress he was under that he acted so out of character. This was no summer outing. Thankfully, George was polite enough to listen to Mary's diatribe. He even succeeded in diverting Mary's attention from the topic, and the latter half of the journey was relatively peaceful. Lucy had to hand it to the valet: he was a man of great patience. How smoothly their house would run with him in charge.

It was strange to be back here in Edinburgh. Lucy's last visit had been with Charlie to visit his parents almost five years ago. It had been an unpleasant trip with her mother- and father-in-law barely speaking to her or when they did, it was to ask if she was *well*. Lucy had to grin and bear it as they spoke of their neighbour's wonderful grandchildren and what a joy they brought. It was all deliberate, of course; Lucy knew they blamed her for the childless state of her marriage. Lucy smiled. So much had occurred since then. She wouldn't be welcome at *their* door.

Where she stood, Lucy could hear the city sounds drifting up to her second-floor suite. She pulled aside the netting covering the window and stepped out onto the tiny balcony. Lucy had always loved Princes Street with its hum of activity. This evening, it was busy with carriages and trams, the pavements bustling with shoppers and workers heading home for the night. It was such a pity that they were here on a case, for she would have loved to explore the city again. But Phineas insisted they came to the hotel straight from Waverley Station. His manner had been brisk, and George appeared ill at ease too. Did they suspect that Menzies had spies on the look-out for them? It made sense, for it was clear Hardwicke considered Phineas a terrible threat; why else would he have tried to frame him for murder or attempted to have him assassinated? Lucy wondered if Thomas's claim that he was leaving for Scotland due to being summoned by his brother was actually true in light of what Kincaid had revealed. Wasn't it more likely he had fled? If Thomas's arrival was unexpected, Menzies might be anticipating they would follow, and he'd hardly be happy about them chasing him down to his island estate.

With a sigh, she let her gaze wander. She was bored and needed some distraction until Phineas returned. Then, to her delight, as her eyes became accustomed to the heat haze which clung low over the city, she could make out the silhouette of the castle perched on its rock, and she recalled a pleasant afternoon she'd spent up there, away from her in-laws. Sudden yapping drew her attention across the road, but it was only a lady with a dog strolling through the gardens. A little further along, however, a man stood at the Scott Monument, looking towards the hotel. It seemed such an odd thing to do. Was it a coincidence, or was he watching out for them? Good Lord! She was becoming paranoid. With one last longing glance towards Carlton Hill, she stepped back inside, even more disgruntled. To be stuck inside was unbearable. It was stuffy and humid in the room. Maybe if Phin returned soon, they could take a stroll up to the castle after dinner. Surely it would be cooler by then?

'I'm all done, ma'am. Is there anything you need?' Mary asked.

'No, Mary. You may go for your dinner now. I'm sure you must be hungry after the journey. If you can come back around half past ten, I'll be ready to retire then.'

'I will for sure, ma'am.' Mary gave her a sympathetic look. 'An early night will do you good. I've asked that your meal be served up here at eight o'clock as you wished, and Mr George approved the choices. Ring if you need me, ma'am.' At the door, she turned and gave her a concerned look. 'Make sure you lock this door after me.'

Lucy smiled and shook her head. 'Mary, we're not in the wilds of Africa now.'

Mary sniffed. 'Aye, maybe not, thank Gawd; but there's devils everywhere,' she said with a dark glance before she closed the door.

. . .

Lucy stopped pacing and glanced at the clock again. Nine o'clock. Where could Phineas be? Her stomach rumbled, and she cast a longing glance at the covered dishes. She doubted the food was still warm. If he was going to be delayed, why had he not sent a message? Then an infuriating notion crept into her head. But it wasn't just annoying: it was very probable! What if he had travelled out to Menzies Hardwicke's island without her? It was the kind of thing he might well do. After all, he hadn't wanted her to make the journey up here. Well, there was one way to find out. If that were his plan, he wouldn't have gone alone. He always took George with him.

Fizzing with irritation, Lucy yanked open the door to her suite, determined to find out what was going on.

'Oh!' she cried. 'You're here. What on earth are you doing sitting out there?'

'Good evening, ma'am,' George said. He rose from his seat, looking incredibly sheepish.

Lucy, now fuming, beckoned him into her room. 'What is going on? Where is your master, George? Has he not come back or sent a message?'

George shook his head but wouldn't meet her eye.

'I see! It's as I expected. He has tricked me.'

George took a step back as alarm flitted across his features. 'I'm not sure what you mean, ma'am.'

'Oh, I think you do, George. Best you confess, now,' Lucy demanded. George hesitated. 'Out with it, man! I'm in no mood for prevarication.'

The valet inhaled deeply, his eyes full of apology. 'Mr Stone returned from the police station within half an hour. He was unable to contact Chief Inspector Fairfax as he's off duty today, ma'am. Rather than wait until tomorrow—'

'He has set off for Kinnock Island by himself,' Lucy finished for him in disgust. 'I knew it!'

George took a step nearer. 'I'm sorry, ma'am, yes. He hoped to catch the last train out to Dalmeny this evening. Mr Stone is impatient to conclude the case.'

'But alone, George? That borders on foolish!' Lucy exclaimed.

George shifted on his feet. 'Mr Stone bade me stay here to protect you, no matter what. My instructions were to stall you from following as best I could.' Was that a guilt-induced blush to George's cheeks?

Lucy was flabbergasted, and for some moments, the power of speech left her as a surge of anger coursed through her entire body. How could Phin do this?

George's brow was creased with concern. 'Ma'am, are you well?'

'Yes, George. I'm sorry. I... am very well.' Lucy sat down with a sigh. 'It is best you tell me all about it.'

'The master felt it was too dangerous for you to go to Kinnock Island as he had no idea what he might be facing there. Mr Stone believes that Thomas Hardwicke fled London because he had been indiscreet at his club, and this was bound to get back to either the police or Mr Stone, exposing the syndicate. Therefore, his unexpected arrival will have forewarned Menzies Hardwicke that pursuit by us is likely. With this in mind, the master is anticipating a reception committee of the unwelcoming variety. He also feared that they might try to abduct you to use as leverage against him, which is why he was anxious you stay in the hotel under my protection.'

'Well, he should have warned me to be on my guard. Indeed, he should have taken me into his confidence. Surely at this stage, he must realise that I'm not content to sit and wait while someone else—' She nearly said *had an adventure,* but instead continued: '—faces such danger.'

'Mr Stone didn't wish to alarm you, ma'am.'

'But we can't leave him to face this alone. What if he walks into a trap or they decide to—' She couldn't finish the dreadful thought. 'We must go to his aid.' She sprang up. 'As soon as possible.'

'Ma'am, I really think you should reconsider. Mr Stone will not be pleased.'

'And I, George, will not be pleased if he comes to harm!'

George spread out his hands. 'So, it is useless that I argue with you?' he said with a glint in his eye.

'Yes, completely!'

'Very well, ma'am. I agree with your assessment of the situation.'

Lucy broke into a grin. 'Don't worry, George. I will tell him I gave you no option.'

George gave a sigh of relief. 'Thank you. I was not comfortable with the idea of him going off without a police escort. It's a matter of grave concern to me. Nothing I could say would dissuade him.'

Lucy smiled. 'George, you are unfortunate enough to have a master and a soon-to-be-mistress, who are inordinately stubborn.'

'Yes, I consider myself most fortunate in that regard,' he replied with a smile. But soon he grew serious once more. 'Unfortunately, the master has a good head start on us.'

Lucy glanced at her watch. 'It's half past nine; perhaps we could still catch a train.'

'I have checked already,' George said. 'They're finished for this evening. The first train in the morning is at half past six.'

Lucy came to a decision. 'And we shall be on it.'

George cast her a bleak smile. 'Yes, ma'am.'

'Very well. We will leave Mary here in case Mr Stone should return before us.'

The truth was Mary would be a liability in a tricky situation, whereas George was ex-army and experienced in unusual circumstances, courtesy of Phin's previous investigations. She'd feel a lot braver if he were with her. 'I imagine Mr Stone, in keeping with his meticulous habits, had planned his route. Do you know the details?'

'Yes, ma'am. A train to Dalmeny from here, then hired equipage at the station or a long walk to the coast. If I may say so, ma'am, Mr Stone is armed and cognisant of what may lie ahead.'

'Is he now?' Lucy took a calming breath before she could continue. 'But he's hardly fully recovered from the attempt on his life. His injured shoulder puts him at a disadvantage.'

'Yes, ma'am, I fear so too.'

'Mr Hardwicke lives on an island. Had Mr Stone made enquiries about hiring a boat?' she asked.

'My understanding, ma'am, is that at low tide a causeway is accessible on foot. At other times, one must use a boat. Mr Stone intended to make enquiries locally once he had a better idea of the terrain. I consulted this morning's newspaper for the high tide times so he would know when it would be safe to cross the causeway to the island.'

'Excellent. When is the first low tide tomorrow?'

'Five in the morning, which means we're unlikely to be on time to use the causeway as it's at least an hour by road, two hours on foot from the station to get there.'

'That is unfortunate, George. We shall have to hire a boat to take us across instead.'

'As you wish, ma'am.'

Lucy bid him goodnight. 'Do not on any account stay out in the corridor all night. I shall keep my door locked. I promise.' George looked as though he was going to object. 'I will check, you know.' The valet nodded with a look of defeat. 'And George?'

'Yes, ma'am?'

'I'd appreciate if you could be ready to leave here at six o'clock sharp,' she said.

Once she'd locked her door, Lucy paced the floor for some time, consumed with worry. Phineas was not usually a reckless man, yet going off alone to confront Menzies was just that. With a groan, she sat down. This was her fault for being so stubborn. Phin was risking his life to protect her. She wished with all her might she had not insisted on coming.

THIRTY-SEVEN

Dalmeny, West Lothian

Lucy should have been half asleep —it was so early— but her senses were buzzing. The journey out to Dalmeny had only taken twenty minutes, and it was as well they were travelling first class as the train was jam-full with workmen taking up every seat in third. Mystified as to where they could all be headed, Lucy had queried George, who informed her they were likely labourers employed on the Forth Bridge which was mid-construction. The railway bridge would span the Firth of Forth and was said to be a wonder of modern engineering. True enough, when Dalmeny station was reached, the workers streamed off the train and down the platform. Lucy held back, reluctant to get caught up in the tide of men and lose her companion.

At the ticket office, George made enquiries about where the best place would be to hire a boat. A station porter gave them directions to the local slipway, where it would be possible to find a boat to take them out to the island.

The porter cast George a peculiar glance. 'Not many folk go

to Kinnock these days. Are you sure you want to go? You're unlikely to get a welcome there, you know. There are more pleasant places hereabouts. I can give you tips if you wish.'

'Thank you, but no, that is where we wish to go,' George replied.

The porter shook his head. 'Well, I've never seen the place so popular. Only yesterday evening we had a gentleman asking for directions.'

George raised a brow at Lucy before thanking the porter again.

Once outside the station, Lucy turned to George. 'I would hazard a guess that was Mr Stone, George. I only hope we aren't too late to help him. A lot could have occurred since last night.'

George harrumphed. 'Ma'am, in my experience, Mr Stone is resourceful and always prepared for the unexpected.'

'I hope you are not mistaken. Lead on, George,' she said.

It only took ten minutes to walk to the slipway, but it was the sight of the Forth Bridge under construction that left Lucy and George standing at the water's edge, gaping in wonder at the structure. Three huge diamond-shaped metal towers rose up from the water, dominating the skyline to the north. On the nearest one Lucy could make out men climbing upwards, tiny specks in the distance. Lucy was impressed by their courage. No one could survive falling from that great height, she thought with a shiver, before turning away.

A little further on, they came across two men sitting on a wall a little distance from the slipway. Both had weather-beaten faces and rugged looks suggestive of an outdoor life. They were watching Lucy and George closely. One white-haired man, who appeared to be the elder, was smoking a pipe; the other was mending a net. On the far side of the slipway, Lucy spotted a couple of large rowboats and hoped the men were the owners. It was time to charm them.

'Good morning, gentlemen,' she said with a smile as she approached.

'All right, hen?' the smoker asked, his eyes crinkling as he took her measure.

'Yes, thank you. Do you know who I should speak to about hiring a boat to Kinnock Island?'

The men shared a knowing look, and the older man took his pipe out from the corner of his mouth and sucked at his bottom lip. 'I dinnae think it's a good idea, lassie,' he replied, pointing out towards the horizon. With a slow shake of his head, he continued, 'Nae; that storm's a-comin' in soon.'

Lucy followed his gaze, and indeed, black clouds clung low and sulky on the horizon. 'But not yet, surely, and I understand it is not that far to the island... I'm prepared to pay handsomely,' she replied, taking a step closer.

The second man looked up from his net and began to chuckle. 'Frasier! Dae ye hear that! Just like that Sassenach last night and that lad the day before.'

'Haud yer wheesht, Angus!' Frasier smiled kindly at Lucy. 'Well, lassie, 'tis temptin', but a poor fisherman can nae afford to lose his boat. That'—he pointed out to sea—'is going to be auld wives and pike staves in an hour. I'll no risk it!' With a sniff, he knocked out his pipe against the wall, his gaze a challenge.

'Yes, ma'am, I must agree,' George said, glancing up. 'I don't like the look of that sky. With the heat we have experienced these last few days, I think we're in for quite a storm.'

'We had better hurry then. We don't want to be stuck on the mainland.' Lucy turned back to the men, hoping one final plea might work. 'It is quite urgent that we get to Kinnock House.'

'I telt that gentleman yesterday. Nae go out tae Kinnock. Hardwicke dinnae like visitors,' Frasier said. Angus nodded in agreement.

'But did you take him out?' Lucy quickly described Phineas, and Frasier tilted his head and rubbed his chin.

'No, but that sounds like 'im.'

'Good. You see, it is very important that I follow him. Most urgent, in fact. As I say, money is not an object.'

Frasier glanced at Angus, then waved across to the horizon. 'Best go back to toon and wait it oot.' Angus nodded in agreement and got back to his repairs.

George stepped up. 'What about the causeway? Is it far?'

'Aye, an hour by cab, two on foot,' the elderly man replied. 'Best hire a cab in toon. But you'd be lucky to make it on time. Tides already a-turnin'.'

'Thank you,' Lucy said, trying to hide her disappointment. They walked back up to the road. 'Let us hurry back to the station, George. There are bound to be equipages for hire there. If luck is on our side, we may get across the causeway on time.'

Lucy's optimism was in vain. As soon as they arrived at the causeway, it was evident they were too late, with the water lapping over the submerged walkway. The wind was beginning to pick up and the sky now brooded over them, black and angry.

'Botheration!' Lucy exclaimed, peering closely as she tried to judge how deep the water was. Then she looked across at the island. 'How long would it take to walk across?'

'As far as I know, at least twenty minutes. I don't think you should chance it, ma'am,' George said. 'We will have to wait for the next low tide.'

'I can't stay here doing nothing, George. Mr Stone may be in trouble,' Lucy replied, looking out in despair at the outline of Kinnock House so temptingly close. It was a square, ugly building—forbidding almost. In the foreground, Lucy could make out what appeared to be the ruins of a church or monastery. It was as bleak a place as she had ever seen. Why on earth did Menzies Hardwicke want to live on such a godforsaken island? Unless, of course, one wanted to hide away from the world to cover up one's crimes.

George stood frowning across at the island. 'I agree. I suggest, Mrs Lawrence, that we take the cab back to Dalmeny and telegram Chief Inspector Fairfax. Perhaps a police boat might be available to bring us out?'

'An excellent idea, George,' Lucy replied.

As if on cue, the first splatters of rain began to fall as Lucy and George climbed back up the embankment. But as she neared the crest, she saw their cab heading off down the road in the distance. 'Stop!' she cried out, but she could only watch in dismay as the cab disappeared from view. 'Now, what are we going to do, George? It's a two-hour walk back to Dalmeny.'

'Shall we shelter from this rain for now, ma'am, while we think about it? The storm is coming in fast,' George said. The valet pointed to a stand of trees further up the shoreline.

A strong gust of wind caught Lucy's hat, threatening to dislodge it. With a sigh of frustration, she clamped it down and followed.

They huddled together, George doing his best to shield her from the rain, which was now almost horizontal.

'What should we do?' she asked. The island was nearly invisible now, obscured by the rain. 'Should we try the causeway? We might just make it.'

'No, ma'am, definitely not. Even without this storm, it would be impossible.' George strained his neck, looking down the beach. 'If I'm not mistaken, I think there are a couple of rowboats further down the shore, just beyond that rocky outcrop. If you wait here, I will go and check.'

'No, George, I will come with you. Time is of the essence,' she replied.

They trudged down the beach, heads bent into the wind. A few yards further and they came upon a small inlet. There were two boats drawn up onto the shore where seaweed marked the high-tide mark.

'They look very heavy, George,' she shouted above the wind. 'And should we not find the owners and ask permission?'

A rumble of thunder echoed in the distance. 'Ma'am, I don't imagine they would grant it. However, whoever the owner is, they will hardly be using the boat for the next hour or so. Only mad men would take a boat out in this weather,' he said with a lop-sided grin. He waved towards the island. 'And, if we do not act soon, it will be too rough to make a crossing.'

'True, we have little choice. Very well. We will borrow one of them,' Lucy said with a shiver. The rain had now soaked through her jacket and her blouse was sticking to her skin. It was unpleasant, but compared to what Phin might be facing...

George gestured for her to go to the opposite side. He bent over, grasping the side of the craft and began to push. Lucy followed his example. Between them, they managed to drag the boat to the water, but it took a good ten minutes. Lucy gasped as the cold waves crashed upon her lower body, but she was determined to carry on. All she could think of was getting to the island.

Once the rowboat was afloat, Lucy climbed into the stern and sat down as George pushed it off. Once afloat, he clambered in, sat down on the centre thwart, and took up the oars. Unfortunately, progress was slow due to the strong onshore wind. The swaying of the vessel was terrifying to Lucy, whose only boating experience had been on the ornamental lake at Somerville Hall. Halfway across, the swell caught the boat, and it tilted precariously to the port side. Lucy knew George was struggling to keep control of the vessel, but there was little she could do to help. She wasn't strong enough to row in these conditions. Holding on to the gunwales, she uttered a prayer. A bolt of lightning crackled above them, and the wind dropped momentarily. George righted the boat back on course, just as the rocky shoreline of the island became visible to Lucy.

'Nearly there, George,' Lucy shouted. 'Keep straight; there is a gravelly spot where we can land.'

She kept her eyes trained on Kinnock House. What kind of welcoming committee were they about to meet? And were they too late to help Phin?

THIRTY-EIGHT

Kinnock Island, Lothian, Scotland

The wind howled about them. 'Nearly there, George,' Lucy shouted, hoping to give him encouragement as she didn't think he could maintain the pace for much longer: he was grimacing with every pull of the oars. Lucy pointed off to the right. George paused and looked over his shoulder. Whatever he said in response was taken away on the wind, but he set to with renewed vigour.

A few minutes later, George was able to jump out into shallow water. Lucy followed and between them they hauled the boat up onto the shingle. Lucy cringed as the heavy boat scraped along the rocky ground and hoped they weren't doing too much damage in case they needed to make a quick getaway.

The ground rose steadily from the rocky foreshore with a few hardy shrubs and trees standing guard at the highest point of the rise. George helped Lucy up the slope, and at the top, they stopped momentarily to take in the landscape. At the far end of the island was Kinnock House, rising above a stand of trees. It was a great, grey, stone Goliath with a scattering of outbuildings to one side. A square house with small mullioned windows, it looked perfect for the terrain: bleak, hardy, and unforgiving. Between them and the house, Lucy could make out the gable of one of the monastery buildings.

She pointed to it. 'Let's take cover there.' George could only nod his agreement. Lucy suspected he needed to rest, but knew his pride wouldn't allow him to admit it.

They scooted down the slope into the hollow where the ancient monastery ruins stood. The crumbling walls provided some much-needed protection from the wind and the rain. Lucy leaned against a wall to catch her breath, hoping George would follow suit.

'Hopefully, no one saw us come in on the boat,' Lucy said after a minute or two.

'We will soon know if they did,' George said. 'There is so little shelter; we're at a disadvantage.'

'To put it mildly, George! However...' Lucy pulled her pistol out of her bag and showed it to him with a grin.

George nodded his approval and reached inside his coat pocket. 'And here is mine,' he said.

Lucy blew out her cheeks. 'That's a relief, George, for I'm not the best of shots.'

'Yes, ma'am, I'm aware of that!'

'Oh dear, yes, of course. But I thought you had forgiven me for that unfortunate incident, George.'

'Forgiven, yes of course. To forget may take a little longer.'

Lucy squirmed but then realised the valet was teasing her. 'George, you are too cruel.'

'Yes, ma'am.'

With a wave of her hand and a weary smile she returned to the problem at hand. 'Do you think Phineas is in trouble?'

'I do, ma'am. Otherwise, he would have sent a message, or indeed, returned to Edinburgh.'

'Why on earth didn't he take you with him?' she asked.

Lucy held up her hand as George began to protest. 'Yes, I know he wanted you to guard me, but the danger is here, not in Edinburgh.'

George smiled gently. 'Can you not guess? You are more important to him than his own safety.'

'Oh, George!' she cried. 'I should not have insisted on coming to Scotland. I'm a selfish and obstinate creature.'

'But you would have fretted back in London,' he replied. He nodded to the pistol in her hand. 'And if you are even a half-decent shot, two of us here now is definitely better than one.'

Lucy squeezed his arm in gratitude. 'What should we do? We can hardly storm the house,' she said.

'Stealth may be of more use. We might be able to find a way in around the back.' George moved along the wall to a window shaped gap. He peered out towards the house in the distance.

'What can you see?' Lucy asked.

George pulled back. 'There is some activity at the front of the house. However, my sight is not good; I do not know who it is.'

'What are they doing outside in this weather?' she asked, puzzled. What could be going on?

Lucy crept past George and took up position on the other side of the window opening. She took a tentative peek, then withdrew quickly. Four figures stood on the front steps of the house. Lucy immediately recognised Phineas's tall form and Menzies Hardwicke. There was no sign of Thomas Hardwicke, however, and the other two men were unknown to her. Nevertheless, even from a distance, she could tell something wasn't right. Lucy darted another look.

To her horror, as she watched, the group moved down the steps, Phineas being supported between the other two men, each of them with a hold under one of Phineas's arms. If she wasn't mistaken, Phin's arms were tied, and his head drooped down onto his chest. How they were treating him must hurt his injured shoulder, and yet he didn't struggle. *Was he ill or drugged?* Either way, he needed their help and urgently.

'George!' She described what she saw.

'This isn't good,' he answered, an edge to his voice verging on frantic.

'Where could they be going?' Lucy watched as the small group disappeared around the far corner of the house.

'I don't know, ma'am.'

'Well, we need to find out,' Lucy replied. 'Come on!'

Despite the wind and rain driving into her face, Lucy picked up her sodden skirts and ran over the rough terrain that stretched between the ruins and the house. It was lethal open ground with hollows, crags, and dense thickets of vegetation, causing her to stumble several times. It was inevitable of course. The wind claimed her hat, whipping it up into the air and taking it out of reach.

A few minutes later, as the gable of the house came into view, Lucy had to jump a low wall which skirted the lawn. Just as she reached the wall of the house, George caught up with her. Panting, Lucy leaned against it to catch her breath. George was almost doubled over and was so white in the face when he eventually looked up that she grew concerned. All of this physical exertion for a man in his sixties wasn't ideal. If anything happened to him, Phineas would never forgive her. But to her relief, he appeared to recover and straightened up.

Lucy threw him a questioning look, and he half smiled at her. 'I'm fine, ma'am, truly. Let us proceed.'

George set off, beckoning for her to follow. They edged along the side of the house towards the corner, ducking to avoid several windows. After a quick check around the corner, he motioned for her to keep close and follow. On this side of the house, facing south, a low balustrade bordered a terrace, which they crept along. The ground dropped away steeply, and below, to Lucy's astonishment, there were the remains of a neglected garden. It was difficult to imagine anything growing in such a windswept and hostile place, and one would have to admire anyone who would attempt it. Lucy surmised it must have been a previous owner. An interest in horticulture was surely out of character for a man like Menzies, whose only obsession was art.

When he reached the next corner, George held up his hand for her to stop. He darted his head around the corner and quickly drew back.

'There's a jetty down there. They're getting into a boat.'

'Oh, no! Let me see,' Lucy said. She slipped past him and peered down. Menzies was already in the craft, sitting in the bow, and the two men were manhandling Phineas in too. One of the men took up the oars, while the other stepped back up onto the jetty. Lucy swung back to George. 'We will have to follow them. Quick!'

They raced back along the terrace and sprinted across the open ground until they reached the shelter of the monastery. But they didn't stop. They slithered down the bank towards their rowboat. Her heart pumping wildly, Lucy grabbed one side of the rowboat, George the other, and they heaved. As soon as the craft hit the water, they both jumped in. George steered the boat around to the southern edge of the island, keeping as close to the shore as he dared. Lucy prayed there were no hidden rocks lurking beneath the surface to hinder them.

'Can you see them yet?' George asked.

'No,' she replied, cursing under her breath. 'They must have gone north towards the Firth of Forth.'

The muscles in George's neck strained once again as he heaved, the oars slicing through the water. As they rounded the eastern end of the island, Lucy frantically scanned the horizon. 'There!' she said. 'They're headed north as I thought. Oh dear, that man is still on the jetty, and he's armed.' Lucy grabbed her pistol and held it up just as the man spotted them. The man dropped onto one knee and aimed at them. 'Just row, George!'

Lucy shouted, discharging the pistol, aiming above the man's head. He dropped down flat, and Lucy fired again.

From his prone position, he trained his gun on her. A bullet whizzed past Lucy. All the while, George rowed as hard and as fast as he could, as they manoeuvred past the jetty.

'I think we're out of range,' she said a few minutes later. When she looked back, the man was walking back up towards the house. Lucy almost cried with relief, but of more concern was Menzies Hardwicke. Why was he taking a semi-conscious Phineas out to sea? The possible answers made her stomach churn. She looked past George towards Menzies' boat. 'They're still a good bit ahead of us, George, but they're stationary. What on earth are they up to?'

An out-of-breath George couldn't even shrug; he just raised his brows with a helpless expression.

'We can catch up,' Lucy encouraged him. With the back of her hand, she swiped the rain from her face. 'One last push, George, please.'

As they drew nearer, Lucy realised that Phineas was half slumped in the stern of the boat, leaning over the starboard side. Now Menzies and his helper were advancing on Phineas. Each grabbed one of his arms and pulled him closer to the edge.

'Oh, no!' she cried. Phineas was barely resisting.

'What? What's happening?' Panting, George rested the oars in the rowlocks and looked back over his shoulder just as Menzies Hardwicke and his accomplice tipped Phineas over the side of his boat and into the sea.

THIRTY-NINE

Lucy screamed. 'Oh my God, George, row faster! We must get to him.' As she looked on in horror, Menzies' accomplice took up an oar and used it to push Phineas away from the boat. Then he turned to Menzies and pointed at Lucy and George. Menzies just shrugged and sat down. His companion then picked up his oars and their rowboat headed further out to sea. Menzies was trailing his hand in the water, watching the struggling black shape that was Phineas being buffeted about by the waves. Lucy couldn't believe how cruel and callous the man was.

'Faster!' Lucy cried. They were still a few minutes away, and the current was taking Phin towards the shore. At this distance, Lucy couldn't tell if he was face down or face up in the water, but he had stopped moving. Perhaps he was trying to stay afloat?

For a split second she glanced at Menzies' boat, now further away. Why were they heading out further into the open water? Still, at least they weren't impeding them from rescuing Phin. But was that because it was too late? She shoved her pistol back into her bag, for they were out of range anyway and concentrated on Phin's form.

'Nearly there,' she called out to George. 'Keep going!'

Minutes later, they pulled alongside Phineas. To Lucy's relief, he was face up but appeared to be barely conscious, just floating. The waves pushed him up against the starboard side of the boat. George rested the oars and made a grab for Phin's coat. Lucy moved to port to counterbalance, but George was struggling to lift Phineas's sodden weight. Side-on to the wind, their craft was dipping in an alarming way. Still, they couldn't leave Phineas in the water. Lucy threw caution aside and moved back across beside George and clutched at the lapel of Phin's coat.

'Let's heave together,' George said, rather breathless. 'Are you ready?'

Lucy nodded and took a deep breath, then pulled with all her might. The starboard side dipped alarmingly as they dragged Phineas in. Lucy lunged backwards, trying to compensate for his weight resting on the gunwale. With one final tug, George managed to pull him in the rest of the way.

For a moment, all Lucy and George could do was take deep, rapid breaths. Phineas lay in a sodden heap in the bottom of the boat, his dark hair plastered to his ashen face.

But he was breathing. Phin was alive.

George was exhausted and sat slumped on the thwart. Lucy began to cry as relief flooded her mind. She slid down beside Phineas and cupped his head in her lap. His eyes flickered and opened. Did he even recognise her?

'Have you a knife, George? I need to untie his hands,' she said.

George rummaged in his coat pocket. 'Use this,' he said, handing her a penknife.

With shaking hands, Lucy managed to cut through the cord binding Phin's hands. Phineas groaned. Then Lucy spotted blood on the bandage on his shoulder. All of the manhandling must have opened up the wound. They desperately needed to get help. In despair, she looked out of the boat. The sea around them was empty but for Menzies' boat, now a little distance away. 'George, look!'

He twisted around. 'Good Lord!' he exclaimed as Menzies Hardwicke slipped backwards off the craft and into the sea. He disappeared under the grey, churning water. The man remaining in the boat did nothing to help him but manoeuvred the rowboat around and began to row for the shore.

George turned to Lucy, shock evident on his face. 'Oh, my, ma'am. What an un-Christian thing to do!'

Lucy gulped several times. 'The man was dying, George. I don't know what was wrong with him, but perhaps it was too much. But it is difficult to feel sorry for him'—she glanced down at Phin—'considering he wanted to kill Phineas.'

'Aye, ma'am. Maybe it's a fitting end for him.'

'Oh, George, we did it!' she said, her chin trembling. 'That is all that matters.'

'Yes, ma'am.'

'What should we do? Phin needs a doctor,' she said, stroking Phin's face, but he didn't respond, and she felt her eyes prickle with tears once more.

'I dare not risk going back to shore,' George replied. 'It will take too long, and we have no transport at the other end. Let us go back to Kinnock House. We need to get him out of those wet clothes before he catches his death. I'll need to clean that wound, too.'

'But that other man is still there, and there could be others,' Lucy replied.

'True.' George gave a weary sigh before taking up the oars once more. 'But the island is our best chance.'

. . .

Lucy was relieved to see the jetty was deserted as they rounded the eastern side of the island. It took a great deal of effort to get the still prone Phineas out of the boat and onto dry land. He was slipping in and out of consciousness the entire time. In the end, George had to half carry him up the steps to the house, Lucy going in front with her pistol at the ready.

The house appeared to be deserted, the front door standing ajar. Lucy cautiously pushed it open, and for a moment, stood listening. Silence. She beckoned George forward, and once over the threshold, she took Phineas's uninjured arm and helped get him down the hallway towards what turned out to be a drawing room. They got Phineas to a sofa and lowered him onto it.

'Now what?' she said, catching her breath. Phin was pale, his breathing laboured.

'I'll look after him,' George said. 'Try to find some bed linen. We can use it to bind up his shoulder and while you are at it, why don't you see if you can find some dry clothes for us all.'

'What on earth!' a voice exclaimed from the door.

Lucy swung around. It was Thomas Hardwicke, swaying in the doorway, half dressed and ill-looking, his cheeks a flaming red.

'Lucy? Is that you? What are you doing here, and where is my brother?' Thomas asked, his words slurred. He took a few steps into the room, then grabbed the back of a chair to steady himself. Even from across the room, Lucy could smell whisky from him. 'Who the devil are you?' he said to George.

Lucy exchanged an impatient glance with the valet. 'Thomas, be quiet and sit down. We need your help. Is there any way of getting a doctor here?'

'Has my brother had one of his turns?' Thomas asked, swaying as he tried to look at the prostrate form on the sofa.

'No, my fiancé is unwell and needs urgent assistance.'

'Oh, yes. I forgot about him. He arrived here the other day. Upset Menzies, he did.'

'That's beside the point, Thomas, he needs a doctor,' Lucy said.

Thomas wobbled around the chair, then plonked down into it. 'None here, m'dear. Just the servants, Menzies and I.'

'Menzies went out in his boat, Thomas, and won't be coming back,' Lucy snapped, but she didn't elaborate any further.

Thomas blinked at her. 'What? In this weather? You must be mistaken, for he is far too ill. He's probably up in his room. That chap Stone barged in, accusing him of the most awful crimes. I tell you, I had strong words with him. I've never seen my brother so upset. Not right, y'know; the poor fellow is on his last legs.'

George cleared his throat and give Lucy a meaningful look. 'Those bandages, ma'am.'

'Yes, of course, George.' As she passed Thomas, the fumes of alcohol were even stronger. From the doorway, she glanced back at George, but he was already pulling off Phin's sodden jacket, tut-tutting under his breath.

Thomas looked on helplessly, slumped in the chair.

FORTY

The Next Morning, Kinnock House

Lucy tapped on the door of Phineas's room, hoping he had passed a comfortable night. Between herself and George, they'd managed to get him into bed the previous afternoon, but he had been feverish well into the early evening. Luckily, George had been able to strap up Phin's shoulder once he had cleaned the wound. There had been no help available in the house, as every servant in the place had vanished. Lucy guessed they knew what their master had been up to and had fled back to the mainland even before she and George had set foot on the island. The man who had shot at Lucy from the jetty was also missing, as was their rowboat when George went to check, once the storm had subsided.

When Thomas had sobered up a little, he hounded George about his brother's whereabouts. Eventually, George informed him of his death, and to his credit, he did it as gently as possible. However, Thomas didn't react well. Demanding a bottle of Scotch, he had taken it back to his room and locked the door. Once she'd found some dry clean clothes in the servants' quarters and changed, Lucy had followed him hither, but all her attempts to question him had failed. Through the keyhole she saw him sprawled on the floor, clutching his precious bottle. He had made little sense, and she gave up in frustration. Thomas could drink himself into a stupor again for all she cared. When she passed his room that morning, all she could hear were loud snores. Lucy hurried past in disgust.

Lucy had stayed by Phin's bedside well past midnight, watching him sleep fitfully. Eventually, George had tried to persuade her to get some rest, promising to stay with his master for the night. She only left when he agreed to procure the services of a doctor as soon as possible in the morning if there was no improvement overnight.

To her relief, when George answered her knock on the door, she found Phineas awake and sitting out in a chair. He was dreadfully pale, but he gave her a wan smile as she rushed over and threw her arms around his neck.

'Are you well?' she asked. 'I thought I'd lost you.'

'I'll live; a bit of a cold, but thankfully nothing worse,' he answered, his voice muffled into her shoulder.

Lucy straightened up and scowled down at him. 'How could you?' She pinched his good arm.

'Ouch!' he said, rubbing the spot. 'Why did you do that?'

'*That* is for going off behind my back. You nearly drowned, and all because of your stupid pride. If it wasn't for George confessing all in Edinburgh and helping me... well...' she frantically sought the words '...you would be at the bottom of the North Sea,' she spluttered, suddenly wanting to cry.

Phin continued to rub his arm. George coughed and discreetly left the room. 'You'll upset George with that kind of talk.'

'He's worth ten of you!' she snapped before blowing her nose.

Phineas nodded, looking contrite. 'You are right, of course.'

'Oh, Phin!' she pouted as she sat down on the bed. 'You could have died and right in front of our eyes.'

His contrite expression almost had her crying again. 'I'm very grateful... to you both for rescuing me. I totally underestimated how devious the man was.'

Lucy shivered. 'He was a monster! And to commit suicide like that. It was horrible.'

Phin sighed. 'You should not have had to witness that.' He sighed again and squeezed his eyes shut. 'I thought I was doing the right thing coming here to confront Menzies, and that I was prepared for anything.'

'But you weren't! What happened, Phin? How could he have tricked you so?'

Phineas took her hand and squeezed it. 'Far too easily, I'm afraid. I crossed the causeway at low tide on Tuesday evening. It was all very civilised. Menzies appeared to accept that the game was up with my arrival. I was invited to stay for dinner and offered a bed for the night. I didn't really have a choice. With the high tide fast approaching, I couldn't leave, and there was no offer of the use of a boat, so I accepted and planned to leave the next morning when the causeway would be accessible once more. Your friend Thomas was here too, of course.' Phin frowned at her. 'He's rather fond of you, isn't he? He spoke about you at some length, extolling your many virtues, none of which was news to me; however, Lucy, my dear, I do wonder if I should be worried?'

Lucy huffed. 'Never mind Thomas Hardwicke. He's nothing but a drunk.' She explained about Thomas's current state of inebriation. 'I want to know what happened next. It all sounds so strange,' she said.

'It was. Over the course of the meal, Menzies explained that he was dying and joked he couldn't take the paintings with him, which upset his brother greatly. Thomas grabbed the nearest bottle of Scotch and disappeared without a word. That was certainly awkward. Eventually, conversation resumed, and I felt obliged to tell Menzies the Edinburgh police were on their way and that his best course of action was to hand over the paintings to me so that I could return them to their rightful owners. For the sake of his brother, I thought he might agree. He found my suggestion amusing but committed to nothing.'

'But *were* the police on their way?' she asked.

'I had hoped they were, having left a message for Chief Inspector Fairfax, outlining the case and requesting his assistance. Unfortunately, he was off duty on Tuesday, but he should have received it yesterday morning. I thought they would arrive sometime after breakfast and help me retrieve the artwork and arrest and charge Menzies.'

'Except that storm blew up. It would have prevented them from making the journey. Isn't it as well you weren't left to the mercy of the Edinburgh constabulary!'

Phin kissed her hand. 'Correct. Don't worry, I know how lucky I am that you are the most determined lady of my acquaintance, ready to brave any obstacle.' He pulled her close and kissed her. When he came back up for air, his arm wrapped tightly around her waist, he said, 'So, where was I? Oh yes, I asked Menzies to do the decent thing. I should have realised I was being hoodwinked. He was merely biding his time. No doubt, once he had given it some thought overnight, he decided to take his own life, along with mine.'

Lucy shuddered. 'He was like a spider waiting to pounce. You took such a gamble in hoping the police would arrive to help.'

With a shrug, Phin gave her a crooked smile. 'McQuillan wouldn't have let me down so.'

'No, that is true,' she replied. 'So, what happened after dinner? Did you sit around the fire exchanging pleasantries?'

'It was almost as strange as that. As I said, Thomas had left us alone to nurse his woes. Menzies talked about his favourite artists for some time. I have to admit, his knowledge of the art world was extensive. Then I asked to see the paintings, for it occurred to me that he might have hidden them somewhere off the island. But no, he invited me upstairs to a special room which had been converted into a small private gallery. In the middle of the floor was a solitary armchair, draped with a woollen blanket and a table with his pipe and tobacco and a decanter of brandy. And there, of course, on the walls were the eight paintings I have spent almost two years trying to find, each now newly framed. As you can imagine, I viewed them with mixed feelings. I got the impression he spent a lot of time in there; in fact, every waking hour in the last few weeks. I won't deny the place had an eerie atmosphere.'

Phin's words sent a shiver down Lucy's spine. 'No doubt gloating over his possessions. How strange, but considering everything else that has happened, I suppose it is the kind of odd behaviour one would expect from a lunatic.'

'I do not know what diagnosis a physician would put forward, but he was perfectly lucid, Lucy. However, it was obvious the physical toll his illness had taken. The man looked wretched: thin, gaunt and his eyes...' Phin paused for a moment, swallowing hard '...dead eyes.'

'Well, I don't feel the least bit sorry for him after all he has done!' Lucy exclaimed. 'Were you able to ascertain if Thomas was involved in all of this?'

'I'm certain he knew what was going on, but he wasn't involved directly in the thefts. However, he was happy to gain from Menzies' activities. I suspect his house contains some works which were procured illegally. McQuillan will have some fun finding out.'

Lucy huffed. 'I bet he orchestrated the stealing of my paintings, though.'

'No, you are mistaken. That was Menzies' doing. He knew Thomas had wanted those Miller landscapes of yours, so he arranged for them to be stolen and delivered to him. He wanted to give them to him as a parting gift before his death.'

'Oh, Lord! How grim!'

'Yes, but when Thomas received them, he panicked. Along with his indiscreet comments at his club that night, he knew he was in trouble by association. He knew that you and I would soon realise he was one of the few people who knew you possessed those particular paintings.'

'And he was implicated by receiving stolen property.'

'Well, yes, that too.' Phin shook his head. 'What a pair.'

'Huh! And to think my mother wanted me to marry Thomas. Well, he shall not have my paintings, if I have anything to do with it!'

'It will be sorted in due course, but you will have to be patient, my dear. You will have to prove your ownership to the Scottish police, as will all the owners of any other paintings found in the house.'

'Do you know if my paintings are here? Did Thomas bring them?' Lucy asked.

Phin nodded. 'I suspect he brought them here, as he would have been afraid to leave evidence behind in London. But, Lucy, stay away from him, please. I will ask George to retrieve them.'

Lucy flicked him a sideways glance. 'Very well, but I still reserve the right to give him a thorough tongue-lashing when he sobers up.'

'That sounds fair. I'll enjoy watching someone else being on the receiving end of one of your—'

Lucy glared at him.

'—admonishments!'

With a sniff, Lucy asked: 'But what happened yesterday morning? How did you end up incapacitated?'

'I suspect it was the porridge. All appeared to be normal over breakfast. We even chatted a little. Menzies' mood darkened, however, when I insisted that the paintings be handed over. But he asked one of his servants to bring them down to the drawing room, and I accompanied him there. However, we were not long in the room when I began to feel woozy. Too late, I realised I had been drugged. I collapsed into a chair and had to sit and watch while Menzies removed the canvasses from their frames, rolled them up and put them into a bag. Then I was trussed up and frogmarched out of the house.'

'And we arrived in time to see you being manhandled into that boat.'

'I recall little of that trip, Lucy. A few images and sensations crept into my consciousness. I remember looking up into your face as I lay in the bottom of a boat. I was unaware of anything else that occurred. George filled me in this morning.'

'Well, once they had dropped you into the water, our focus was on rescuing you. I didn't even try to save Menzies. We were too far away, anyway.'

'I doubt you could have. He never intended to survive and would have ensured he was weighed down with something.'

Lucy shivered. 'You may be right, for he disappeared under the waves very quickly. It was almost as if time stood still. I suppose it was the shock of seeing someone do that.'

Phineas frowned. 'Do you recall if he had a brown leather bag with him?'

'I don't know. He could have, but we were a good distance away, as I said. Why do you ask?'

'Unfortunately, I believe Menzies took his precious canvasses with him to the bottom of the North Sea.'

Lucy gasped. 'All eight paintings?'

Phin nodded. 'I'm sure he brought that bag with him onto the boat. I have an image in my mind of the bag at his feet. George has searched the house and can't find it. The memory is hazy, however, so I could be mistaken. Those paintings were both rare and valuable.'

'That is awful, Phin.'

Phineas shrugged. 'I no longer care, Lucy. I'm just grateful to be alive.'

There was a knock on the door and George came in. 'Sir, the police have arrived, and Chief Inspector Fairfax wishes to speak to you.'

'I'll see him shortly, George, once I have explained everything to Mrs Lawrence.'

'Very good, sir,' George replied, slipping out the door.

'Well, hurrah for the cavalry!' Lucy exclaimed. Phin quirked a brow and laughed, which set him off coughing. After a few sips of water, he recovered.

'Tell me, did you find out about the syndicate? Did Menzies reveal what we wanted to know?' Lucy asked.

'Oh, yes. He was very proud of the entire affair. Although, he claimed it was all for his personal use. I had thought there might have been a ring of international clients, but he denied it.'

'I see, and how did Edward Vaughan get involved?'

Phineas began to cough again, and it took several minutes before he could continue. 'Drat! I really do have a cold.'

'And there I was thinking sea bathing was beneficial to one's health,' Lucy said.

'You can be quite cruel, madam.' But he didn't look cross. 'Well, we were mistaken, Lucy. Edward wasn't Apollo, though he was involved, just in a different capacity.'

'But the painting in his armoire. If he didn't steal it, then... Oh, my goodness!' She grabbed Phin's arm. 'Alice! It was Alice! She's Apollo! We just assumed it was a man.' Lucy's mind was in a whirl. 'The message on Apollo's card. It was signed with an 'A'. 'A' for Alice, *not* Apollo. Was she the woman the maid saw in Thomas's house that night?'

Phineas nodded, his expression bleak. 'Yes, fresh from stealing your paintings and delivering them as per instructions from Menzies.'

'This is fantastical! But how did she become involved?' Lucy asked.

'Menzies met her at a house party, shortly after she and Edward married. At Sidley, in fact.'

'Sarah and Geoffrey's place?'

'Yes. It was before Menzies became seriously ill. All his life, he was a strong supporter of the Tories and was often to be found on the country house political circuit.'

Lucy sat up straight. 'Yes! I remember now. Sarah told me he helped fund Geoffrey's campaign.'

Phineas didn't quite meet her eye and hurried on: 'Menzies was very taken with Alice that weekend and realised that she found the social scene jaded and her marriage a bore. Alice was looking for adventure. They fell to talking about art, of course, and she introduced him to Edward, who, as we now know, was the grandson of Tandy Robinson and was almost as knowledgeable about art as Menzies.'

'And they formed the perfect little group!' Lucy exclaimed. 'Menzies' greed, Alice's ennui and Edward's lack of funds and the ability to spot a good painting. I do feel foolish, Phineas, to have jumped to such a conclusion about Apollo when I was only recently hoodwinked by a woman burglar when I was in Egypt.'

'But we all were duped by Alice. Menzies cultivated the couple over the course of several months. Once he had gained her trust, he arranged for Alice to be trained by a lock picker as a bit of a lark at first, and then ensured that the couple were included on the guest lists of prominent art lovers around the country. When he suggested a bit of judicious stealing, they were happy to oblige.'

'So, Edward identified the paintings, Alice came back and stole them at a later date, and what then? Did she take them to White?' she asked.

'Yes, or Edward did. White arranged the transport of the

paintings up here to Menzies. He was the go-between as such. That ensured Menzies protected himself by staying at arm's length.'

'But what went wrong? Why did he have Edward murdered?'

'Try not to be too upset, but I'm afraid the announcement of our engagement was the catalyst. Alice insisted to Menzies that I was getting close to uncovering the syndicate—for her own ends, I might add. Unfortunately, he believed her and panicked. He couldn't risk exposure. Once White informed him of your visit and connection to me, he decided to act. Alice begged Menzies to arrange Edward's murder so she could be free of him and at the same time get her revenge on me, so they cooked up a plan that benefitted them both.'

'Dear Lord! If Alice couldn't have you, she wanted to ensure no one else would either. And she was on hand that night to throw the accusation at your head and to ensure McQuillan acted upon it.'

'Yes, she's quite the actress, is she not? Our engagement party was common knowledge in society circles and the perfect opportunity to set me up for a fall with all the main players present,' he said. 'I have to admit it was clever.'

'But it could have been fatal for you, Phin; I wouldn't be too impressed, if I were you,' she said. Phin just shrugged. 'And White's murder?'

'Again, Menzies knew that both Kincaid and I had realised White was the middleman, and that knowledge could potentially lead us here to Kinnock Island,' Phin replied. 'If White talked to the police, the game was up. Menzies knew he was running out of time. He had confirmation that he was dying on that visit to London.'

'The day I met him and Thomas at Brown's Hotel!' Lucy gasped. 'Thomas made some remark about you being accused of Edward's murder and how sorry he was for me. I was extremely annoyed and insisted you were innocent, despite the speculation in the newspapers. Menzies knew our connection and must have realised his plot to frame you was suspected. Why else would I be so adamant that you were innocent? And Phin, there is something else!'

'Yes?'

'Thomas told me that his brother insisted on staying at Brown's Hotel instead of at his home. The Royal Arcade is just around the corner. He must have had a meeting with White before he returned to Scotland.'

'Probably, my dear. Of far more concern to Menzies was White's exposure as part of the chain. Menzies couldn't risk him being questioned by the police. He had to be despatched as quickly as possible.'

'But we still don't know who the assassin is.' Lucy gnawed at her bottom lip. 'Surely it wasn't Alice who bludgeoned Edward to death?' She shivered at the memory. 'Though I have to admit, Seb and I always suspected she organised it, but I could find no way to link her, and Coffin Mike could find no clue either.'

'That's because he was looking in the wrong place. We assumed the Collector was London-based, whereas Menzies had surrounded himself with a group of thugs from the slums of Edinburgh. Through them, he hired an assassin.'

'Really? How does one even go about such a thing?'

'I'm not sure that is the kind of knowledge I want you to have,' he said with a grin. Lucy swiped at his arm. 'As I said, he had some dubious connections,' he continued. 'The assassin posed as a waiter at our engagement party. The rest you know. Unfortunately, I couldn't get Menzies to give me his name, but I do know he's Russian and escaped the country directly after White's murder. McQuillan, through his connections, might be able to get more information.' Phin paused. 'Unfortunately, there is more, my dear. The assassin had help the night of our party. It was no coincidence that our celebration was held at the Strawbridge house.'

Lucy frowned. As she thought about it, she recalled her own surprise at the Strawbridges' insistence on the lavish party when Sarah had previously mentioned financial difficulties. Lucy didn't like where this appeared to be leading. 'What are you saying, Phin? Surely Sarah had nothing to do with this?'

'No. She's entirely innocent. I'm afraid it was Geoffrey. He was in serious debt to Menzies and had been indiscreet in certain quarters, leaving himself open to blackmail.'

When she looked at Phineas, her heart almost stopped. His expression was grim as he continued: 'Menzies told Geoffrey to put Sidley Manor on the market in an effort to get his money back. Unfortunately for Geoffrey, he couldn't find a buyer. Then Menzies told him he could clear the debt by helping him with something else.'

'Edward's murder! That is why he was anxious that Sarah didn't travel down to Oxford. She would have discovered he was trying to sell the house. It was never anxiety over her health. Oh, no, Phin, this is terrible. This will destroy Sarah! Are you saying he facilitated the whole thing?'

'He had little choice but to do as he was told. Menzies threatened to expose him to the party and the press. Geoffrey was simply trying to save his career and his marriage. He may not have known exactly what was planned that night, but once the murder had taken place, he was guilty by association. You saw how distressed he was when the body was found?'

'Yes, he was deeply shocked. But it is small consolation to know he didn't kill Edward.'

'Indeed.'

'What *was* his involvement?'

'Firstly, he encouraged Sarah to host the party. He knew which agency Sarah would use and tipped off Menzies. Our Russian friend slipped in that night, unchallenged. Most of the hired servants didn't know each other and assumed he was one of them. The note enticing Edward from the party was given to one of the footmen who handed it to Edward. Meanwhile, the assassin lay in wait, knowing the servants were all busy downstairs. He did the deed, changed, left the house and disposed of his bloodied clothes in the garden a few houses away.'

'And walked away into the night! Oh my God! I can't believe it. Geoffrey stood by while you were arrested for a crime you didn't commit. How cowardly! And the same assassin then went on to try to kill you and succeeded in killing White.' Lucy gripped Phin's arm. 'We must let McQuillan know about Geoffrey, immediately.'

'Don't fret. Chief Inspector Fairfax will put things in train. It is over, Lucy. At last.' He stood. 'And we have more important matters to consider, do we not?'

'We do?'

He pulled her up and into his arms. 'We never did set a date for our wedding.'

EPILOGUE

August 1888, Thorncroft, Kent

Dawn painted the tiny puffs of cloud pink and gold. Lucy sat on the shore, her arms wrapped around her knees, watching the colours ebb and flow until at last a pure blue sky peeked through. A shiver went through her, but not because she was cold. It was excitement. Later this morning she would marry Phineas Stone. Tomorrow, she would wake, not in an empty bed, but beside him. And every morning after that. *Lucy Stone*. It didn't quite roll off the tongue, but she would get used to it. With a contented sigh and a smile, she stood and made her way back through the dunes, humming 'The Wind That Shakes the Barley'. The song was stuck in her head, courtesy of Mary. It was a favourite ballad of hers, often heard floating around Phillimore Gardens whenever Mary was in one of her homesick moods.

In the lead up to the wedding, Lucy had even found herself thinking about Somerville Hall and her family, none of whom would attend this, her second wedding, but most decidedly the most important. Some of Phin's siblings couldn't come either, but after such an eventful summer, a quiet, intimate wedding seemed more appropriate somehow.

Lucy took the path through the trees and came out onto the rear lawn near the summer house. She paused briefly, recalling that awful row she and Phin had witnessed between Alice and Edward all those months ago. And, for a moment, Lucy was sad. That weekend, when everyone realised that Phin was going to propose, had been the catalyst for two murders, Phin's attempted murder, and eventually, a suicide. But at least, justice had been served, though not in the conventional sense. If she'd been superstitious, she might have taken Edward's murder at her engagement party as a bad omen, but helping to investigate the Apollo syndicate had only strengthened her relationship with Phineas. No, if there was anyone to feel sorry for, it was Lady Sarah. It had come to light that Geoffrey had spotted Lucy's note deferring their trip to Sidley and mentioning going to Scotland. He knew the game was up and had bolted. Just like that! Leaving Sarah alone to face the scandal. By the time Lucy and Phin had arrived back in London, Sarah had escaped to her father's estate, hounded out of London by the press. Lucy had written to her, offering to visit, but Sarah's tear-stained note in response had begged her to leave her be for now. There had been no communication since.

Another victim was Lady Muldoon, now living alone in that great Mayfair mansion, echoing with memories. Alice's antics as Apollo had been declared the actions of a woman not in her senses. The authorities were just as eager to avoid such a notable and embarrassing arrest, and the Muldoon family found it convenient to have Alice permanently committed to an asylum. Lucy didn't believe she was mad at all, but rotten to the core. It bothered her that Alice would never stand trial. If she'd been a girl from the slums of the East End, and not an heiress, Lucy was sure it would have been a very different outcome.

To her credit, Lady Dot had travelled down to Kent for

their wedding once she'd been assured by Phin that it was to be a very quiet affair with only close family and friends. Harry had been making a special effort to ensure his wife's oldest friend was content and free from any embarrassing comments or situations. However, Lucy had caught Lady Dot's wistful looks, particularly when Seb and Phineas were indulging in nonsense and banter as they were inclined to do. Lucy's heart went out to her: all the money in the world couldn't cure loneliness.

The house was blissfully cool as she entered. However, the servants were bustling about, preparing for the wedding breakfast, and in the middle of the hall, her hostess, Gertie Stone, stood looking slightly bewildered. Lucy greeted her before escaping up the stairs to her suite. She always found Gertie a disconcerting presence. Thankfully, most of the organisation for the wedding had been handled by Harry's very efficient housekeeper, Mrs Mullet, who was discreet enough to seek Lucy out when actual decisions had to be made.

Much to her surprise, Lucy was greeted by Mary, standing hands on hips and glaring at her as she came through the door.

'Well, there you are, ma'am! I thought maybe you'd had second thoughts and scarpered, so I did!' Mary declared.

Lucy burst out laughing. 'You do talk nonsense, Mary. I woke early and couldn't sleep, that is all. I went for a walk down on the beach.'

'Hmm,' was the maid's response. 'I suppose that is understandable with the day that is in it. Perhaps if it isn't too much trouble, you'd sit down here now, ma'am, and I can get started on your hair.'

'Don't fuss, Mary, please, and don't be cross with me, not today,' Lucy said. She obeyed Mary's command and did her best to look contrite. But she couldn't help but grin, and eventually, she coaxed an answering smile from her beleaguered maid.

In the mirror, Lucy caught a glimpse of her wedding dress hanging on the front of the wardrobe. It was such a contrast to the travelling ensemble she'd worn when she'd eloped with Charlie all those years ago. It was such a pity she couldn't have worn white or cream today, but as a widow, she felt it best to conform. As it was, her past wasn't easy for some of Phin's family to accept. If she wore white, it would cause a sensation.

Mary caught her eye in the mirror. "'Tis a fine dress, ma'am. Sure, he'll be bowled over when he sees you.'

'I certainly hope so, Mary,' she replied.

Lucy had ordered the dress from Paris from a modiste she'd visited the year before. It was a huge extravagance, and although the lilac ribbed silk with the tiny pearl buttons down the bodice had been expensive enough, the Carrickmacross lace collar, suggested by Mary, had been worth every penny. The fine and delicate workmanship added a sumptuous quality to what was otherwise a plain, though beautifully cut dress. Mary had lovingly attached the lace around the square neckline as Lucy had looked on, marvelling at the tiny delicate stitches Mary employed.

Her pleasant thoughts were interrupted by Mary muttering under her breath. Lucy raised a brow at her through the mirror. 'Out with it!'

The maid paused, brush in hand. 'It's all tangled from the wind, and I'm sure the salty air won't have done it any good. I had it lovely and smooth last night before you retired.'

Lucy had to pull on her upper lip to stop from smiling. 'Sorry.'

Luckily, she was saved any further scolding by a knock on the door. Mary slapped the brush down on the table with a grunt and marched over to answer it. It was Harry.

'May I come in?' he asked.

Lucy swung around in her chair. 'Of course, Harry.'

Her father-in-law-to-be approached, a smile on his face.

'Good morning! I have something for you, my dear.' He held out a purple velvet box. 'Please, open it,' he said. 'It was my wife's, and I would like you to have it.'

Lucy opened the box and gasped. Inside was a pearl choker of five strands, held together at the back by a sapphire of the deepest blue.' Lucy gulped, glancing down at her engagement ring, which matched beautifully. When she looked up at him, her eyes were full of tears. 'Thank you. It is beautiful. I will treasure it always, but surely it should go to one of your daughters?'

'Not at all. They already have so many of her pieces. I kept some back to give to my son's wives.' Harry bent down and kissed her cheek. 'Welcome to the family, Lucy.'

Andrew was waiting for her down in the hallway two hours later. On her arrival a few days earlier, he had taken her aside and offered to give her away.

'I understand your father is deceased and your brother... is unable to attend the wedding. It would be an honour to give you away, Mrs Lawrence'—he still insisted on calling her that—'as I can see how happy you have made Phin. You appear to be a perfect match for each other.' The colour rose sharply in his face, and he had harrumphed several times. 'You will always be welcome here at Thorncroft.'

As much amused as delighted—as Thorncroft was Harry's estate still—Lucy accepted the olive branch, realising how much it cost Andrew to make the offer. From what she knew of him, swallowing his pride was not a common occurrence.

Now, as she stood at the top of the stairs, if she wasn't mistaken, Andrew's eyes widened—could it be in admiration? Lucy made her way down the steps, suddenly self-conscious. For several moments, he just stared, then appeared to come to his senses. 'Shall we go?' he said, at last. 'Everyone is waiting at the church.'

'Yes, please,' she answered him, then turned. 'That will do, Mary,' she said feeling a tug on her train. 'Just fold it over my arm.'

Andrew offered his arm and escorted Lucy down the steps to the waiting carriage. 'It isn't far to the church,' he said as he handed her up; then he did the same for Mary. The maid grinned at her once inside and proceeded to fold Lucy's train so that it wouldn't be crushed.

A young man clutching a large bouquet of flowers rushed across the gravel and up to the carriage.

'Here you go, ma'am,' Mary said. 'The head gardener brought them for you.' She handed Lucy a beautiful bouquet of lilies just as Andrew joined them inside the carriage, taking the seat opposite.

'Is this your doing?' Lucy asked him, holding up the flowers.

'Eh, yes, of course,' he muttered, not meeting her eye.

'It is such a pity that neither of your sisters could attend,' Lucy remarked as the carriage pulled away.

'Indeed. They were both extremely sorry, but Elvira's youngest child has been ill, and she didn't wish to leave her. And Clarissa rarely leaves Cornwall these days.'

'It was exceedingly kind of Clarissa to invite us to visit. We shall certainly do so before the year is out. I have always wanted to explore that part of the country.'

'Yes, it is quite beautiful,' he said in such a tone as killed any further conversation. Andrew coughed, treated Mary to a curious glance, barely concealing his astonishment at her presence in the carriage, then fixed his gaze somewhere above Lucy's head.

The silence, although welcome to Lucy, was not conducive to the calming of one's nerves. A tight knot of anxiety had pitched its tent at the bottom of Lucy's stomach about an hour earlier and showed no inclination of decamping. Was it nerves? Excitement? She couldn't recall feeling this way the first time around, as she and Charlie had absconded in a hired carriage early one morning. Who would have thought she would get a second chance of happiness? Lucy's hand flew up to the choker at her neck, and suddenly she felt calmer. Harry's gesture had been so sweet. Marriage to Phin would be different. She'd never been more certain in her entire life.

'Here we are!' Andrew announced unnecessarily as they drew up before the lychgate minutes later.

Heart thumping, Lucy paused at the entrance of the little church, the aisle stretching out before her. The setting was perfect and just how she'd imagined. Large vases, holding a profusion of white roses and ferns, adorned the church, releasing their delicate perfume into the air. And there Phin was at the top of the aisle. Waiting. Grinning. So handsome. Seb, his groomsman, beaming beside him. She wanted to laugh with happiness, but one glance at Andrew's stern expression curtailed it. She must not let Phin down by being silly.

Lucy felt a pull on the back of her dress: the agreed sign from Mary that she was to pull herself together. Sometimes, it was unnerving the way Mary guessed her thoughts. But she was so glad Mary was with her: her stalwart companion through so many dangerous adventures. Her insistence that Mary be one of her witnesses and present for the ceremony had caused a few raised brows, but when Phineas had insisted likewise for George, the objections had melted away.

Andrew glanced down. 'Shall we?' he asked gently. Was that a hint of a smile in his eyes?

. . .

The ceremony went by in a flash or so it seemed to Lucy. Once the register was signed, she began to relax only to be overwhelmed by happiness. And soon her face hurt from smiling. Then to her surprise, Gertie and Lady Dot kissed her cheek in turn, while Harry and Seb slapped Phin on the back as Andrew looked on, slightly bemused. Phin offered his arm, and they walked down the aisle. At the back of the church, Lucy saw George and Mary, heads together. They were as thick as thieves already, she realised—the Stone household would be an efficient and happy one. As they left the church, she smiled her thanks to them both.

Outside, Lucy held onto Phin's hand tightly as a photographer took their picture. Who would have thought that day in the mortuary, over the body of Charlie, that she'd meet her soulmate? The beginning had been so fraught. She'd known despair, poverty, and scandal, but he had stuck by her, accepted her many failings, and most important of all, loved her.

Once the photographer was finished, Sebastian threw rice most enthusiastically as he grinned from ear to ear. Poor Andrew's admonishments fell on unheeding ears, as usual. As Lucy climbed up into the carriage, Seb winked at her. The door closed and they were off.

'Well, Mrs Stone, how do you feel?' Phin asked.

'Splendid. And you?'

'I've had worse days,' he replied, trying not to smile, but before she could scold him, he swooped in for a kiss.

'A successful day, I believe,' Phin murmured, as they stood on the terrace at the back of Thorncroft, looking out to sea later that evening.

'How does one measure such things?' she asked, leaning into his shoulder.

Phin put his arm around her and squeezed her waist. 'No

dead bodies,' he replied with a grin. Then he sighed. 'We had better go back inside to our guests, Mrs Stone.'

'You don't have to keep saying *Mrs Stone*, you know,' Lucy said.

'But I like the sound of it.'

'So do I, but you may grow tired of it or wear it out,' she reasoned.

'I don't believe so, dearest Lucy.' He looked down at her, his expression serious. 'Are you happy?'

'Never more so, for now I will know where you are and what you are up to at all times, to quote your good self.'

His eyes widened in mock horror. 'I see—I have been trapped!'

'Don't worry; I may release you on good behaviour,' she said.

Phin chuckled. 'Well, then, I intend to be very, very bad.'

They remained standing in companionable silence for a few more minutes.

'I wonder how the trial went today,' she said at last. The previous day, the trial had begun of Menzies Hardwicke's companion who had assisted his suicide from the boat. Chief Inspector Fairfax's men had caught him in Dalmeny, and he had been charged with the attempted murder of Phineas and possession of eight stolen and extremely valuable paintings. The artworks had been returned to their rightful owners, but on receiving his commission, Phin had immediately donated it to charity. Kincaid, however, had accepted his share with delight, left the country and not been heard of since.

'I'm sure the papers will give a good account of it.' Phin tilted his head and looked down at her. 'We have far more interesting things to think about.'

'Certainly. And today was wonderful. I only wish...'

'Ah, Lady Sarah,' he said. 'I'm sure you feel her absence today. What a dreadful business! But Geoffrey should not have absconded as he did. He should have stayed and faced justice. Instead, he has left his wife in the most awful circumstances.'

'Her family has been wonderful, at least, and are standing by her. Her father, the earl, is very protective of her, but she has been left with nothing.'

'Geoffrey's debts were substantial; such a shame the townhouse had to be sold, but there was little choice with his creditors clamouring for payment.'

'But how sneaky of him to try to sell Sidley, unbeknownst to her, all those months ago. No wonder he tried to keep her from travelling into Oxfordshire,' she says.

'It would never have covered his debts to Menzies Hardwicke, but I suppose he felt he had to try.'

'That is nothing, Phin. The fact he was implicated in Edward's murder... how will she ever recover from that?'

'I think you underestimate her, Lucy. Sarah is strong and will bounce back, and she will have us to fight her corner, too.'

'Thank you, Phin. I can't abandon her. Sarah stuck by me when things were bad. And now she has to face the birth of her child without Geoffrey to support her. At least she has little James, and perhaps the baby will help her recover. Do you think Geoffrey will ever be found?'

Before Phin could respond, they were interrupted.

'Hey! You two! Time enough for all that lovey-dovey stuff when you are on your honeymoon,' Sebastian called out from the doorway. 'Father is opening another bottle of champagne, do hurry up!'

The following morning, Lucy and Phin sat in the carriage, ready to depart on the first leg of their honeymoon to Paris. Lucy was incredibly happy, for her wedding night had been everything she'd hoped. Phineas exchanged an impatient glance with her then drummed his fingers on the wood panelling. Lucy smiled to herself. *He's as anxious to depart as I am!*

At last, the remainder of their bags were stowed, and the footman knocked on the side of the carriage as Mary and George joined them for the short journey to the train station. Earlier Mary had muttered darkly about boats and seasickness, but when Lucy suggested she stay behind, her maid had drawn herself up to her full five feet and exclaimed: 'Over my dead body!'

Lucy looked out at the family gathered on the front steps to wave them off. Sebastian waved to her, making a cheeky remark which made Harry laugh and Andrew squirm. Andrew turned on his heel and stormed into the house. Seb really was her favourite brother-in-law.

With a jolt, they moved off. As the carriage travelled up the driveway through the ancient fir trees and towards the road, Phineas sighed and relaxed. 'What a relief to get away at last!'

'Sir,' George piped up. 'This telegram arrived for you just before we left.' He handed the envelope to Phin and discreetly glanced out the window.

Lucy assumed it was another message of congratulations. They'd received many of them from their friends the previous day, including Chief Inspector McQuillan. She watched Phin's face as he read it. But he frowned and drew in a sharp breath. 'We may have to change our plans, my dear,' he said. Their eyes met as he handed her the telegram.

Phin, Luca missing! I need your help. Come to Italy at once. Elvira.

A LETTER FROM THE AUTHOR

Dear reader,

Many thanks for reading *The Art of Deception*, Book 3 in The Lucy Lawrence Mystery series. I hope you enjoyed Lucy and Phin's story. If you would like to hear more about new books, you can sign up here:

www.stormpublishing.co/pam-lecky

For news about my writing, upcoming deals and recommendations, you can check out my author newsletter:

subscribepage.io/jf9sWM

If you enjoyed this book and could spare a few moments to leave a review, that would be hugely appreciated. Even a short review can make all the difference in encouraging a reader to discover my books for the first time. Thanks so much!

I think by now, readers, you have realised that mischief follows Lucy Lawrence around like a faithful hound! And poor Phineas, in this instance, falls victim to her unfortunate actions. However, I think you will agree that their partnership is consolidating as Lucy realises that Phineas respects and welcomes her opinions and is happy to work alongside her. (Not something many Victorian men would have done, but then Phineas isn't your typical 19th century male!) So, what could be next for our newly-married pair as they hare off to Italy? Well, you will have to wait for book 4, which will be published in autumn 2024.

Thanks again for being part of my writing journey.

Pam Lecky

- x.com/pamlecky
- instagram.com/pamleckybooks
- linkedin.com/in/pam-lecky-b0b646109
- bookbub.com/profile/pam-lecky

ACKNOWLEDGEMENTS

Without the support of family and friends, this book, and indeed my entire writing journey, would not have been possible. My heartfelt thanks to you all, especially my husband, Conor, and my children, Stephen, Hazel and Adam. I am very grateful to my chief beta readers, Lorna and Terry O'Callaghan, who have read every draft and given me invaluable feedback.

Special gratitude is owed to my agent, Thérèse Coen, at Susanna Lea & Associates, London, whose belief in me, along with her sage advice, helped to bring Lucy Lawrence to life.

Producing a novel is a collaborative process, and I have been fortunate to have wonderful editors, copyeditors, proofreaders, and graphic designers working on this series. To Kathryn Taussig, my editor, and all the team at Storm Publishing, thanks for believing in this series and taking it to the next level. A massive thank you to Bernadette Kearns, my original editor – all the books in the Lucy Lawrence series benefited hugely from your input.

I am extremely grateful to have such loyal readers. For those of you who take the time to leave reviews, please know that I appreciate them beyond words. To the amazing book bloggers, book tour hosts and reviewers who have hosted me and my books over the years – thank you.

Last, but certainly not least, I am incredibly lucky to have a network of writer friends who keep me motivated, especially Valerie Keogh, Jenny O'Brien, Fiona Cooke, Brook Allen and Tonya Murphy Mitchell. Special thanks to the members of the

Historical Novel Society, RNA and Society of Authors Irish Chapters, and all the gang at the Coffee Pot Book Club.
Go raibh míle maith agat!

Pam Lecky
July 2024

Printed in Great Britain
by Amazon